A WILD FEY HAS APPEARED!

A WILD FEY HAS APPEARED!

FANTASIA

BOOK ONE

UNICE5656

Podium

To my writing group.
You know what you did.

All rights reserved. No part of this publication may be reproduced, stored in a retrieval system, or transmitted in any form or by any means electronic, mechanical, photocopying, recording, or otherwise without prior written permission from Podium Publishing.

This is a work of fiction. Names, characters, places, and incidents are either products of the author's imagination or used fictitiously. Any resemblance to actual events, locales, or persons, living, dead, or undead, is entirely coincidental.

Copyright © 2023 by Tsu-Yu Unice Chang

Cover design by Podium Publishing

ISBN: 978-1-0394-2814-0

Published in 2023 by Podium Publishing, ULC
www.podiumaudio.com

Podium

AUTHOR'S NOTE

(Welcome to the weird and wonderful world of Fantasia! This story is an irreverent romp through adventure and comedy tropes, with layers of meta-humour that cheerfully trample over literary convention and story immersion alike. In addition to the typical prim and proper narration, expect these parenthetical snark-filled asides sprinkled liberally throughout the story. Enjoy!)

A WILD FEY HAS APPEARED!

CHAPTER 1
SIDE PURCHASE

Arwyn walked into the electronics store, telling herself, *I'm just here to buy a new laptop.* Her old one had valiantly carried on for almost a decade before breaking down, and it was time to turn it in for a partial discount on a new model. She had already done her research online and knew exactly which one she wanted; a quick word to the store employee and she had it in hand within a few minutes.

Business done, she could not resist drifting over to the video game section.

The first thing she saw was a huge display proclaiming, *Fantasia: Fantasy Life* in fancy, glittering lettering. Beneath the words, a screen showed an attractive blonde girl lying down while wearing a sensor-helmet. It faded into an image of the same girl, now a powerful cleric, blasting undead monsters with holy magic.

A new virtual reality game! Fantasy themed this time. Arwyn was a huge fan of fantasy books, games, and comics, a passion she had not outgrown through her teenage and young adult years. (Outgrow? Now she has *money* to pour into it. She's just getting started.) She had tried other virtual reality games, but everything released until now had been first-person shooters—not that you could play in third person in virtual reality—or real-life-based socialization worlds that she actively disliked.

Looking at the unreasonable price tag, Arwyn tried to convince herself not to buy it. *This price is ridiculous. You should never buy a game when it first comes out; the price drops so much after a few weeks. I'm swamped at work and won't have time to play right now anyways.*

Smaller text on the sign caught her eye: "Play in your sleep!" It appeared that the new immersion console was able to induce a dreamlike state for gameplay that met the body's requirements for sleep.

Oh my. Self-control crumbling, Arwyn quickly did some calculations in her head. Knowing herself to be very reluctant to spend money on unnecessary expenses, she set a small fraction of her income aside in a "guilt-free spending" fund. If she spent every cent in there and lived an ascetic life for the next month, she could afford it.

The second employee she asked for help was much friendlier than the first. (She assumed it was because of the huge commission he was about to earn.) In addition to the sensor-helmet that served as the game console, she ended up buying the reclining chair that was designed to align the spine in an ergonomic fashion while wearing the helmet. The employee went so far as to help her carry the bulky item to her car. *Just how much am I earning this guy?* Driving home, she felt a growing sense of excitement. *This is going to be fun!*

It took two trips to lug everything into her house, one for the recliner and one for everything else.

First things first. Full of virtuous work ethic, Arwyn opened her new laptop and began setting up her user account along with installing the programs she used for work. While she waited for them to load, she read the instruction manual for *Fantasia*.

Welcome to *Fantasia*!

You're about to enter a world full of magic and excitement. Become a warrior or a mage, an elf or a beastman. Whether you want to reign as the lord of a city or become the most famous craftsman on the continent, it can all happen here! *Fantasia's* revolutionary game design allows 99% realism and the ability to play in your sleep. Your adventure awaits!

Huh. Is this for real? I might actually consistently get enough sleep from now on. A natural night owl, Arwyn frequently stayed up too late relative to societal demands, such as regular work hours, which were unfairly biased toward early birds.

The setup instructions seemed quite simple, so Arwyn got to work unpacking the recliner and attaching the console to a power source. She set up the system in her dining room–turned–games room, managing to cram the recliner in amongst the shelves of books and games.

Looking at the clock, Arwyn saw that it was only seven o'clock. Resisting the urge to jump into the game before bedtime, she heated leftovers for dinner and started the file transfer from her old laptop to the new one.

While she was online, an instant message popped onto the screen:

Leah-IfIHadAMillionDollars…: Hey, Ari, what's up? How was the laptop buying?

ArwynTheElf: Well, I kind of made a side purchase . . .

Leah-IfIHadAMillionDollars...: Really? What?

ArwynTheElf: It's called Fantasia.

Leah-IfIHadAMillionDollars...: *squeal* Oh my god, it's out?? I've wanted to get it ever since I saw it on VirtualRealities.com! I'm going to go get it right now, and we can play together tonight! See you in Fantasia!

Leah-IfIHadAMillionDollars... *is offline.*

Arwyn sighed at her friend's exuberance. If Leah did not make such a huge amount of money as a highly successful public relations representative, her financial stability would be in a question. As it was, Arwyn was glad that she had helped her friend set up an account that automatically saved part of Leah's income every month.

Looking back at the file transfer, she saw that it was still at a measly 2 percent. Glad to have an excuse not to work, she resumed reading the *Fantasia* manual.

Getting started

When you first log on to *Fantasia*, a biometric reading will be done of your body. Your character's appearance will be based on your own appearance, with modifications depending on the race you choose and a limited range of options. Appearance modules can be bought on the VirtualRealities website to further alter your appearance.

This I have to see, thought Arwyn, bringing up the VirtualRealities website on her laptop. Choosing *Fantasia* from the many games on the website, she found the items you could purchase with real money. She ignored the vanity weapons and armour and skipped to the list of appearance modules:

Beauty – Increase your overall attractiveness by 1.

Hair colour – Expand the allowable hair colour range by 30.

Eye colour – Expand the allowable eye colour range by 30.

Skin colour – Expand the allowable skin colour range by 30.

Height – Change your height by up to 5 cm.

Proportions – Change your body measurements by up to 5 cm in total.

Age – Change your apparent age by up to 10 years.

Special modifications can by requested by emailing VirtualRealities. Prices will vary depending on request.

Each of the regular modules cost ten dollars. *Wow. Just cheap enough that I'm tempted, and just expensive enough that you pay through the nose if you want to dramatically alter your appearance. Meh, I'll create my character before deciding whether I need any of these.* She went back to reading the manual.

Choosing a race

There are many races and sub-races to choose from in *Fantasia*. Choose carefully; to change race after starting the game, you must delete your character and start back at level 1 for all skills.

Human – The most versatile of the races, humans are a balance between all attributes. The youngest and most populous of the races. No sub-races available.

Heh, of course there are no sub-races; that would be like printing "SUE ME" in bold across the front of the game. Making generalizations about race . . . bad idea.

Elf – Elves are magical creatures at home in nature. They are naturally faster and more dexterous than humans, as well as having more affinity with magic, at the cost of brute strength.

Arwyn already knew that she would choose to be an elf, having been fascinated with them since she had learned to read.

Sub-races

Dark elves – Distant cousins of surface elves, dark elves moved underground millennia ago and have developed the ability to see in pitch blackness with infrared vision. Their eyes are so sensitive to light that their sight must be shielded at all times above ground.

Sun elves – Originally from desert climates, sun elves are a race of extremes, from vivid colouring to highly specialized talents. There are no shades of grey amongst these people.

Moon elves – The original race of elves from which the other sub-races evolved, moon elves are at home in the forest, always in harmony with the trees—especially the Mana Tree, which is their main source of magic.

Avariels – Upon attaining level 50, all elves (regardless of sub-race) may embark on a quest for the Mana Tree and, upon completion, be granted a set of wings to soar in the sky.

Eee! Wings! I'm not stopping until I hit level 50 and finish that quest!

Impatient to start playing, Arwyn skimmed through the rest of the races: dwarves, goblins, beast-kin, celestials, dragonkin, elementals, undead, and merfolk. The manual also said that new races would soon be added, but Arwyn doubted she would come across something more appealing than a winged elf.

Classes

Ever felt frustrated at having to keep and train separate characters to play different classes? *Fantasia* is the game for you! Learn all the skills and abilities you want, as long as you can find the non-player character (NPC) or manual with the knowledge. Some skills can even be taught from player to player.

It is recommended that low-level players focus on one or two classes in order to gain combat levels quickly, as each class's skills must be learned separately, from beginner level. Only one character can be created per player.

The four main classes were warrior, mage, archer, and rogue, each with countless sub-classes and skill sets. After some deliberation, Arwyn decided to first focus on becoming a warrior wielding dual blades, like her favourite elven character, Drizzt Do'Urden[1]. *I really hope I can actually coordinate two swords; it would be painful—and pathetic—if I ended up cutting my own hand off.*

Skills

If fighting does not appeal to you, there is still much to do and explore in the world of *Fantasia*! In addition to the various combat skills and abilities, there are many non-combat skill sets to master, including several crafting skills, enchanting, art, cooking, and trading. Unlike in other games, the items you create are only limited by your skill level and imagination. Make highly customized items that are absolutely unique!

Cool. I'll definitely try that.

The rest of the manual was about advanced gameplay and standard navigation common to all games of this type, so Arwyn decided to jump into the game without reading further. Getting ready for bed, she lay down on the recliner in her pyjamas. *Wow. This is actually really comfortable.* Putting the sensor-helmet on, she set the time when she wanted to wake up and then turned on the game.

CHAPTER 2
SIDEKICK

Arwyn was plunged into complete darkness.

"Performing scan," said a disembodied female voice, the kind one would expect to hear announcing floors in an elevator. "Scan complete. New player detected."

A rotating form of Arwyn appeared, with a spotlight from above.

"Please select a race. This will affect your starting location."

A virtual screen appeared with the word "Human" as well as arrows on either side. Arwyn toggled through the different races, seeing her base features shift and distort depending on the option. She stopped at "Elf" and studied the change. Her facial features took on an exotic cast, her eyes gaining a catlike tilt while her cheekbones and nose were more accentuated. *Elves sure are a good-looking bunch.* She selected "Confirm."

"Please select a sub-race. This will affect your starting location."

The word "Elf" faded and "Moon" appeared. Flipping through the three choices, the only difference she noted was her skin changed from very pale to very tan to jet-black. Shrugging, she picked moon elf because it was the closest to her natural skin tone. (She was an indoorsy kind of girl.)

"Please select your hair colour." A colour palette appeared, a red dot indicating her actual hair colour, while a red circle around it showed how far she could shift without purchasing an appearance module. She was pleased to find that if she did not change the darkness level, she could shift the hue to purple, her favourite colour. Her natural hair was dark enough that the shift to purple could only be seen in bright light, but she was pleased with the subtle effect. Her eyes were slightly lighter than her hair, and the resulting purple slightly brighter.

"Would you like to purchase any appearance modules?"

Arwyn was tempted to make herself taller—she was already above average for female height, but nothing that would make her stand out—but controlled herself. "No, I'm satisfied."

"Character appearance confirmed. Please choose a character name."

"Arwyn, A-R-W-Y-N." Her mother had actually named her after an elf on purpose; no sense in letting it go to waste.

"Sorry, that name is taken. Please choose another."

Are you serious? Arwyn was terrible at coming up with names on the spot. After thinking for (quite) a while, she thought, *Hmm, elves . . .* "Fey, F-E-Y."

"Welcome to Fantasia, Fey. Your adventure begins."

At a blinding flash of light, she shut her eyes.

◊◊◊

Fey opened her eyes to an elven village, the (creatively named) Moonwood. True to elven style, all the buildings were living trees magically induced into creating hollows and bending growth to create rooms, steps, and even furniture. If you did not know it was a village, you would not recognize it as one.

A small stream of people travelled throughout the village, bypassing the obvious newbie in their midst. Wondering where to start, Fey's eyes alit upon an NPC who appeared to be carving a bird out of a block of wood. There was no icon floating over his head or any other virtual display, but she instantly knew that he was Hyurnnan, the village headman, and he had a quest for her. At her approach, he looked up.

"Ah, Fey. You are ready to leave the village and find your place in the world. Before you stray too far from the safety of the village, you must build your strength to be able to deal with the monsters you will encounter."

Since he seemed to be waiting for a response, Fey asked, "How should I do this?"

"Take this," said Hyurnnan, producing a dagger, complete with sheath, out of thin air and handing it to her. "And these," he continued, handing over twenty thin vials of red and blue liquid similarly conjured out of nothing. "Go into the Elvenwood and defeat ten slimes. Bring back three slime bubbles as proof of your victory. They live fairly close to the Moonwood; do not go too far beyond the village outskirts or risk encountering monsters far beyond your level."

At that, Hyurnnan seemed to lose all interest in her and went back to his carving.

Okay . . . Fey headed over to an out-of-the-way area at the edge of the village (or what she guessed was the edge of the village; it was hard to tell when the buildings were trees) to take stock of the situation.

The first thing she did was locate the small pouch she was wearing at her waist and stow her potions away. The pouch was fitted with a clever liner that divided it into many individual pockets but could be removed to accommodate larger objects. *I guess these are "item slots."*

Next, she looked at the dagger. *How do I "equip" this?* There did not seem to be an equipment slot mechanic, so she shrugged and tied the sheath to her belt. *As long as I can stab things with it, I guess that's equipped enough for me.*

Okay, am I ready to go defeat slime monsters? To check her stats, she called up the character menu in her head:

<Fey, level 1 moon elf.>

<No class(es).>

<HP: 25/25, MP 10/10.>

<Exp: 0/10.>

<No skills.>

. . . This is rather pathetic. I feel like I'll die if I trip over a tree and skin my knee.

Speaking of knees . . . (#RandomTangent) Fey looked down at what she was wearing. Her outfit consisted of calf-length leather boots over brown leather leggings and a white linen shirt, none of which would provide her much protection against serious injury. Her hair, which appeared completely black in the shade of the trees, was tied back in a single long braid.

Let's go level! (And become less pathetic!) Drawing her dagger, Fey set off into the forest, alert for any slime monsters about to attack.

When she reached the slimes (yeah, drop the "monster" part), Fey felt rather silly for her caution. Instead of huge (or medium) monsters with sharp teeth and claws, she encountered teardrop-shaped bags of slime with huge eyes that would sit comfortably in the palm of one hand. A thin, whippy appendage extended from the top point of the teardrop, ending in a small bubble of slime that bounced merrily as the slimes hopped around. In short, these were some of the cutest creatures she had ever seen.

The slimes, in an assortment of cheerful rainbow colours that reminded her of candy, bounced around, making occasional cute squeaks and generally ignoring her presence, obviously not the type of monster that would attack a player on sight.

Walking up to a green one, Fey gingerly picked it up by the bubble. It dangled, looking surprised.

"Aww," she said, placing it gently in the palm of her other hand. "You're just too cute. I can't kill you." As she pondered how she could advance in the game if she could not complete the newbie quest, the slime bit her. (How it did this without teeth is somewhat of a mystery.)

Yelping in surprise, Fey jerked her hand sideways, sending the slime flying to the ground with a fatal-sounding splat. She was rather surprised when the system notices dropped into her head:

<Fey has defeated the slime!>

<Fey has gained 3 experience.>

<Fey has learned Slam!>

Huh? I learned a skill? Calling up the skills menu, she read the description:

<Slam: throw the enemy to the ground with devastating force.>

<Level 1: opponents 2 kg or less.>

Cool. Or lame, considering the two-kilogram limit. I guess that will increase as it levels.

Remembering that the quest involved collecting slime bubbles, she looked at the slime's remains. Of its body, nothing remained but a pile of goo, but fortunately, the bubble was still intact. Gingerly fishing it out of the puddle, she wiped it off on a leaf and tucked it into her pouch. *I'd better not do that again; the bubble might not survive impact.*

The slime also appeared to have ingested a coin, which she also wiped clean and stowed away. *I really hope that's not where all monsters keep their gold.*

Looking around, Fey picked her next target, a red slime. (She's already murdered a slime, so might as well go all in, apparently.) Aware now that they would attack once provoked, she approached cautiously. *So . . . I stab it?* Still rather unwilling to kill the adorable creatures, Fey poked it with her dagger, jumping back when it snarled in a cute, high-pitched voice.

The slime hopped toward her, but every time it jumped, slime leaked out of the small hole Fey had made. By the time it had closed the metre between them, it looked distinctly deflated and half dead. It made a half-hearted bump against her boot, leaking even more, then stopped moving.

<Fey has defeated the slime!>

<Fey has gained 3 experience!>

<Fey has learned Bleed!>

Okay, this is ridiculous. You call this combat? And you learn skills by doing such random things? A wry smile appeared on her face. *I guess this game is really suited to me.*

Calling up the skills menu, she read:

<Bleed: create a bleeding wound that causes damage over time. Cannot be negated by a health potion; can only be negated by an all-cure or bleeding potion.>

<Level 1: Cause 10 damage over 5 seconds.>

Not bad.

The third slime (green again) was dispatched with little excitement, but after the fourth—orange this time—Fey levelled up:

<Fey has reached level 2!>

<Fey has gained 5 attribute points.>

<Vitality: 6 | Strength: 6 | Dexterity: 2 | Agility: 2 | Intelligence: 2 | Willpower: 2.>

<Unspent attribute points: 5.>

In order to create a certain level of balanced development that would also benefit players when using the game's multiclass system, each base attribute automatically went up by one per level in addition to five free points that could be assigned by the player. Fey, remembering her plan to become an agility-based warrior, put three points into strength and one each into agility and dexterity.

As Fey went on killing slimes, they seemed to sense the danger and began to flee. Seeing as they made a squishing sound with every hop and moved quite slowly, she had no trouble keeping track of the colourful creatures. *I feel like a murderer,* she thought mournfully, slashing one open (blue) from behind and killing it instantly. Upon accidentally stepping on one that tried to hide in leaf litter (colour unknown), Fey learned Stomp.

When she killed the ninth slime (yellow), she levelled up again and stopped to apply her attribute points. By the time she refocused on her surroundings, the slimes had all successfully reached hiding places.

Fey spotted a beautiful purple slime unsuccessfully attempting to camouflage against a contrastingly brown tree. *Aww, my favourite colour, too.*

Steeling herself, she walked up to make the kill. Deciding to train Bleed, she poked the slime lightly with her dagger. Instead of attacking her, it just cringed away. *Gah, now I'm a bully and a murderer,* she thought, resisting the urge to break into hysterical laughter (. . . or tears).

Since it was not moving, the slime did not appear to be leaking much. Sighing, Fey picked it up by the bubble. It gave a squeak of distress but continued to passively cringe away instead of attacking her.

Nuuu . . . I can't take this. Realizing she would probably regret it, Fey put the slime on the ground and dug out a health potion. Unsure of how to go about making it drink the potion, she just dumped the liquid on its head. Instantly, the wound started healing and it reinflated.

"Okay, now shoo," she said, flapping her hand at it. "If you bite me, I *will* kill you."

Instead of taking either option, the slime just hopped up and down, looking happy and squeaking adorably.

Gah, cute overload. I have to go find some ugly monsters to fight before I'm reduced to skipping through fields of flowers and befriending the woodland creatures.

When the slime continued to hop in place rather than flee, Fey crouched down for a better look. *Great. I broke the game already; nobody heals the damn monsters.*

In a surprisingly large leap, the slime landed on her head.

<Fey has tamed the slime!>

<Fey receives a pet!>

<Fey has learned Monster Tamer!>

<Please select a name for your pet:___>

Are you kidding me? I nearly kill this thing, and it wants to be my pet? Picking it up off her head, she stared at it sternly.

It smiled back, its translucent body nearly sparkling in a patch of sunlight.

"I'm going to be creative and call you Amethyst."

<Name confirmed.>

<Amethyst, level 1 slime.>

<HP: 5/5, MP: 5/5.>

<Exp: 0/10.>

<No skills.>

Oh man. If I accidentally drop it, it's going to die. Holding it carefully in one hand, she quickly dispatched a tenth slime with the other and headed back towards the village.

When she arrived back in town, Hyurnnan looked up from his carving. "Have you completed your quest?"

"I have," Fey answered, pulling three slime bubbles out of her pouch and handing them over.

"Good. Continue building your strength. You may now venture farther into the forest. As you gain strength and riches, buy more powerful weapons and armour to match your abilities. At level 10, you may seek out an instructor to teach you the basics of your first chosen class."

<Quest complete!>

<Fey gains 10 experience. Amethyst gains 5 experience.>

"Um, sir? What do I do with these?" Fey asked, pulling out seven more bubbles, having carefully saved one from each slime. They looked remarkably like round candies.

"Sell them to the healer," he replied dismissively. "They're good for making salves." He returned to his carving.

Amethyst wriggled forward, looking interested in the bubbles, so Fey held them closer for inspection. The slime hopped onto her other hand, then ate three in quick succession. (That candy comment suddenly became foreshadowing.)

It's . . . a cannibal . . .

Appalled, Fey just stared as the slime bubbles gradually dissolved and disappeared within Amethyst's translucent body. Once they were fully absorbed, the slime grew very slightly bigger and became less . . . squishy.

<Amethyst has gained Double Membrane!>

Having become more accustomed to the randomness of *Fantasia*, Fey made no mental comment and simply called up the pet menu. She found Double Membrane in Amethyst's Abilities section.

<Double Membrane (passive): increases the amount of force needed to inflict any damage.>
<Level 1: 2x damage resistance.>

So it won't die if I drop it accidentally, only if I throw it. Sarcasm aside, Fey was quite pleased. The skills and abilities she had gained were weak, but she assumed that would change as she used them and they levelled up.

Now all I need is money . . . . Following Hyurnnan's advice, Fey wandered into the healer's shop. Rows of prepared herbs and bottles were lined up neatly on tree-shelves, while fresh herbs were strung out to dry along the walls. Something that appeared both healthy and nasty-tasting brewed in a pot over what appeared to be the magical equivalent of the type of hot plate found in a chemistry lab.

"Greetings, adventurer. How may I be of assistance?" A pretty (they were all pretty), gentle-looking elf appeared in the opposite archway from where Fey had entered. The knowledge that this was Kallara, the village healer, was automatically deposited in Fey's head.

Feeling the need to match the formal cadence the NPCs used, Fey answered, "I have recently obtained some slime bubbles and was told you might have use for them."

Kallara smiled. "I was just about to start a new batch of healing salve. If you like, I could purchase any bubbles you have. Alternatively, if you help me collect all the ingredients, I will give you a portion of the salve."

Fey did not have any other pressing tasks, and obtaining some kind of healing item seemed like a good idea, so she accepted the quest. "I would be pleased to aid you in the creation of the salve." She wanted to add something flattering about the nobility of the healing art but could not think of how to word it without sounding ridiculous and did not continue.

"Excellent! I already have most of the necessary ingredients. All I need are three buckets of water, ten slime bubbles, and a flask of slime."

Oh god, I have to kill more slimes?

Either not noticing or ignoring Fey's pained expression, Kallara continued, "You can use this bucket to fill at the stream."

Relieved at the reprieve from killing slimes, Fey grabbed the bucket and headed toward the sound of running water.

At the stream, Fey took the time to take a drink, kneeling at the edge of the water to scoop it up with her hands. (Bold of her to assume the devs wouldn't infect her with a parasite[2].) As she leaned forward, Amethyst hopped (or fell) into the shallow water with a splash. And started swelling.

<Amethyst has learned Osmosis!>

Remembering from biology class what happened to animal cells in a hypotonic environment,[3] Fey hurriedly snatched Amethyst out of the water. The slime had doubled in size but did not appear to be harmed. Curious, Fey opened the pet Abilities menu:

<Osmosis (active): absorb water to increase in size.>

<Level 1: maximum 2x size.>

Just how big is she going to get? And how do I make her shrink? She's a lot heavier now . . . . Determined not to have to carry any more weight than necessary, Fey barked, "Amethyst, shrink!" She was relieved when the slime began to shed water and returned to its original size, reminding Fey of a kitchen sponge.

Hmm . . . Fey dipped her bucket into the stream, only able to fill it halfway due to the shallowness of the water. Putting the bucket down, she then put Amethyst into the water and called, "Osmosis!" The slime obligingly swelled in size. Holding her[4] over the bucket, Fey said, "Shrink!" The bucket filled with a small amount of water, but more than Fey would have been able to manage with just the use of her cupped hands.

Finding the whole process unreasonably entertaining, Fey used Amethyst to fill the bucket to the top before picking it up. *Oof. Water is heavy.* She tottered her way back to the healer's shop, trying not to spill any.

Back at Kallara's, a large, empty pot had been set up over a new hot plate. "Pour that in here," directed the healer. Eyeing the amount of liquid, she said, "Just one more trip to the stream will suffice." The healer began gathering tools and materials while Fey returned to the stream.

After the second trip—made faster when Amethyst's Osmosis levelled up and she could triple in size—Fey faced the hysteria-inducing task of killing more slimes. Armed with a flask and instructed to fill it with liquid from the slimes' bodies as well as collecting more slime bubbles, she set off to the training grounds.

The task was, physically, very easy. When Fey found a slime, she stuck it in the flask and injured it with Bleed. It only took a few seconds before the monster met its demise, with no slime innards lost in the process. (Mentally, Fey had to deal with the very strong sensation that she was going to an unpleasant afterlife for her sins.)

The slimes appeared to remember her, starting to run away when she arrived. (The word "run" is used very loosely here.) By the time she had captured the first few, the remaining slimes had reached cover. She knew where many were, but none were in easy reach. Just as she had resigned herself to climbing a tree, she heard a squeak.

Amethyst, on an overhanging branch, hopped to the ground, dragging a red slime by the bubble. Fey was horrified. She had initially stowed her pet in her belt pouch with a whispered, "Don't watch," and here the diabolical slime was, dragging a comrade to its death-by-bleeding with a cheerful expression on her face.

What does it say about me that the slime that I tamed is a merciless cannibal?

Grabbing the red slime and dropping it into the flask, she tried to rationalize Amethyst's actions. *Maybe they're enemies or something. There are totally people I wouldn't be sad to see bleed to death in a flask of slime. Yeah, that must be it.* She cheered up when the slime died and she reached level 4. (The end justifies the means?)

Fishing the bubbles out of the flask, she fed the extras to Amethyst, who gained experience in the Double Membrane ability. *I hope I can feed her something else . . . Actively encouraging cannibalism isn't great.*

Kallara had the pot of water boiling and was cutting up leaves when Fey returned. She took the flask and bubbles and examined them closely while Fey stood around nervously, wondering what defect might be present. Appearing satisfied, Kallara poured the contents of the flask into the pot and gave Fey a glass tool to stir it with while she went back to cutting leaves.

Fey watched with interest as Kallara pressed oil from the thick, triangular leaves. "What kind of plant is that?"

"Aloe. Salve is quite easy to make. I'm just . . . " And she was off, providing a running commentary of what she was doing, with practical tidbits on how to optimize the process that made it clear she was a master potion-maker.

Hmm . . . maybe I should learn some of this. Having extra potions and stored healing abilities could never hurt.

Kallara eventually popped the slime bubbles and mixed their contents with aloe oil. The boiling slime was strained out of the water, cooled, and added to the mix. "Now, this mixture would help with cuts and burns," she said, still in lecture mode, "but its most important property is its ability to absorb healing magic."

Placing her hand just over the salve, she said, "Blessing of Health." A golden glow began to emanate from her hand, seeming to be absorbed by the mixture. Kallara closed her eyes in concentration, and the light began to pulse in a steady beat, about once a second. This went on for two to three minutes before the healer opened her eyes and let her hand drop to her side, cheeks flushed as if she had just undergone physical exertion.

To Fey's surprise, Kallara asked, "Would you like to try?"

"Me?" Fey said, eyes wide.

"The task is quite simple. Concentrate on infusing the salve with healing energy, then say, 'Blessing of Health.' Continue to focus on the healing energy; it's useful to say or think the word 'heal' repeatedly."

"If you say so," Fey answered, doubting that it was as easy as the healer made it look. She gave it a try anyway. Feeling somewhat silly, she held her hand over the salve, focused on healing, and said, "Blessing of Health."

When her hand actually began glowing, she mentally jumped up and down with excitement and gave herself a high five. (How one high-fives oneself is mysterious but nonetheless possible in the imagination.)

Taking a calming breath, she decided to speak aloud to lessen the need for mental concentration. "Heal."

The light pulsed, making her even more excited. She felt a mildly pleasant tingling sensation running down her arm and out through the hand held over the salve. *Is this what magic feels like? So cool!*

Smug at her success, Fey continued with a second "Heal," only to be totally deflated when the result was a stab of pain between her eyes and:

<Failure. Insufficient mana.>

Aww, so lame.

Kallara made her feel slightly better when she said, "That was well done. Not everyone is able to invoke healing power on their first try. As you increase in magical reserves, you will surely be able to create powerful potions, perhaps even lay healing directly on people."

Is she saying I should become a healer? I hate having to be dependent on other people, though.

While Fey pondered her future, Kallara filled a small ceramic flask with the newly made healing salve and handed it over, along with a 20-gold piece.

"You don't have to pay me," Fey protested. "My reward was just supposed to be a portion of the salve."

"Take it; you've earned it," Kallara said with a smile. "You finished collecting ingredients quite quickly, and the slime you collected was exceptionally pure. You saved me the time it usually takes to filter out all the dirt and leaves."

I guess most people don't just let them bleed to death in the flask . . . Fey took the money.

<Quest complete!>

<Fey gains 20 experience. Amethyst gains 10 experience.>

<Amethyst has reached level 3!>

<Fey has learned Blessing of Health!>

"Thank you," Fey said to the healer, happy with the unexpected earnings as well as the learned spell.

"Return anytime and I will teach you more potion-making," Kallara said with a smile.

Fey left the tree-shop, feeling the beginnings of friendship with Kallara.

Wait, she's just an NPC . . . Those were all programmed responses.

Somewhat subdued, she went to find her next task.

CHAPTER 3
KICK START

Walking around the village, Fey noticed a notice board (haha, it fulfilled its function) at the edge of the village's central clearing. On it were flyers from players and NPCs alike requesting items to be collected, tasks to be performed, and expeditions to be joined.

Most of the tasks were far beyond what Fey could accomplish at her level, so she skimmed past them quickly.

A flyer with an illustration caught her eye, titled Twiggy Collection. The drawing was of a woody monster that looked like a large branch that had suddenly developed feet, eyes, and a mouth. The task was to collect thirty—presumably dead—twiggies and deliver them to the village tavern. The reward was 30 gold and the monsters were only level 2, so Fey decided to accept the task. Following the directions on the flyer, she left the village by a different trail than had led to the slimes.

The twiggies looked nearly as harmless as the slimes, though thankfully less guilt-inducingly cute. Each one was as tall at the "head" as Fey's knee, with smaller branches splitting from there and reaching up to hip level. The main trunk was only about twice as thick as Fey's forearm (and she was a skinny child).

Eyeing the woody creatures, Fey looked doubtfully at her dagger. Stabbing or slashing one seemed like a recipe for a very dull weapon. Just in case the game had an unrealistic damage system, she slashed a twiggy experimentally, putting a moderate amount of force behind the strike.

Nope, all real. Fey's attack knocked the twiggy flat and left a barely perceptible cut on its bark. Pressing her thumb carefully to the edge of the dagger, she found a section had become quite dull.

"Hmm . . . " Fey pondered, putting the dagger away. The twiggy slowly struggled to its feet and began to attack, but it walked so slowly that taking a step back every half a minute or so was sufficient to stay out of its reach.

As if in response to Fey's vocalization, Amethyst squeaked from her position on Fey's shoulder.

Oh yeah. How am I going to use her in combat? Looking at the twiggy's pointy branches, she rather doubted the slime's membrane would hold up well against an attack.

Nearby twiggies were also converging on Fey's position to attack, but she simply took another step backward while poking and prodding Amethyst to determine the slime's strong and weak points (*pokepoke*).

The strong points were few. Despite the Double Membrane ability, Amethyst's body was still quite soft and squishy. The bubble-arm as well as the bubble itself seemed to be made of firmer stuff.

"Hmm . . . " Fey repeated. Holding the slime in front of a twiggy, she used her index finger to flick the bubble at its trunk.

"Now do that on your own," Fey told the slime.

Amethyst obligingly tapped the twiggy with her bubble, then looked to her owner for approval.

Fey was unimpressed. "Like you're actually trying, please."

Amethyst doubled her efforts. The resulting strike was still pathetically weak, but a system notice appeared:

<Amethyst has learned Whip!>

The vague beginnings of a plan began to take shape. Fey returned to the village to gather supplies.

Fey located the tree-shop that was the general store and entered. Boxes and shelves that extended straight from the walls and floor held a variety of gear and supplies.

An elf that looked to be in his mid-twenties was stacking potions in a decorative pyramid to one side of the store. Fey's system-granted knowledge told her this was Jeral, the shopkeeper's nephew. "Greetings. How may I be of assistance?"

"I need a rope."

"Rope, is it?" Jeral went over to a different shelf and picked up a coil of thin rope. "Would this fit your needs?"

Fey took the item and examined it. Despite how thin it was, it appeared expertly crafted and quite strong. Satisfied, she asked, "How much is it?"

Jeral smiled charmingly. "For such a beautiful maiden? Naught but five gold."

The elf had classically elven good looks and was clearly used to taking advantage of them. Fey could feel herself starting to blush and quickly paid and left before she could embarrass herself. Gold was the only currency in *Fantasia* (none of that nonsense with bronze and silver) and one gold the lowest denomination, so there was no point in trying to haggle over such a cheap item.

She did not notice Jeral watching her leave with an amused smile on his face.

By the time Fey returned to the twiggies, they had forgotten about her earlier attacks and were going about their normal business. Fey quickly seized an individual by both ends and ran off a short distance from the rest of the monsters. Ignoring its feeble attempts to escape, Fey briskly tied it up at both ends and secured it against a tree.

Satisfied that it was unable to move enough to harm her pet, Fey put Amethyst on the ground in front of the twiggy and said, "Whip!"

Obediently, the slime sent her bubble flying out. It bounced harmlessly off the monster without leaving the slightest mark.

Tsking at the weak attack, Fey pulled up the skill description:

<Whip: strike a foe with a lashing motion.>

<Level 1: 1 pound of force.>

Fey stared mutely at her incredibly weak pet. "Just . . . practice. A lot. Hit the twiggy until it dies." She really hoped the amount of force scaled reasonably quickly with the skill level, or the slime would never be able to do any damage whatsoever.

Amethyst gave a squeak of understanding and got to work, pounding away at the wriggling twiggy.

Putting thoughts of her pet aside, Fey moved on to considering her own fight against the twiggies. Ideally, she would get a heavy, bladed weapon like an axe, but it would be a waste of resources to acquire one when it was not something she could see herself using as a long-term weapon.

Short of an axe to inflict heavy cuts, she supposed the next best choice would be bludgeoning damage. Fey decided to try out her real-life tae kwon do skills and see what she could accomplish.

Walking up to a twiggy, she raised her knee and snapped out a front kick. The vertically oriented kick sent the light creature flying several paces upward and outward, where it began the slow struggle of climbing to its feet.

<Fey has learned Snap Kick!>

Fey squinted at the now-distant twiggy, trying to determine whether she had actually done any damage. The experience of fighting such light creatures was considerably different from fighting human opponents, most of whom easily outweighed her by at least ten kilograms.

Changing strategies, Fey next went for a roundhouse kick, turning sideways to orient her kick horizontally. She exaggerated the turn more than usual to give the kick a slight downward component and avoid sending her new target into the air. She felt a much more satisfying impact this time as it was partially caught against the ground before being knocked flat.

<Fey has learned Roundhouse Kick!>

The twiggy started struggling to its feet, but compared to the one she had sent flying, it was visibly struggling. Encouraged by the signs of damage, she followed up by raising a foot high above her head and slamming her heel straight down at the twiggy's head level.

<Fey has defeated the twiggy!>

<Fey gains 6 experience. Amethyst gains 3 experience.>

<Fey has learned Axe Kick!>

<Stomp, Snap Kick, Roundhouse Kick, and Axe Kick have merged into the passive ability Kicking!>

<Kicking: all kicking attacks gain a strength bonus.>

<Level 1: 105% strength.>

Niiice. Compared to the earlier skills Fey had learned, mostly by accident, the kicking skills felt more like a retroactive description of something she could already do, with no sense of a skill "activating" when she kicked. Having the passive bonus suited her quite well.

Encouraged, Fey let loose and attacked the rest of the twiggies, using snap kicks to send them flying if too many converged on her at once but otherwise relying primarily on axe kicks for damage. When she had defeated a whole group of them, she gathered up the bodies in a tidy pile of firewood, finding occasional coins stuck in odd crevices.

Task done, she went to go check on Amethyst's progress. There was now a definite bubble-shaped indent in the twiggy's trunk, but it was still struggling as vigorously as before against the ropes. "Keep going," she told the slime, who had paused to cast a questioning look at her approach.

A new wave of monsters appeared, but Fey still had plenty of time to distribute her attribute points from levelling up before the slow creatures got anywhere near her.

The second group died even more quickly than the first as Fey became more accurate at hitting their weak point (the face) and her Kicking skill levelled up. Counting the number of bodies she had collected, she estimated that a third wave of monsters would be sufficient to bring her quota to thirty. She glanced over to gauge Amethyst's progress. The middle of her victim's trunk was definitely battered and pulpy, but it was still struggling weakly. *I hope she's done by the time I'm ready to go . . .*

"Faster," she told the slime, who obligingly increased the pace of her repeated Whip attacks.

When the third wave of twiggies appeared, Fey noticed one individual hanging back instead of attacking with the rest. Keeping an eye on it as she fought, she noticed that it seemed to be watching her fighting, an unusual amount of intelligence in its expression.

Acting on instinct, Fey went out of her way to show off, sending twiggies flying more often than necessary as well as using flashy kicks that involved spinning and jumping. She even managed to hit a twiggy in midair on a second kick after sending it flying with the first.

With a final axe kick on a standing twiggy that left it partially split where its main forks met the trunk, only Fey and the last twiggy were left. (In spirit. In body, they were all still there.)

With a look of respect in its cartoonish eyes, the twiggy bowed.

Feeling rather silly, and not quite sure what she was doing, Fey bowed back.

<Fey has tamed the twiggy!>

<Fey receives a pet!>

<Monster Tamer has reached level 2!>

<Please select a name for your pet:___>

Oh, so that's what the hell I was doing. I guess I'm going to have a small army by the time I reach level 20 (#Foreshadowing).

The twiggy started walking toward Fey, but it did not look like it would close the metre or so between them anytime soon.

"Feh, your legs are so short, you're more of a stumpy than a twiggy," she muttered.

<Name confirmed.>

<Stumpy, level 2 twiggy.>

<HP: 12/12, MP: 10/10.>

<Exp: 10/25.>

<No skills.>

"Hey," she yelled indignantly. "I didn't actually want to name it Stumpy!"

The system notice made no reply.

"Aargh, stupid game."

Moving on from her irritation, Fey finished piling up the twiggy bodies (we could probably just call them "logs" now).

<Amethyst has defeated the twiggy!>

<Amethyst gains 6 experience. Fey gains 3 experience.>

Huh. I guess she gets half my experience and I get half her experience. Or is it a third and two-thirds?

Fey realized that the rhythmic sound of Amethyst's repeated attacks had not stopped. "It's dead, Amethyst, you can stop now," she called, walking over to untie the dead twiggy, now with a fist-sized area of pulpy mush in its centre.

"Good job, Amethyst!" Fey praised, looking at the damage.

Amethyst jumped up and down and squeaked.

Fey used the rope to tie the logs into three linked bundles and slung the contraption over her shoulder to haul back to the village.

Ugh, heavy. The trip back felt a lot longer than the journey out.

Her mood was vastly improved at the three-quarter point of the walk, when she received a system notice:

<Fey's strength has increased to 24 (+1)!>

Ooh, you can actually improve your attributes through practice. Hefting her bundles a little higher on her shoulder, she finished the trip with less internal complaint.

CHAPTER 4
WINDFALL

The tavern-keeper, Fey was surprised to see, was human. *I guess elves don't aspire to start taverns?*

As she approached the tree-building, he came outside to collect wood from a rather small pile near the entrance. The game system informed Fey that this was Tallen, who had moved to the Moonwood about ten years prior.

Compared to the slender elves everywhere, Tallen's tall and burly build looked even larger. He might have looked intimidating, but the cheerful smile he sent her way gave her the impression of a friendly bear.

"Ah! So somebody answered my notice. I was just about to run out of wood."

"Yes, sir," said Fey, "but why do you need all these twiggies?"

"For cooking fires, of course. You can't cut down trees in the Elvenwood. Well, not unless you want to die," he said with a chuckle. "But twiggies work just fine, so I can't complain."

So . . . we can't kill trees for wood, but killing animals is okay?

"Anyways, just pile those over here." He gestured at the woodpile. "And here's your reward," he said, pulling a 5-gold and 25-gold piece from a pocket.

<Quest complete!>

<Fey gains 20 experience. Amethyst gains 10 experience. Stumpy gains 10 experience.>

"Would you like a meal as well? On the house."

"That would be great, thanks," Fey said, noticing that her exertion had indeed made her somewhat hungry.

"Just come in and seat yourself wherever there's room," said Tallen, disappearing through the tree-tavern's entrance.

"Sure. I just have a few things to take care of and I'll be back in a few minutes," said Fey, going back to retrieve her pets.

Amethyst was right near the end of the trail, having kept up with Fey's slow walking pace reasonably well. Fey scooped up the slime and continued down the path.

Stumpy was still closer to the twiggy monster area than the village. Sighing, Fey picked him up and braced him on her shoulder before marching back to the Moonwood. *Ugh, more trouble than it's worth. I don't want to have to carry something this heavy everywhere.*

Entering the tree-tavern, she found the décor more human-looking than the other shops she had visited. The long tables and benches that took up most of the space were still grown directly out of the floor, but someone had taken the effort to sharpen the corners and edges so that they looked more like carved furniture.

"There you are! I was wondering if you'd been eaten by wolves," Tallen called out. (Fun image.) "Sit down and I'll bring you some stew. Ale or cider?"

"Cider, please." Fey retained a childlike aversion to all things bitter, including alcohol, dark chocolate, and coffee. She sat at one of the long tables, several seats down from the tavern's only other patron. Judging from her clothes, Fey guessed she was a mage, and relatively high level given the newness of the game.

The mage looked up from reading a book. Her eyes fixed on Amethyst, seated on Fey's shoulder. "Why do you have a monster on your shoulder? How do you keep it from attacking?"

"Well, actually, it's a pet. You can tame monsters and turn them into pets," Fey explained.

"You don't say!" exclaimed the mage. She patted Amethyst, who had hopped to the table in exploration. "It's so cute! I don't suppose you'd consider selling it to me?"

"Uh, no, thanks. I'm kind of fond of her." (Diabolical cannibalism and all.)

The mage sighed. "Oh well. It looks like its main element is water, anyways. If you had an earth element pet, I'd really have to buy it from you. I'm an earth mage."

"Well, actually . . . " Fey picked up Stumpy and put him on the table.

"A twiggy! It's perfect!" the mage exclaimed. "I really *have* to have it. How about a thousand gold for it?"

"A thousand," Fey repeated, stunned by an offer two orders of magnitude larger than the amount of money she currently had.

"No? Two, then."

Fey's mind finally caught up to the conversation and she said, "Deal," before the poor stranger could start offering even higher sums of money.

"Great!" she said with a smile, opening a trade dome.

<Welcome to *Fantasia* trading!>

<A trade dome has been activated. If a player leaves the dome without both sides having agreed to a trade, all items and money will be returned to their original owner and the trade will be cancelled.>

"Okay," said the mage, taking out two crystal coins and placing them on the table. "Do you accept two thousand gold in exchange for your pet twiggy?"

"Yes."

<Trade confirmed.>

<Fey gains 2,000 gold.>

<Pet ownership transferred.>

"What did you name it?"

" . . . Stumpy," Fey confessed.

"Stumpy," the mage repeated. "Well. I think I'll go with 'Alder.' I'm Terra, by the way." She held out a hand, and Fey shook it.

"I'm Fey."

"Fey. I'll remember that name."

<Fey's fame has increased to 1 (+1)!>

Now that's just silly.

Tallen came over with a bowl and tankard, the mouthwatering aroma of stew sharply increasing Fey's appetite.

"Enjoy your meal. I'm off to experiment with my new familiar."

Carefully stowing away her 1,000-gold coins, Fey took a bite of the stew. It tasted even better than it smelled, driving all extraneous thoughts from her head.

I wonder if there are any negative effects from binge-eating in game.

Despite the thought, the hearty stew quickly filled Fey's stomach. Thanking Tallen for the meal, she left the tavern.

The slight jingle of her belt pouch reminded Fey of the crystal coins inside, triggering the I'm-going-to-get-robbed feeling that she always experienced when carrying large amounts of cash. She walked speedily toward the bank to deposit her windfall, taking the opportunity to exchange the numerous 1g coins she had collected from monsters for larger denominations.

It occurred to Fey that she could go shopping for better equipment, but it would make more sense to wait until she reached level 10 and joined her first class. She checked her status page again:

<Fey, level 6 moon elf.>

<No class.>

<HP: 79/79, MP: 30/30.>

<Attributes: Vitality: 14 | Strength: 24 | Dexterity: 10 | Agility: 10 | Intelligence: 6 | Willpower: 6.>

<Pet: Amethyst, level 5 slime.>

That's more like it. While she was by no means strong yet, she no longer felt so fragile that she might accidentally die.

Let's get levelling!

Fey headed back to the notice board, where a few more quests were now open to her. Some were item collection requests for herbs and mushrooms; she ignored these for now.

She considered a request for wolf pelts. The monsters were at level 7, which she should be able to handle as long as she was careful not to provoke a whole group at once. *Maybe I could get a wolf pet. That would be pretty cool.*

Just as she was about to accept the quest, it occurred to her that her tolerance for danger in a virtual reality environment was lower than in other games she had played. She considered wolves' sharp teeth and looked down at her oh-so-rippable clothing and complete lack of armour.

. . . Maybe later . . . Fey did not enjoy pain. (Not that there's anything wrong with that kind of thing.)

Looking back over the requests, Fey realized that the mushrooms being requested were actually monsters she could fight for experience. Better yet, there were no exact numbers requested; the reward was stated in gold per mushroom. There were five different varieties: white, yellow, green, blue, and poison. Wary of poison, Fey decided to go after the level 4 blue mushrooms.

CHAPTER 5
MAGIC

There were other people out hunting mushrooms. Fey briefly considered joining a party but quickly decided against it. With a group of newbies, the lack of specialization meant that there was no particular increased efficiency in banding together. *Also, eew, strangers.* She was able to talk to people she did not know, but she certainly did not enjoy it.

Avoiding the noise of the other players, Fey found a separate clearing full of blue mushrooms.

As mushrooms went, these were huge, each one roughly the size of a soccer ball.[5] Other than their size and vivid blue caps, they did not have any particularly distinguishing features. (Well, other than having eyes and being able to jump around.)

The mushrooms hopped around, gaining more height and distance with each jump than the level 1 slimes. They were fairly cute, but not unbearably so.

Again blatantly disregarding normal behaviour during combat, Fey picked up a mushroom for examination. It was quite light and spongy in consistency, with no teeth or other pointy bits that she could identify.

Pretty sure it can't hurt Amethyst. Fey put the slime on the ground and dropped the wriggling mushroom on top. The two bounced off each other, looking none the worse for wear.

"Okay, Amethyst, attack!"

Slime and mushroom charged at each other (if you could call hopping along at a moderate speed "charging"). The resulting collision sent both of them bouncing backward, tumbling around in disarray. Determinedly, they rolled upright and charged again.

With iron self-control, Fey refrained from falling to the ground in helpless laughter. *I really need a camera.* Remembering that she was in a game, she used the system's camera function to record one charge and collision, then left the two to "fight it out," turning her attention to the other mushrooms.

Drawing her dagger, Fey slashed at a mushroom. As expected of a mushroom, it did not bleed. Less expected was the way it launched itself at her with bruising force.

"Ow!" Mad now, she threw it to the ground and stomped on it multiple times until it stopped moving (*dead*). It then desiccated quickly, shrinking to less than half its former size in the process. She even found a coin. *That is remarkably convenient,* she thought dryly, tucking both the mushroom and the coin away in her belt purse.

Sixteen mushrooms and several bruises later, Fey had reached level 7 (woot) and discovered the secret to killing the mushrooms effectively. They had a vital spot in the centre of their stems, the discovery of which coincided with Fey experiencing the intense satisfaction of a one-hit kill.

After assigning her new attribute points, Fey glanced over at Amethyst and her mushroom adversary. Both appeared to be either sleeping or unconscious from exhaustion. Fey picked them up and placed them against a tree, sure they would be back at it as soon as they woke up. *Aww, they're so cute together.* She snapped another picture.

Just the few minutes' break was enough for Fey to stiffen and start to really feel the bruises she had collected in fighting. Checking her health bar, she saw that it had fallen by a significant amount: 66/88.

Health in the game did not drop linearly outside of special statuses such as curses and bleeding. In order to more accurately depict physical injury, minor injuries such as superficial bruising were unable to drop health points below certain set points, and hitting vital points had a much larger impact on damage than in most games. Fey could continue fighting the mushrooms all day and her health would not drop much further than it already had.

Still, the bruises hurt, so Fey decided to test out her healing balm. She seemed to feel better just scooping some ointment onto her finger. *Whoa, this stuff is powerful. Or maybe it's just the placebo effect.*[6]

Any doubts as to the effectiveness of the salve were put to rest when she dabbed a tiny amount onto a bruise on her arm; not only did that bruise disappear, but she was instantly restored to full health, all her aches melting away.

With the guilty, sinking feeling she always felt when she was wasting money, Fey scraped the rest of the balm back into the container, resolving to save it for when she had gained a few levels (let's say, 50 or so) or she was actively dying.

Another thirty mushrooms later, Fey had reached level 8 and exceeded the meagre capacity of her belt pouch. She decided to round off her total to fifty mushrooms and then go make a delivery. She pounced (*stab*stab*stab*), then went to collect Amethyst.

The slime was jumping up and down on the blue mushroom's head. "Go, Amethyst!" Fey cheered, seeing her pet finally getting the upper hand in the fight.

As she approached, however, it became clear that Amethyst was *not* pounding the mushroom into the ground; both creatures were smiling, and Amethyst's aerial activities appeared to be a team effort. (Just then, she performed a backflip.)

"What are you doing, Amethyst?" Fey groaned. Here she was with a pet who would drag one of its own kind to certain death, then start using a mushroom as a trampoline. . . . *It's not normal. I feel like it's a failed mutation that should be put out of its misery for the good of the species . . .*

At the sound of Fey's voice, mushroom and slime broke apart to "stand" (or whatever the verb is for footless creatures) side by side, looking expectantly at her.

Fey stared at them for a long moment. She scooped Amethyst up to hold the slime at face level. "You're screwed up, you."

Amethyst just blinked.

Sighing, Fey put the slime on her shoulder and turned to the mushroom. Other than turning its head to watch the exchange, it had not moved.

Bowing to the inevitable, Fey picked it up.

<Fey has tamed the blue mushroom!>

<Fey receives a pet!>

<Monster Tamer has reached level 3!>

<Please select a name for your pet: ___>

Okay, so I don't even necessarily have to do *anything to tame a monster?* Fey bounced the mushroom up and down in her hand while thinking. (It looked delighted.)

Name, name, name . . . Fey was careful not to think aloud lest the system pick another dumb name out of her words. *Mushroom. 'Shroom.* She could not think of a witty name that included "mush" or "shroom." (Because there aren't any.)

Her mind flitted to the drugs and medicine unit of her high school chemistry class (because she is that random). "Magic," she declared triumphantly.

(For the poor, unrandom souls who were not able to follow that thought progression, this is a reference to "magic mushrooms," which contain the psychoactive compounds psilocybin and psilocin and are taken for their hallucinogenic effects.)

<Name confirmed.>

<Magic, level 4 blue mushroom.>

<HP: 36/36, MP: 20/20.>

<Exp: 58/121.>

<Skills: Spore.>

Ooh, it came with a skill.

<Spore: release spores that induce various status effects.>

<Level 1: random effect, 10% chance of success, 5 m effect radius.>

Fey tried to think of the kinds of random effects she could expect; her mind promptly delivered a list of moves from Pokémon. *Stat debuffs, poison, paralysis, sleep, confusion. Maybe a mesmerize/ attract. Probably not burn?* Fey was sure the developers of *Fantasia* had come up with effects beyond her limited imagination.

She shrugged; presumably they were all detrimental to her opponents and therefore her strategy (quote-unquote "strategy") would be to cast Spore and then attack. *I wonder if I could just keep casting Spore and get all the effects to stack.*

"Okay, let's go." Arms full of the pile of dead mushrooms that would not fit into her pouch, she set off for the designated drop-off site, Amethyst sitting on her shoulder and Magic bouncing merrily along behind.

Fey successfully arrived in the area she intended. (Pretty amazing that she didn't get lost. Fey-dar[7] works!) There was a rather suspicious-looking cloaked figure in the clearing, scribbling away in a notebook. She could not make out many features, just a faint outline of limbs that suggested an adult male and the glint of heavy, round glasses that looked almost cartoonish.

Who wears glasses in a fantasy video game? Arwyn was heavily nearsighted and had been wearing glasses since elementary school. She was so used to the sensation of frames around her eyes that she sometimes forgot she was wearing them, but even she appreciated the game's correction of her eyesight in a world where things might be attacking her head on a regular basis.

Mentally shrugging, she called out, "Are you the one who put out a notice for mushroom collection?"

"Oh—ahem, ye-yes, it was," he said, stumbling over his words and his feet as he hastily stood up.

"Well, I have fifty blue mushroom caps here," she said, when he said nothing further. (*awkward pause*)

"Oh, okay," he said, producing a sack from somewhere in his cloak and opening a trade dome.

Riiight. Fey dropped the mushrooms into the sack.

He thrust two 100g pieces at her. "Do you accept two hundred gold for fifty blue mushroom caps?"

"Yes," said Fey, attempting to sound normal while all her instincts screamed that she had somehow managed to get caught in a sketchy situation.

<Trade complete.>

<Fey gains 200 gold.>

<50 blue mushroom caps transferred.>

"So . . . what are you using the mushrooms for?" Fey asked, making one last attempt at normal social interaction.

"I, uh, can't tell you."

"Okay . . . I'll be going now," Fey said, backing away in a somewhat sideways fashion so it would not look like she was backing away. She had initially intended to hunt for more mushrooms, perhaps even challenge the level 5 poison mushrooms, but it no longer seemed like a good idea.

It'll be fine, she tried to reassure herself. *What trouble can you get into with fifty measly blue mushrooms?*

She would have been less nonchalant had she had at the time more knowledge regarding the Spore ability.

Instead of returning to the mushrooms, she headed back to Moonwood village.

CHAPTER 6
SLUGFEST

Back at the notice board, Fey decided to pick only NPC-given tasks to minimize the chances of getting into another sketchy situation. She scanned the requests for monsters at or below her level. The monsters' movement speeds and attack abilities inevitably increased with level. *Noo . . . I don't want to die,* Fey thought, being melodramatic. While they would likely be able to inflict minor damage, beginner monsters were almost all diminutive in size, and to die from fighting one would be quite the feat.

Just as she was about to prod her weak-minded, pain-intolerant self into just picking a quest and accepting the inevitable injuries, a posting caught her eye: Clear giant slugs from Pine Grove. The slugs were at level 10, two above her own, but given how slow they were, she was confident she could avoid any attacks and leisurely inflict damage, eventually defeating them even if it took more time.

Following the directions on the post, Fey headed toward Pine Grove.

The path took her far deeper into the forest than she had been before. Fey walked for more than an hour, passing various monsters as she went; thankfully, it appeared that none would attack as long as she stayed on the marked trail.

As she went farther into the wilds, the trees became larger. Alarmingly large. Really, really big. At first, Fey was simply impressed with the wonder and majesty of nature, but when they continued to get even bigger, she started to suspect they were starting to exceed even the largest trees in real life. *What happened to 99% realism? Rawr.* (Really, she was just annoyed at first tripping over then having to climb over giant tree roots.)

The path turned into more of an obstacle course, weaving over, under, and around roots thicker than her body, and she did not complete it entirely unscathed, a few small falls adding to her collection of bruises.

<Fey's dexterity has increased to 15 (+1)!>

. . . I feel like someone's trying to make me feel bad for my entirely justified mental whining. (Oh no, she might figure out she's a Main Character! Initiate distraction.)

The minimap finally indicated she had arrived at her destination. Fey was confused to see a giant clearing, too perfectly circular to be a random occurrence. *Uh, isn't a grove supposed to be full of trees?*

Her eyes focused on a huge, dark object in the middle of the clearing. As she stared, her brain finally interpreted it correctly: a tree trunk that made even giant sequoias[8] look miniature. The circular clearing was simply the space beneath its massive branches.

Okay, this is going from unrealistic to physically impossible.

"Greetings, adventurer." The voice came from directly behind Fey, causing her to jump and spin in startlement.

An aged, wise-looking elf had appeared, seemingly out of nowhere. With long white hair and a white robe entirely untouched by dirt, he perfectly fit the "wise sage" stereotype. "Have you come in response to my request for aid, or has some other business brought you here?"

"I came to help with the . . . slug problem," said Fey, unable to think of a sophisticated way to mention slugs and feeling like she was failing at the whole role-playing aspect of the game.

"Yes, the parasites plaguing the Pine." *Ah, so that's how you say it. The alliteration is a bit much.* "As you can see," he said, pointing, "many of them infest the tree's base, leeching its vitality. Destroy them all, and you shall be awarded the Guardian's Blessing."

Fey followed the line of the sage's arm and saw slimy spots near the bottom of the tree. "Base" was a relative term, as the highest of the slugs were still many times her height above the ground.

Ugh, so many. Might as well get it over with.

With a respectful nod to the sage and an "I will do my best to complete the task," Fey strode toward the Pine. It took a good five minutes to reach the trunk, and she muttered comments about the ridiculousness of mega-trees the whole time.

When she was finally within touching distance of the trunk, Fey inspected a giant slug up close. It was a slimy, tan-white oblong blob longer and wider than Fey's whole body. Thin eyestalks protruded from one end, distinguishing head from tail. Where it stuck to the tree and along the mucus trail behind it, Fey could see blackened, dead bark. It made extremely slow progress across along the trunk, with no clear goal that she could discern.

Inspection over, Fey was left to ponder how to kill such a massive creature armed with only a dagger, a slime, and a mushroom. Most of them were at least head height off the ground, and she was not inclined toward courting death by stupid-looking fall by trying to kick them.

Let's see what this Spore thing can do. Fey picked Magic up, pointed him at the slug, and said, "Spore!"

A cloud of golden powder wafted out from the underside of Magic's cap to envelop the slug.

<Spore successful. The slug has fallen asleep!>

Uh . . . If there had not been a system notice, Fey would have thought the attack had failed, for all the difference being asleep made. She tried again. "Spore!"

<Attack failed.>

"Spore! Spore! Spore!"

After making Magic cast Spore until his magic points ran out, the slug was asleep, paralyzed, and slowed. Spore had failed numerous times and levelled up, and Fey was extremely exasperated. She put Magic down and dropped Amethyst off as well. *Time for plan B.*

She drew her dagger, looking dubiously at its short length compared to the size of the slug. *Is this even long enough to do critical damage? Maybe if I hit it in a vital spot?*

She aimed at the head end of the slug, somewhat behind the eyestalks. *Do slugs even have brains?*[9] Bracing herself for the squishy consistency, she stabbed downward.

A spasm ran down the slug's body.

<The slug has woken up!>

Nothing else happened. Fey stabbed a few more times in the same general area, to similar (lack of) effect. *I knew it. No brain. The heart, maybe? Slugs totally have hearts, right?*[10]

Having no idea where the slug's heart might be, she stabbed rather randomly along its midsection, leaving wounds that slowly oozed green-blue blood. The slug was moving, but so slowly that she could not tell if it was trying to run away, curl up defensively, or counterattack.

On her sixth stab, the slug convulsed particularly violently. *Vital spot?* she thought hopefully. She carefully noted the location of her dagger before pulling it out.

This turned out to be a fortunate decision. As soon as her weapon was free, the slug exploded, showering her with slime.

<Fey has defeated the giant slug!>

<Fey gains 30 experience. Amethyst gains 15 experience. Magic gains 15 experience.>

In the face of extreme ickiness, Fey stayed calm and rational. She carefully wiped her face clean, ensuring that no slime was left around her eyes, nose, and mouth. There was a coin stuck to her forehead, which she put away.

Only then did she screech, "EEEEWWW!" so loudly that a flock of birds was startled into flight.

Hidden in a lookout spot, the sage chuckled.

Adding injury to insult, the system notice announced:

<Fey has been poisoned!>

The thought of dying of poison far from a healer or antidote put Fey into a panic until she checked the status effect:

<Slug poison: −1 health/30 seconds.>

<Duration: 5 minutes.>

Fey did the math. *Ten damage?? What's the point of coding such a lame status effect?*

It was all too much; the shock and disgust from the slime explosion combined with the panic-turned-indignation at the poison to fill Fey with angry, violent energy. She loosed a cry halfway between a shriek and a roar, sending fear into the hearts of every creature that heard it.

Unfortunately for the slugs, they lacked hearing organs and legs to run away quickly (#Doomed). Fey raced to the nearest slug, stabbing it repeatedly without bothering to aim for vital organs. When it finally exploded, she ran to the next, then the next, then the next. Only when she had killed all twenty or so slugs within reach from the ground did she stop, panting with exertion, to survey the carnage.

A few seconds later, as if even the system notice were intimidated by her excessive violence (in reality, it was just struggling to fit her behaviour into its algorithms), she was informed:

<Fey has learned Rage!>

<Fey has learned Terrify!>

The abilities seemed self-explanatory, but she looked at the descriptions:

<Rage: harness the strength of your anger to increase your attack. Can only be activated after the player or a party member has taken damage or a negative status effect.>

<Level 1: Attack +10%, accuracy −50%.>

<Terrify: a cry to inspire fear in your enemies.>

<Level 1: radius 10 m, attack 10%, attack initiative −1.>

Attack initiative was a measure of monster aggression, which determined how likely a monster was to attack without provocation. Beginner monsters, such as slimes, had an initiative value of zero and would never attack unprovoked. Most monsters had a moderate initiative and would attack what looked like easy targets based on player strength and intimidation ability, while highly aggressive monsters would attack everyone in their vicinity, even much higher-levelled players who would almost certainly kill them.

Hmph. Fey felt like a pouting child being offered a cookie to get her out of a bad mood. The skills looked quite useful, but she was covered from head to toe in a layer of thick, foul-smelling slime, accented by pieces of slug skin and organs. (Realism isn't always great.)

In addition to her newly learned skills, Fey had decimated (in the sense of destroying approximately one-tenth of) the slug population, all the ones within reasonable reach from the ground, and one that was not. *How did I get the one all the way up there?* she wondered, looking at the distinctive remnants of a slug explosion a good three metres above the ground. (That's about ten feet for you weirdo Americans.) *Did I jump? Did I throw something?* (We'll never know, as the irresponsible author never bothered thinking through the logistics of this feat before putting it into the story.)

Dismissing the question as a mystery she was unlikely to solve, Fey looked for her pets. "Amethyst," she called. She followed the sound of squeaking until she found her wayward companions, who appeared to be playing in the poisonous remains of a slug. *Aww, crap. Can pets die of poison?* As she watched, Amethyst opened her mouth—"No! Don't!"—and ate some slug slime.

"Gah! What did you do that for?" Fey rushed over and plucked the slime-slime out of the slug slime.

Instead of her pet being poisoned, Fey was surprised by a different system notice:

<Amethyst has learned Poison Slime!>

<Poison Slime: secrete learned toxins to deal touch poison.>

<Current poison: Slug poison (–1 health/30 seconds; duration 5 minutes.>

So . . . Can she only learn one poison? Will she do the most recent poison or the most poisonous poison? Holding Amethyst by the bubble, Fey rapidly whirled the slime in a circle until all the slug slime splattered off (#Centrifuge). "Don't just go *eating* random crap," she scolded.

Amethyst squeaked, appearing to enjoy the ride. Her membrane appeared to have nonstick properties, as there was no residue at all after only a few spins. She returned to her spot on Fey's shoulder.

Magic, on the other hand, had no such properties. He also appeared entirely immune to the poison, standing in the puddle of slug slime with no system notices appearing at all. "Come along," she told him, walking to the base of the tree directly below a surviving slug.

Fey examined the trunk. The Pine's rough bark had ridges running down its length, wide enough in such a massive tree that she could wedge her feet into them, making climbing fairly easy. Belatedly realizing she could possibly be ruining her boots, Fey made her way up to the slug. She knew approximately how far along the body to attack based on her first slug kill, but it still took a few random stabs in that area before it spasmed. Grimacing, Fey turned her head away before withdrawing the dagger, protecting her face from the ensuing slime explosion. Bearing the state stoically (well, if you couldn't hear all the mental whining), she moved on to her next target.

On her way up, she noticed Magic hopping along beside her as if the tree trunk were the ground. She paused to investigate. *Does he have some kind of suction cup?* She plucked Magic off the tree and examined his underside. It was white and smooth and suction-cup-less. She put him back on the tree. He stuck. She picked him up and put him cap-first on the tree. He rolled "upright"—that is, perpendicular to the tree trunk and parallel to the ground—and stuck.

Okay, this tree is ridiculously huge, but not enough to generate enough gravitational pull for this to be possible.

"How are you doing that?" Fey asked.

Magic squeaked. ("Do what?")

Fey shook her head and moved on.

It took Fey over two hours to kill the rest of the slugs, most of that time spent climbing around. She was repeatedly poisoned, until finally:

<Fey has gained Immunity!>

Eventually, Fey dropped to the ground, covered in slime and thoroughly tired from all the climbing.

Before she could start looking for the sage, he appeared at the edge of her peripheral vision.

"Well done, adventurer."

<Quest complete!>

<Fey gains 200 experience. Amethyst gains 100 experience. Magic gains 100 experience.>

"As promised, I will endow you with a Guardian's Blessing," he continued. Raising his hands, he began humming, the sound expanding until it sounded like many voices at once.

"Guardian. Grant this child your blessing."

From between his hands appeared a glowing, translucent flower that rather resembled a butterfly. The glow began a warm yellow, but as the flower drifted toward Fey in a roundabout, butterfly-like fashion, the colour gradually shifted to violet, shrinking and brightening as it moved. By the time it reached Fey, it was a bright spark the size of her fingertip.

Gently landing near the outer corner of her left eye, it flashed and transformed into a tattoo-like marking where it had landed. (Not that Fey could see this.) Fey was infused with a sense of well-being.

"You have been made known to the Guardian of the Forest," the sage said mysteriously. "While in the forest, the Guardian may lend you strength. In return, do your best to help preserve nature's balance."

Not really understanding what had happened, Fey said, "Thank you. I will do my best."

Formalities over, the sage's face suddenly transformed with a warm, teasing smile. "I am Jerendal."

"Well met," Fey replied. "I am called Fey."

"I will remember that name." After a pause he added, "It is not often that I see an adventurer driven to battle-rage by slugs." His smile turned into a chuckle as Fey looked away, mortified.

Son of a—He saw that?

By the time Fey looked back up, Jerendal had disappeared again, the ghost of his chuckle still in the air.

<Fey's fame has increased to 2 (+1)!>

Not even close to being worth that much embarrassment.

CHAPTER 7

FIRST CLASS

On the long, slimy walk back to town, Fey realized she had reached level 10 and could advance to her first combat class (#AwkwardHappyDance). Checking the system clock, she saw that she had several hours left before she had to wake up. Time passed three times as quickly in game compared to real life, so players could experience a full day's adventure in eight hours of sleep. Fey had plenty of time to finish her advancement quest and acquire some class-related skills. Expression bright with anticipation, she set off to find the warrior class instructor.

As it turned out, there were two warrior instructors. Fey found them sparring in a clearing just off the town centre, the sound of clashing metal preceding them. Leaning against a tree, she quietly watched their skilled movements.

Based on their identical platinum hair and glacier-blue eyes, she guessed that they were siblings, perhaps even fraternal twins. The system informed her that the female, armed with a double-ended spear that fanned out into five sharp points at either end, was Irrilana; the male, using a more traditional sword and buckler, was Irrilathan. The sparring took the pair all over the clearing as Irrilathan tried to close the distance between them and bring his sword to bear, while Irrilana tried to keep him far enough away to take advantage of her weapon's superior reach. Though their movements were fast and deadly serious, they were clearly enjoying themselves.

This game really is realistic in most ways. The warrior trainers actually spar in their free time rather than waiting around for players to talk to them. Fey had even forgotten for a moment that they were NPCs.

Finally, Irrilana managed to bind Irrilathan's sword between two spear prongs and send it flying with a twist, a move that forced her to drop her weapon as well. She charged forward, barehanded. Irrilathan set his stance to absorb a tackle, but instead, Irrilana dove just beyond the reach of his grasp to pop up behind him in a lightning-fast move that must have been magically enhanced. Throwing her arms around his neck, she kissed his cheek and said, "I win."

Irrilathan laughed and simply said, "Fine," before walking toward Fey as if his sister weighed nothing at all, and as if she made him carry her around all the time. Casually holding a hand out to the side, he spoke a word that brought his sword flying into his grasp. (Coolness factor off the charts.)

"Greetings, adventurer. I assume you have come because you wish to begin the journey towards becoming a warrior."

"Yes," Fey affirmed.

Irrilana released her grip and dropped lightly to the ground, also summoning her weapon. "Warriors have many skills and strategies, but what they all have in common is fighting at close quarters, dealing and avoiding death by inches. Are you prepared for this? If not, another class will be more to your liking."

In an honest evaluation of herself, Fey knew she was really more suited to being a mage, being rather physically uncoordinated, pain-intolerant, and generally weak. Based on her experience with Kallara, it appeared she even had a knack for spellcasting in this game. She still wanted to be a warrior. It was partly out of habit, as she had always picked warrior classes in the non–virtual reality games she had played before this, and partly out of the same enjoyment of pushing her limits that had her going to tae kwon do in real life despite the same weaknesses. She also wanted to have a class that could survive solo adventuring, being highly reluctant to deal with strangers, team cooperation, and anything remotely resembling drama.

This time, she knew, clumsy mistakes would not just deplete her health bar; they would *hurt*.

Suck it up, she told herself. *The pain intensity is only 20% of real life*. "I am prepared," she told the trainers. Just to add something corny, she said, "I will look death in the eye and not flinch."

"Then go deep into the forest," said Irrilathan, pointing away from the village, "where the shadows are deep and creatures of the dark reign. Defeat ten different creatures and bring back tokens of your victories. If you succeed, you will be deemed worthy of the title of warrior."

Nodding, Fey marched off in the indicated direction.

When she was out of earshot, Irrilathan chuckled. "'Look death in the eye and not flinch'? Was she serious?"

"Nobody could say that and be serious," said Irrilana with an amused smile.

Stopping along the way to let Amethyst cannibalize some more slime bubbles, Fey reached a part of the forest where the leaves abruptly turned a darker shade of green. The game system notified her:

<Elvenwood: Dark Forest.>

Do the leaves literally have to be darker? Okay now— "Ahh!"

Fey's internal monologue was interrupted by a flying creature swooping toward her face. She reflexively flailed her hands wildly, managing to swat it away. It hit a nearby tree with a *splat* and slid to the ground, momentarily stunned.

Upon examination, the creature resolved into a small, humanoid shape equipped with dragonfly wings. *Crap. I've killed a fairy. I'm going to the fantasy equivalent of hell, where I'll be eaten and tormented and—* "Eeek!"

The creature raised its head, revealing blood-red irises surrounded by obsidian sclera. It hissed at her in a highly unnerving manner before again launching itself toward her face. Being slightly more prepared this time, Fey managed to whack it on her first try, slamming it into another tree.

It got up more gingerly this time, clearly injured. Apparently changing tactics, it started chanting in a strange, hissing language. Deciding it would be best if she did not find out the hard way that the creature was cursing her rather than just cursing *at* her, she looked around hastily for a way to interrupt its speech.

Fortunately, an answer to her problem was (literally) at hand. Fey grabbed Amethyst off her shoulder and threw the slime at the fairy monster, yelling, "Interrupt its casting!"

Given Fey's terrible aim, Amethyst landed a pace away from the fairy. She hopped over and jumped onto its face, cutting off the chant mid-syllable.

<Amethyst has learned Interrupt!>

"Good job, Amethyst!" Fey praised.

Amethyst jumped up and down happily, which the fairy did not appear to appreciate, given the slime had not moved away from its face.

Magic nudged Fey's foot, wanting to participate as well. The mushroom had alternately hopped along at Fey's walking pace or stuck to her boot in the same inexplicable manner that it had stuck to the giant Pine. Fey decided to train Magic's Spore to help it improve its success rate. "Use Spore, but don't hit Amethyst, okay?"

Nodding, Magic sent a cloud of spores that somehow parted to avoid the slime.

<The possessed fairy has been poisoned!>

"A damage effect! Good job, Magic!" Fey was so pleased that she bent down to pat him several times.

<Fey has been poisoned!>

<Blue mushroom poison: −2 health/10 seconds.>

<Duration: 5 minutes.>

Two times six times five is . . . sixty! Fey's maximum health at this point was 122, and letting it drop to half would result in significant weakness, leaving her a prime target for whatever other monsters might want to ambush her. She was so busy panicking that she almost missed the second part of the system notice:

<Level 1 Immunity effect: decrease 1 damage per poison infliction.>

<Net effect: −1 health/10 seconds.>

<Duration: 5 minutes.>

Phew. Thirty damage I can handle. Fey was almost glad she had spent the better part of an hour being coated in multiple layers of poisonous slug remains.

After the two good smacks she had gotten in, Fey was fairly confident that the unadulterated blue mushroom poison was enough to kill the fairy monster. To be on the safe side, she told Amethyst to add her slug poison, adding a few extra points of damage per minute. Stabbing a tiny humanoid felt a bit icky, so Fey settled down to let the poison do its work.

Near the end of the five minutes before the poison would wear off, the possessed fairy started convulsing, with violent, writhing motions that did not look voluntary. Fey jumped up, dagger at the ready, calling, "Amethyst, get out of there!"

A black fog rose out of the fairy's body and coalesced into a vague shape with demonic red eyes. Thankfully, instead of attacking, it dissipated into the wind.

"Thank you," said a small, weak voice.

Startled, Fey's attention was drawn back to the now unpossessed fairy. Its eyes had turned a beautiful shade of blue, and it smiled weakly at her, pale in an unhealthy way.

"You freed me," it continued. "Thank you."

Uh . . . " . . . You're welcome."

"That evil spirit possessed me several weeks ago and has been wreaking havoc in this body ever since, but it left rather than die from the poison you inflicted. I can die in peace."

"Wait—" *Die in peace?? Oh crap, I'm killing an unpossessed fairy. I'm going to the fantasy equivalent of hell, where I'll be eaten and tormented and— Wait! I know!* Remembering the way she had saved Amethyst, Fey pulled out a health potion and dumped it on the fairy, who coughed and spluttered even as its pallor receded and it became visibly stronger.

After catching its breath, it stood up experimentally, then rose into the air with a buzz of its dragonfly wings. Laughing delightedly, it zipped around in dizzying patterns.

"Thank you!" it exclaimed again, hovering in front of Fey's face. Seeing the butterfly marking next to Fey's eye, it said, "You are one of the Forest Guardian's! No wonder you came to my aid."

<Guardian's Blessing has reached level 2!>

Huh? Fey had not realized that the blessing she had received at Pine Grove could increase in level. She checked the description.

<Guardian's Blessing: Due to the blessing of the Mana Tree, you feel more vigorous when travelling in a forest. Increase the strength of your connection with the Guardian by helping creatures of the forest and preserving the balance of nature.>

<Level 2: 115% health and mana regeneration.>

That is a pretty freaking awesome bonus.

The fairy caught Fey's attention again by executing a graceful bow while still hovering in midair. "I am Stelli, and I am in your debt."

Looking at the fairy's androgynous face and body gave Fey no clues as to whether Stelli was male or female, but it felt wrong to continue thinking of a non-hostile humanoid creature as an "it." *Fairies might not even have genders; they could spawn out of mushroom spores and fairy dust for all I know.*

Idle thoughts aside, Fey replied, "My name is Fey." She did not address Stelli's comment about being in her debt, more concerned as to whether the possessing spirit counted as a monster she had defeated or whether she still had ten more to go.

"Is there any way I could be of assistance to you?" Stelli persisted.

"Well, I'm on my warrior quest," Fey said. "Not sure if you can help with that."

"I can! I can!" Stelli exclaimed. (He/she/they seemed rather excitable.) "You need to defeat monsters in the Dark Forest, correct? I can help you find them, and I am quite adept at support magic."

"Your aid would be welcome," said Fey, figuring she might as well accept the offer of help. It was unlikely that Stelli was so bad at casting buffs that Fey would be better off without the fairy . . . *Right?*

"Here we go!" Spinning quickly in the air, Stelli said, "Blessing of Vigor!"

<Blessing of Vigor: 2x health regeneration, +5 speed.>

"Come on!" Coming out of the spin with no sign of dizziness, Stelli sped into the trees, forcing Fey to jog to keep up.

Where is he/she/they even going? Fey thought, vexed. *I—* "Eeek!"

Stelli had led her straight to a giant beetle, twice the size of Amethyst, armoured with a shiny black carapace and armed with mandibles that looked like they could easily take a finger off.

The fairy flew in wobbly circles around the beetle and cried, "Dizziness!"

<Dizziness: −5 speed, −30% accuracy.>

Fey was impressed. With that much penalty to speed and accuracy, Stelli had essentially rendered the beetle several levels weaker.

My turn. Putting her pets on the ground with the nonspecific command of "Attack!" Fey advanced on the disoriented beetle. Magic and Amethyst hopped along beside her.

The beetle, despite its unrealistic size, only reached up to Fey's ankle. She shrugged and tried plan A. *What does one do when one wants to kill a bug?* She stomped down on it as hard as she could, the action boosted by her Kicking skill.

Ow. The beetle's shell felt more like a layer of stone than a chitinous exoskeleton.[11] Rather than breaking, the beetle simply bounced off the ground after sending a jarring impact up Fey's leg. Provoked, it went after Fey's ankle with its huge mandibles, forcing her to jump around awkwardly to save herself.

Plan B arrived in the form of Magic and Amethyst. They hopped forward and tackled the beetle; this had so little effect that the beetle did not even pause in its attack on Fey's feet.

They're not very smart. Physical attacks, really? With soft, squishy bodies and very little mass, the slime and the mushroom were particularly unsuited to direct physical combat. She thought that she could probably do more damage by hitting her opponents with a pillow.

"Do something else, you two!" Fey ordered (just as unhelpfully vague as her first command). She kicked the beetle, which succeeded in knocking it several paces back and hurting her foot. *Stupid boots,* she grumbled, wishing she was wearing a pair with more substantial defence. Unfortunately, pet intelligence was proportional to level, so Magic and Amethyst milled around confusedly rather than coming up with any different tactics that might be useful. (Not very effective…)

Thankfully, Stelli chimed in with some helpful advice. "Go for the underbelly."

"Oooh," Fey said, enlightened. Nudging a toe under the beetle, she flipped it onto its back. It rocked back and forth, legs waving helplessly in the air. Before she could chicken out from the ickiness of touching a giant insect, she sent her dagger plunging down into its underside, where the beetle's thinner exoskeleton broke easily under the pressure.

The beetle spasmed, but its legs continued to wave.

Eeweeweeweew. Praying that it would not explode and spray her with beetle guts, she stabbed again, closer to the head.

<Fey has defeated the giant beetle!>

<Fey gains 30 experience. Amethyst gains 15 experience. Magic gains 15 experience.>

The beetle died by desiccating in a most convenient way, leaving behind a coin and the hard part of its exoskeleton, which Fey picked up for possible usefulness later.

"Come on!" Stelli cried, zipping away through the trees before Fey had even finished packing away her loot. She hastily broke into a jog, scooping up Magic and Amethyst and chasing after the fairy. Halfway along, she tripped over a tree root but managed to stay on her feet with some minor flailing.

Tripping along, she nearly stepped on her next opponent. This would have been bad, because the monster was covered in thick, pointy spikes as long as her hand. In fact, the creature appeared to be a pair of eyes, spikes, and nothing else.

Fey's nearness appeared to offend it, and it bristled, spikes tilting threateningly in her direction. *How do I even—*

Stelli flew in wide circles around the spike monster, glowing brighter and brighter. "Blind!" The fairy's body burst with intense light.

<Blind: −70% accuracy.>

"Ahh!" As Stelli had not warned Fey to cover her eyes, she was affected by the debuff as well. Her vision became a mess of afterspots.

The spike monster did not appreciate the light either; it went from bristling to shaking violently in such a way that spikes were thrown in all directions, somehow immediately replaced by more spikes on its body.

"Oww!" With such an attack, the spike-thing did not need accuracy; it simply filled the 2π steradians[12] around it with a never-ending supply of spikes. Shielding her pets with her arms and back, she sidled over to the monster, drew her dagger, and viciously slashed it in half.

<Fey has defeated the spikester!>

<Fey gains 30 experience. Amethyst gains 15 experience. Magic gains 15 experience.>

<Fey has learned Vicious Strike!>

Vision still spotty from the blinding, bleeding from a hundred small wounds in her arms and back, Fey glared at Stelli.

"I thought you were going to cast *helpful* magic."

The fairy's hovering dipped guiltily. "Sorry." Making a complicated gesture in the air, Stelli called, "Minor Heal!"

The wounds in Fey's skin healed, ejecting spikes to litter the ground. Unfortunately, the holes and bloodstains in her clothing did not likewise disappear. Fey groaned; while she could probably deal with the bloodstains (that sounds highly suspicious but is perfectly normal), she had no ability to repair clothing. She called upon her favourite ability when dealing with minor problems, formally known as "procrastination," and went back to her quest.

Looking up her new skill, she read:

<Vicious Strike: attack suddenly and harshly for critical damage. Can only be used on the first hit against an opponent.>

<Level 1: 300% damage.>

. . . Wow. That's worth a bloody shirt or two. Fey had the feeling that this would be one of her favourite moves.

Hiding her satisfaction, Fey gave Stelli a stern look. "Let's be careful from now on, okay?"

The fairy nodded guiltily and led the way at a slower pace.

Seven unlikely creatures later, Fey headed back toward Irrilana and Irrilathan to present her tokens.

"There are only nine items here," Irrilana said with a raised eyebrow.

Stelli darted forward to hover in front of the warriors. "Fey defeated the evil spirit that was possessing my body," he/she/they explained.

"Indeed? That must have been quite an undertaking," said Irrilathan. Had Fey not been able to stop the spirit from casting, she would have been in serious trouble against its curse magic.

"If this is true, you have completed your warrior quest."

<Quest complete!>

<Fey gains 500 experience. Amethyst gains 250 experience. Magic gains 250 experience.>

<Fey has reached level 11!>

<Amethyst has reached level 9!>

<Magic has reached level 9!>

<Fey has gained the warrior class!>

"Take this sword," said Irrilana, producing a short sword, sheath, and belt out of nowhere, "as a symbol and privilege of your warrior status. You may now begin your education in close-range combat, whether armed or hand-to-hand."

Fey accepted the blade with caution, aware of how easily she could dismember herself with it.

"As well," added Irrilathan, "we will teach you your first skill exclusive to the warrior class: how to channel arcane energy into your blade and increase its destructive potential. Draw your blade."

Fey pulled the short sword out of its sheath.

"Focus your energy and *push* it into your blade."

Having already experienced the tingling rush of a successful spell during her quest with Kallara, Fey imagined a similar feeling travelling down into her sword. The metal began to glow a radiant white.

"Impressive control," said Irrilana, "but you need the energy to burst free of the blade to do any damage."

Fey mentally pushed more magic down her arm, imagining it bursting free from the sword. Angry white flames with an inner purple heart flared out, several times the width of the blade.

"Good. Now tone it down so you do not deplete your mana too quickly," said Irrilathan, and Fey reduced the flow of energy until the flames were barely visible flickering above the sword's edge.

"Very good. The flames take little energy to maintain passively, but can be flared at need to increase your destructive power. Use it wisely, warrior. We will see you back at level 20, when you may begin to learn subspecialist skills."

<Fey has learned Mana Blade!>

Irrilathan had clearly dismissed her, but Fey had a question. "Do you teach any skills related to dual-wielding?"

Irrilana's eyes sparked with interest. "Dual-wielding? Now that is an interesting and difficult path. People naturally favour their dominant hand," she said, nodding toward Fey's right hand, which she had used to draw the sword. "Weapons held in the other are wielded with less strength and skill. There is no specific skill that can help with this; you must simply strengthen your weaker hand until you no longer *have* a weaker hand."

Irrilathan chimed in. "I suggest you find yourself a second weapon for your left hand, perhaps a long dagger. Be cautious of how long your blades are; when dual-wielding, they can get in each other's way and leave you less maneuverable."

"Thank you for the advice." Fey bowed and left.

Just outside the Moonwood, Fey turned to Stelli. "Thanks for your help." Indeed, despite the spikester incident, the fairy had been extremely helpful and had enabled her to finish her quest quite quickly.

"Thank *you*. Blessing of the Guardian always upon you." Stelli quickly zipped away into the forest.

Fey took the opportunity to inventory her character.

<Fey, level 11 moon elf.>

<Class: warrior (unspecialized).>

<HP: 145/145, MP 60/60.>

<Pets: Amethyst, level 9 slime; Magic, level 9 blue mushroom.>

Not bad for a day's work. Seeing that it was almost time for her wake-up call, Fey decided to log out rather than get stuck in the middle of an activity.

CHAPTER 8

BROKEN BLADE

Arwyn sat up and removed her headset, imagination still occupied with the game. Mechanically, she ate breakfast (cereal) and got dressed for work (boring businesswear). Checking her new laptop, she saw that the file transfer was complete. Having been on the computer for less than a minute, she got an instant message:

Leah-IfIHadAMillionDollars...: Hi!!! Did you play Fantasia last night?

ArwynTheElf: Yes. I didn't see you around. What's your avatar name?

Leah-IfIHadAMillionDollars...: It's "Sirena." I picked a mermaid race, and it turns out that I don't learn how to breathe above water until level 30. You? I know you picked an elf.

ArwynTheElf: "Arwyn" was taken, so I picked Fey.

Leah-IfIHadAMillionDollars…: "Fey" for an elf. How creative.

ArwynTheElf: I wouldn't be throwing stones, "Siren."

Leah-IfIHadAMillionDollars…: It's "SirenA," with an A.

ArwynTheElf: "Siren" without an A was taken, wasn't it?

Leah-IfIHadAMillionDollars…: Hmph. I shall not deign to answer that question.

With an amused chuckle, Arwyn shut the laptop. *Looks like I'll be playing solo for a while.* She would rather deal with the difficulties of playing on her own than the headache of being annoyed by strangers. She would meet up with Leah once her mermaid avatar reached level 30. Busily planning what she would do in-game the next night, she headed off to work.

◊◊◊

Leandriel dodged yet another flying shard of rock debris and shot a blast of holy light at the demon Beloth. He was a level 100 celestial, on the final quest to earn his angel wings by slaying the demon lord.

The black-skinned humanoid he was fighting was about three storeys tall and capable of throwing huge fireballs that exploded on impact, making it nearly impossible to get close enough to bring his sword to bear; all he could do was continuously dodge and send holy light attacks. He was a class of celestial warrior called a guardian, so his holy magic was on par with that of a human paladin, but not nearly as powerful as that of a cleric or celestial wizard.

Wistfully, he thought of how much easier the battle would be if he could fly, but that was the whole point of the quest.

It was reaching the third hour of combat and he was getting tired, his limbs heavy and slow to respond, but Beloth seemed to be weakening as well.

It was time to take some risks.

No longer attempting to conserve his mana stores, Leandriel blasted the demon lord with a continuous stream of holy light, blinding it. He set down an anchor point for the magic, continuing to hit the demon from the front while he snuck behind.

Using the strength and agility gained from a hundred levels of fighting, Leandriel leaped three storeys to land on Beloth's forehead. The demon sent a massive hand to catch him, but it was too late: Leandriel plunged his sword into its vital spot, the tattoo of a third eye in the middle of its forehead.

<Leandriel has defeated the demon lord Beloth!>

<Leandriel gains 2,588 experience.>

<Leandriel's fame has risen to 7,455 (+1,000)!>

<Quest complete!>

<Leandriel gains 1,150,000 experience.>

<Leandriel has advanced to angel!>

As Leandriel received the flood of system notices, Beloth's massive hand completed its journey despite the demon lord's death. The hand, longer than his entire body, smashed into him with the force of a car at highway speeds, pulverizing what felt like every bone and organ in his body.

<Leandriel has died.>

<Level decreases to 99.>

<Please wait. You will be reborn at the nearest rebirth point.>

◊◊◊

"Oww," Leander groaned, pulling off his game helmet before his avatar could be reborn. He rubbed his arms and legs, trying to dispel the phantom pains that coursed through his body. Even with the game's pain decreased to 20% of real life, it was not easy to shake off devastating injuries.

He breathed calmly until the pain faded, past experience a guide. As a beta tester, Leander had been playing *Fantasia* since the outset, when pain had been the same as in the real world. This had been decreased to 50%, then 30%, and finally 20% after too many testers had reported being debilitated by what should have been minor injuries.

It was almost noon; he had stayed logged in particularly late in order to finally finish the quest. He opted for breakfast food anyway, making himself scrambled eggs with toast. Leaving his apartment on the VirtualRealities company campus, he headed to the athletic centre. Company policy dictated a minimum of two hours of exercise daily, to keep employees at peak fitness despite sometimes spending ten to twelve hours a day asleep and motionless.

Leander ran around the track, managing to lose the last of the phantom pains after half an hour. He walked in a cool-down, then lifted weights, ending his workout with stretching. Other employees nodded at him in greeting but left him alone, knowing he preferred to focus on his exercise while in the athletic centre.

Hitting the shower, Leander contemplated his tasks for the day. Other than giving feedback to the programmers, almost all of his work was accomplished in *Fantasia* while asleep. Even extending his sleep to ten hours a day, it left him with a lot of free time during the day.

Leander's job was to test quests and monster areas for glitches and appropriate difficulty level. Although the game had already been released to market, many of the higher-level features were still in development. *Fantasia* had an extremely steep experience curve but no maximum level, meaning that the developers could leisurely create new and ever-more-difficult quests and monsters as the average player level rose. It had taken Leandriel over two years to reach level 100, even with his employee-only ring that boosted experience gain by 15%. There were still details that needed to be worked out, but the developers already had much of the level 300 areas built, so they were in no danger of players quitting the game due to boredom.

Leander decided to consult with the programmers, then see if he could get an exception to log back in to *Fantasia* early. He still had to figure out how to control his new wings. Controlling a whole new set of limbs had no real-life parallel, so there were bound be to be a few problems.

Arwyn returned home after a busy but routine day at the office. Barely resisting the urge to immediately start playing *Fantasia*, she cooked and ate dinner, then prepared for bed. Even then it was only eight o'clock, but none of the activities she usually did in the evenings held any appeal as much as the matte-black gaming helmet that seemed to beckon to her. (She's not addicted at all. *denial*) She put it on. It was Friday, so she did not bother setting a wake-up time.

◊◊◊

Darkness.

"Scanning," said the same disembodied voice Fey had heard the night before. "Player detected. Welcome back, Fey."

A pause. "Due to the decreasing number of available unique names, please select a surname to go with your character name."

Noo, not more naming. Wait a minute, if they'd thought to do this in the first place, I could have used Arwyn as my avatar name!

Cursing the short-sightedness of whoever was in charge of the naming system (*cough* the author *cough*), Fey tried to figure out what her last name should be. Elves' last names in books were always some strange combination of unpronounceable syllables, punctuated by apostrophes.

After many minutes of dithering, Fey decided. "E'lan. E-apostrophe-L-A-N." She thought it was appropriate; "elan" meant "impetus" and "vigour," and the sound reminded her of eladrin high elves from the Dungeons and Dragons universe.

"Welcome back to *Fantasia*, Fey E'lan. Your adventure continues." A blinding flash of light.

◊◊◊

Fey reappeared in the spot she had logged off. The first thing she noticed was that she was miraculously clean. Not a trace of blood or slime slug from her previous adventures remained. She took a mental note of the handy form of cleaning that was logging out and back in.

Unfortunately, her clothing retained the damage it had sustained from the spikester attack.

Wait, I have a class now, so that means . . . NEW EQUIPMENT!!! Yay! Fey mustered far more excitement for the prospect than she would a shopping trip in real life.

Her excitement had to be shared, so she plucked Amethyst off her head and cooed, "I'm getting new equipment."

Amethyst blinked, not really understanding the significance of Fey's words.

Mood undampened, Fey plucked Magic off her boot and repeated the process. The mushroom likewise blinked.

"Hmm. Can pets wear armour?" Trying to imagine the strange armour that would fit a slime and a mushroom, Fey walked over to the armour shop.

Inside the tree-shop were several other players, mostly wearing the same newbie outfit as Fey (minus the holes). She browsed displays of armour sets, realizing that virtual reality equipment would function significantly differently from other games. Rather than adding up to a total defence that would apply to all attacks she was hit with, each piece of armour would only protect the body part it was covering. The designs before her were significantly more pragmatic than the typical fantasy armour, though efforts were made to satisfy both form and function.

"Oh my, what an adorable slime! And a little mushroom, too!" The speaker was a green-haired elf who the system informed Fey was Senaia, the blacksmith's daughter and keeper of the armour shop.

In response to Senaia's eager expression that nearly had anime-like sparkles, Fey handed over her pets. "This is Amethyst, and that's Magic."

The shopkeeper spent several minutes petting and cooing over them while Fey awkwardly hovered between going back to browsing and staying within conversational distance in case Senaia suddenly started talking.

The green-haired elf eventually regained her senses and said, "Oh my, but where are my manners? Greetings, adventurer, my name is Senaia."

"Greetings, I am called Fey."

"I will definitely remember the owner of such cute pets!"

<Fey's fame has increased to 3 (+1)!>

"What brings you in today? Are you just browsing?"

"No, I have recently advanced to the warrior class, and was wondering if you could recommend some equipment suitable for me."

"Of course! Follow me." Senaia led the way to two particular armour stands along the wall, one holding a set made of blackened metal and the other of hardened leather. "One has higher defence, but the other has greater mobility," she explained.

. . . They kind of look like BDSM outfits . . . While the armour covered all the skin it was supposed to, it conceded to fantasy armour aesthetics by shaping the plates and grooves to suggest a plunging neckline and tiny waist, as well as being extremely form-fitting.

When Fey did not say anything, Senaia prompted, "Are you planning on a strength-based or agility-based strategy?"

"Agility-based," Fey answered absentmindedly. Before she realized what was happening, she was alone in the changing room with the leather armour. *Am I really going to try this on? I guess I have no choice unless I want to waste money on custom armour at such a low level.* She reached for the basic clothing, close-fitting pants and shirt in some kind of black cloth, followed by a stiff leather vest, thigh-high boots, and arm guards. The helmet design made the greatest concession to looks, looking more like a wide headband that allowed her hair to flow freely around it.

When Fey emerged out of the dressing room, she attracted not a few stares from the predominantly male players. Senaia bustled over from the counter (where she had been playing with Magic and Amethyst) and began pulling on the ties that adjusted the fit of the armour.

Looking in the mirror, Fey had to admit the overall effect was not as bad as she had feared. She had a thin, willowy build that played well with the elven appearance modifications, making the outfit more "at one with nature" than "sex kitten."

She twisted and moved her limbs, testing the leather's

flexibility. The armour was cleverly grooved and composed of overlapping sections in a way that allowed her full range of motion despite the tight fit.

"Do you like it? Would you like to try the other set?" Senaia asked.

"I'll take this one. How much does it cost?"

"With the full set discount, nine hundred gold."

Not wanting to have to remove the armour, Fey left her pets behind as collateral while she went to the bank and withdrew enough money to pay.

Senaia reluctantly returned Magic and Amethyst after she had the gold in hand. "They're just so *cute*," she sighed wistfully.

" . . . Would you like one?" Fey asked, taking pity on the enamoured shopkeeper.

Senaia's eyes widened. "You would sell me one of your pets?"

"I meant I could go and tame another mushroom or slime for you," Fey clarified. She was not quite sure how exactly she had tamed either pet in the first place, but she figured that, with the Monster Tamer ability and some experimentation, she could manage it again.

"Would you really? I would *love* to have a slime for a pet. If you obtain one for me, I'll give you a permanent twenty percent discount at the store."

Fey had not expected a quest, but this one had a reward she could not resist. "It's a deal," she said immediately. She began to head out, then turned back and asked, "What colour would you like?"

"I think a yellow one would be nice and cheerful."

Fey nodded and stepped out.

The slime territory in the forest was quite large to accommodate the large number of newbies who wanted to train on them. Fey managed to find an unoccupied area for herself, out of sight of anyone who might stare at her unusual activities.

At her approach, slimes began to flee in terror; she was uncertain if this was because her level 11 basic intimidation was too high or if they had some kind of racial memory regarding evil players who did particularly cruel things to them.

Fey began setting up her slime-taming system. Putting Amethyst on the ground, she said, "Go ahead and eat slime bubbles, but leave the yellow slimes alone." Remembering Amethyst's terrible strategy when fighting in the Dark Forest, she added, "Use Whip."

Amethyst nodded and hopped cheerfully into the trees. Squeaks of terror that abruptly cut off with a splat began to sound.

Ignoring the cannibalism that she had just authorized, Fey picked up Magic and put him on her head. "Cast Spore in a big cloud, but don't hit me."

Obediently, Magic cast Spore to the maximum extent of his range, ten metres in radius.

<Attack failed.>

<The slime has been paralyzed!>

<Attack failed.>

Fey smiled and began to walk.

Fey's analytical mind had come up with a fairly efficient way to train her pets' skills and collect yellow slimes. Sending Amethyst off to kill—and presumably eat—all but the yellow individuals would increase the concentration of yellow slimes as they respawned with a random colour assignment. The system notices that appeared whenever Magic cast Spore let her know how many slimes were in the vicinity, even if the debuff failed. Spore itself gained experience whenever it successfully inflicted a status effect, so casting it on the plentiful slimes made it level up quite quickly.

After about fifteen minutes, Fey started seeing piles of goo that sometimes had coins in them, clearly the result of Amethyst's activities. Not wanting any loot to go to waste, she called out, "Amethyst, collect any coins you see." Hearing a squeak of acknowledgement, Fey continued her activities.

Another two hours, many respawns, and countless piles of goo later, Fey had collected four yellow slimes and Magic's Spore had reached level 6. Since her level 3 Monster Tamer skill had a 27% chance of success, she decided to try her luck with the four before collecting any more. (Also it was starting to get troublesome carrying around so many slimes trying to get away.)

She dumped the slimes unceremoniously onto the ground (*plop*) and sat down beside them. Barring getting her fingers bitten, she was fairly immune to any damage they might inflict, and she handled them with impunity.

Rather than attack, the slimes immediately began to run away. Fey let them get about two hops away, then grabbed them by the bubble to drop them back in front of her, enjoying herself immensely.

This process repeated itself for several minutes before one of the slimes stopped trying to escape, shivering in fear. She grabbed the other three slimes' bubbles in one hand (*dangle*) to watch it more carefully.

"Hi?" She extended a careful hand.

The slime squeaked in terror and started running away again.

Sighing, Fey put it back in place. Dumping the other three slimes, she continued her activities, leaving the stationary slime alone.

Another half hour later, all the slimes had stopped running away. *Now what?* They still fled in terror if she tried to touch them.

She tried talking. "Hi, little slimeys," she said in a baby voice. I'm here to take you to a nice new home with a nice lady named Senaia. She'll take very good care of you, and play with you, and feed you, and you won't have to worry about any mean people trying to kill you. Doesn't that sound nice?"

She continued babbling soothing nonsense while inching her hand forward. Miraculously, the slimes did not run.

"That's it, I'm not going to hurt you," she crooned, fingers touching the first slime that had stopped running. It flinched but stayed in place. She gently pet the slime until it snuggled against her hand, then picked it up.

<Fey has tamed the slime!>

<Fey receives a pet!>

<Please select a name for your pet: ___>

"Topaz," she decided, continuing with the gemstone theme. Standing up with the new acquisition, she contemplated the other three slimes, still huddled on the ground at her feet. She thought that she could probably tame at least one more of them but did not know what she would do with an extra slime pet. Still, it seemed a waste to just leave them here, half-tamed.

I guess I could find buyers for them. But wouldn't it be better to have a selection of different colours, then? Ah well.

She looked around for Amethyst, having lost track of her surroundings while playing catch-a-slime. Magic still sat on her head.

What she saw pushed her into a sprint, the slimes on the ground forgotten: Amethyst was halfway across the slime territory, with another player's sword descending in an attack.

"Stop!" she screamed. She had never run so fast in her life.

<Fey's agility has increased to 22 (+1)!>

Blade was a level 15 human warrior, having started playing *Fantasia* on the day it was released. Level 15 was strong enough to take the relatively safe route between beginner cities, and so he had wandered over to the Moonwood from the human starter town, (the even less creatively named) Newtown.

After exploring the village and talking to several NPCs, he had decided to hunt down the King Slime, a boss monster that appeared whenever a certain number of slimes were killed. Boss monsters were considerably stronger than their normal counterparts, but given how weak slimes were, Blade felt that he could handle the King Slime on his own.

He had been leisurely wandering around the slime territory, killing any slimes he encountered, when he spotted a strange-looking slime that appeared to have coins floating around inside its body.

Aha! The King Slime! Eagerly, he thrust his sword toward it.

"*Stop!*"

The cry seemed to send a shiver of fear down his spine. Distracted, he turned toward the sound, his blow losing most of its force, but the sword still connected with the slime with more than enough force that a normal one would be severely wounded or killed.

Blade was dumbfounded when his weapon simply bounced off the slime, which appeared completely unharmed. His attention was split between the invulnerable slime and the figure sprinting toward him when the slime sent its bubble flying forward to connect with his boot.

He heard a cracking sound before the pain registered. "Ouch!" he yelled, grabbing his foot and hopping away a few steps. (The word wasn't "ouch," if you know what I mean, but we're a family-friendly story over here.)

<A bone in your foot is broken. This will require a healing spell two levels greater than your health requirements or a specialized bone-healing spell to repair.>

Completely uninterested in his plight, the sprinting figure flew straight past him and snatched up the slime, checking all over its body for injury before hugging it in relief. He had time to register the figure of a female elf with long, dark hair and leather armour.

"You can give me those coins now," said a low, feminine voice. The slime spat out a large pile of gold coins, leaving it with the exact same appearance as a normal slime.

Blade was starting to get the feeling that he had made a mistake, though the sharp pain in his foot made it hard to think. "Hey, uh . . ."

"You idiot!" the elf yelled, surprisingly loud given how slender she was.

"I, uh, didn't know that was your friend or whatever," he said, unable to muster up a better explanation in the face of that much rage. "I was looking for the King Slime." He shifted uncomfortably, wincing as he put weight on his broken foot.

A cold, clear gaze evaluated him from head to toe, appearing to catalogue everything from his human-round ears to the semi-spherical indent in his boot without actually registering him as a person. Her lips twitched at the foot injury, some of the rage fading.

Without another word, the elf began walking back to town.

"Hey, wait!" called out a voice as Fey prepared to return to the Moonwood. "What are you doing with that slime? Actually, is that a second one?"

Fey was amused because Amethyst was perfectly fine, and had in fact broken the human warrior's foot, but she was still angry at the threat to Amethyst's life. She certainly was in no mood to explain the monster taming system. "None of your business," she said without turning around.

She had only walked a few paces when a giant green slime hopped out of the trees, a hundred times bigger than Amethyst.

"King Slime?" she heard muttered behind her.

This huge thing looks nothing like Amethyst at all! (Well actually, other than size and colour, they were identical.)

The boss slime seemed hostile, so Fey sent her mind into analysis mode to come up with a battle plan. (Loading . . . please wait.) Then she exploded into motion.

Drawing her sword in her right hand and her dagger in the left, she sprinted at the King Slime. When she was within reach of its bubble-arm, she dodged sideways, neatly anticipating and avoiding its first Whip attack.

She activated Mana Blade and combined it with Vicious Strike, running along the King Slime's side and cutting as large a wound as she could. She used a glancing strike with her off hand to inflict Bleed.

Guh, so awkward. Fey had enough martial arts training to know when a movement felt right, and the way she was using the sword definitely felt wrong. Against the soft-bodied slime, it was sufficient, inflicting gaping slashes in its membrane, but she was going to have to practice if she wanted to fight anything tougher.

Taking advantage of its flinch, Fey attacked in a flurry of slashes, inflicting as many Bleed wounds as she could. Slime oozed out, coating her weapons and making her grip slippery.

She saw the King Slime's bubble whipping out again but was too slow to dodge; a sphere approximately the size of a grapefruit slammed into her left arm.

"Ow," Fey said. (It really was "ow" this time. Fey tries not to swear unless it's important.) She could still use her arm, so she guessed it was not broken. *Gotta love armour.* Deciding that with an opponent so large, she could sacrifice accuracy for damage, she activated Rage.

Fey had determined that slimes had no vital spots and simply died when they lost too much slime, so she kept up a barrage of continuous strikes, aiming for large wounds and activating Bleed whenever the cooldown allowed. As the King Slime weakened, its counterstrikes lost power, so she did not sustain any injuries worse than the bruise on her arm. Her mana ran out quickly and the flames of Mana Blade disappeared, but she continued holding the upper hand in combat.

Faster than she would have thought possible for a boss monster, the King Slime lay deflated on the ground.

<Fey has defeated the King Slime!>

<Fey has gained 108 experience. Amethyst has gained 54 experience. Magic has gained 54 experience. Topaz has gained 54 experience.>

<Topaz has reached level 2!>

<Topaz has reached level 3!>

<Topaz has reached level 4!>

<Mana Blade has reached level 2!>

<Vicious Strike has reached level 2!>

<Rage has reached level 2!>

<Bleed has reached level 3!>

<Bleed has reached level 4!>

<Fey has attained level 1 Slime Mastery! (Details in Bestiary.)>

The skill increases were expected, given the tiny amount of experience it took to go from level 1 to 2. She had to look up what

Slime Mastery meant; Monster Mastery added useful information to her personal Bestiary about a monster's stats, location, and item drops, and was increased by observing (i.e., killing) a large number of monsters or their boss counterparts. As an added bonus, it made taming the particular monster easier.

What Fey was not entirely aware of was exactly how many slimes Amethyst had killed and eaten. When a pet went beyond a certain distance from the owner, she no longer received system notifications about their activities. Amethyst had in fact eaten so many slime bubbles that her Double Membrane ability had gone from level 1 to 6, which was how she had survived the human warrior's attack. Combined with the extra boost to mastery from killing a boss monster, Fey had easily crossed the threshold for level 1 Slime Mastery.

Amethyst hopped over, having collected the loot from the battle as part of her simplistic understanding of Fey's earlier command to collect coins. She spat a 100g coin, a small blue gem, and a thin copper ring into Fey's hand.

Fey examined each item. "Description."

<Small water gem (uncommon): can be used to enchant items. Gives 10% water affinity.>

<Minor ring of speed (common): gives +1SPD when worn. Multiple rings can be worn for stacked effects.>

Coool. Fey put the gem in her pouch and the ring on her left middle finger. Just before she headed back to the Moonwood, she remembered to collect the King Slime's bubble as well. *I bet Kallara will have a use for this.*

Having completely forgotten about the player she had just yelled at (who had watched in frustration with his broken foot as Fey killed the boss he had spent hours hunting for), she set off for the town in a cheerful mood.

CHAPTER 9
PARTY TIME

Fey's first stop was the armour shop, where she delivered Topaz to a delighted Senaia.

"Oh, it really is so adorable," she cooed, poking at its bubble playfully.

"It's for you," Fey replied.

<Pet ownership transferred.>

<Fey has completed the quest!>

<Fey gains 500 experience. Amethyst gains 250 experience. Magic gains 250 experience.>

<Fey receives a 20% Moonwood Armour Discount.>

"What did you name it?"

"Topaz."

"Wonderful name; I will keep it. Oh my, it's level 4 already!"

"I ran into the King Slime on the way back, so it gained some experience," Fey explained.

"You defeated the King Slime? What a feat!"

<Fey's fame has increased to 4 (+1)!>

I guess bragging is part of getting fame? "It was nothing," Fey answered modestly. Her Bleed skill just happened to be super effective against slimes.

"I expect great things from such a promising adventurer; come back whenever you need your armour upgraded," said Senaia. "Oh! Here," she added, pulling 180g from her pocket and handing it to Fey. "We'll make the discount retroactive."

"Thanks!" Fey said, losing some of her natural reserve at the unexpected refund.

"Come back anytime so Amethyst and Topaz can play together," Senaia invited with a smile.

Quest complete, Fey went to the bank to store away the water gem and most of her money before bringing the King Slime bubble to Kallara.

"You!"

The exclamation came simultaneously from two different mouths as Fey stepped into the healer's tree-shop.

The human warrior was seated on a bench, left foot bare and suffering an ugly-looking bruise, while Kallara went about gathering supplies from various shelves and cupboards.

Blade had slowly limped to town while Fey finished her errands and had in fact only just sat down on the healer's bench when Fey (whom he mentally referred to as "that scary elf lady") walked in.

"I see you two know each other," Kallara commented, hints of amusement in her expression.

"That slime broke my foot!" Blade accused, pointing at Amethyst.

"You totally deserve it after trying to kill her," said Fey, exhibiting zero signs of remorse or sympathy.

"I see." Kallara wisely made no further comment on the subject. "What brings you here today, Fey?"

Fey pulled out the King Slime bubble, which the healer recognized immediately.

"Defeating the King Slime at your level? Impressive."

<Fey's fame has increased to 5 (+10)!>

Wow, I should go around telling all the NPCs about this. Fame was minorly useful at gaining quests from NPCs, though not enough that Fey seriously considered going around bragging about such a minor feat. "Is the King Slime bubble used for making any potions?" she asked.

"Of course!" Kallara's enthusiasm for rare potion ingredients was winning out over her usual calm demeanour. "It can be used as the base material for quite a few potions. Not just healing potions, but even tonics that can temporarily boost your base attributes!"

"Nice," Fey said. What she was really thinking was, *Profits.*

"What would you like to make?" Kallara asked. "I'll help you brew any tonic you'd like as long as you also gather the other ingredients."

"How about a strength tonic?" Fey suggested, guessing that would be one of the most valuable.

Completely distracted from her injured patient, Kallara pulled a book off the shelf and opened it to a particular page before handing it to Fey. "Here's a list of the ingredients. Fresh-killed herbs have the most potency. You can find everything in the garden out back."

"Fresh-*killed*?" Fey muttered. "I don't like the sound of that. Kallara, just what level are these monsters?"

"None of them are over level 20," Kallara answered with a smile. (Whether it was an evil smile is up for debate.)

I'm going to need to be extra careful so I don't die. Fey figured that if she gathered the weaker herbs first, she could level up enough that tackling a level 20 monster would be relatively safe.

"However," Kallara continued, "there are herbs of up to level 40 in the garden. Take care not to disturb them."

Fey stared at the healer with a doomed expression while Kallara ushered her out the back exit. "Goodbye, world," she lamented before heading into the garden.

Kallara waved. "The rebirth point is located in the town centre," she called after Fey cheerfully. (Whether her smile was evil was no longer up for debate.) Mischief done, she turned to her injured patient, who now felt decidedly less safe.

"Are you sure it's a good idea to send her out to such a dangerous place alone?" Blade ventured as Kallara smeared some sort of soothing ointment over his foot.

"Oh, she should be fine. I go out there to collect herbs all the time," Kallara said unworriedly. Blade had a sneaking suspicion that this did not mean much for Fey because the healer was actually at an extremely high level.

"However," the healer continued, "if you are worried about her, you could always go help." While he was distracted, she pulled sharply on his foot to align the bones.

"Oww!" he yelled. (The word wasn't "oww.")

"Watch your language, young man," Kallara chided. "Hold still. Bone Heal. Minor Heal."

A warm glow began emanating from the healer's hands, seeming to sink into Blade's skin and melting away the pain of his injuries. By the time the glow faded, even the last trace of a bruise had disappeared.

"There you go, all done." Kallara patted his foot and moved away.

"Thanks." Blade replaced his footwear and got up, leaving a 50g piece on the bench as payment.

He hesitated, looking between the two exits from the healer's abode, one leading to the main clearing and the other to the herb garden.

With just about anybody else, Blade would not hesitate to go and offer his help, but he was certain that the scary elf lady, or "Fey," as he had heard Kallara call her, would not welcome his presence.

Still, it went against his nature to leave someone in danger without at least trying to help. Bracing himself for dangerous monsters and hostile conversation, he followed Fey into the herb garden.

"Good luck!" Kallara called after him, eyes laughing with mischief.

Behind Kallara's tree-shop was a fairly large area where the trees were far enough apart for patches of sunlight to reach the ground. Fey could see different kinds of plants growing in various levels of sunlight or shade, some planted in neat rows while others looked wild.

She advanced cautiously to a spot clear of all plant life, sword at the ready. When she was not immediately beset by carnivorous plants, she felt safe enough to sheathe the weapon and examine the potion book Kallara had lent her.

The tome was more of an ingredients compendium than a recipe book for potions, listing the locations where each component could be found, ideal harvesting and storage conditions, and any special considerations, along with detailed colour sketches of the plants. What it did not list was the level of each herb monster. In fact, the drawings all looked like normal plants, with no eyes, mouth, legs, or any other feature that indicated they might rear up and attack.

This is scary . . . In the absence of concrete information, Fey's fertile imagination was conjuring up endless scenarios where herb monsters killed her in cruel and unusual ways.

She sighed. *Might as well get it over with.* (The quest, or dying in a cruel and unusual manner?)

"Magic, Amethyst, come look at this." Fey pointed at a particular plant illustration.

Magic hopped up Fey's back to sit on her right shoulder (*defy gravity*) while Amethyst simply leaned forward from her position on Fey's left shoulder to stare attentively at the page.

"This is sweetgrass," Fey said. She had chosen to go after the plant required in the largest quantity, reasoning that it was unlikely to be the most difficult to obtain, and therefore unlikely to be the level 20 monster. "Go find plants that look like this and come tell me when you've found them, but *don't touch anything.*"

Squeaking their understanding, the slime and mushroom hopped off to explore. Fairly quickly, excited squeaking led her to an herb patch situated in a sunny spot, full of clumps of long, broad leaves that matched the drawing in the book.

"Good job, you two." Fey patted her pets affectionately, then moved them a safe distance away before approaching the sweetgrass. Sword in one hand, she yanked a plant out of the ground.

She stared at the round root ball attached to the leaves, equipped with a pair of black button eyes and stubby legs kicking futilely for freedom.

" . . . Odd." (Or should we say, odd-ish?)

After struggling for a while, the creature opened its mouth and uttered a cry. Suddenly, all the other clumps of grass uprooted themselves and began running away.

"Oh no you don't! Magic, Amethyst, after them!" The chase was on. Unfortunately for Fey, the sweetgrass's stubby legs were still enough to make them faster than her legless pets, so she had to do all the chasing herself. She ended up in a graceless half-bent position, grabbing clumps of sweetgrass while jogging.

How to kill the creatures became an issue. Stabbing them would likely sever at least part of the root and make collection more difficult. She tried stomping on a few, but they simply got up and continued running.

When she had collected ten, her hands were completely full. Making a snap decision, she tied them into a bundle with her rope and dropped them, still wiggling, on the ground. "Amethyst, Whip!" She ran off after the remaining sweetgrass.

Returning with another squirming bundle, Fey saw that Amethyst was still repeatedly Whipping the first group. *What, are they still alive? What kind of insane defence do they have?*

" . . . Eew." Upon closer inspection, she found that Amethyst had actually been mashing the long-dead creatures into unrecognizable paste. "Amethyst," Fey groaned, "you're supposed to stop when they're dead."

Amethyst stopped attacking and blinked, appearing to absorb that bit of wisdom as a new revelation.

"Ehh . . . I don't have time for this right now." Fey swiftly tied up the second bundle of sweetgrass. "Whip, but *stop* when they're dead," she said before again running off to collect more.

Assuming that the sweetgrass paste was unusable, Fey ended up collecting ten more plants than the recipe called for. Watching Amethyst bash the last group, she saw that the slime was able to kill them with a single Whip attack, causing their bodies to shrivel into normal-looking roots. She winced, wanting an excuse to run away again. In contrast, Magic looked completely unconcerned at the one-sided massacre.

Packing everything up in her pouch, she opened the book to look up the next ingredient. "Thornweed," she read aloud. The plant looked rather like a rosebush without flowers. *This does not bode well for my hands.* Fey's equipment did not include gloves, and she foresaw some nasty scratches.

Alas, woe is me, and other cries of lament. Let's get it over with. "Amethyst, Magic, find this plant."

Instead of the thornweed, Fey found something far more irritating. "What are you doing here?" The human warrior was in the herb garden, apparently looking for her.

"I, uh, thought you might need help." Blade had rather been expecting Fey to be fighting for her life against some high-level monster, so the whole "totally fine" thing was throwing him off.

Fey rolled her eyes and was about to reply when she heard a squeak. She turned and walked off in the direction of the sound.

Blade followed. "Where are you going?" Not owning pets, he had not particularly registered the squeak, so Fey's actions seemed completely random.

Fey was not in a particularly talkative mood, and the answer would be self-evident when they got there, so she ignored the question, coming across the thornweed a minute later. It resembled a rosebush without flowers, all stems and thorns.

Assuming the plant would attack by thrashing its stems around, Fey stopped beyond its reach and told Magic to cast Spore five times.

<Attack failed. The thornweed is unaffected.>

<Spore was successful. The thornweed's speed is decreased by 20%.>

<Attack failed. The thornweed is unaffected.>

<Attack failed. The thornweed is unaffected.>

<Spore was successful. The thornweed has been paralyzed.>

"Good job, Magic!" she praised, wading into the bush to start harvesting.

To Blade, who did not have the benefit of Fey's system notices, the mushroom had not done much of anything, but he walked forward as well. "So, uh, you need to gather these?"

"Would you leave already?" Fey asked in a voice that could only be described as unimpressed.

"Hey, you heard the healer; there are level 40 monsters in here. You might need help."

Fey paused to give him a measuring look. *Well, I suppose I could use him as a meat shield if we get attacked.* "Fine."

Blade sighed in relief at being released from the unnerving stare.

"Help me cut this plant," she continued imperiously (#UnpaidLabour).

Encouraged by the shift from words to action, Blade drew his sword and slashed at the thornweed with a two-handed grip. The flexible stems whipped sideways from the force of the blow before returning, gently swaying, to their upright position with barely a scratch.

Well, I see my meat shield isn't very clever. Does that make him a better meat shield or a worse one? Fey idly pondered the question while grasping a stem near the base and sawing away at it with her dagger. Her technique was far more effective, though it still took many cuts to get through the woody stem.

Blade sheepishly copied the movement, though it was more awkward with a blade as long as a sword.

Ugh, this is taking forever. There has to be a faster way, Fey thought. While her hands automatically repeated the slicing movements, she searched through her skill menu for anything that might help the situation.

Hmm. Maybe Mana Blade? Remembering how she had been able to affect the shape of the magic flow while learning the ability, she activated it and imagined the flames solidifying into an extremely sharp, thin edge.

Her magically sharpened dagger slid through the rest of the stem like a hot knife through butter (yay, clichéd similes) and Fey narrowly avoided giving herself a nasty cut.

<Fey has learned Mana Edge!>

<Mana Edge: with the finest control, shape Mana Blade into a sharp edge to increase armour penetration.>

<Subskill: takes the same level as Mana Blade.>

<Level 2: +6 armour penetration.>

Noticing Fey staring off into space in a way that suggested looking at a virtual screen, Blade asked, "What are you doing?"

"Experimenting," Fey answered unhelpfully. Grasping another stem, she sliced through it in one clean stroke.

"Hey, how did you do that?"

Fey gave Blade another long look while she considered whether to answer. *You gotta give him credit for not running in the face of hostility.* Fey's hostile act (is it really an act?) was sufficient to send the vast majority of people packing.

"Uhm, is there something on my face?" Blade asked, again unnerved by the staring.

Fey sighed and reluctantly started communicating like a normal person. (Well, more like a normal person, anyway.) "Do you want to share the quest?" she asked unenthusiastically.

"Sure."

"What's your name?"

"Blade."

<Fey has invited you to join her party.>

<Blade has accepted the party invitation.>

<Fey's party: Fey (leader), level 11 moon elf; Blade, level 15 human.>

"I modified Mana Blade to sharpen the edge of my dagger," Fey explained.

"What? How do you do that?" Blade activated his own Mana Blade, the regular magical flame appearing around his sword.

"Lower the mana flow until it barely extends from the edge of the blade, then shape it into a hard, sharp line."

Frowning in concentration, Blade stared at his sword until the flames shrank unevenly down, eventually solidifying into a wobbly line that was not quite as perfect as Fey's version but was still quite effective against the thornweed.

<Blade has learned Mana Edge!>

"That's amazing," Blade exclaimed enthusiastically. This was only the second ability he had gained, after Mana Blade itself. His straightforward style of fighting did not seem to lend itself to spontaneous skill gains.

"Eh," Fey said, not as impressed given the number of other abilities she had already gained. She continued steadily harvesting thornweed stems, and Blade followed suit.

<Thornweed's paralysis has worn off.>

Fey immediately jumped up and backed out of range, but Blade, unaware that the thornweed had been paralyzed in the first place, was slow to react.

"What— Ow!"

The monster plant whipped its remaining limbs violently, leaving a scratch across Blade's cheek.

<Blade has been poisoned!>

<Thornweed poison: −2 health/5 seconds.>

<Duration: 5 minutes.>

"Crap," Blade muttered, reaching into his pack for an antidote. Most adventurers bought antidotes after their first encounter with a poisonous monster and tried to avoid them as much as possible because of the extra expense. He was flabbergasted when Fey reached out and deliberately let the thornweed graze her hand. "What are you—"

<Fey has been poisoned!>

<Thornweed poison: –2 health/5 seconds.>

<Duration: 5 minutes.>

<Level 1 Immunity effect: decrease 1 damage per poison infliction.>

<Residual poison effect: –1 health/5 seconds.>

<Duration: 5 minutes.>

Without Immunity, taking the full brunt of the thornweed's poison would result in 120 damage, where Fey's maximum health was 145. Her Immunity halved it to a much more manageable 60 damage, allowing her to let it run its course and continue training her ability.

Blade's mind was boggled at what seemed like a high-level class ability appearing in a newbie. "Where did you learn that?"

Fey came to the realization that if she continued working with Blade, he would end up learning all of her hard-earned (*cough* randomly acquired *cough*) skills and abilities. She considered not answering the question, but the path to Immunity seemed too obvious to bother with evasion.

"You just have to get poisoned a lot."

"That's it?"

Fey thought back to the hours spent covered in slug slime. "That's it," she said sardonically. "Want to try it?"

"Well, the thornweed—"

"Oh, no, I have easy access to a weak poison," Fey said with a smile. "Amethyst, slug poison."

The slime became shiny as she secreted a layer of slug slime.

"Here." Fey dropped Amethyst into Blade's hands, which had automatically come up when she held the slime out.

<Blade has been poisoned!>

<Slug poison: −1 health/30 seconds.>

<Duration: 5 minutes.>

Blade was hit with a wave of nausea from the poison. He grimaced. "Ugh. How long do you have to stay poisoned for?"

"Just a few hours," Fey answered cheerfully. She had Magic cast Spore until the thornweed was again paralyzed and went back to cutting stems.

Blade grimaced again and joined in.

By the time they had collected thirty stems, the thornweed bush was looking quite denuded.

Fey realized that they had not received any system notifications about defeating a monster or gaining experience points. "No experience?" she muttered in annoyance.

"We didn't kill it," said Blade, pointing at the remnant of the plant where it came out of the ground. "It's probably a big monster with high HP."

"Let's kill it!" Fey said (bloodthirstily).

"Uh, it seems pretty tough. Maybe we should just—"

Blade stopped talking as Fey began ordering her pets around. Magic began to cast toxic clouds of spores every few seconds while Amethyst pounded away where the plant extended from the ground with Whip.

Fey activated the normal variant of Mana Blade and flared the magical flames, holding them over one of the remaining stems.

"What are you doing?" Blade asked.

"Seeing if I can set things on fire with Mana Blade. Looks like not." Fey shrugged and went back to severing thornweed stems.

"Uh, I don't think you can kill it like that," said Blade.

"Yeah, this is just to keep it from being able to do damage. Magic and Amethyst are working on the killing thing."

"I don't think . . . " Blade sighed and went back to helping.

<Spore was successful, but the thornweed's attack cannot go any lower.>

<Spore was successful, but the thornweed's speed cannot go any lower.>

<Spore was successful, but the thornweed's defence cannot go any lower.>

<Magic's Spore has reached level 7!>

"Why. Won't. It. DIE??" Fey gritted in frustration twenty minutes later. They had removed all of the thornweed's stems, while Magic had debuffed its stats to the minimum and Amethyst had turned the remaining plant into a pulpy mess, and yet there was no indication that the plant-monster had died. The only status effect the thornweed had not received was poison, which Fey assumed was because the thornweed itself had stronger poison than either of her pets.[13]

"Maybe we should give up and hunt for the other ingredients?" Blade suggested again.

Fey sighed. "You can stop casting now," she told Magic, who looked distinctly worn out. The mushroom tiredly hopped to the shade of a nearby tree, wiggled around until it had made an indent in the dirt for its stem, and appeared to go to sleep.

"What's it doing?" Blade asked.

"Absorbing nutrients?" Fey answered vaguely. Most of her attention was focused on using the game's camera function to take a video of the adorable scene.

<Thornweed's paralysis has worn off.>

Given that the plant no longer had any stems to attack with, Fey was not particularly concerned with the system notice until the ground began to tremble.

"Oh, dung," said Blade. (He didn't actually say "dung.")

The thornweed uprooted itself, revealing a very large root ball and eight large roots, resembling an earthy octopus with short "hair" where they had cut all of its stems off. It normally would have revealed itself after losing more than half its stems, but the paralysis effect had kept it underground.

Fey spotted a small purple spot on the thornweed's root-head. Amethyst, having continued bashing cheerfully away at the remains of the stems, had been surprised with a free ride several metres above the ground.

"Amethyst, get away from there!"

Squeaking cheerfully, the slime jumped off the octopus head and slid down one of the root-tentacles to arrive safely (and stylishly) on the ground.

"We should run," Blade said. "This is clearly the level 20 monster Kallara was warning us about."

Fey did run, but as part of a forward charge to hit the thornweed with an augmented Vicious Strike. The plant flinched, wrapping a root rather feebly around her waist. Fey easily severed the appendage with a few cuts. "Nah, look how weak it is. Magic's debuffs are still in effect."

Indeed, the thornweed was the strongest monster on the ingredients list. Kallara had mainly been teasing when she made the quest sound dangerous, as they should have been able to harvest enough of the plant without causing it to uproot itself and fully attack. (In fact, they had done so and then Fey had decided to poke the plant-kraken.) At full strength, this would have been quite a dangerous fight, but with its attack, defence, and speed all maximally weakened, the thornweed was currently no stronger than a level 10 monster. Furthermore, it generally relied on its poisonous stems to do damage even after it had uprooted itself, leaving it essentially "declawed" in this situation.

Emboldened by the demonstration, Blade waded into the fight. It was only minutes before the thornweed toppled.

<Fey's party has defeated the thornweed!>

<Fey receives 30 experience. Amethyst gains 15 experience. Magic gains 15 experience.>

<Blade gains 42 experience.>

"Hey, why did you get more experience than I did?" Fey exclaimed indignantly.

"My level is higher?" The experience shared in a party was distributed based on the members' relative levels, and Blade was level 15 to Fey's 11.

"I did more damage!"

"Well, that wouldn't be a fair metric to go by in a party that might have support classes," Blade pointed out. When Fey did not look satisfied with that answer, he sighed and said, "You can change the experience allocation to 'individual' if you want."

Fantasia had a variety of settings to customize party gameplay, including several configurations of experience allocation. (All of these were listed in the Advanced Gameplay section of the game manual, which Arwyn had not bothered to read. Bad player.) The "default" setting was based on players' relative levels, while the "individual" allocation treated experience distribution as if no party was formed, based on factors such as relative damage and who struck the killing blow.

Fey changed the setting and then began bundling up the thornweed stems. They had ended up collecting double what they needed, so she divided them in half and tied each bundle up with her rope. She marched off to the next task, leaving Blade to pull up the rear.

CHAPTER 10
SALVATION

Opening the potion book, Fey read, "Fifteen dryad-blessed apples."

Wandering the entire garden yielded no obvious dryads but only a single apple tree, so by logical deduction, there was a dryad somewhere near it.

"Hello?" Fey called out. "I'm Fey, and this is Blade. We're looking to get some dryad-blessed apples, and we're happy to help out or trade for them."

After a few seconds, she heard a loud whisper. "Make him go away."

"Make him— Oh. Blade, go away."

"What?"

"You heard her." Giving him the book, she pushed him away from the apple tree. "You can go collect the next ingredient. Oh yeah, Amethyst, go with him and maintain the poison effect."

Amethyst nodded and hopped over to Blade's shoulder, smearing his cheek with poisonous slime on the way.

Blade grimaced and started walking.

Once he was out of sight, Fey turned back to the tree. "Hel-lo. Oh, hi."

A small, green-skinned humanoid had appeared to sit on one of the lower tree limbs, wearing a dress made of autumn leaves. "Hello, guardian."

Guardian? Oh, yeah. Fey's Guardian's Blessing had allowed her to talk directly to the dryad, whereas most players would have had to obtain apples by researching dryads and making offerings to the tree based on their general preferences. "Greetings. My name is Fey."

"I am Pom, the guardian of Malus."[14] The dryad gestured to the tree as she spoke the second name.

"I'm looking for fifteen dryad-blessed apples as part of a recipe to brew a strength tonic. If you could help me with this, I would be happy to help you in turn."

"It just so happens that Malus here is looking a bit tired," said Pom, patting her tree fondly. "If you bring me a flask of enchanted or holy water, I will happily grow some apples for you."

Eyeing the tree's vibrant green leaves, Fey thought the tree already looked extremely healthy, but she was not about to argue with such a straightforward task. "I will be back with your water," she told the dryad, then left to find Kallara.

⸺◦◦◈◦◦⸺

Blade felt sick. Even as mild a poison as slug poison had its associated symptoms, which in this case were nausea and general weakness. (Fey hadn't particularly noticed because the discomfort was in fact weaker than what Arwyn put herself through if she stayed up too late reading a book and then had to get up early the next morning. Also, she thought it was normal to feel nauseated when covered head to toe in slug remains.) "This Immunity better be worth it," he muttered to himself, shooting a baleful glance at the slime on his shoulder, who blinked innocently. "First my foot, and now this." It appeared that Blade was not impressed by Amethyst's adorableness and saw through to her evil nature. The slime cast Poison Slime every five minutes to the second, ensuring that Blade was not given a break from the poison's effects.

Upon reaching level 10, Amethyst had gained a small bonus in power and intelligence and was now capable of a limited amount of independent thinking. Because of this, she noticed when Blade—letting his discomfort dull his sense of his surroundings—walked right past the flowers he was supposed to collect. She squeaked.

Not being particularly attuned to pet squeaks, Blade ignored the sound and continued walking. Amethyst began jumping up and down on his shoulder, which finally caught his attention. "What?"

Amethyst pointed her bubble in the direction they had already come. Unfortunately, the flowers they were after—tiny red flowers called "blossums"—were already out of sight. Blade glanced in the indicated direction, shrugged, and kept moving forward.

Amethyst felt that she was not getting her point across. She expressed it more forcefully by smacking Blade in the eye with her bubble. (She considerately refrained from destroying that eye by activating Whip, but this forbearance went unappreciated.)

"Ow! Ow!" Blade yelled. (The second "ow" wasn't an "ow.") "What the [censored word] was that for?"

Amethyst pointed more forcefully in the direction they had come. Glaring, Blade walked angrily in the right direction for a few seconds before asking, "What?" in an annoyed tone.

Amethyst now pointed at the ground, where Blade spotted the blossums.

"Oh." He cleared his throat sheepishly. "Thanks."

Amethyst secreted another layer of poisonous slime.

<Blade has been poisoned!>

<Slug poison: −1 health/30 seconds.>

<Duration: 5 minutes.>

Blade groaned as he was hit with another wave of nausea. Narrowing his eyes, he said another, "Thanks," this one much less sincere.

Amethyst squeaked cheerfully.

Bending down, Blade reached toward the plants. Amethyst took this opportunity to jump to the ground and hop to safety. (None of that "leave no man behind" nonsense for our pragmatic slime.) She was therefore unharmed when the blossums reacted to Blade's proximity by releasing leaves that spun rapidly in the air and cut his bare hands with dozens of stinging wounds. (*cough* If anyone is noticing certain similarities to a famous gaming/anime franchise, it's a coincidence . . .)

Blade yelled, throwing his hands up to protect his face. He wore fairly heavy armour, but the plants were clever enough to attack gaps in the joints. Mostly blinded by the need to cover his face, he eventually managed to kill all the blossums by stepping on them and grinding them into the ground.

Panting, he finally lowered his arms, skin stinging fiercely from a hundred shallow cuts. "What *is* this?" he asked disgustedly. Before meeting Fey, all of his adventures had been straightforward fights with animal-based monsters. (He hadn't yet identified Fey as the root cause of his woes.)

Amethyst returned from her hiding spot and hopped back onto Blade's shoulder while he gathered the blossum remains.

"Some help you were," he muttered.

Amethyst squeaked. A few minutes later, she secreted more poison.

Blade groaned, sincerely wishing his adventures would return to normal.

———◦◦◦◦◦———

"Kallara?" Fey called out, re-entering the healer's tree-shop from the back. "I need some enchanted water for the dryad's tree. Or holy water, but I assume enchanted water is more up your alley."

Kallara raised an elegant eyebrow. "How do you know this?"

"The dryad told me."

"Dryads do not speak to strangers," said Kallara, surprised. Her eyes focused on the small butterfly-shaped flower at the corner of Fey's left eye. "Ah! The Guardian's mark. Forest creatures will trust you instinctively."

"How does everyone know I have this Guardian's Blessing, anyway? Is it some kind of magical sense?"

Kallara blinked in surprise. "You have the marking of a mana tree blossom at the corner of your left eye," she said, tapping the equivalent spot on her own face. "Here." She retrieved a small mirror and handed it over.

Fey was somewhat dismayed at (finally) discovering the marking. *It's so . . . froufrou.* She would describe her personal style as pragmatic and simple to the point of severity at times, all clean lines and solid colours. She wore makeup and accessories maybe once every two years, on special occasions, and otherwise restricted herself to glasses that suited her face shape and a hair tie for when she needed to do chores or run around. She honestly enjoyed looking somewhat unapproachable, and the little butterfly-flower really ate into the image.

Still, there was little Fey could do to remove the tattoo, and the hefty bonuses were worth a sacrifice to appearance. *After all, I can always be extra mean to scare people off.*

She returned the mirror and asked, "So, do you know how to make enchanted water?"

"Of course. It's a very simple process, though it takes quite a bit of mana. The only ingredient is water, quite a bit of it."

Fey grabbed the bucket she had previously used for the healing salve and headed off to the stream.

Once she arrived, Fey sighed as she realized she had sent her slime-sponge off with Blade and would have to make do with her hands when it came to filling the bucket in the shallow waters.

"I don't suppose you could help me with this," Fey remarked to Magic as she scooped.

Magic was still at level 9, and the lack of intelligence clearly showed when he obligingly hopped into the water without any clear plan as to how he could possibly be of help. Being quite buoyant, he promptly began floating down the stream.

Fey hastily snatched him out of the water before he could be swept away. "Okay, scratch that. Don't help."

Obligingly, Magic stayed out of the water.

It took a total of six trips before Kallara judged they had enough water to enchant. "Do we really need to make this much?" Fey asked, eyeing the small cauldron she had filled.

Kallara smiled. "This will yield only one flask of enchanted water," she said, indicating a cylindrical container on the counter that could easily be held in one hand.

Fey's gaze travelled between the cauldron and the small flask, trying to figure out where the extra volume would go.

"The enchanting process invokes the existing properties of the object and concentrates it," the healer explained. This did not noticeably lessen Fey's confusion.

Placing her hand over the water, Kallara closed her eyes and said, "Water."

The liquid flared with pale blue light and visibly shrank in volume.

"Water."

"Water."

Each time Kallara spoke, the water flared with light and shrank in volume. With fifteen repetitions, the water was down to half its original volume.

Looking a bit pale, Kallara sat down on her patient bench.

"Are you okay?" Fey asked.

Kallara smiled despite clear weariness. "I am fine. Sudden mana depletion results in fatigue and dizziness. I shall recover momentarily."

"Can I help?" Fey asked. Judging by how much the water would need to condense before it could fit into the small flask, Kallara would need to drain her mana reserves several more times, so Fey thought she should offer to throw her meagre mana into the effort as well.

"Each invocation takes quite a bit of mana, but you are welcome to try. Focus on the essence of water and invoke it."

Essence of water. Right. Instead of starting to philosophize about water and its reason for existence, Fey began filling her thoughts with all of the physical and chemical properties of water that she knew, as well as visualizing the electron clouds of the atomic bonds in the molecule. (Hey, whatever works.)

"Water."

Fey felt a sharp jolt of pain in her head and suddenly became dizzy.

<Spell efficacy decreased due to insufficient mana.>

<Fey has learned Enchant!>

Looking into the cauldron, Fey could barely discern a change in the water level. *Lame.*

"You really are quite talented," said Kallara, impressed. "It takes much skill to cast a spell without sufficient mana reserves."

<Fey's fame has increased to 6 (+1)!>

Not so lame? Wobbly, Fey sat next to Kallara. "How much does each invocation normally require?"

"Two hundred points."

Fey checked her status: 0/60. *Well. Looks like I'm not going to be much help.*

Kallara closed her eyes and meditated to speed her mana recovery. Fey did not have the mage-only ability, so she just rested quietly. Whenever either one of them had fully restored their mana reserves, they would cast Enchant; Fey did this more often due to her low maximum mana, but it made very little difference to the volume of water. After her fifth partially successful spell, her persistence in the face of stabbing headaches and waves of dizziness paid off.

<Fey's intelligence has increased to 12 (+1)!>

Kallara condensed the water to the volume of the flask with sixty casts of Enchant. (Let's face it, Fey didn't actually help.) She used a complicated series of chains and pulleys on the ceiling to raise the cauldron to the counter and tip it sideways, pouring the enchanted water directly into the flask.

"Go ahead and take it," the healer invited with a mischievous smile.

Fey closed one hand around the flask and pulled. It did not budge. She put more of her weight into the task, with a similar lack of success. Eventually, she managed to heave it off the counter with both hands.

Bracing her legs to keep them from collapsing under the ridiculous weight of the small container, she gritted, "Why is it so heavy?"

"The enchanted water weighs as much as the original volume of water used to make it," said Kallara, eyes twinkling in amusement. (What a prankster.)

Six buckets of water. Why me? The ultra-dense liquid was on the outer edge of Fey's ability to lift, let alone carry any distance.

If Fey were male and/or obsessed with proving her manly strength, she would have walked out with the flask, no matter the toll on her lower back. Not having high levels of testosterone to impair her thinking (sorry guys, but it's true), she asked Kallara if it was okay to get the flask dirty. Permission granted, she lowered it to the ground and rolled it outside, the action made awkward by the small object.

After a long trip through the herb garden, Fey reached the dryad's tree. "Pom, I have the enchanted water," she called out.

The dryad stepped into view. "Excellent. Pour it on the ground anywhere near here." Seeing Fey crouched over the diminutive flask, she asked, "Why are you on the ground?"

"It's too heavy for me to lift," Fey answered absentmindedly, fiddling with the lid and allowing the enchanted water to soak into the ground near the tree's roots.

"Ah." Pom nodded sagely, presumably having encountered many things too heavy to lift during her life as a miniature humanoid creature.

Within a few seconds, the apple tree seemed rejuvenated, its leaves becoming even more vibrantly green. Several of its fruit ripened, deepening in colour to a luscious red.

"Wonderful, wonderful," said Pom, looking at the tree in satisfaction. Walking along the branches, she began picking apples and throwing them to Fey. (Or, given Fey's catching abilities, *at* Fey.) "Fifteen, was it?"

Ahh! Incoming! "Yes," Fey managed to respond while trying to catch the falling fruit. In the end, she had five caught and ten fallen (ignominiously) to the ground. *Yay, I caught five!* (It really says something about her physical ability that she is proud of that accuracy.)

Gathering up the rest of the apples, Fey said, "Thanks!"

"Malus and I appreciate your help as well," said Pom.

Picking up the now-empty flask, Fey headed off to find Blade.

He should be done gathering the next ingredient, since I spent so long with Kallara making the enchanted water. Using the party menu in the game system, she located the warrior on her minimap and walked to his location.

"What the . . . " It looked to Fey like she had walked into a recent war zone; the ground was pocked with craters that seemed to be the result of small explosions. "What happened?" she asked Blade, who was grimly—and grimily—digging in the dirt at the centre of a crater.

"Self-destruct," Blade said shortly, pulling what looked like a slightly charred potato out of the ground.

Fey winced in sympathy. *He looks terrible.* In addition to a layer of dirt and several dents and scratches in his armour, Blade's hands were covered in scratches, and he looked pale from poison. Fey looked particularly healthy and clean in contrast.

Ignoring the mood, Amethyst and Magic enjoyed a cute, squeaky reunion.

Fey's sense of empathy and guilt kicked in. She could easily see how, if she had collected all the ingredients herself, she would have ended up in a similarly dishevelled and miserable state. Given how she had ended up after her slug-killing adventure the night before, she felt that she had somehow transferred today's misfortune to Blade. The human warrior was enduring it all with commendable stoicism, which made her feel worse than if he had been whiny or angry about it.

Sighing, she pulled out her probably-super-expensive, hope-I-never-have-to-use-it-again jar of healing salve and offered it to Blade. "Here."

"What's this?" Blade asked, examining the jar's contents, a pale green gel.

"Healing salve."

Blade scooped out a large glob on one finger, making Fey wince. Experimentally, he dabbed it on a cut; instantly, all his wounds began healing and he felt much better. He enthusiastically spread the salve over both hands as well as on several cuts on his face, all of which healed without a blemish. Even his pale complexion recovered to its normal state.

As a bonus, Blade's continuous poisoning finally paid off:

<Blade has gained Immunity!>

"This stuff is great!" he said enthusiastically.

"Yep," Fey agreed, lips tight at the amount of wasted salve. *Don't think about it. It's fine. Really.* She successfully kept her comments to herself.

"What's next on the list?" Fey asked (to distract herself).

"This is the last thing on the list," Blade said, gesturing to the potatoes. "When I saw you weren't at the apple tree, I went and got the rest of the plants."

"Great!" Fey was genuinely pleased at the news, as there had been five more ingredients on the list. The saved time made her feel better about the use of the healing salve. "Let's get brewing."

Kallara looked up from reading a book as Fey and Blade entered her tree-shop. "Back so quickly?"

"Blade collected the rest of the ingredients while we were making the enchanted water," Fey explained.

Blade had no idea what they were talking about but assumed it was related to getting the dryad-blessed apples. Instead of asking about it, he spent his time more productively and emptied his backpack of several types flowers, leaves, and roots. Fey added her own ingredients to the pile.

"Excellent," said Kallara, beginning to sort the components for processing. "I take it you two have formed a team?"

Blade said, "Yes," at the same time Fey answered, "Temporarily."

They exchanged a look.

Why do I suddenly have the feeling that I'm in a lovers' quarrel? Fey broke eye contact, making sure to look bored rather than flustered. As far as she was concerned, Blade was a generically nice guy but not particularly interesting in a way that would make her want to seek him out for future adventures.

"I see," said Kallara with thinly veiled amusement. She cast a spell that seemed to make any dirt on the plants fall off, then began grinding the sweetgrass roots with a mortar and pestle.

"Uh, do you need that turned into a paste?" Fey asked.

"Yes. Why do you ask?"

"Amethyst could probably help with that." Fey put the slime on the counter next to the mortar and said, "Use Whip to mash the roots, but don't break the bowl, okay?"

Squeaking in acknowledgement, Amethyst began to hit the roots, gradually increasing her speed until she resembled a very cute food processor.

Kallara watched this for a few seconds before saying, "My, isn't this convenient?" She reached for the next ingredient.

Just as Blade was about to suggest that they return in a few hours to pick up the finished product, Fey asked, "Can I help?"

Surprised, Kallara looked up from the blossum petals she was counting. "I . . . Yes, of course." Most people treated her somewhat like a vending machine, visiting to have their injuries healed or to buy ready-made potions. Unless she put a quest out for ingredient collection, she rarely got the chance to brew more interesting and complex potions, and even then, the players would simply leave the ingredients with her and return to pick up the finished product. Fey was one of the few who had expressed interest in Kallara's craft, but the healer had not expected Fey to want to help with the tedious aspects of cutting, peeling, grinding, boiling, and mixing potion ingredients.

Gathering her thoughts, Kallara smiled with genuine warmth. "Could you remove the thorns from the thornweed stems?" To Blade, she said, "Could you collect water from the stream?"

Blade was too polite to say that he had not intended to get involved with the actual potion-making process. Resigned to his fate, he took the bucket and headed out.

Fey picked up the paring knife Kallara offered and got to work. "So, do you only need the thornweed stems for the potion?"

"That's correct. The stems have important strengthening properties, but the thorns are quite toxic," said Kallara, most of her attention on the blossum petals. Every time she had a pile of ten, she pressed it down on the counter with her palm, somehow ending up with a single petal that emitted a pleasant fragrance.

She won't be needing these . . . After Fey de-thorned all the stems, she swept the poisonous remains into her pouch for future use.

With three people and a slime to share the labour (Magic was particularly useless due to his lack of limbs and just hopped around looking cute for moral support), the strength tonic ingredients were processed in just over an hour. "It will need to steep overnight, but everything is done," Kallara told the players. "Thank you for your help!"

"Thank you for your expertise," said Fey. "I'll come back later to pick up my portion."

"And how should I divide it up?" Kallara asked.

"Give . . . Blade . . . half," said Fey, her sense of fairness warring with her greed.

Kallara smiled at Blade. "Looks like someone has taken a liking to you."

Fey grimaced but did not comment.

Blade took one look at Fey's expression and wisely decided to stay out of the subject of her feelings. "Yeah . . . I'll come by later as well."

"Have fun, you two. Keep an eye out for more rare potion ingredients for me."

"Will do," Fey said, waving goodbye as she left the shop. Blade followed.

CHAPTER 11
FLIGHT

Fey was hungry from all her exertions, so she headed toward the tavern.

Blade fell into step beside her. After a few seconds, he asked, "Where are we going?"

"I am going to get something to eat. I have no idea where you're going."

Blade had also worked up an appetite and continued keeping pace with the elf. He was not quite sure why, but Fey's obvious desire to ditch him seemed to make him want to convince her to team up.

"Hey, we did pretty well together collecting those herbs. Why don't we keep working as a party?"

"I don't need a me—" Fey cleared her throat. "I mean, two warriors don't make a particularly effective party." Playing alone in the game, she had done away with the thought-to-words filter she employed in public, and had only barely managed to keep the phrase "meat shield" out of her speech. She covered up her rudeness with logical argument, pointing out how she and Blade had no complementary abilities that would make them more effective as a team compared to fighting alone.

Instead of being put off, Blade took the words as a suggestion. "Let's look for more party members, then."

Eew. More people. Fey let her expression convey how she felt about the idea.

When they entered the tavern, Tallen came bustling up to greet them. "Welcome! Party of two?" Recognizing Fey from earlier, he brightened. "Ah, the young elfess!" (Making words up now, are we?) "Have you brought me more twiggies?" he asked hopefully.

"I'm afraid not. Are you running out of firewood again?"

"Ah, well, our stock is always pretty low, but you can make a little go a long way with the right cooking skills. Here to eat, then?"

"Yes, please."

"Have a seat wherever there's room," Tallen invited, disappearing into the kitchen.

Fey found an empty spot along one of the tavern's long tables and Blade sat across from her, looking curiously after the tavern-keeper. He had noticed that Fey treated Kallara like a real human being rather than an NPC (and was in fact nicer to her than to a certain PC), and her interaction with Tallen followed the same pattern. Being still rather incompetent at dealing with Fey (#Understatement), he broached the subject.

"Hey Fey, you know that the NPCs aren't real people, right?"

Out of the many, many things that annoyed Fey, number one was probably having her intelligence insulted. If Fey's liking for Blade had been graphed from their first interaction, it would have started at a small negative value (–10), gradually creeping up to a small positive value (+4) as they collected herbs. The new comment plunged the scale abruptly into the far negatives (–1,000).

Fey plunged into heavy sarcasm mode, her voice dropping an octave and words dripping with scorn. "*Really?* Oh, but they look so real! What a surprise! I never would have been able to figure it out without you explaining to little dumb me!"

Blade backpedaled, holding his hands up defensively, sensing that he had sparked true irritation, if not outright anger. "Hey, sorry."

The human warrior would have been in for more tongue-lashing followed by many minutes of icy silence had he not been saved by Tallen's arrival with two heaping plates of food. Fey's attention was instantly diverted by the mouthwatering aroma of fish and chips, looking perfectly golden and crispy. On each plate was a small bowl of ketchup, her preferred condiment when it came to potato-based foods.

"That looks *amazing*," Fey breathed as Tallen set the plates on the table, accompanied by tankards of cool cider.

The tavern-keeper grinned at her unfeigned enthusiasm. "It tastes even better," he boasted.

Fey ate a fry dipped in ketchup; her eyes closed involuntarily at the amazing taste. "Mm" was all she could manage to say.

"I'll just let you enjoy your meal," Tallen said, still grinning, going off to serve another party of players.

Fey continued eating, having mostly forgotten about Blade and any petty irritation she might feel toward him. (The like/dislike graph now had a blank section where no data was collected.)

Curious, Blade tried the food. It was good, but fried foods were not his favourite, so nothing to go into raptures over. Deciding to take Tallen's interruption as the blessing that it was, he stayed quiet as they ate. He was rather amazed at the amount of food Fey consumed. After devouring the generous portion of fish on her plate, she slowly but steadily savoured and consumed the chips, which in and of themselves could have served as a decent-sized meal. He had rather expected someone as thin as she was to eat very lightly.

In reality, Arwyn's food intake was directly proportional to how much energy she burned. If she spent the day lazing about at home reading a book or playing video games, she could get by with a single meal and a cup of hot chocolate, whereas during days or weeks of increased training at tae kwon do, she needed to eat three to four large meals a day to avoid losing weight. Given how she had spent the virtual day hiking around the forest, running after monsters, and crushing and grinding plant parts without any meals, Fey had worked up quite the appetite.

Amethyst nudged at the food curiously and Fey offered the slime a ketchup-dipped fry. "Here. Try eating things that aren't slimes or poison."

Amethyst obediently opened her mouth and accepted the offering. The fry was visible through her translucent membrane for several minutes until it was gradually dissolved and disappeared. It was unclear whether the slime had any sense of smell or taste to appreciate food.

"You like?" Fey asked, popping another fry into her own mouth.

Amethyst gave a squeak that somehow sounded like, "Mch."

"A wasted fry, then. How about you, Magic?"

The mushroom shook his head, uninterested in human food.

Even lost in her bubble of food appreciation, Fey was not so oblivious as to miss the female player who sat down directly next to Blade despite the ample amount of free seating in the tavern. The player was an elf dressed in the same newbie outfit Fey had been wearing the day before, though she had removed the default hair tie and allowed her hair to cascade past her shoulders in an attractive but impractical arrangement.

Evaluating the stranger's appearance, Fey guessed that the newbie had made some unfortunate choices regarding her avatar's appearance. Fey guessed that in real life, the girl had a round, cute face, something that did not mesh well with the angular modifications applied for the elven race. The result was a rather nondescript appearance that was neither cute nor elegant. Additionally, she had either kept her original blonde hair or chosen the warm, yellow hue, one that clashed with the cool, pale skin of a moon elf and made her look washed out and unhealthy.

All of the inspection and judgement on Fey's part was carried out with brief, indirect glances as she continued eating, her main attention still on her food (*omnom*).

The player cozied up to Blade in a blatantly flirtatious manner. "Hi, do you mind if I join your party?"

Fey instantly found the voice annoying, both for its slightly whiny tone and its assumption that Blade was the party leader. She resented having her fry time polluted by the negative emotion.

Blade, to his credit, did not appear affected by the overly friendly body language. He did, unfortunately, miss Fey's subtly narrowed eyes and responded to the question with enthusiasm. "We were just talking about getting more party members." He did notice when Fey shot him a full-on glare and hastily tacked on, "What do you think, Fey?"

Despite her initial negative impression of the girl, Fey proceeded logically and asked, "What's your level and class?"

The girl looked resentful at the questioning but answered, "I'm still level one."

. . . She didn't even do the slime quest! Fey could not help but form the impression that the newbie was lazy, not very smart, and looking for a guy to mooch off of.

"Oh . . . " said Blade, disappointed. "We're, uh—"

"But I'm sure with *your* help, I could level up really quickly," she interrupted. "What do you say?" The blonde elf was really invading Blade's personal space in a way that Fey felt highly awkward witnessing.

"No," Fey said flatly. She spoke mainly to Blade, the subtext being something along the lines of, "If you want me to even *consider* forming a long-term party with you, we are not going to join up with the likes of Ms. Moocher here."

"Nobody asked *you*," said the newbie, the whiny tone in her voice becoming more pronounced.

Fey did not bother to point out that Blade had literally asked her opinion less than a minute before. It was becoming clear that the girl was trying to play some sort of female dominance game that would establish her as higher in the hierarchy of some sort of societal structure, the details of which Fey did not quite understand. Normally, Fey would not hesitate to inflict the kind of emotional wounds that would take years of therapy to resolve (Vicious Strike isn't just a move, it's a way of life), but refrained for two reasons. One, she did not want her fries to get cold while she delivered the verbal attack, and two, the dubious prize of winning this particular game was Blade's continued company, which she had been passive-aggressively trying to rid herself of. She settled for giving the girl a patronizing look, which caused a gratifying amount of irritation.

Down to the last few fries, Fey dipped, chewed, and swallowed. Blade still had not said anything after the last hostile exchange, so Fey assumed that he actually wanted to join parties with the blonde. In actuality, he simply disliked openly hostile confrontations and did not know what to say.

Fey stood. "Well, Blade, I shall leave you in the company of this *charming* young lady." The amount of sarcasm loaded into the word "charming" would have been enough to make a small child cry. Having had a good idea for her next adventure, she hurriedly dissolved the party and left the table before Blade could say more than, "Hey—!"

Blade tried to get up and follow but was hampered by the charming young lady, who grabbed his arm and said, "We don't need *her*." (Ooh look, even the dignified non-parenthetical narrator is getting in on the snark. Elf girl be annoying.)

Ignoring the minor scene evolving between Blade and his new arm shackle (oof, the snark is strong in this one), Fey went over to

Tallen to pay for her meal. "Hey Tallen, is there a stronger monster than twiggies to hunt for firewood?"

Tallen's eyes lit up at the question. "Indeed there is! Treants live up past the twiggy clearing, just before you reach the Dark Forest. Each is about a man's height, big enough for a whole day's cooking. Bring me a load of those, and I'll make sure you never have to pay for a meal again."

"What level are they?"

"Fifteen."

Perfect. "I'll go after some right now. Hope you have some delicious food waiting for me when I get back!"

Tallen waved the words away as a matter of course. Eager for Fey to bring back as much fuel as possible, he gave her some advice. "You'll want to get one of those magical backpacks that shrinks and lightens items. They're sold at the general store."

Fey thanked him for the advice and headed to the general store.

Jeral was again on duty and remembered Fey from her earlier visit. "Ah yes, the fair maiden who was in need of rope. How may I be of assistance today?" he asked with a charming smile. He was somewhat disappointed that he failed to elicit a blush as he had on Fey's first visit.

Fey had in fact mentally fortified herself prior to entering the tree-shop, deciding that she was going to find the smile manipulative rather than attractive given the way Jeral used it as a sales tactic. "I'd like to look at the magical backpacks, please," she said, all coolness and politesse.

Still looking disappointed, Jeral led the way to the correct shelf, stocked with several backpacks made of sturdy leather. They were all very similar in size and shape, the main distinguishing characteristic a small set of numbers branded into a corner of the opening flap.

Jeral explained the marking system. "This number at the top with the star mark refers to how many times the enchantment can shrink the object relative to its original size, while the bottom number with the feather tells you how many times lighter it can make its contents."

Seeing the enchantment effects and marked prices sent Fey into analysis mode. Jeral quietly wandered away after she stared at the shelf without talking for a minute. There was a very cheap unmagicked backpack at 10g, a series of weight-reducing backpacks, a series of size-reducing backpacks, and a more expensive set that reduced both size and weight. The prices for each went up by a factor of ten, while the enchantment effect only went up by a factor of two to five, making the cheapest enchantments the most cost-effective.

Can't you just . . . Fey stuck a weight-reducing bag inside a size-shrinking bag. When nothing terrible happened, she stuck the size-shrinking bag inside another size-shrinking bag. This failed to rip a hole in reality or cause a fatal explosion, so Fey assumed enchantment stacking in this fashion was allowed in the game.

Fey went to the bank and withdrew almost all of her savings before returning to the store. "I'd like eleven of the tenth-size packs and four of the half-weight packs, please."

Jeral raised an eyebrow at the unusual purchase but went into the back storage to retrieve the requested items, the quantities more than what was available in the front display. "That will be fifteen hundred gold."

Fey handed over the money and left the shop carrying a considerable pile of leather.

Jeral shook his head bemusedly. "That's a strange one," he muttered to himself.

Fey started on the path toward the treants, waiting until she was alone in the trees before she dealt with her purchases. She stuck ten of the size-reducing packs inside the eleventh, then stuck that successively into each of the half-weight packs, effectively creating a pack that reduced size by a factor of a hundred and weight by a factor of sixteen, all for a fraction of the price of a single pack with the equivalent enchantment.

Jeral would have stopped me if sticking a bag inside a bag would have transported me to a hell dimension or something. Right?

—◦◦◇◦◦—

Leandriel stood at the edge of Skyhaven, the (not-so-creatively named) major celestial city that floated amongst the clouds. Looking down, he saw the endless green forest canopy and concluded that the city was currently floating over the Elvenwood.

Taking a deep breath, he stepped off the edge and into thin air.

With his wings spread, Leandriel waited for his descent to change from stomach-churning free fall to a controlled glide before cautiously beginning to beat his wings. The past few days had been quite the challenge as he adjusted to his two new limbs. First of all, the wings were *huge*. The game developers had decided that for angels in particular, their wings would be large enough to actually support their weight in flight, rather than relying on magic or weight reduction. In the case of Leandriel's muscled 75 kilogram frame, plus full plate armour, that meant a colossal wingspan of a full six metres. (That's 165 pounds and 18 feet for you weirdo Americans.) When folded, the wings jutted far above his head and trailed all the way to the ground. He had not yet seen himself in a mirror, but, judging from the reactions of people around him, he guessed he cut quite the imposing figure. It was a good thing that people automatically avoided crowding him now, as he still felt clumsy doing something as simple as turning around when walking.

His second challenge had been simply learning to move his new limbs when his brain was only used to controlling four. It had taken hours of experimentation before he had learned what his wings "felt" like and he could reliably move them as intended. Fortunately, the correct series of movements required to beat his wings in flight was programmed instinctively into the wings, or he was sure that his first forays into flight would have ended in fatal falls.

Last but certainly not least was the enormous amount of stamina required for flying. While the huge muscles and lungs that would theoretically need to accompany the huge wings had been eliminated in favour of aesthetics, he certainly felt the exhaustion that came with using the phantom muscles. His wings felt somewhat like an extra pair of arms, but the amount of exertion with each wingbeat was more like what his legs went through with vigorous jumping or sprinting exercises. As a level 99 warrior, Leandriel had truly superhuman levels of strength and stamina, but he was already starting to feel out of breath after the first few minutes of flight. He went back into a glide to conserve energy, circling lower over the forest due to the lack of thermal updrafts to ride over the sun-absorbent canopy.

Still, Leandriel thought the power of flight was definitely worth the trouble. He did not particularly enjoy adrenaline-inducing activities like roller coasters or extreme sports, but he savoured the thrill and freedom of self-sustained flight.

He beat his wings to gain height. His breathing was definitely deepening, but he was not yet desperate for air. He could savour the blue skies and amazing view for just a little longer.

⸺◦◦◦◦◦⸺

On the rather long walk to the treants, Fey did some experimenting. She pulled out a thornweed thorn she had saved, and held it out to Amethyst. "Here, eat this." The slime opened her mouth and engulfed the thorn. (Do not try this at home. Ingesting toxic substances generally leads to ill effects, like death.) Fey could see it floating inside the slime until it was gradually digested.

<Amethyst has improved Poison Slime!>

<Current poisons: slug poison, thornweed poison.>

Interesting. It appeared that instead of only being able to secrete one kind of poison, Amethyst could memorize and copy all poisons she was presented with. (Way OP[15], just for fun.) Fey considered having Amethyst learn Magic's blue mushroom poison, but gave up that idea given the number of times the mushroom would have to cast the random ability to get a poison effect. Instead, she pulled out another thorn and pricked herself.

<Fey has been poisoned!>

<Thornweed poison: –2 health/5 seconds.>

<Duration: 5 minutes.>

<Level 1 Immunity effect: decrease 1 damage per poison infliction.>

<New poison effect: –1 health/5 seconds.>

<Duration: 5 minutes.>

Fey got a minor headache from the poison but persisted in training her Immunity ability as she walked. She repeated the cycle of poisoning herself then waiting for her health to replenish a total of eight times before arriving at her destination.

<Immunity has reached level 2!>

<Immunity has reached level 3!>

CHAPTER 12
IMPACT

Arriving at the treant territory, Fey put her thornweed away and surveyed her surroundings.

So . . . where are all the treants? She double-checked her minimap to confirm she was in the right location. All around her she saw only trees.

After several minutes of staring, Fey realized that some of the trees around her must be treants. Unlike the twiggies she had fought before, these monsters appeared to have an inactive state that made them fairly indistinguishable from regular trees.

"Now what?" she muttered. Given Tallen's dire remarks about harming real trees, she had a feeling that if she accidentally picked the wrong target, something would show up to make her regret it.

She racked her memory for any details about treants. *Something about being a man's height?* All of the trees around her were considerably taller than that, but if she considered only the height of the main trunk, several of the younger trees would fit the description.

Here goes. Fey sent Magic and Amethyst to hide, reasoning that none of their attacks would be particularly effective against the treants' thick bark. Hoping she had guessed correctly, she hit the tree with a side kick, turning sideways to the tree and snapping her foot out with picture-perfect technique, making sure her planted foot had its toes facing in the opposite direction of the kick. She was grateful for her footwear as the impact reverberated up her heel.

Fey landed in a fighting stance, waiting tensely for a counterattack. For a moment, nothing happened, and she cringed, imagining an irate elven ranger popping up out of nowhere to berate her for the dent she had left in the tree's bark. She was relieved when the treant woke up, opening spooky yellow eyes and uprooting itself from the earth.

Fey easily dodged as the treant swiped at her with a branch-arm, its ponderous movements easy to read. She kicked it again, this time with a back kick, turning so that her back faced the target and allowing the large, powerful muscles in the gluteus area to do the work. (Her butt. The muscles are in her butt.)

Unfortunately, Fey did not have the mass to back up her kick, so when her foot collided with the much heavier treant, she was the one sent backward (#ConservationOfMomentum). She grimaced but kept her balance, very much used to this phenomenon. She was thin enough that there was rarely anyone in her weight class to spar against, so she ended up being paired with opponents who outweighed her by fifteen to thirty percent. (In case you were wondering, no, our heroine doesn't have miraculous combat ability that allows her to make up for this liability and yes, she usually gets her butt kicked pretty soundly.)

The kick left a second dent in the treant's bark, but she was not sure she was doing any real damage. Given that she had no heavy, bladed weapon such as an axe, she could only continue dealing blunt damage and hope it accumulated in a meaningful way. Given how slow the treant was, she was able to attack at her leisure, whaling on it with a series of powerful kicks, sometimes adding jumps and spins to the basic kick to add force to the attack.

Fey was now breathing heavily and wanted to sit down to rest. The energy expenditure required to kick with maximum force was not something she could maintain for extended periods of time, especially with movements that required jumping and spinning. Her rate of attack slowed considerably as she spent half a minute catching her breath between combinations of kicks.

<Fey's stamina has increased to 101 (+1)!>

Fantasia did not have a stamina bar, relying instead on the players' feelings of exhaustion to let them know when they were running out of energy. The stamina stat was instead a descriptive marker of cardiovascular fitness. New players started with stamina of 100, which was the equivalent of a reasonably healthy young adult. Level 150 was around that of a world-class athlete in peak physical condition. The game did allow stamina to surpass the biological limits of the human body, allowing people to experience the fun of truly superhuman feats of endurance.

The requirement to build stamina was less fun. Similar to real life, players had to push their bodies to their limits in order to increase them, and in the case of stamina, that meant punishing physical exhaustion.

Still, having the concrete stat increase gave Fey considerable motivation to continue fighting, as did the increased levels in her Kicking ability, which reached level 5 after several more rounds of blows.

Okay, seriously, am I accomplishing anything? Despite the increased attack power with every level of Kicking, the treant appeared to be moving just as vigorously as it had after her first attack. *I need to get past that stupid bark.*

Keeping half her concentration on dodging the treant's attacks, she examined her skills and abilities.

Mana Edge, maybe? Using a sword against a tree seems like it wouldn't be good for the sword.

As Fey mused over the problem, it occurred to her that there was no rule that stated she had to channel her battle magic through the sword. She focused on sending her mana into her feet.

The tingle she associated with magic went down her legs easily enough, then seemed to encounter a certain amount of resistance as it reached the leather of her boots. She was able to push it through, and a visible glow began to emanate from her feet.

Fey had partial success with her experimentation. She was able to manifest the flames of Mana Blade by designating her shoes as weapons, but given the lack of actual edged blade, she was unable to sharpen the mana flow into Mana Edge. The ability was burning up her mana reserves at a faster rate than normal, which she suspected had something to do with the sense of resistance she had felt channelling the magic through leather.

Fantasia had no hard limitations on the types of equipment players could use, no item slots that could be locked by level or class. In order to give lighter armour a viable place in combat and guide tactics into falling within the classic combat classes, the developers had introduced the property of magic conductivity into materials. For classic magic as cast by a mage, organic materials such as wood, cotton, and silk made the best conductors, while metal acted as an insulator and hampered spell efficiency. Warrior skills, which were not considered "magic" but nonetheless consumed mana, had the opposite conductivity and took to metal the most readily. The leather in Fey's boots was not the ideal conduit for Mana Blade, limiting her flexibility to adjust the shape of the magic and forcing her to burn more mana to manifest the effect. (Fey doesn't actually know any of this, having not done any research into the game system before jumping in.)

Even without the armour penetration of Mana Edge, the increased attack power gave Fey enough of a boost that she was eventually able to cause a significant wound in the treant's trunk, a thin layer of sap soaking through its damaged bark. She focused her attacks in that one area, encouraged by the fact that it actually seemed to make the monster flinch. Eventually, the treant toppled to the ground, nearly squashing Fey in the process.

<Fey has defeated the treant!>

<Fey gains 50 experience. Amethyst gains 25 experience. Magic gains 25 experience.>

The treant's leaves shrivelled and fell off and its eyes closed and disappeared, leaving it looking like a log that had been uprooted by some sort of natural disaster. Fey sat next to it, leaning against a tree and catching her breath. She had spent far too long kicking ineffectually at the treant and only had a single log to show for all her trouble.

Magic and Amethyst descended from the tree they had been hiding in to inspect their exhausted owner. Sweaty and flushed, Fey let her head loll gracelessly back against the tree, limbs splayed out with an equal lack of consideration for appearances. She gradually caught her breath, which only served to lessen the obviousness of her breathing and increase her resemblance to a recently dead body.

Amethyst jumped onto Fey's head and squeaked concernedly. Fey lazily took the slime down and placed her on the ground. Magic hopped up one bent leg and surveyed Fey from his vantage point on her knee. She patted him absently, then let her hand drift back to the ground and resumed her corpse imitation.

Several minutes later, Fey revived (#Undead) and heaved herself off the ground. She would have liked nothing more than to find a relaxing, labour-free activity for the rest of the day, but she had firewood to collect. It had also not escaped her notice that she had not gained a single level since logging in, most of her time taken up with potion-making.

As she got up and moving, she noticed that she did not have any of the lingering fatigue she would have expected after exertion of that magnitude, the kind that would take hours to days to completely recover from. This was because the muscle microtears that contributed to delayed-onset muscle soreness were treated as damage and subject to the same accelerated healing as other injuries in the game. The discovery made her considerably more enthusiastic about continuing to fight.

Determined to have some progress to show for her day's adventures, she found another shorter tree and kicked it, Mana Blade activated from the beginning.

After defeating her third treant, Fey levelled up.

<Fey has reached level 12!>

<Fey's stamina has increased to 102 (+1)!>

<Mana Blade has reached level 3!>

In addition to her own stat gains, Magic had caught up to Amethyst in level and received the same boost to intelligence.

Sending her pets out to gather scattered coins, Fey wrestled her three logs into her pack to clear the ground before she fought any more treants. It was a rather surreal experience to handle items that shrank and lightened as she moved them, but she soon got them fitting neatly into the six-layered pack arrangement she had created.

She had just gone to look for her next target when the sound of breaking branches above her head made her look up.

Leandriel was having fun. As he gained confidence in his flying abilities, he attempted more complex maneuvers, climbing, diving, and turning sharply in the air. He wobbled a few times during the exercises but managed to recover his balance with an exhilarated grin.

The mistake he could not recover from was when he swooped down too close to the treetops. The air currents flowed differently as they travelled over the forest canopy, causing his wings to dip unexpectedly. The first crash of branch against wing hopelessly upset his balance, sending him into a skewed fall into the trees.

Not wanting to damage the delicate bones in his new limbs, Leandriel gave up on regaining flight and tucked his wings tightly to his back, letting himself fall and trusting his high vitality and strength to allow him to survive the impact. He crashed through several layers of branches that slowed his descent before breaking through the canopy.

His first instinct was to attempt some kind of roll on impact to dissipate the force, but with his new wings hampering his maneuverability, he overruled the urge and let the ground slam into his legs and arms, forcing his muscles to relax despite the bruising collision.

Finally, blessedly still, Leandriel took a breath to recover his orientation and catalogue his injuries. Multiple bruises and scrapes, quite a few lost feathers, but no broken bones. He gingerly picked himself off the ground, only then noticing the figure below him.

His heart raced anew as he realized he had crashed into an elven woman, and she appeared far more injured than he was.

Fey was fairly sure that at least one of her ribs was broken. She had never experienced such an injury, but there was a sharp pain every time she inhaled. Her left arm was numb in a way that seemed ominous.

She tried to regulate her breathing, taking slow, shallow breaths. She had looked up barely in time to see a large object hurtling down just before being crushed under its weight.

She gasped as the weight shifted, her pain sharpening as bone ground against bone. Involuntary tears leaked from her eyes and her vision blurred.

Distantly, she heard a startled exclamation before a young man's face entered her field of vision.

"Are you okay?" the man asked in a low, urgent voice.

"My ribs . . . arm . . . " Fey managed to whisper.

The man muttered angrily at himself and fumbled in his belt pouch. When he produced a healing potion, Fey saw the silver sparkles in the liquid that indicated it was a medium healing potion, capable of restoring up to 500 health points. Given that her maximum health was currently 172, she opened her mouth to tell him it would be a waste. The man took the opportunity to pour the potion into her mouth.

Well, too late now. She stopped worrying about money and swallowed the healing liquid, sighing in relief as the pain was soothed away and her injuries gradually knitted themselves back together.

Rustling noises and small tremors in the ground announced the awakening of several treants in the area, disturbed by the crash.

The man wore an annoyed expression, as if a fly had buzzed near his face. Not bothering to stand up from his kneeling position beside her, he drew a longsword and unleashed a single attack. A circular arc of white light flew out and bisected all the monsters at once, each half toppling lifeless to the ground.

He sheathed the weapon in a smooth, automatic movement and focused on her again. "Are you still hurt anywhere?" he asked anxiously.

Fey took a deep breath, luxuriating in being able to do so without pain. "I'm good. You didn't need to use a medium healing potion, you know; my health is only one seventy-two."

Startled at the pragmatic response, Leandriel answered honestly. "That is the smallest healing potion I have."

Fey belatedly noticed the man's huge, pure white wings. "Are you an angel?" she asked, then smiled because it sounded like she was delirious with pain.

He nodded. Due to her obsession with the winged races, Fey knew that meant he had reached at least level 100, which would explain his lack of lesser healing potions. It also told her that he must be an NPC, given how impossible it would be for a player to have reached that level in the short time since *Fantasia* had been released.

Deciding that she had spent enough time lying on the ground, Fey sat up. This failed to elicit any pain, so she moved on to standing. The angel hurried to assist her, and she accepted a supporting hand around her waist despite not needing the help. She put as little of her weight on the angel as possible, pushing straight up with her legs and gaining her feet in a single lithe movement.

Upright, Fey noticed her braid had been knocked askew. Grimacing, she pulled out the hair tie and began combing out the braid.

⚬⚬⚬

As the elf finger-combed her hair, she stepped into a patch of direct sunlight created from Leandriel's fall through the canopy. He could not help but notice that her hair was a rich, deep purple rather than black.

Shaking the irrelevant thought away, he spoke to the player he had nearly killed with his clumsiness. "I really cannot apologize enough for crashing into you like that."

—◦◦◇◇◦◦—

Fey listened absently to the angel's lengthy, sincere apology while retying her hair. She would be angry except that he radiated such pure remorse that yelling at him would feel like kicking a puppy. She considered her hairstyle options. She generally wore her waist-length hair loose or in a simple ponytail; the first was not a viable option for running and fighting, while the second did not feel appropriate for the elegant aesthetic of an elf. She ended up with a very simplified version of the stereotypical elven hairstyles she had seen in movies, pulling back the sides to keep it out of her face while leaving most of it free to flow down her back. (She did not attempt any of the intricate braids common to those styles, knowing through experience that trying them on herself was a recipe for disaster.)

Leandriel was winding down the apology section of his speech and moving on to explanations. "I only recently earned my wings and am still in the process of mastering flying. When I came too close to the treetops, I lost control and fell."

Fey nodded her understanding, realizing that she had not previously considered the difficulties inherent in learning how to fly in a virtual reality setting.

Hair dealt with, Fey took a few seconds to examine her drop-in visitor. (Ah, puns, the spice of life.) He looked every inch the stereotypical warrior angel, tall and dark-haired, with piercing blue eyes that reminded her of the heart of a glacier. His wings were such a pure white that they haloed in direct sunlight, and his armour was equally shiny and impressive.

The overall effect was intimidatingly gorgeous, so much so that it tipped all the way into the realm of unrealistic and made Fey relax. *Just an NPC. One who is very sorry.*

Sensing that the angel would continue apologizing for at least another five minutes if she did not intervene, Fey placed a gentle hand on his arm. "It's fine. I'm all good now."

"That does not in any way excuse the amount of pain and distress I caused you."

"No, seriously, if all my injuries could heal that quickly in real life, I'd be golden."

"'All your injuries'?" Leandriel repeated, eyebrows creasing in concern.

"During training. In tae kwon do class," Fey clarified, realizing how sketchy it sounded that she casually referred to incurring painful injuries on a regular basis. "Not that I've ever broken anything, but I've gotten some nasty sprains and bruises." She belatedly realized that it might not be the best idea to refer to "real life" when talking to an NPC, but Leandriel did not seem particularly confused by what she was saying. *I suppose they wouldn't make it easy for players to confuse the NPCs if they wanted to make trouble.*

Leandriel's expression cleared of confusion, but guilt remained.

With the exception of a couple of spectacular falls, the vast majority of Arwyn's injuries in tae kwon do class were incurred at the hands (well, usually feet) of other people, and the vast majority of those people were athletic young men. She therefore had a certain amount of experience in dealing with the guilt they tended to feel when she got hurt.

The key, she had found, was to act normal so that it was clear she had not come to serious harm and find some way for them to assist her that would serve as an act of penance.

Fey looked around and spotted the treants the angel had neatly felled. "Do you mind if I take these?" she asked, gesturing.

"Of course not." Leandriel was quick to help her collect the logs and store them in her pack. The angel had such casual strength—able to pick up logs one-handed—that the task was complete within a few minutes, Fey ending up holding the bag open while he dropped them in.

She nodded in satisfaction, having made more progress on the wood collection than she would have been able to by fighting. "Thanks! Um, do you need directions to town or something? It might be hard to fly out of here," she said, glancing up at the trees, which were still mostly intact.

———◦◦◇◦◦———

Leandriel felt his emotions click into place like the final piece of a complex puzzle. His dismay and concern at finding the elf he had injured, his surprise and confusion at her calm and forgiving response, his appreciation of her consideration—all of it coalesced into a level of fascination and attraction he had never felt before.

"May I have the honour of knowing your name?" he asked.

"Oh, sorry. I'm Fey."

He took the opportunity to offer his hand, which she shook readily, her grip firm but not aggressive. "My name is Leandriel. Please allow me to assist you."

CHAPTER 13

DIVINE INTERVENTION

You really don't have to feel bad, you know," Fey said. She certainly was not averse to the idea of Leandriel's company, but having a level 100 angel help her fight level 15 treants seemed akin to using construction equipment to play in a sandbox.

"I will feel better if I can leave you feeling that meeting me today was a fortunate occurrence."

Fey felt oddly flattered by the words. "Well, as you can see, I'm hunting treants for firewood. You already did help, but if you really want to, you can help me gather more logs."

"It's settled, then." Leandriel drew his sword and, showing off a little, unleashed one of his area-of-effect attacks.

"Holy Impact!"

He stabbed into the ground, and a shock wave of holy energy travelled outward to a radius of thirty metres, purifying anything that touched the ground. One of the conveniences of holy element attacks was that they left non-monster plants and animals unharmed; three seconds later, fourteen treants toppled to the ground while the real trees were unaffected.

Fey was suitably impressed, but . . . "Do you think you could leave one or two for me?" she asked. "I'm trying to do some training."

"Oh. Of course." Leandriel looked rather embarrassed at having thoughtlessly committed the gamer crime of kill-stealing, which Fey found rather endearing. *You shouldn't be allowed to be cool and cute at the same time. The devs just had to be extra.*

Considering their disparate combat strength, elf and angel came to the same logical conclusion. "We should split up," Fey said. There was simply no viable way they could fight effectively as a team.

Leandriel nodded in agreement. "I'll go this way," he said, indicating a direction. "How many do you need?"

Good question. "Uh . . . I don't have a quota. I was planning on bringing back as many as I could carry."

Leandriel accepted the vague (i.e., half-baked) goal without any qualms, and even helped her plan. "We should form a party so we can find each other later."

<Leandriel has invited you to join his party.>

<Fey has accepted the party invitation.>

<Leandriel's party: Leandriel (leader), level 99 angel; Fey, level 12 moon elf.>

"I'll set the experience allocation to 'individual,'" Leandriel added considerately. With such a huge difference in level, Fey would be lucky to get a single experience point per kill on the default weighted setting.

"Level 99?" Fey asked curiously.

"I died shortly after completing my advancement quest," Leandriel explained.

"Ah." Fey nodded her understanding. About to set out on her own, she realized she should introduce the angel to her pets so that he would not accidentally kill them.

"Leandriel?"

"Yes?"

"I have pets. Amethyst, Magic, come out!"

Leandriel expected Fey to have unusual pets, and smiled when he saw the little slime and mushroom hop over.

The slime went straight to her owner and spat out a small pile of coins she had collected. Fey bent to pick her up, murmuring, "Good job."

The mushroom, in contrast, hopped forward until it landed on Leandriel's foot. He looked down at the mushroom, and it looked curiously back at him.

Fey swooped down and plucked the mushroom off his sabaton, chiding, "Magic! Don't go randomly sticking to people like that; it's rude."

Something about the absurdity of someone attempting to teach a mushroom manners made Leandriel's lips twitch in amusement.

Holding a pet in each hand, Fey made the introductions. "This is Amethyst, and this is Magic."

Leandriel could see why a purple slime would be named Amethyst, but a mushroom . . . "Magic mushroom?" he murmured.

"Yup!" Fey said, delighted that somebody had understood the reference. Leandriel could not help but smile in response.

Magic was hopping excitedly and leaning forward, eager to explore the new person, so Fey passed him over to the angel. Leandriel handled the mushroom deftly, allowing Magic to hop in spirals up and down his arms without worrying about petty things like gravity.

"So how did you tame them?" Leandriel asked.

"Well, there's a Monster Tamer skill," Fey began.

"I meant, what did you do specifically to tame these two?" he clarified. He had fairly extensive knowledge of most of the skills and monsters within the game, having spent a lot of time with the artists and developers who had created them.

Magic was now dangling upside down from the tip of one finger, looking delighted at the experience.

"Oh. Well, during my first quest, I poked Amethyst with my dagger, but then I felt sorry for her and dumped a healing potion on her head. Then later, I told her to attack Magic and they ended up bouncing off each other until they passed out, then somehow ended up as friends when they woke up."

Leandriel chuckled softly, both at Fey's misadventures and at the programmer who had designed the monster-taming system.

Fey grinned. She did not mind being laughed at, as long as the laughter was not malicious, and it made her feel good to make the angel laugh. She had the impression that he was generally quite serious, but laughter was a good look for him. (Okay, but, like, what would be a *bad* look for him?)

With reluctance, Leandriel said, "We should probably get to work. Message me when your pack is full and we can meet up." With a last pat, he returned Magic to Fey's possession.

Before they parted, Leandriel cast a buff on his party member.

<Helping Hand: increases player attack and defence by 10%.>

<Duration: 1 hour.>

While a guardian class like Leandriel did not have as powerful buffing abilities as a priest, they were certainly a great help to anyone lucky enough to benefit from them.

"Thank you," Fey said, somewhat surprised to see that Leandriel had magical abilities.

Leandriel nodded and disappeared into the trees. Fey turned in the opposite direction and went to work.

With her newly gained level, improving skill, and boost from Helping Hand, Fey could now defeat treants slightly more quickly. It was still quite a time-consuming process that involved many, many attacks. Fey thought wistfully of the effortless ease Leandriel had demonstrated while killing a dozen treants at a time.

After each kill, Fey loaded the resulting log into her pack and checked to see if she could still carry it. Somewhere between twelve and eighteen logs, it went from heavy to painfully heavy. Out of stubbornness and a liking for round numbers, she added another two. Heaving the pack onto her shoulders, she winced. The pressure of the straps was starting to give her a tension headache, and she felt faintly nauseated.

She messaged Leandriel:

<**Fey:** I'm done.>

<**Leandriel:** I am walking toward you now.>

Opening up the minimap, she located Leandriel and walked to meet him halfway. (More like quarter-way, given how slowly she was walking.)

———◦◦◇◦◦———

When Fey came into sight, Leandriel could immediately tell that she was carrying too much weight. There was a tightness to her mouth and shoulders that indicated she was in pain, and her stride looked short and laboured compared to the easy walk she had had before.

His first instinct was to help, but he thought that Fey might be the independent type who would insist on accomplishing everything by herself. He waited until they were on the path back to the Moonwood before cautiously broaching the subject.

"Would you like me to take some of your logs?"

He was somewhat surprised when the elf replied, "Yes, please," without any hesitation. (She was really more of the make-others-do-the-heavy-lifting type than anything else.)

Fey was moving quite slowly, so it was easy to remove logs from her backpack while they continued walking. The logs enlarged as they left the enchanted space, then shrank much farther as they came under the influence of his belt pouch. After he had gained his angel wings, both weight and bulk became huge disadvantages to flying, so he had obtained a pouch that reduced both weight and volume by an incredible factor of 10,000. As an added bonus, it also came with a magical inventory system that allowed him to view and locate items quickly.

Leandriel transferred logs one by one, keeping an eye on Fey's posture. By the time he had removed five, her shoulders were no longer painfully tight, so he stopped and moved to walk beside her. He could have easily taken all twenty logs but did not want to belittle her efforts.

Fey sighed in relief, stretching her neck from side to side and picking up her pace with an easy stride. Beside her, Leandriel kept up easily.

Fey kept an eye on the angel in her peripheral vision, trying very hard not to stare. At this point, the sun was setting, gilding his wings with splashes of gold among the lengthening shadows of the trees. She was not someone who was particularly appreciative of visual aesthetics, but even she had to admit he was a moving work of art.

Leandriel called up a tiny ball of light to help them see. It floated ahead of them, casting a gentle luminescence that did not ruin their night vision.

"What class are you?" Fey asked curiously. Leandriel seemed to be able to wield sword and magic with equal ease.

"A celestial-specific class called a guardian. It is similar to a regular paladin, except it does not require devotion to a particular god and relies on our intrinsic affinity to the holy element."

"Guardian angel, eh?" (A wild Canadian-ism has appeared!)

He smiled. "I did not name the class. You are a guardian yourself, I see." He tapped the corner of his eye, referring to Fey's Guardian's Blessing.

Fey grimaced, reminded of her flower-butterfly tattoo. "It's very useful, but I rather wish that it had a different physical manifestation." (Yes, our heroine does sometimes talk like that.)

"I think it rather suits you," said Leandriel.

"Um, thank you." Fey rarely received either positive or negative comments about her appearance, which was how she preferred it. She tended to aim for neutral to slightly intimidating rather than cute or pretty in the way she styled herself, which allowed other traits to shine through. It generally annoyed her when someone did compliment her on her appearance because it implied that outer beauty was something she should find important. Leandriel's unassuming words somehow managed to avoid triggering that annoyance, leaving her feeling . . . pleased, but somehow vulnerable.

Leandriel wisely turned the subject back to the game. "If you can, you should get the Guardian's Blessing up to level ten."

"What happens then?"

Leandriel decided to be mysterious and only said, "It will unlock a useful ability."

"Okay," Fey said, not really understanding but willing to take his word for it.

The sight of an actual angel in the Moonwood caused quite a bit of staring and whispering among the players, but no one impeded their progress as they made their way to the tavern.

Tallen stepped outside as Fey approached. "What have you brought me?" he asked, rubbing his hands in anticipation at having his firewood troubles solved for a few weeks.

"I'm not actually sure how many we collected," Fey said, starting to unload her pack at the small pile of wood next to the entrance.

"Fifteen logs," said Tallen, pleased. "Very good. I'll go get your reward."

"That's not all of it," Fey said, indicating Leandriel, who began to unload his share of the logs. As they left the influence of his carry-pouch, they expanded from splinter-sized to longer than even his impressive height. To the gathered audience of passers-by, it appeared that he was pulling them out of thin air.

Tallen's expression underwent a gradual change as the angel stacked his gatherings neatly against the tavern, going from pleased to surprised and eventually blank shock as the supply of logs did not end.

Leandriel surveyed the pile he had made, now as tall as he was. He could easily continue the stack to well above his head, but it would pose a danger if the pile suddenly collapsed while someone tried to retrieve a log. "I will stack the rest of these in the back," he said, walking into the tavern's small yard and continuing his labour.

Fey followed the angel, unable to suppress a small giggle at the absurdity in front of her.

Leandriel caught the sound and smiled in response. "What is it?" he asked, hands continuing their work.

"It's just . . . so excessive," Fey said, giggling again. She had been aware that Leandriel would be able to kill treants much more quickly than she could, but it appeared that he had made a concerted effort to gather as many logs as possible while she was training rather than go at a leisurely pace. Giving someone way more of something than they expected fell squarely into her brand of humour.

Leandriel appeared to take her comment seriously, though his eyes were warm with amusement. "Maybe slightly excessive," he agreed. Fey giggled again at the understatement.

In total, 547 logs were stacked neatly in the two piles. Leandriel had in fact nearly caused the extirpation[16] of treants within the outer Elvenwood; only the fact that he had cut a wide berth around Fey allowed a few individuals to survive.

Tallen disappeared into the tavern and came back holding a handful of coins. It took Fey a moment to recognize that some of them were made of the same crystal that she had previously seen during her trade for Stumpy the twiggy.

"Good job, lass," Tallen praised. "I've never seen so many logs in one place."

<Quest complete!>

<Fey gains 5,470 experience. Amethyst gains 2,735 experience. Magic gains 2,735 experience.>

<Fey has reached level 13!>

<Fey has reached level 14!>

<Amethyst has reached level 11!>

<Magic has reached level 11!>

<Fey has earned the title Wood Collector!>

<Fey's fame has increased to 16 (+10)!>

Tallen had set the reward for Fey's quest at 10g and ten experience per treant, expecting her to collect ten to twenty logs. Leandriel had taken advantage of the fact that the quest had no formal upper limit to help Fey as much as possible. He supposed he should report the loophole to the devs, given that it was supposed to be difficult for high-level players to power-level their friends.

Accepting 5,470g from Tallen, Fey turned to Leandriel to share the reward.

"Keep it," Leandriel insisted. He was always being given new weapons and armour to test and had almost no expenses to speak of. He often did not even bother picking up loot from monsters he had defeated, but even so, he had savings that could be issued in the mithril coins that were worth one thousand crystal each, or 1,000,000g.

Fey briefly considered the merits and likelihood of success of arguing and decided it would be a waste of energy. "Thank you," she said instead.

"I should return to my duties," Leandriel said with reluctance. He had quite enjoyed helping Fey, and collecting treants had been a nice break from the dangerous fights he generally got into.

Fey accompanied Leandriel to the town's teleportation gate, the Moonwood's only stone structure. Compared to the organic shapes of the tree-buildings, it stood out as clearly man-made, with four circular pillars joined by archways that stood over an intricately carved magic circle. The gates were present in all major settlements in the game and allowed teleportation to places a player had previously visited, cutting down on transportation time given that the game world was literally the size of Earth. (The first trip still had to be done the tedious way, though.)

Leandriel activated the gate and set his destination to Skyhaven. The gate pillars and carved glyph slowly brightened as the gate powered up, bright strands of magic appearing to weave together into a glowing portal.

He turned to Fey. "May I add you to my friend list?" he asked formally, more nervous than he should have been for such an everyday request.

Fey blinked, rather surprised that NPCs had friend lists, but said, "Of course."

<Leandriel has sent you a friend invitation.>

<You have accepted Leandriel's friend invitation.>

None of Leandriel's life experience gave him any clue as to the appropriate etiquette for leave-taking from a person he had nearly killed and whom he strongly hoped he would see again. He settled for, "Goodbye."

"See you later," Fey replied.

Though he knew the words were not a declaration of intent, they made Leandriel smile. Reaching out, he renewed the Helping Hand buff on Fey just before stepping into the portal and disappearing in a flash of light.

See you later.

CHAPTER 14
BOAR-ING

As soon as the angel disappeared, Fey noticed that there was a small crowd, and far too many people staring at her. Some of them even looked like they might approach and talk to her. To prevent this (horrible?) fate, Fey quickly slipped into the forest (#Escape). She found a trail and walked quickly toward the monster territories, wanting to take advantage of Leandriel's Helping Hand before it wore off.

The strength of monsters in the game was approximately proportional to how far from town they lived, with the slime territory just outside the town limits. Fey was on her way through that area in search of stronger monsters to fight when Amethyst suddenly jumped off her shoulder and started hopping away.

"Hey, where are you going?" Fey grabbed the slow-moving slime, who immediately began wriggling for freedom. After a few seconds' struggle, Fey finally resorted to dangling Amethyst by the bubble to prevent her escape.

The slime began to swing rhythmically in a single direction like a cute divining rod.[17] Curious, Fey turned to face a different direction, and the slime reoriented herself to continue pointing at a particular path between the trees.

"You want me to go that way?"

Amethyst squeaked an affirmative.

Fey sighed and followed her slime-compass.

As Fey walked, the sun fully set, only faint traces of moonlight reaching through the trees. She noticed that her night vision was much better than it was in real life, one of the perks of being a moon elf. As well, Amethyst appeared to be faintly bioluminescent, just enough to make out her outline and colour in the darkness. Fey saw other players hunting similarly glowing slimes and shaded Amethyst with her hand. *That sure is convenient. The developers really thought of everything.*

Passing the first group of newbies, Fey started having second thoughts when she heard faint shouts and screams in front of her. Looking up, she saw the unmistakable streak of bright light that signified a player travelling to the rebirth point.

Dubiously, she asked Amethyst, "You sure about this?"

The slime squeaked and swung even more insistently in the same direction (#Hypnotize).

"If I die, I'm going to be really mad at you," Fey grumbled, continuing her forward journey.

Reaching the cause of the ruckus, Fey laughed. The King Slime—blue this time—had respawned and was avenging his slain subjects by attacking the hapless newbies in the area. (Bad author, recycling adventures.) Most of them were between level 1 and 3 and had very little chance against the level 15 boss.

Like Amethyst, the King Slime travelled quite slowly, which made his powerful Whip attack seem startlingly fast in comparison. Fey wondered why the newbies were all scrambling around risking death instead of taking the wiser path of fleeing the area.

The answer became apparent as she noticed one particular newbie shouting instructions to try to organize the others in a concerted attack. The King Slime soon put an end to that nonsense, sending the newbie flying away in a second flash of light.

Fey had gotten the measure of the situation and had a plan. "I'll take care of this," she told her pets, shooing them up a tree for safety. Pitching her voice to carry, she called out, "Scatter and run back to town! It can't catch us if we run!"

Hearing the calm advice amidst the chaos made most of the newbies automatically obey, running off in all directions, with one particularly unlucky player being chased by the King Slime.

Fey stepped in smoothly to intercept the boss, activating Terrify. As she had assumed, she was not able to use the intimidation skill without producing the same feral shriek she had released when she first learned it. The sound hurt her throat, but it succeeded in making the King Slime end its chase and focus on her.

Fey took her chagrin at having to make such an undignified sound and channelled it into an extra-vicious Vicious Strike as she drew her sword and made her first attack. A fight that she had been able to win at level 11 was almost effortless at level 15. She kept the same basic strategy as before, using Mana Blade and Bleed to inflict large wounds, but added a few forceful kicks that made slime gush out more quickly. Before long, the King Slime was reduced to a lifeless pile of faintly glowing goo.

<Fey has defeated the King Slime!>

<Fey gains 108 experience. Amethyst gains 54 experience. Magic gains 54 experience.>

This time, the boss dropped coins worth a few hundred gold as well as a thin bracelet in the same copper as Fey's ring.

<Minor bracelet of magic (common): gives +1 intelligence when worn. Multiple bracelets can be worn for stacked effects.>

Fey put the bracelet over her wrist, where it conveniently shrank to the exact dimensions of her forearm so that it did not slide around and interfere with her movements.

Fey's pets came out of hiding now that it was safe to do so.

"So, what? Did you want to eat the King Slime or something?" Fey asked Amethyst.

Amethyst did indeed hop over to the King Slime bubble, which was larger than her entire body. Even stretching her mouth comically wide, she was unable to engulf the entire sphere. After several attempts, she gave up and hopped away, her own bubble-arm drooping in disappointment.

"Looks like another present for Kallara, then." Fey reached for the bubble.

Magic surprised Fey by hopping onto the sphere. He appeared to "plant" himself into the membrane, his stem merging with the surface. After a few seconds, the bubble began to deflate like a leaky beach ball.

<Magic has learned Drain!>

When the bubble was nothing more than a flat, empty membrane, Magic detached himself and hopped off, squeaking an invitation to Amethyst. ("Here you go.") Amethyst bumped against him in the armless equivalent of a hug and happily ate the remains.

<Amethyst's Double Membrane has reached level 7!>

"Oookay . . . No present for Kallara, then." Fey did not think she would ever get used to how weird her pets were. She looked up Magic's new skill:

<Drain: absorb the opponent's health to replenish your own.>

<Level 1: Drain 1 HP/5 seconds, recover 10% of drained health.>

That . . . really doesn't explain how Magic was able to deflate that bubble, but okay? Fey gave up on trying to understand the logic of the whimsical game world and simply appreciated the useful ability her mushroom had gained.

Resetting herself, she remembered her original goal, to find some stronger monsters to train on. "Any more detours?" she asked her pets. They shook their heads. "Good." Scooping them up, she continued deeper into the forest.

Fey decided that her next training ground would be the territory of the level 12 miniature boars. Each monster was the size of a young piglet but fully mature with strong musculature and small, sharp tusks that gleamed white in the moonlight. They were much faster than any of the monsters she had fought before, but small enough that she thought she should be relatively safe from serious injury.

The first thing she did was kidnap two boars, one at a time, and tie them up with her handy-dandy rope. They squealed angrily and struggled vigorously, but she was able to secure them with a moderate amount of effort.

Fey then placed (sicced) a pet on each monster. "Drain," she told Magic, who obediently hopped up and planted himself on the squirming boar.

To Amethyst, she said, "Use thornweed poison on this one."

Amethyst secreted a layer of toxic slime and then cruelly hopped onto the boar so that it dripped into its eyes. The boar squealed in pain.

<The boar has been poisoned!>

<Thornweed poison: −2 health/5 seconds.>

<Duration: 5 minutes.>

<Bonus effect: The boar has been blinded!>

"Whoa." Fey was equal parts impressed and seriously disturbed at Amethyst's ruthless approach to inflict maximum damage through targeting mucous membranes.[18] "Uh, yeah, just keep doing that." Half fleeing from her cute but deadly slime, she drew her sword and dagger and went off to fight the rest of the boars.

Fey's combat with the miniature monsters was both ungainly and dangerous. They were aggressive creatures that attacked by repeatedly charging and attempting to gore her (specifically her ankles) with their tusks. At shin height at the tallest, the boars were difficult for Fey to reach with her bladed weapons, so she resorted mainly to kicking attacks while dodging multiple monsters and trying to keep her balance. She had a feeling that she would be in far greater danger if she fell down, so she made very sure she was never in a position to be tripped.

As more boars noticed her presence and the number of attackers increased to five, Fey was forced to give up attacking and focus solely on dodging. After much ungainly hopping around and several close calls, she resorted to using Terrify, a shriek ripping from her throat.

With fairly high attack initiative, the boars only hesitated for a second before resuming their attack, but it was long enough for Fey to swoop down and slash the nearest monster with a Bleed attack.

<Bleed (level 4): 70 damage/20 seconds.>

Fey went back on the defensive, but the boar she had injured was bleeding profusely and quickly lost the strength to chase her. *Bleeding like a stuck pig, haha.* (Clearly, this fight isn't tense enough if she has time to pun.) Keeping an eye out for another opportunity, she slashed another boar while sidestepping its charge. With each opponent taken out of commission, it became easier to hit the remaining ones. The bleeding status was insufficient to defeat the boars by itself, but dropped their health below half, significantly lowering their strength and speed and allowing her to finish them off quite easily.

Like the treants and twiggies, the boars' bodies failed to disappear upon death. *I guess because they're edible? Maybe I should bring them to Tallen.* Since each was fairly small and portable, she piled them into her backpacks to bring back to the village.

While she waited for the monsters to respawn, Fey went to check on her pets.

Amethyst's boar (or more accurately, victim) was long dead, her thornweed poison inflicting a whopping 120 damage if allowed to run its full course. *I probably shouldn't bring back poisoned meat.* She untied the carcass and left it on the ground, where it abruptly disappeared five minutes later.

Magic's boar was still alive and kicking, but weakly. His Drain skill had increased to level 2, but even so, only drained 1 health every 4 seconds.

Watching the small creature's dying struggles caused a wave of guilt. It was not in her nature to prolong the suffering of innocent creatures. (Actual enemies were a separate category.) When the boar finally grew too exhausted to fight its bonds, she could not help but tell Magic to stop his attack.

Magic obediently hopped off the boar and Fey untied it, reassured by its ongoing breathing. She picked it up, hoping for an easy trigger of her Monster Tamer skill.

No such luck; the miniature boar remained inactive and no system notices popped up. Fey sighed and sat, putting the small creature in her lap.

As it regained health, the boar began to struggle more and more vigorously. Fey had, however, figured out that if she kept her hands wrapped firmly around its round abdomen, it was unable to reach her with its short legs or tusks. This made its struggles almost comically cute, and she giggled more than once as it tired itself out and eventually went to sleep.

<Fey has tamed the miniature boar!>

<Fey receives a pet!>

<Monster Tamer has reached level 4!>

<Please select a name for your pet:___>

This time, a name came to Fey quite quickly. "Boris," she decided. It was not a particularly elegant name, but the boar was not a particularly elegant creature.

<Name confirmed.>

<Boris, level 12 miniature boar.>

<HP: 160/160, MP: 72/72.>

<EXP: 4,886/6,841.>

<Skills: Rage, Charge.>

Nice, two intrinsic skills.

With the experience from the boar kills, Magic and Amethyst had also just reached the threshold to level 12. (This is totally just a coincidence and not because the author is too lazy to keep track of the pets' levels separately . . .)

Fey laid Boris on the ground to continue his nap, then sneaked up on the respawned miniature boar herd and kidnapped another two.

<Fey has learned Isolate!>

Huh? Fey looked up the skill:

<Isolate: separate a single opponent out of a group without alerting the other members>

<Level 1: opponents' awareness range is 1 m less than usual. Sight and sound are dampened.>

This was not the first time that Fey had suddenly grabbed a monster out of a group, but one of the only times she had tried to be even remotely sneaky about it, explaining why the ability had taken so long to form.

She repeated the same process as the first time, tying up victims for Magic and Amethyst to practice on and taking on the rest of the herd by herself. Gradually, she brought Amethyst more victims at once, until the entire herd of eight was tied up and Fey had to find a second herd to fight. (You'd think she'd run out of rope, but nope, miniature boars can be trussed up pretty easily.) Once Magic's Drain got to level 3, he was able to kill the boars before Fey got back from her hunting. Isolate quickly jumped to level 4, while Bleed improved to level 5. She filled her packs with boar meat at a fairly steady rate, avoiding the bodies her pets left behind. While Magic's kills were not poisoned, they looked strangely shrunken and dry, which Fey guessed would not be good for the meat's taste or texture.

When Boris woke up, Fey decided to head back to town rather than distress her new pet with the sight of fallen herd-mates. (Though the way things have been going, he would probably be entirely fine with the systematic slaughter of his people.)

"Hi, buddy," she said, sitting down to pet her new animal friend. Simply by nature of being miniature, the boar was extremely cute. Boris responded by butting at her leg affectionately.

"Okay, let's go." Shouldering her backpack, Fey headed down the trail towards the Moonwood, Amethyst on her shoulder and Magic sticking to her boot. Boris trotted along beside her, the first pet to be able to keep up with her walking pace. (Yay, Boris!) Fey nodded in approval, thinking that she was running out of places on her body to carry small pets.

In the distance off the trail, Fey noticed the orange glow of a fire. Judging by the distance, it seemed too big for just a modest campfire. She decided to investigate.

Long before she could see the fire, she heard loud voices and raucous laughter, the kind she associated with excessive alcohol use. Even worse, she heard the thud of an axe against wood.

Keeping to the shadows of a larger tree, Fey peeked at the fire and saw a party of a dozen well-armed humans, drinking and shouting at each other as inebriated people sometimes did. One of the humans was hacking at a large tree branch with an axe, and she saw many scars on the nearby trees that indicated the source of the fuel for the large bonfire they had going.

Isn't an angry forest ranger supposed to show up and punish them? Fey felt a strong sensation of revulsion for the group's actions. She chalked it up to general distaste for drunken obnoxiousness as well as an appreciation for the beauty of untouched wilderness and failed to suspect that her Guardian's Blessing had given her the instinct to investigate the area in the first place.

Despite this lack of insight, Fey decided to take on the job of protecting the forest from further damage, as well as the more fun job of punishing the wrongdoers and teaching them a lesson. She did not have any delusions about being able to take on the whole group at once and began thinking up some underhanded tactics.

She positioned Magic in a high tree branch. "Cast Spore at them as many times as you can," she told the mushroom.

Clouds of sparkly dust drifted through the clearing. Some of the humans noticed the phenomenon, but no one seemed concerned until the status effects began piling up.

<Slayer has been poisoned!>

<Diablo has been paralysed!>

<Mysticist has been slowed!>

<Skillz has fallen asleep!>

<Eleet's attack had been lowered!>

<Victor's defence has been lowered!>

<Warlord has become confused!>

Fey could not help snorting at the number of ridiculously overdramatic names in the party. Thankfully, the sound was covered by the eruption of confused shouting around the fire. Other than the sleeping and paralyzed individuals, the players were all scrambling to locate the source of the attack. Someone tried unsuccessfully to shake the sleeping player awake. Another shouted, "Who's there? Show yourself!"

Fey rolled her eyes and stayed hidden. The real fun came when the axe wielder, now confused, began to swing wildly at hallucinations. His friends shouted at him and scrambled to get out of the way.

In the chaos, one of the players stumbled close to her hiding spot. Unable to resist, she snuck up on him with Isolate. Pulling a thornweed thorn out of her pouch, she scratched him with poison before giving him a quick shove and ducking back under cover.

The player panicked at the strong poison, yelling and gesturing at the spot where he had been attacked. Fey quietly sneaked to the other side of the fire while the humans attacked the bushes where she had been hiding.

By now, status effects were piling on top of other status effects, leaving the players considerably handicapped. Fey felt a particular sense of satisfaction whenever one of them pulled out a green antidote to counter a poison effect. (Because making people waste money was the worst fate she could imagine?) The sleeping player had woken up, but now three people were paralyzed. The confused axe-man eventually charged into the forest, screaming at the top of his lungs, and did not return.

Fey felt this was a good time to move on to the next phase of the plan. (Wait, she has a plan?) Leaving Magic to continue sowing chaos, she snuck off to the nearby stream and used Amethyst as a water bag with Osmosis. She then created another diversion by poisoning a player with the thornweed, using the distraction to run to the bonfire. She scattered the logs and kicked dirt over the fire, using Amethyst's water to put out any remaining embers. She ran for cover before anyone could see more than a shadowy figure in the sudden darkness.

Fey's night vision was significantly better than the humans', so she had no trouble picking her way back to Magic's hiding spot. "You can stop now," she told the tired mushroom, patting his head in appreciation.

Hunkering down, she settled in to wait. Without any fresh attacks, the players gradually quieted down. Believing the danger over, they began to discuss. "What the [swear word] was that?"

"I don't know. I never heard of invisible attackers or cursed areas."

"It was a person!" insisted the first victim of the thornweed poison. "We should keep looking for them! And when I find them, I'm gonna . . . "

Fey rolled her eyes at the expletive-ridden threats that spewed from his mouth. *Crude.* She waited until everyone was free from paralysis, then told Boris, "Give me a nice, angry squeal."

The boar screamed, the sound eerily similar to a human voice. The players were silenced by the unsettling sound, then cautiously advanced to the source of the noise.

Fey used Terrify. Against players, the ability caused a visceral sense of fear that could be resisted depending on the individual's mental constitution. However, tired, injured, blinded, and confused, the players were ripe to fall victim to the intimidation effect. Fey used it again, this time holding the shriek for twice as long and gradually increasing the volume as if she were walking toward the players. They broke and ran.

Serves 'em right, Fey thought with satisfaction. She walked over to the fire and made sure every last ember was put out.

<Guardian's Blessing has reached level 3!>

CHAPTER 15

APOLOGIES AND WAKE-UP CALLS

Fey made it back to the Moonwood just as dawn began to lighten the shadows of the forest. She had been logged in for nearly a full game day; with the threefold time acceleration built into *Fantasia* and how early in the evening she had started playing, it was currently 4:00 a.m. in the real world. *This could really turn night owls into early birds,*[19] she mused. She wondered if the sleep-induction portion of the virtual reality headsets had ever been developed and marketed separately. (The salespeople are way ahead of you, buddy.)

Having worked up quite an appetite from her exertions, Fey headed to the tavern. Tallen was happy to see her and even happier about the stock of fresh miniature boars she had brought with her. Each one was the perfect size to roast whole and sell as a single serving, and she could practically see the gold coins piling up in the tavern-keeper's eyes as he whisked the meat off to the kitchen and its magical refrigerator. He paid her 15g for each; she could tell he was planning on making the money back several times over, but considering the amount of work it would take to clean and cook each animal, she considered the exchange quite fair.

"I'm serving breakfast now," said Tallen, "but would you like me to save you one for later?"

"Oh no, thank you," said Fey. "I can't eat that much meat in one sitting." Most of her calories came from carbohydrates, and she liked it that way. "Speaking of breakfast . . . " she continued, widening her eyes meaningfully.

Tallen chucked at her "starving waif" impression. "Go sit yourself down. I have just the thing."

Fey sat next to a window—an opening that the tree-tavern had been induced to grow around—and admired the forest sunrise as she waited for her meal. She turned her attention back to the table as Tallen deftly slid a plate in front of her.

Oh. My. God.

In front of Fey was a large waffle topped with generous slices of banana and strawberry, drizzled in chocolate syrup, and sprinkled with powdered sugar. Not only did it look worthy of its own social media page, it emanated a heavenly aroma that had her mouth watering.

"How did you know?" she breathed, reverently admiring the carb-heavy goodness. It was the exact thing she would have ordered at a fancy breakfast restaurant. (The author is not sure whether the above passage counts as food porn but apologizes if reading it caused waffle cravings.)

Tallen just winked. "Enjoy," he said, leaving without answering the question. (Clearly, he has some kind of scary mind-reading abilities.)

Picking up her cutlery, Fey dug in. The taste and texture were perfect, and she was hungry enough that before long, only traces of syrup remained.

Fey felt sluggish after ingesting that much sugar but managed to get herself moving. She had the presence of mind to ask Tallen for portable snacks she could eat on the road and was rewarded with fruit and some kind of meat jerky. She decided it was best not to ask what kind of meat it was.

Now that it was morning, Fey returned to Kallara's tree-shop to collect the strength tonic that had been brewing overnight. Walking through the entranceway, she called out a friendly greeting.

Looking up from a pile of herbs she was sorting, Kallara smiled. "Good morning! The strength tonic turned out quite well. I'll have it bottled in a minute."

The healer pulled out two glass vials and filled them from the pot that had been cooling away from the fire.

"Wow, it's so pretty." The potion was a translucent gold, similar to honey in colour but with the viscosity of water.

"I make nothing but the best," said Kallara with a wink.

Fey saw that Kallara's words were not just empty boasting when she examined the tonic's item information:

<Strength tonic: temporarily boost strength on consumption.>

<Base effect: +15 strength | Duration: 1 hour | 10 doses.>

<Fresh herbs bonus: +15% strength.>

<Master apothecary bonus: +100% duration, +10% doses.>

<Perfect brewing bonus: +15% strength, +15% duration.>

<Net effect: +20 strength| Duration: 2 hours 9 minutes | 11 doses.>

"Wow, Kallara, you really are the best. Thanks!" Fey said, eyes wide at the bonuses that more than doubled the value of the tonic.

"Oh, it was no trouble," the healer said modestly, though in fact it was extremely troublesome to get the "perfect brewing" bonus, with less than five seconds and five degrees Celsius of leeway for every single step of the brewing process, from adding each ingredient to heating and cooling down. Kallara did not usually bother with the relatively small bonus but had made the effort because she liked Fey.

"By the way, your young man came looking for you," she added.

"My *what?*"

"Your young man," the healer repeated. "The one who helped collect the ingredients for the strength tonic?"

Fey shuddered. "Eew. Blade is not, and never will be, 'my young man.' Eew." (Aww, come on, that's mean. Blade's a nice guy.)

Kallara had seen enough of the two players interacting that she had determined the lack of romantic compatibility between them, but found it amusing to continue teasing Fey. (Because she's evil under all that niceness.) "Whyever not?" she asked, feigning confusion. "He's quite handsome, and quite gallant, from what I've seen."

"He's all right, but he's no Leandriel," Fey muttered under her breath.

"Leandriel?" Kallara repeated, her pointy ears picking out the syllables with ease.

Fey felt her face heat up. *Oh my god, am I blushing? I do not blush. Crap, I think I'm blushing. Stop it RIGHT NOW.* She took a deep breath and blanked out any thoughts of blue-eyed warrior angels. (Well, she tried to, anyway.)

"Oh, nobody," she said, the attempt at a casual lie ruined by the fact that her voice was an octave higher than usual. Changing the subject with no attempt at subtlety, she asked, "Oh, by the way, Kallara, could I have an empty flask?"

Having already gotten payment in the form of entertainment (#Evil), the healer pulled a clear, cylindrical flask out of a cupboard and held it out. "Will this do?"

"Perfect. Thanks. Gotta go. Bye." Fey bid a tactical retreat and escaped into the forest.

"Bye!" Kallara called cheerfully while waving at the disappearing figure.

Fey power-walked down the forest trail, muttering to herself. "Argh. Gah. Eek. Okay, stop. Stop. Gah. No, stop." She took another deep breath and held it until she felt her heartbeat slow down.[20]

Fey rarely ever became emotionally perturbed, but once she did, it was very difficult for her to calm down. After several unsuccessful minutes of trying to clear her mind, she sighed and gave up. Fighting feelings was always a losing prospect.

She mentally turned around and faced the issue. *Okay, so I thought Leandriel was really cool and nice and handsome. Happy, brain? I admitted it. There's no reason why he wouldn't be, given he was literally designed that way. Real people like that don't exist.*

(This is the literary device known as "dramatic irony."[21])

With that internal admission, Fey was able to return to some semblance of her usual self. She reached the stream and filled up her new flask. "Here, Amethyst, get in." She dropped the slime into the water. "Osmosis."

Amethyst swelled to triple her original size, taking up a third of the roomy flask.

"Okay, now shrink. Now grow. And keep going."

Fey was so entertained by the sight of the expanding and contracting slime that she simply sat watching for several minutes. Belatedly, she wondered if slimes needed to breathe. Amethyst seemed as lively as ever after several minutes immersed in the water, and Fey noticed that the slime kept her bubble floating above the surface. Curious, she poked it down, causing Amethyst to start looking rather uncomfortable and turning a bluer shade of purple. (This doesn't make any physiological sense given that slimes don't have any blood or hemolymph.) Fey allowed the bubble to float back up and the slime returned to normal.

"So slimes come equipped with snorkels," she mused. "Or is this more the equivalent of an elephant's trunk?"

Amethyst squeaked, the sound altered by its path through water.

<Osmosis has reached level 3!>

Fey's amusement was interrupted by approaching footsteps. She stood, flask in hand, to see Blade appear between the trees. (Yay! . . . ? He's back . . .)

Still in good humour from the previous entertainment, Fey's tone was fairly pleasant when she asked, "What are you doing here?" Looking behind the human warrior, she did not detect the presence of any other players.

"Kallara told me you went this way."

Well, that's what I get for walking in a straight line, Fey thought resignedly. *Also, Kallara needs to stop with the whole matchmaking thing.* She was trying to figure out what to say into the yawning silence when Blade exhaled noisily, raked a hand through his short hair, and said, "Look, I'm sorry."

Fey blinked in surprise. Her mouth opened and closed silently once before she managed to say, "What?"

"I'm sorry."

"For what?" she asked suspiciously.

Blade honestly did not know exactly what he was apologizing for. He simply knew that Fey was not happy with him and was following the wise advice his elder sister had once given him to "just say sorry." It was quite an effective technique, though many people would find it difficult to swallow their pride and apologize even if they did not feel they had done anything wrong. Figuratively, Blade was a much bigger man than most. (Literally, he falls just slightly short of the coveted 6-foot/180-centimetre benchmark for male romantic leads.)

He took a guess. "Uh, for trying to kill your slime?"

Fey acknowledged the point. She had not been expecting an apology for that particular incident, but she appreciated it. "Okay."

"Okay what?"

Fey smiled enigmatically, the smile growing into a grin at how confused Blade looked.

<Fey has sent you a friend invitation.>

Fey decided to pull a dramatic exit and announced, "I'm logging out now." Her avatar faded out of existence while Blade was still staring at the system message.

"That's one weird girl," Blade muttered.

<You have accepted Fey's friend invitation.>

—◦◦◇◦◦—

Leandriel's sword, imbued with holy light, sizzled as it sliced through the undead banshee. The withered creature opened its mouth and shrieked, but Leandriel had purchased a silence charm to protect himself from the banshee's devastating voice, and the fight took place in eerie soundlessness.

Leandriel neatly lunged and beheaded the creature before turning to meet the other monsters. Creatures with dark affinity instinctively hated creatures with holy affinity, having a much higher sensing range and attack initiative when facing their opposing element.

Dodging, blocking, slashing, and spinning, Leandriel used basic sword work in order to defeat the monsters. He was gradually getting used to the altered balance required to fight effectively with wings, training the necessary adjustments into his muscle memory.

He had not realized that he was keeping an eye on his friend list until he noticed the green "Online" next to Fey's name change to a red "Offline." The distraction cost him a scratch on his arm in the gap between two pieces of plate armour.

Hissing with pain, Leandriel seared the wound with holy light before it could start rotting from the dark creature's unclean claws. He turned his mind back to battle; he had a dungeon to clear.

◊◊◊

Arwyn pulled off her game helmet, feeling strangely sluggish. Looking at the clock, she saw that it was eight o'clock; she had been playing the game for a solid twelve hours, and her body had not taken kindly to such an extended period of inactivity. Groaning, she rolled off the side of the recliner, managed a wobbly landing on her feet, and trudged to the kitchen for sustenance.

The majority of her calories in the morning consisted of black tea with what could be considered "way too much" sugar and cream, but since she had woken up unusually early for a Saturday, she made herself a proper breakfast with scrambled eggs and toast.

What exactly am I supposed to do with all this extra daytime? The urge to jump right back into *Fantasia* was strong, but Arwyn was determined to settle into a proper sleeping pattern and stay out of the game until bedtime. She ended up calling Leah to set up a lunch date followed by a shopping trip. It was the sort of thing Leah really enjoyed, and while Arwyn did not particularly care about following the latest trends, she acknowledged the need to clothe herself and did occasionally pick out pieces that stood out from her baseline "generic neutral" look.

The friends met up at a restaurant that was a step up from fast food but by no means gourmet.

"Hi! How's *Fantasia* going?" Arwyn asked.

"It's really fun! I'm finding different parties to train with—nobody cool enough to hang around for more than one trip yet. The fish and the corals are *beautiful*."

"Sounds like a tropical vacation," Arwyn commented.

"Yeah. My only complaint is that there are almost no guys around."

Arwyn raised an eyebrow unsympathetically. "They are called mer*maids* for a reason." She could not see the majority of male players wanting to play a race that was so commonly associated with femininity.

Leah flapped a hand. "Yeah, yeah, I know. I didn't stop to think about it. Now tell me about the Elvenwood. There must be some cute guys there, right?"

Leah's gaze sharpened at Arwyn's shift in expression. "There are! Tell me," she demanded.

Arwyn pulled out her phone and accessed an image file she had taken in *Fantasia*, a snapshot of Leandriel standing in front of a glowing teleportation gate. She knew it was somewhat creepy and obsessive to have done so, but comforted herself with the fact that NPCs were made to be admired.

Leah grabbed the phone with a high-pitched sound of excitement (*squee*). "An angel? Where did you find an angel?"

"He kind of fell out of the sky. Okay, well, he literally fell out of the sky."

"Tell me the whole story *right now*."

Arwyn obediently recounted the events starting from the angel's crash landing to his exit via teleportation gate.

Leah sighed in admiration. "Wow, just wow."

Arwyn sighed more wistfully. "I wish they hadn't made him that amazing."

"Who made what?"

"Leandriel. As an NPC."

"*What?* No! He's an NPC?"

"He's level 99. It's the first week since game release. Do the math."

Leah pouted, then sighed. "I should have known he was too good to be true."

"Tell me about it," Arwyn grumbled.

Finishing their food, the friends headed over to the nearby mall.

(No mention of Blade occurred throughout the afternoon.)

CHAPTER 16
DOUBLE TROUBLE

Alwyn came home pleasantly tired after a fruitful shopping expedition and dinner with Leah. She dumped her purchases on one end of the couch and settled lazily on the other. (Based on historical data, the clothing would not be put away until after she wore it the first time.)

In the quiet of her house, she could hear the seductive voice of *Fantasia* calling out to her. *"Come rest on this comfortable recliner,"* it coaxed. (Yes, she is having a conversation with an inanimate object. Just go with it.)

Her gaze was dragged toward the game helmet in the next room as if by gravity.

"Come," it whispered.

No, she thought, sounding unconvincing even in her own head. *I have to stay off until bedtime.*

"But why?" asked the game helmet, a pout in its voice. *"Don't you want to play with me?"* (Okay, this is was supposed to be funny but now it's getting creepy.)

Resolutely, Arwyn turned away from the games room.

"Come back," whispered the game.

Just for something to do, she sat at her desk and turned on her computer. *Fantasia* still foremost on her mind, she ended up spending several hours watching semi-educational videos about melee combat and sword-fighting in particular. She was sure that it was a terrible way to actually learn how to fight with a weapon, but she noted a few basic moves she thought she could try once she logged in.

She also came across numerous rants on the inaccuracies of weaponry and fighting as depicted in fantasy. This would have made her sad because they were generally the coolest aspects, but fortunately, the actual magic available in *Fantasia* neatly sidestepped most of the considerations required in real life for things such as "practicality" and "physics".

After a chain of "related videos" that went increasingly off-topic, Arwyn closed her laptop and got ready for bed, sliding on the game helmet slightly before eleven o'clock.

◊◊◊

A disembodied female voice said, "Scanning. Player detected. Welcome back to *Fantasia*, Fey E'lan."

Fey blinked as she materialized in the game world at the same spot she had logged out. Her pets flashed into existence as well, and she petted them in greeting.

Blade was not present in her vicinity; peeking at her friend list, she saw that the human warrior was not online. The angel warrior on the same list, on the other hand, was; presumably, NPCs never went offline. Fey idly wondered how the artificial intelligence behind the characters was programmed to interpret the fact that the players regularly disappeared from existence, only to pop up several game days later.

Continuing her musings, Fey plopped Amethyst back into the flask of water and had her train Osmosis while she walked back to the village and looked for a quest on the notice board.

Emboldened by the fact that she had yet come to serious injury (surprise attacks by level 99 NPCs notwithstanding), Fey felt confident enough to go after monsters slightly higher than her level 14. A post caught her eye:

<Dubbles and trubbles from human lands have infested the eastern forest. Help clear them out before they spread.>

<Reward: 2,000g for clearing all dubbles, 3,000g for clearing all trubbles, Guardian's Blessing for clearing both.>

No image of either monster was provided, but the notice stated that dubbles were level 16 and trubbles were level 18. The quest would be challenging, but she figured she would level up as she fought, and the prospect of improving her Guardian's Blessing was too good to pass up. She headed east down the appropriate trail, wondering what kind of creatures would be called "dubbles" and "trubbles."

<Amethyst's Osmosis has reached level 4!>

"Good job, Amethyst," Fey cooed through the glass of the flask. The slime flicked her bubble to make herself spin in the water before going back to training the ability.

Figuring she should also use the travel time efficiently, Fey pulled out a thornweed thorn and poisoned herself to train Immunity.

A few minutes in, a disembodied voice said, "Hey."

Private messaging in Fantasia came in three levels. The most basic and least intrusive was text-based messaging, which Fey had used with Leandriel the day before. The second level was audio chatting, similar to a phone call without the need for a device. The third level was video chatting, during which a virtual screen would pop up to show the other player.

Fey thought it was a bit presumptuous for Blade to initiate audio chat on the first call (and she didn't like sudden and unexpected noises in general) but answered anyway. "Hi."

"Where are you?" Blade had just logged in, materializing near the stream where they had logged out the night before.

"Heading to the eastern forest on a quest."

"Need some help?"

"No."

An awkward silence ensued.

Fey sighed internally and added, "You can come if you want," in such an unenthusiastic tone that both her pets flattened under its weight, cautiously regaining their normal shape after a few seconds.

"I'll catch up. See you soon!" Blade answered, apparently immune to apathy.

Fey sighed (externally) and kept walking.

As she neared the eastern edge of the forest, the trees dwindled in size until they looked only decades, rather than centuries, old. She stopped training Immunity when it reached level 4, wanting to be in peak condition to fight the dubbles and trubbles. Amethyst continued with Osmosis and had passed level 5 by the time they arrived at the area indicated on the map.

Fey pulled the slime out of the flask and looked around. She saw trees and little else.

"Where are the monsters?" she asked aloud.

As if in answer, something crashed into Fey's mid-back hard enough to knock her off her feet. Her breath left her lungs in a forceful whoosh as she dropped Amethyst and broke her fall with her hands.

Instinctively turning toward the attack, Fey saw a flash of pastel green streaking away into the trees.

"What the—" she muttered, picking herself up and positioning her back against a tree so it would be protected. She drew her weapons and waited tensely for another attack.

After several minutes of inactivity, Fey grew annoyed and yelled, "Come out, you stupid monster!"

Provoked by the sound, a flash of bright green streaked toward her. Fey crossed her forearms in front of her face just in time for the monster to smack into them, the impact slightly painful even through her armguards. She had a good look at the creature as it made contact; it appeared to be a pair of green bouncy balls connected by a stretchy line as thick as one of her fingers.

" . . . A double bubble is called a dubble? Who invented this game?" (The author, who spends way too much energy coming up with extremely dumb puns.)

Fey sighed. Aggravating or not, she had a quest to complete. "Come back here, you stupid bouncy balls!" she yelled. This time, when the dubble came streaking out toward her, she managed to hit one of the bubbles with her sword, but the creature seemed to bounce harmlessly off the blade and went back into hiding.

Deciding she would have to change tactics, she said, "Magic, cast Spore."

As a glittering cloud of particles spread through the trees, Fey was inundated with system notices:

<Spore was successful. The dubble's speed has decreased.>

<Attack failed. The dubble is unaffected.>

<Attack failed. The dubble is unaffected.>

<Spore was successful. The dubble has fallen asleep.>

<Spore was successful. The dubble's attack has decreased.>

<Attack failed. The dubble is unaffected.>

<Attack failed. The dubble is unaffected.>

<Attack failed. The dubble is unaffected.>

<Spore was successful. The dubble has become confused.>

<Attack failed. The dubble is unaffected.>

. . . *Oh crap,* was all Fey had time to think before every dubble in the area attacked at once.

The next ten minutes were a twisted game of dodgeball straight out of a nightmare as dubbles attacked from every angle. (They also rudely ignored the rules against headshots.) Fey quickly ushered her pets up against the tree and stood guard in front of them, fearful that the attacks would pound their soft bodies to mush. She acted in pure defence, managing to protect her head and abdomen at the cost of layered bruising all over her arms and legs.

In the corner of her vision, Fey watched her health point display steadily drop under the barrage of attacks. Before she could start planning on a strategic retreat (i.e., running away) to avoid dying, she noted that her health bar had stabilized at around 150/225. The force of the dubbles' attacks was simply not strong enough to cause more than superficial bruising, so while her injuries certainly hurt, she was in no danger of losing her life. This was part of *Fantasia's* newbie-friendly game design, where weaker monsters would simply overwhelm an unprepared player instead of killing them.

As she grew accustomed to the attacks and stopped worrying about her health, Fey's brain kicked in. "Magic, cast Spore every five seconds," she said, choosing a pace that Magic could keep up without exhausting his mana stores.

As the status effects piled on, sleeping and paralyzed dubbles dropped to the ground. Fey was unable to leave her pets undefended in order to go after the disabled monsters, so she focused her attention on the ones still attacking.

She made a breakthrough when, by chance, one of her sword strikes slid off a dubble at an angle and ended up shearing the rubbery appendage that connected the bodies of the twin creature. Both halves of the dubble dropped to the ground, severed limb twitching, apparently unable to move without the connection.

"Yes," she growled in anticipated victory, fed up with the stupid creatures and their painful attacks. Changing the focus of her attacks, she was able to sever more and more of the dubbles' linking arms, ending up with a semicircle of grounded monsters. (Honestly, it looked like a ball pit in a playground.)

In the middle of fighting, Fey's attention was caught by a system notice different from the others flooding in:

<Spore was successful. Blade has been poisoned!>

Magic's skill was now at level 8, with a success rate of 45 percent and range of twenty-five metres. "Magic, stop casting for a bit," Fey said. In a louder voice, she called out, "Blade?"

"Dammit, stop poisoning me!" came an irritated voice somewhere behind her on the right.

"You literally walked right into it," Fey muttered to herself while fending off more dubble attacks. More loudly, she called out, "Sorry!" her voice cheerfully insincere.

She heard a loud smacking sound in the same direction, followed by swearing. "What the hell was that?"

"It's called a dubble," Fey explained cheerfully (#Schadenfreude[22]). "Cut the line that connects their heads and they can't move."

Eventually, Blade came into view, kicking along a group of severed half-dubbles and sporting a circular red mark on one cheek. "You really know how to pick quests," he complained.

Fey refrained from pointing out that nobody had asked him to come help (although her expression probably conveyed it fairly clearly). She went to invite Blade into a party so that Magic could cast Spore without harming the human, then realized she was still in a party with Leandriel, his name greyed out in the menu to indicate that he was out of range for sharing experience points and other party-related effects.

She sent him a quick private message to explain what she was doing.

<**Fey:** Hi. I have to leave your party to join another one for the quest I'm on.>

<**Leandriel:** Have fun. I do not believe my duties will allow me to join you today.>

Fey had not expected the angel to even be interested in adventuring with a newbie like her, let alone have time for it. Hiding her feelings of pleased surprise, she replied in a lighthearted tone.

<**Fey:** Too bad; these dubbles could use some trouncing.>

She could almost hear the quiet amusement in the words when he answered,

<**Leandriel:** Indeed, you must trounce some extra in my stead.>

The words made a silly smile appear on Fey's face, and she pressed her lips together in an effort to hide it.

<**Fey:** I will. Bye.>

<**Leandriel:** Goodbye.>

<Fey has left Leandriel's party.>

In the few seconds that it took for the conversational exchange, Blade had sent Fey his own party invite, only to be informed:

<Fey is already in another party.>

Three seconds later, he received Fey's party invitation and accepted, assuming that the elf had found other players to do the quest with.

<Fey's party: Fey (leader), level 14 moon elf (warrior), Blade, level 16 human (warrior).>

"Where's the rest of the party?" Blade asked, confused.

"What rest of the party?" Fey asked, equally confused.

"When I just tried to send you a party invite, it said you were already in a party."

"Oh. I just left a party that I joined yesterday."

For no reason that Blade could discern, Fey seemed rather embarrassed about the mundane explanation. (It's because she has a *crush*. Fey and Leandriel sitting in a tree, K-I-S-S-I-N-G.) He was about to press for more detail when he noticed that Fey had jumped from level 11 to 14 in the short time they had been apart. He himself had only gained one level.

"Holy [censored word]! How did you gain three levels so quickly?"

"Oh, you know, hunting quests," Fey said vaguely, looking rather shifty as she avoided eye contact. She was relieved when a new wave of dubbles attacked, forcing them to stop casual conversation.

With Blade free to move around and disable any dubbles downed by Spore, it was only a few minutes before all the bubble monsters were split apart and unable to move. Fey cautiously stepped away from the tree, revealing her three pets.

"And you got another pet, too?" Blade asked incredulously, looking at the miniature boar industriously gathering dubbles into a pile.

"Ehe" was all Fey said, somehow looking both sheepish and smug.

The dubbles were all still alive despite their disabled state. Their rubbery skins were extremely durable, but by bearing down with all their weight on a sword, Fey and Blade were able to puncture and kill the monsters. Unlike slimes, the dubbles appeared to be filled with nothing but air, deflating quickly and then crumbling away in a pile of dust.

<Fey has defeated the dubble!>

<Fey has gained 53 experience. Amethyst has gained 27 experience. Magic has gained 27 experience. Boris has gained 27 experience.>

<Blade has defeated the dubble!>

<Blade has gained 53 experience.>

The party's experience allocation was set to "individual," and Fey and Blade divided the kills exactly in half, each getting 15 dubbles.

<Fey has achieved level 15!>

<Fey gains 5 attribute points.>

Fey's boar hunting from the night before had filled her experience bar close to full, so the experience from fifteen dubbles was sufficient to level up.

Spending her attribute points, Fey looked to the task ahead and sighed.

"What?" Blade asked.

"There's probably at least a couple hundred more of these."

"So what? Did you accept a quest to kill all of them?"

"Yes. And also all the trubbles."

"What's a trubble?"

"I have no idea."

Trubbles turned out to be groups of three linked yellow bubbles, which travelled with a spinning motion like a boomerang that made it quite difficult to cut their linkages. As the battle raged on, Magic proved to be quite helpful, but Amethyst ended up going back in the flask to practice Osmosis while Boris was told to stay in the areas they had already cleared. Fey was pleasantly surprised when the boar came back from his explorations with several rare plant roots.

Settling into the fighting, Fey and Blade were getting along quite well. The straightforward combat showed the human off to advantage as he moved with a natural athleticism that contrasted sharply with Fey's own awkward movements. She judged that Blade probably played a variety of sports in real life but had no formal training in martial arts. Fey herself had years of kicks and punches drilled into her muscle memory, but it was only tangentially applicable given unfamiliar weaponry and the strange creatures she was fighting. She was fairly slow at picking up new physical skills and more than once found herself copying Blade's movements when he made a particularly effective attack.

Every few hours, Fey would drop unceremoniously to the ground to rest. It took Blade several episodes to get used to this, as the rest stops appeared disconcertingly similar to collapsing in exhaustion. Around noon, Fey decided that it was lunchtime and took out the travel food Tallen had given her.

She handed Blade an apple. "Here." Her lips twitched in amusement as he cautiously examined the fruit. "It's not poisoned," she assured him, though the words had somewhat the opposite effect.

Blade eventually took a bite (and wasn't poisoned), and the party shared an amiable meal before tackling the rest of the bubble monsters.

Fey and Blade spent the entire game day fighting the animated bubbles. Without Magic to immobilize a fraction of the monsters and Blade to disable them while they were down, the quest could have easily taken three days to complete. With the advantage, the party levelled up ferociously, Fey reaching level 19 and Blade level 20 after putting down hundreds and hundreds of the creatures; Fey's pets reached level 15 from the passive experience gain, and Spore reached level 10, evolving the ability so that Fey could choose what status effect to inflict, though each individual status effect had a cool-down of one minute.

It was well into night when the last trubble burst into dust.

"Well done," came an unfamiliar female voice. Startled, Fey and Blade looked up to see a figure leaning against a tree only a few metres away. The NPC ranger was dressed in mottled browns that made it easy for her to blend into the forest, and she carried an enormous longbow strapped to her back.

"Hello?" said Blade cautiously.

"Hello." The ranger straightened and approached the party. "I am Eliana," she introduced herself.

Fey's keen night vision picked out the shape of a mana blossom on the ranger's cheek. "Are you the one who put up the request?" she asked.

"I am. And you are the ones who fulfilled it." On closer inspection, Eliana asked, "Might you be Fey?"

"Uh, yes?" Fey answered, confused as to how the ranger would know her name.

Eliana chuckled. "Jerem— Jerendal told me about you the other day." Fey was so embarrassed remembering the slug incident that she failed to note Eliana's stumble over Jerendal's name.

"You already have the Guardian's Blessing, of course," Eliana continued, "But you . . . " She turned to Blade. "We do not have any human guardians."

Blade had no idea what Eliana was talking about, having not read the quest or reward descriptions. He glanced uncertainly between the two elves.

"Aww, come on, give him the blessing," Fey urged. She thought it would be hilarious if Blade were to get a flower marking on his face as well. "It's really helpful," she assured Blade with slightly too much enthusiasm, making him suspicious as to whether he actually wanted whatever they were talking about.

"Uh, it's okay," he said, his hands rising a few inches, palms out, as his subconscious tried to defend him from Fey's sense of humour.

As if his reticence paradoxically made Eliana want to bestow the Guardian's Blessing (a contrary people, the elves), the ranger said, "Fine," and began chanting.

Blade nervously backed up a step, then halted when nothing more threatening than the glow of light appeared. This time, golden light coalesced into a blue butterfly whose wings resembled a mana blossom. It fluttered in its butterfly way indirectly toward Blade. Fascinated, the human warrior put up a hand in invitation, and the magical butterfly landed on the tip of his index finger (as opposed to on his face). In a flash of light, the butterfly disappeared, transformed into a solid blue tattoo of the silhouette of a butterfly in profile.

"Cool," said Blade, infused with a sense of well-being.

"That's not fair," complained Fey, "Why does he get to have it on his hand and I have to have it on my face?"

Eliana raised an eloquent eyebrow (apparently a racial trait common to elves, based on our sample population so far). "If you did not desire the marking on your face, why did you let it land there?"

"Nobody told me not to let it land on my face," Fey grumbled.

"Nobody told him, either," Eliana pointed out reasonably.

"Bleh." Fey hated it when she was on the unreasonable side of the argument.

"Well, if that is all, I will be leaving. Goodbye." Eliana leaned against another tree and disappeared (#MagicalRangerPowers).

<Quest complete!>

<Fey gains 850 experience. Amethyst gains 425 experience. Magic gains 425 experience. Boris gains 425 experience.>

<Blade gains 850 experience.>

<Fey's Guardian's Blessing has reached level 4!>

<Blade has gained Guardian's Blessing!>

In the place where Eliana had disappeared lay a small pouch holding the reward for the quest in the form of ten 500g pieces, which Fey and Blade split evenly.

The party travelled back toward Moonwood village, Fey feeling childish from the fact that her prank had not worked. Her mood was reflected in her gait, with her feet dragging along close to the ground and her upper body leaning slightly forward, making her resemble a really tall five-year-old shuffling along, hugging a flask instead of a stuffed animal. Blade was bemused at how easily his companion could switch between poise and intentional gracelessness.

Near their destination, Fey's alarm chimed, letting her know that she had been asleep for eight hours. "I'm logging out," she announced.

"See you tomorrow?"

Fey made a non-committal sound—"Muh"—and exited the game.

◊◊◊

CHAPTER 17

WAKE-UP CALL

Arwyn pulled off her game helmet and sat up, the bright morning light coming in through the windows in sharp contrast to the deep night she had been experiencing in-game. Squinting, she glanced at the clock and saw that it was just after seven.

Sunday mornings were when Arwyn went to tae kwon do class, the one day of the week when having a substantial breakfast was mandatory.

She enjoyed the quiet of the morning, with only the small sounds of her dishes and cutlery interrupting the peaceful silence. While she was not an extreme introvert and was certainly able to enjoy herself in the company of others, quiet alone time was when she recharged her mental energies. She enjoyed the internal dialogue that helped her make sense of the world and added interest to even the most mundane aspects of life.

Dressing for class, Arwyn put on the traditional uniform of loose pants and long-sleeved top in white and fastened her red belt with the traditional double knot. Her impractically long hair was confined to a sleek ponytail, and she filled up her large water bottle before heading out.

Arwyn was enrolled in a peripheral branch of a larger school that had several locations throughout the city, and classes took place in an elementary school gymnasium that was rented out for the weekend. Taking off her socks and shoes at the entrance, she bowed as she entered, then bowed again as one of the assistant instructors walked by and said hello.

Bowing was an integral and frequent part of tae kwon do: when entering or leaving the room, at the formal start and end of class, before and after doing an exercise with a partner, when handing over or receiving an item, and whenever the grandmaster happened to be walking by. Arwyn enjoyed the physicality of the gesture and the genuine respect it embodied, one of the many elements of the ancient tradition that centred and grounded her.

The students lined up by belt level, then age; Arwyn was in the back, as she was in the advanced class for red belt and up. They began with the traditional saluting of the flags and bowing to the instructor, then began warm-up and conditioning exercises.

Much of tae kwon do class was spent doing mundane exercises to improve stamina, strength, and flexibility. Passers-by who peeked in hoping to see flashy stunts or intense fighting were often disappointed to see people running laps, doing push-ups (or whatever you called what Arwyn did given her utter lack of upper-body strength), and stretching quietly (although whimpering was not uncommon). It was not until the muscles were warm and loose—even slightly fatigued—that tae kwon do–specific exercises appeared.

There was quite a bit of variation in what they worked on during this part of class. Sometimes they practiced tae kwon do patterns, also called forms, sets of linked kicks, punches, and blocks that were part of the standard curriculum and tested during exams to advance to the next belt rank. Also common were classes spent on improving one or two specific kicking techniques with drills to improve speed, balance, power, and accuracy. Occasionally, they learned "street fighting," self-defence techniques that would be useful in a real fight but would get one banned from competition.

Today's class was focused on the simple axe kick, where the foot was brought as high as possible and then chopped down to smash the heel into the target. The general technique was straightforward and quite powerful, but its usefulness was limited depending on the height you could achieve. The foot achieved maximum speed about a third of the way into the kick, so to be effective at head height, it had to start well above the head.

Arwyn paired up with one of the other girls in class and accepted a hand target from the assistant instructor with a bow. Both she and her partner wore subtle grins as they bowed to each other and began to practice. While neither of them could compete with the majority-male students in terms of pure strength, they generally far exceeded them in flexibility and active range of motion. (That being said, the other girl was still considerably stronger than Arwyn while having basically the same flexibility, so our MC really has no excuse for being so weak.)

Each partner held the target for the other to kick several times before switching roles. The height of the target depended on who was doing the kicking; for some of the older students in their forties and fifties, they started at waist height, while Arwyn and her partner started at head height.

Settling into a relaxed fighting stance, Arwyn brought her foot up and sent it snapping down through the target with a brief yell on the downward motion. Known as a "ki-up," the cry was both a psychological device to increase force and effort during attacks as well as a physiological technique to coordinate breathing and core muscle activation during the movement.

Hitting the target in the centre resulted in a satisfying slapping sound, and Arwyn repeated the action with each leg several times before taking her turn holding the target. Time passed with a sense of camaraderie as they gradually raised the target higher and higher until it was well over head height, technically impossible to hit even if you were flexible enough to do front splits. They cheated through this limitation by rising up on the balls of their feet during the kick to gain an extra few inches of height. In terms of pure technique building, neither of them had very much to improve on, but sometimes the point of an exercise was to simply have fun and appreciate what the body could already do.

After an hour, class ended (with bowing), and Arwyn headed home tired, sweaty, and relaxed in the best possible way. After showering and eating lunch, relaxed turned into sleepy. She had technically been getting more than enough sleep since purchasing *Fantasia*, but she had gone three days without the full unconsciousness associated with regular sleep—six if you counted the accelerated time experienced in-game. Mind weary though her body was rested, she headed to her bedroom and sank into the queen-sized bed for a nap. (Tsk tsk, going to bed with wet hair. This is how weird hairstyles are born.)

An hour later, she woke up feeling completely refreshed, having had one of those perfect naps with no residual grogginess or any of the small discomforts sometimes associated with sleeping, like a sore neck or a dry mouth. (Even her hair looked fine; when it's long enough, gravity tends to overrule any kind of messy configurations it wants to shape itself into.) She indulged herself by lazing about like a cat among her excessive number of pillows (five) for several minutes before getting up.

Contentedly, she turned on her computer. Technically, she did not have to work on weekends, but deadlines were deadlines and getting things done now meant less stress in the coming week. Taking advantage of an unusually focused state, she spent the next few hours immersed in spreadsheets and emails.

After dinner, an instant message popped up on her screen:

Leah-IfIHadAMillionDollars...: How was TKD?

ArwynTheElf: Great. You should take it with me.

Leah-IfIHadAMillionDollars...: I will if you take yoga with me.

This was an ongoing negotiation between the two friends as each tried to convince the other of the superiority of their chosen form of exercise. Leah contended that tae kwon do was too violent and too high risk for injury, while Arwyn maintained that yoga did not even count as exercise (and wasn't violent enough).

ArwynTheElf: I'd rather . . . go to tae kwon do by myself.

She had been about to write something melodramatic like, "I'd rather eat low-fat ice cream" but then realized she didn't find yoga *that* distasteful.

Leah-IfIHadAMillionDollars...: Good, because I'd rather not have somebody stomp on my foot and have to hobble around for weeks.

ArwynTheElf: That only happened once.

Leah-IfIHadAMillionDollars...: What about the time you sprained your ankle and hobbled around for weeks?

ArwynTheElf: That also only happened once.

Leah-IfIHadAMillionDollars...: And the time you twisted your knee?

ArwynTheElf: Okay, that one doesn't even count. It wasn't a full sprain, I wasn't hobbling, and I didn't even have to skip a TKD class.

ArwynTheElf: Anyways, are you going to list every injury that I ever had? Because been there, suffered that.

Arwyn did not actually get injured frequently in tae kwon do class, but after almost a decade of weekly and twice-weekly classes, the incidents added up.

Leah-IfIHadAMillionDollars...: Actually, I wanted to check on your *Fantasia* progress. I trained hard last night and got to level 15.

ArwynTheElf: . . . 19

Leah-IfIHadAMillionDollars...: *swear word* Seriously? HOW?

(Leah actually wrote "*swear word*"; she swears infrequently, like Arwyn.)

ArwynTheElf: I got the Magic (*song reference*[23]). Oh, and sometimes hunting is more efficient in a party.

Leah-IfIHadAMillionDollars...: >_> Of course I hunt in a party. Solo mages are just asking to die, and I'm not antisocial like you.

ArwynTheElf: I'm only antisocial toward stupid people.

Leah-IfIHadAMillionDollars...: And everyone is stupid.

ArwynTheElf: You understand me so well. ^_^

Leah-IfIHadAMillionDollars...: Well, it's the least I can do, since you're so great at helping me destroy the evidence.

(This was an ongoing joke that Leah and Arwyn played on whatever agency might be monitoring their chat history. They are both law-abiding citizens.)

ArwynTheElf: I'd patent the process if its only use weren't so illegal.

(Still joking. Really. There is no process. #DothProtest-TooMuch[24])

Leah-IfIHadAMillionDollars...: - k, well, I'm going to go try to catch up with you in *Fantasia*. Bye and good night.

ArwynTheElf: Nightnight.

Leah-IfIHadAMillionDollars... *is offline.*

Arwyn took Leah's game-playing as permission to do so herself. Saving her work, she shut her laptop and prepared for sleeping. She brushed her teeth (and flossed; good dental hygiene is important to overall health) before climbing onto the recliner and putting on the game helmet. *"Welcome,"* it whispered seductively. Setting the alarm for work the next morning, Arwyn turned on the game.

◊◊◊

Darkness.
    "Scanning. Player detected. Welcome back to *Fantasia*, Fey E'lan."
    A flash of light.

◊◊◊

Fey blinked into existence a short distance from Moonwood village. Almost immediately after logging on, she received a private message:

Leandriel: Hello. Are you busy today, or can we meet?

Fey felt a jolt of nervous anticipation at the prospect of seeing the angel again.

Fey: Of course we can meet. I'll meet you at the Moonwood teleport gate?

Leandriel: I can be there in half an hour.

Fey: Okay, see you.

After the chat disconnected, Fey gave herself a stern talking-to while walking back to the village. *Okay, we're going to get all of the squealing and giggling over with before he gets here so we don't embarrass ourselves by acting like an idiot.* (Rather than the royal "we," this "we" referred to the various Feys of various mental ages and dispositions hiding inside her body. Fangirl Fey giggled and made no promises.)

Since she had time before the angel's arrival, Fey wandered into Kallara's shop.

"Fey! How are you?" the healer greeted. Noting Amethyst still practicing Osmosis, her eyes crinkled in amusement. "Ah, so that's what you wanted the flask for. I thought you might be practicing Enchant."

"I'm going to do that later." Despite the fact that the idea had never crossed her mind, Fey said it as if she had been planning that all along. (Classic tactic for looking smarter than she actually was.)

Getting to her actual purpose for visiting, Fey opened her backpack and pulled out the plants that Boris had collected while she was fighting dubbles and trubbles. (Despite her previous herb-gathering adventures, she had entirely failed to realize that the miniature boar had actually fought and defeated plant monsters in order to return victorious with their corpses.) "I brought these for you."

Kallara exclaimed in delight while examining the collection. "Some of these are quite rare! I cannot manage to grow all of them in the garden, so it is always a hassle to obtain."

"Boris found them for me," said Fey, indicating the miniature boar. Struck by an idea, she offered, "Would you like to take him? He could gather herbs for you." Boris's straightforward fighting style did little to complement Fey's own, especially given how small and vulnerable he was. She thought this might be a good opportunity to find him a more suitable owner.

"Oh no, I couldn't," said Kallara. "It would be irresponsible to send him into the forest alone, and I cannot leave my shop for long periods of time. You keep him and bring back the plants he finds."

Showing a more humanlike facial expression than a regular animal could, Boris looked distinctly disgruntled at almost being given away.

While talking, Kallara's hands were busy sorting the plants into piles. At the sight of one particular plant, she took a pair of tongs from a drawer and used them to pick it up.

"What's that?" Fey asked, examining the plant, which consisted of a cluster of broad, reddish-purple leaves without separate stems or flowers.

"This is furyweed, and it is quite poisonous."

"I didn't notice any effects when I picked it up," Fey commented.

"It has to enter the body through a cut in the skin or be swallowed[25]," Kallara explained. "I am just being cautious."

Hmm . . . Fey grabbed a few of the furyweed leaves and stuck them in her pouch for later experimentation as Kallara neatly categorized and stored the herbs.

After weighing each plant, Kallara said, "I can offer you 300g for all of them." This was double the amount Fey could expect from selling them at a general store, as the healer could use her considerable potion-making skills to turn a large profit.

"Oh no, they're a gift," Fey said, "You've helped me so much already." She had a feeling that the ferociously potent healing salve she owned was worth a lot more than her newbie self had saved so far.

"In that case . . ." Kallara opened a cupboard and pulled out a very large flask, about the same volume as an unenchanted backpack. "You can continue training Amethyst in this. The glass is spelled, so it's not as fragile as it looks."

"Wow, thanks!" With Amethyst's Osmosis steadily levelling up, the slime was about to outgrow the small flask she had been practicing in. Out of curiosity, Fey asked, "What would you normally use such a big container for?"

"There are certain more dilute potions that are meant to be absorbed through the skin, like a medicinal bath," Kallara answered. "The vast majority of them are vanity charms, so I do not make them very frequently, and when I do, I charge outrageously for them," she added with a wink.

"Iiinteresting," Fey said, always up for learning ways to make a profit. "I have a few minutes before I need to go meet someone. Do you need help with anything?" Fey offered.

Not trusted with actual ingredient preparation that might downgrade the effectiveness of the final potion, Fey was sent to collect yet more water while Amethyst was recruited for her food processor–like abilities to mash things into a pulp. Magic hopped around in exploration, eventually ending up on the ceiling, looking at the drying herbs hung on lines strung between the walls, while Boris retreated to the doorway after an encounter with a powder resulted in a sneezing fit.

"Your visitor is almost here," Kallara remarked while tying up bundles of the new plants with string.

"How do you know?"

"I can sense the teleportation gate activating." Healing was considered a subcategory of magic in *Fantasia,* so Kallara was actually a high-level mage and sensitive to large flows of mana in the vicinity.

"Oh, uh. I'd better go!"

"Slow down," the healer chided when Fey suddenly became clumsy with hurry while collecting her pets. "It takes the gate several minutes to fully activate, and I am sure your visitor will not mind you not being present the second it does."

Fey's rushed pace only marginally slowed down before she was out of the tree-shop. "See you later, Kallara!" she called behind her.

Kallara closed her eyes and used a small spell of farsight to determine who the visitor was. Her eyebrows rose in surprise. "Not who I was expecting," she said to the empty shop.

Fey's rushing lasted until she arrived at the teleportation gate, which was still brightening with magical energy. She tried to calm her breathing as well as her general mental state. It was only partially successful, but she had at least an outward semblance of composure when the gate flashed in activation.

Fey was far from the only person gathered to watch. This early since game release, it was still fairly rare for players to have enough gold or to have explored enough territory to consider using the gates worth the expense. Curious onlookers waited in anticipation of the arrival of a high-level player; the appearance of a warrior angel with huge, white wings, mithril armour, and an obviously enchanted two-handed sword did not disappoint.

The dramatic entrance was ruined when, seconds after his arrival, greedy players rushed forward.

"Can I have some gold?"

"Can I have your old equipment?"

"Let me use your gate key!"

Fey's nose wrinkled in disgust at the shameless behaviour. *Does anybody actually get anything from begging like that?* Rather than get involved with the crowd, she stayed near the back, trusting Leandriel to deal with any obstacles between them.

Leandriel was not entirely unfamiliar with this type of reaction, though he generally stayed away from newbie areas like the Moonwood. Looking over the heads of the crowd (because he's *so* tall), he spotted Fey. She smiled and waved when they made eye contact, mouthing a "Hi," whose sound was lost to the demanding voices around him.

Leandriel tried to edge forward while ignoring the people around him, but a few players refused to take the hint and remained stubbornly in place, blocking his path to Fey. Fed up, he snapped his wings open with an audible snap and held them half spread in a threat display. As threats went, a seven-metre wingspan certainly gave everyone a reason to back up and get out of the way; one player even stumbled and fell during their hasty retreat.

Fey's greeting smile shifted to one of smirking satisfaction as she watched the scrambling crowd. She really appreciated people who were not so nice as to let others walk all over them. She had not thought it possible before it happened, but her rating of the angel's coolness rose another notch as he walked, graceful and dangerous, in her direction.

"Hello," Leandriel greeted (as if he had not just knocked someone onto his butt).

"Hello," Fey echoed cheerfully (as if she had not just been smirking at said individual).

"Shall we?" Leandriel asked, indicating a trail out of the village.

"Lead on," said Fey, and the pair made their way into the forest.

CHAPTER 18

TO INFINITY AND BEYOND

As Fey and Leandriel travelled through the trees, Magic left his owner in favour of exploring the more interesting person (#Abandoned). The mushroom hopped up Leandriel's leg until the angel picked him up. "Hello, young spore."

Magic squeaked animatedly back, causing Fey to stifle a laugh.

Remembering she had a new pet to introduce, Fey said, "This is Boris." She picked up the boar and held him out.

"Hello." (Leandriel was too dignified to rhyme with himself and say, "Hello, young boar.")

Boris grunted and wiggled until Fey put him back on the ground. He trotted off, trying to regain some lost dignity.

"So what brings you to this neck of the woods?" Fey asked, laughing as she was unable to resist the obvious pun.

Smiling in response, Leandriel said, "I brought something for you."

"What is it?" was Fey's immediate response. Belatedly, her manners kicked in and she added, "You shouldn't have brought me anything."

Before Leandriel could answer, Amethyst began jumping up and down with emphatic squeaking, pointing her bubble off the trail.

"What is she doing?" Leandriel asked with a curious expression.

"Well, the last time she did that, she led me to the King Slime. She's kind of a cannibal," Fey admitted.

"By all means, let us follow her direction," Leandriel said. (Remarkably unbothered by the cannibalism.) The pair diverted their path.

As expected, their detour ended at the sight of a King Slime, yellow this time, hopping around and smashing its grapefruit-sized bubble at a group of hapless newbies, who were scrambling to avoid it.

After dispassionately observing the panicked scene for a while, Fey asked, "What happens if no higher-levelled player shows up to kill it?"

"I believe if it is not defeated for an hour after it spawns, a request will be put up in the village to hunt it down." Leandriel had to actively suppress his basic intimidation aura to keep the weak boss from fleeing in terror, and even then, he kept his voice quiet.

Fey briefly considered letting the boss monster continue to rampage so she could earn quest rewards for killing it, then decided it was too likely that some other player would end up fighting it in the interim. "Well. Be right back." Drawing her sword and dagger, she quick-stepped forward, leaving her pets in Leandriel's company.

(*slash*slash*slash*kill*) With Fey now at level 19, the King Slime was quickly dispatched into a lifeless puddle on the ground.

<Fey has defeated the King Slime!>

<Fey has gained 45 experience. Amethyst has gained 23 experience. Magic has gained 23 experience. Boris has gained 23 experience.>

<Fey has attained level 2 Slime Mastery! (Details in Bestiary)>

With level 2 monster mastery, Fey could now see the special abilities (none), strengths (none), and weaknesses (everything) of slimes in her personal Bestiary.

The only loot the King Slime left this time was a small number of coins. Fey was not particularly disappointed, as her main goal was a snack for her cannibalistic slime. Cutting the boss's bubble free, she offered it to Amethyst. The slime had to augment her size through Osmosis, but was able to engulf the bubble without help this time (*omnom*).

<Amethyst's Double Membrane has reached level 8!>

"Hey, thanks!" came an unfamiliar voice. It was echoed by multiple other players, newbies who were grateful for the timely intervention. For each one who thanked her, Fey's fame rose by 1:

<Fey's fame has increased to 17 (+1)!>

<Fey's fame has increased to 18 (+1)!>

<Fey's fame has increased to 19 (+1)!>

<Fey's fame has increased to 20 (+1)!>

<Fey's fame has increased to 21 (+1)!>

<Fey's fame has increased to 22 (+1)!>

<Fey's fame has increased to 23 (+1)!>

"Uh, you're welcome," Fey said awkwardly, feeling a bit of guilt at having considered abandoning them for the sake of quest rewards. "Gotta go now," she said, bidding a fast retreat.

Leandriel fell into step beside Fey, and they continued deeper into the forest. Fey had completely forgotten what they had been talking about before the appearance of the King Slime, but Leandriel still had a present that he wanted to give.

He decided to sidestep any protests by simply handing the item over. Reaching into his pouch, he pulled out a length of cloth that unfolded into a luxurious purple cape. "Here."

"Oh my god, it's a cape. I love capes." Fey's hands came up to accept the item without conscious volition, her hands automatically closing at the pleasure of its downy-soft texture.

She petted the cloth for a while before holding it up, admiring the flutter of cloth. She loved the dramaticism of capes and the way they flowed and moved around their wearer. *I want it so bad,* she thought, struggling against the thought of how ruinously expensive such an item must be. Just to confirm her suspicion, she checked its description:

<Purple angel-down cape (ultra-rare): woven from angel's down and personally blessed by the Angel Queen Chryssiel, this cape grants the wearer some of the holy attributes of the angel race. When worn, +50 defence, +15 speed, +10% holy affinity.>

Holy [censored word], it's even more expensive than I thought it would be. "Personally blessed by Angel Queen Chryssiel"???

"I couldn't possibly take this. It's worth more than all the equipment I might buy for the next 50 levels," Fey said, starting to fold the cape back up.

Leandriel stopped her with a gentle hand over hers. "I have not been able to use it since I gained my wings," he said, slightly unfurling the appendages to accentuate the point. "It has been sitting unused in my storage for quite a while, and I would be honoured if you would make use of it." He failed to mention the series of special quests he had undertaken to earn the ultra-rare item in the first place, or the fact that he had gone to some time and expense to dye the formerly white cape a dark purple that would complement Fey's colouring.

Fey bit her lip in uncertainty, looking up at Leandriel's face with a conflicted expression.

He smiled and took the decision out of her hands by taking the cape and fastening it to her shoulders, attaching it by buckles on her armour that she had previously thought were purely decorative.

Oy vey. Fey stood stock-still, and yet the airy fabric still fluttered slightly with the lightest of air currents. Unable to resist, she took several steps and then made a large turn that made the cape billow out dramatically.

Leandriel watched Fey's antics with warm amusement. To him, the cape had just been a piece of equipment, but through her childlike enjoyment, he saw it in a new way. When she tripped over her own feet in the course of her spinning and turning, he could not help but chuckle.

Reminded of her audience, Fey wrestled control from her inner cape-loving nine-year-old and returned to stand next to the angel. "So, I obviously really, really love this," she admitted.

"I am glad you enjoy it so much," said Leandriel with a smile.

Fey briefly squeezed her eyes shut in a combination of sensory overload from the smile and situational dilemma from the absurdly expensive gift. *Did they have to make him a master gift-giver on top of being perfect in every other way?*

" . . . Okay. I'm going to keep it," Fey decided after a moment. "But I owe you a gift, and you can't bring me another one."

"Ever?" Leandriel asked with some disappointment. He had enjoyed Fey's reaction to the cape enough that the gift-giving felt more like a treat for himself than an expense.

"Okay, fine, on major gift-giving holidays," Fey conceded. (If "conceded" was the right word when forbidding someone else from buying you things.)

"Not minor gift-giving holidays?" Leandriel asked, poking fun at her wording.

"No, so don't go looking for obscure holidays no one's ever heard of."

Leandriel thought about it for a moment. "Agreed." They had stopped walking during their exchange, so he resumed his steps. "You forgot to specify the number of gifts," he added with a grin.

"One!" Fey hurried after the angel, enjoying the flare of her new cape. "One! Do you hear me?" When Leandriel did not respond except to continue to grin, she grew agitated enough to grab his arm for emphasis.

Leandriel smoothly tucked her arm into the crook of his elbow as if he were escorting her to a ball. "I hear you," he assured her. "I agree to nothing," he added, surprising himself with his mischievous mood, "but I hear you."

The rest of their trip was covered in animated negotiation where elf and angel argued over conditions and wording. A gift war[26] had begun.

"So where are we going?" Fey eventually asked. She had a bad habit of unquestioningly following people she knew without paying much attention to her surroundings, leaving her vulnerable to getting completely lost if her guide disappeared.

"A dungeon."

"There are dungeons? With monsters?" Fey asked. From her limited observation of the game world so far, it seemed to her that the monsters were more integrated into the natural ecosystem than a classic dungeon would allow.

"They are fairly rare," Leandriel answered. "Each one is a laborious creation of magic."

"Sounds fancy," Fey commented. Belatedly, she asked, "Uh, I won't get killed in this dungeon, right?" It seemed unlikely that someone would bother to spend a ton of magic just to build a dungeon populated with newbie monsters.

"You will be safe as long as you remain within the first two floors," Leandriel assured her.

Since Fey had absolutely no interest in exploring places that might be hazardous to her health, she was unbothered by the restriction. (She gave the term "healthy curiosity" a new, more cautious meaning.) "How many floors are there?"

"In theory, an infinite number. I have only explored the first eleven."

Infinity dungeons were magical constructs populated with monsters from all over the game world. The monsters became progressively stronger deeper inside, which made the dungeons excellent training grounds for players of all levels. The difficulty was in finding them; scattered across the world, finding their entrances was a matter of random exploration and luck. Leandriel had personally tested three such dungeons and knew the locations of all of them.

Fey and Leandriel arrived at what appeared to be a slight crack in the stone of a small hill. It turned out to be the entrance to a cavern, narrow but navigable even for Leandriel in full armour and with wings. The path inside sloped downward, opening up to a cavern large enough to run laps in. Faintly luminescent patches of moss provided enough light to see in black and white.

<You have entered Elvenwood Dungeon: B1.>

A rippling wave of shadow flowed ominously toward the pair. Fey jumped back toward the dungeon entrance, but Leandriel stood his ground and cast a spell.

"Purifying Light."

The angel suddenly lit up like a thousand-watt lightbulb, the effect particularly blinding on his pure-white wings. The nearer edge of shadow simply disintegrated, leaving behind small coins, while the farther monsters retreated as far as the cavern walls would allow, keening in distress.

"What are those?" Fey asked, cautiously moving up to stand beside the angel. Amethyst hopped off her shoulder and began cheerfully collecting coins.

"They are called glooms. These are the beginner monsters from the Dark Side," Leandriel answered.

Reassured that the monsters were no stronger than a slime, Fey walked to the far side of the cavern to get a better look. "Aww, they're so cute." She scooped up one of the shadowy creatures, which resembled a short-eared rabbit composed entirely of shadow and was almost as insubstantial in weight. It had been their hopping form of movement that made a group of them look like rippling shadow. In texture, the creature had a matte appearance and feel, like fine velvet.

Fey turned to show Leandriel the gloom, but it began to struggle as soon as it was exposed to the holy light. She also noticed that a group of the creatures had conformed to the exact outline of her shadow in an attempt to avoid being purified out of existence.

She could not help but feel sorry for the creatures. "Could you turn off the light?" she asked Leandriel.

"They may swarm," Leandriel warned while turning off the spell. He was not worried about his own safety—his passive health regeneration was high enough that even if he were completely covered in glooms in an unarmoured state, his health would stay at 100%—but seeing multiple creatures climb up Fey's legs made him tense. He resisted the overprotective urge by reminding himself that even six of the level 1 monsters would not be sufficient to damage Fey's level 19 avatar.

Fey was in fact not being attacked:

<Fey has tamed the gloom!>

<Fey has received a pet!>

<Please select a name for your pet: ____>

<Fey has tamed the gloom!>

<Fey has received a pet!>

<Please select a name for your pet: ____>

<Fey has tamed the gloom!>

<Fey has received a pet!>

<Please select a name for your pet: ____>

<Fey has tamed the gloom!>

<Fey has received a pet!>

<Please select a name for your pet: ____>

<Fey has tamed the gloom!>

<Fey has received a pet!>

<Please select a name for your pet: ____>

<Fey has tamed the gloom!>

<Fey has received a pet!>

<Please select a name for your pet: ____>

<Monster Tamer has reached level 5!>

<Fey has attained level 1 Gloom Mastery! (Details in Bestiary).>

"All six of them?" Fey muttered. *They must have* really *hated that light.* She proceeded to come up with six unimaginative names for shadow creatures. "You'll be Onyx, Inkblot[27], Ebony, Midnight, Shadow, and Obsidian," she told the glooms, saving the last name for the one she had first picked up.

<Name confirmed>

<Onyx, level 1 gloom.>

<HP: 5/5, MP 5/5.>

<Exp: 0/10.>

"Look, I tamed them!" Fey called out cheerfully, walking back toward Leandriel with the glooms clinging to her in a way that suggested that they did not particularly feel the need to obey gravity.

Leandriel relaxed and said, "Good. Shall we move on?"

They made their way through a series of caverns populated by monsters whose levels were always one higher than the monsters in the cavern before them. Other than dark-element monsters, whose hatred for the holy element caused them to make suicidal attacks, the creatures were terrified enough by Leandriel that they pressed against whichever side of the cavern was farthest away from the warrior angel, allowing the pair to quickly traverse the first floor.

After the tenth cavern, they arrived at a spiral staircase roughly hewn into the stone of the floor. "Watch your step," Leandriel cautioned at the uneven steps, ready to catch Fey should she stumble.

<You have entered Elvenwood Dungeon: B2.>

"This would be a good floor for you to train on. The monsters range from level 11 to 20."

"Sounds g—" Fey's words abruptly cut off as she spotted the inhabitants of this particular cavern. Giant spiders the size of dogs scuttled across the floor and walls, multiple eyes gleaming menacingly in the low light.

Fey was not enamoured of the group of animals colloquially known as "bugs," which she was aware was not a scientific classification based on phylogeny[28] but which nonetheless made sense in terms of activating the instinct to run away in panic.

Suppressing impending hysteria, Fey pressed her lips tightly together and stiffened.

"Are you okay?" Leandriel asked in concern.

"Fine." Fey's voice had a slightly strangled quality that belied the claim.

Seeing her owner's (wimpy) distress, Amethyst decided to be proactive in eliminating the problem. With a commanding squeak ("Feypets, engage the enemy!" or some such superhero motto), the slime jumped from Fey's shoulder onto Boris's back, and they charged off to engage the enemy. Magic hopped forward to provide backup support, while the new glooms demonstrated an intrinsic ability, casting a shadowy aura over the spiders that seemed to make them hesitate.

<Gloom: −5 accuracy, −1 attack initiative.>

The resulting slaughter was remarkable in a macabre way. Amethyst ruthlessly crippled spider after spider by destroying the legs on one side with well-placed blows of Whip, causing them to topple over, leaving them defenceless against Boris's Charge attack. Fey had not noticed earlier, but upon reaching level 10, Whip had evolved so that Amethyst could extend the length of her bubble-arm, giving her a 1.4-metre radius of destructive range, which she put to good use.

<Amethyst has defeated the cave spider!>

<Amethyst has gained 33 experience. Fey has gained 17 experience. Magic has gained 8 experience. Boris has gained 8 experience. Onyx has gained 8 experience. Inkblot has gained 8 experience. Ebony has gained 8 experience. Midnight has gained 8 experience. Shadow has gained 8 experience. Obsidian has gained 8 experience.>

In between casting clouds of toxic spores, Magic contributed to the macabre scene by hopping onto spiders' backs and using Drain to reduce them to dried-up, brittle husks.

Fey's glooms quickly gained enough passive experience from their fellow pets' kills that they reached level 5, at which point they felt confident enough to tackle the spiders head-on. Working as a group, the six shadow-bunnies swarmed an individual and sank their shadow teeth through its exoskeleton.

<Gloom poison: −10% speed, −1 stamina/minute.>

As with many dark-element creatures, the injuries the glooms inflicted came with an associated malady, in this case a lethargy that impaired the victim's ability to move.

Fey cringed at the carnage, not because of the one-sided slaughter, but because she really disliked the crunch of exoskeleton associated with squishing spiders. She was not sure which was less visually appealing, the gory remains Amethyst and Boris were producing, or the dried-up husks Magic was leaving behind. The glooms were fairly neat in their killing, leaving their victims mostly intact.

Leandriel watched the pets with bemusement. "Did you signal them to attack?" he asked Fey.

"Uh, no. I think Amethyst figured out I don't like spiders," Fey admitted sheepishly.

"Oh." He grinned at a sudden thought. "They say pets resemble their owners. It looks like it would be a poor idea to get on your bad side."

Fey opened her mouth to deny any resemblance to what was now her small army of pets, then closed it. It was true that she was not particularly violent in real life, but there was a certain straightforwardness to the way she approached the world that could be called a cousin to that violence. Translated into a world where monsters were designed to be killed for goods and money, she could not confidently say that her pets were not operating under the same mindset. "Ehe. Fear me," she said jokingly.

She cringed again at a particularly loud crunch of exoskeleton. "I wanna leave."

Leandriel escorted her across the cavern, considerately clearing the path of any spider remains with a purification spell. *So reliable,* Fey thought thankfully, adding yet another point to the list of reasons why the angel was perfect. The pets eventually left off attacking the few remaining cave spiders to catch up with their owner, bringing with them coins and spider fangs as loot.

Fey was not entirely sure she should encourage the type of behaviour she had just seen, but nonetheless praised her pets for their efforts and stowed the items away. She had no idea what use she might have for the non-venomous spider fangs, but that was not going to prevent her from keeping them, just in case (#Hoard).

CHAPTER 19

PLAY BALL

Fey and Leandriel managed to travel to the last cavern of the dungeon floor without further incident, Leandriel's passive intimidation aura more than enough to ward off such weak monsters. In the last space were level 20 monsters that resembled a cross between giant black tortoises and armadillos, with hard shells that were jointed in a way that allowed them to curl into a fully armoured ball. When uncurled, their heads and legs were vulnerable targets for attack. With their slow movement speed, they made good targets for Fey to train against.

"*Excellent*," Fey said in her best evil villain accent, earning her an odd look from Leandriel. "Are you going to go train on a lower level?" she asked the angel, having guessed his reasoning for choosing this place for an outing. With monsters of all levels, the infinity dungeon was the perfect place for them to train separately, together (or is that "together, separately"?).

"It would be rude of me to bring you here and immediately leave you behind . . . " Leandriel started, intending to stay a while to help Fey adjust to the new conditions before attending to his own training.

"Oh, no, you've done me a huge favour showing me this spot. You go on ahead, and we can hang out during breaks or something." When Leandriel continued to hesitate, she added, "I won't get mad." Grinning at his resulting expression, she said, "And I won't say I won't get mad and then get mad. Really, I promise."

Despite all of Leandriel's life experience indicating that Fey's words were a trap, he could find no evidence in her tone or body language that she would be upset at his departure. "I will depart for the eleventh floor, then. Message me if you encounter any problems and I will return as quickly as I can."

"Okay," Fey said cheerfully. She thanked the angel as he cast Helping Hand on her before descending the stairs to the next floor.

With Leandriel gone, Fey could relax the mental ropes tying up her inner fangirl and focus on fighting. (She still needed a small amount of her mental energy to corral her inner nine-year-old because she was wearing a cape.) Eyeing the tortoises, she noted that there were two varieties, one with rounded bumps on the shell and one with pointy spikes. The ones with bumpy shells looked somewhat less dangerous, so she decided to attack one of those first.

Drawing her weapons, she frowned, glancing between the blades and the monster's thick shell. She guessed that as soon as she launched her first attack, it would curl up defensively, rendering her unable to do further damage.

Better make the first hit count, then. Thoughtfully, she pulled a furyweed leaf from her pouch. "Here, Amethyst, eat this." (Remember, children, it is generally a bad idea to feed your pets poisonous substances.)

<Amethyst has improved Poison Slime!>

"Okay, some furyweed poison, please." Amethyst obediently secreted a thin layer of poison, which Fey carefully dabbed along the flats of her dagger and sword. Preparations complete, she hid her pets in a safe corner before aiming at her target. Charging her sword with Mana Blade, she ran forward and chopped at its head with Vicious Strike.

<The volly has been stunned for 3 seconds!>

<The volly has been poisoned!>

<Furyweed poison: −3 health/second.>

<Duration: 5 minutes.>

I wonder why it's called a volly, Fey pondered as she took advantage of the stun effect to do as much damage as possible before the tortoise retreated inside its shell. (Hint: it's a really bad pun.) Even the skin on its head and neck was quite tough, so she was only able to inflict surface wounds that bled sluggishly (tortoise-ly?).

As Fey had predicted, the volly curled up in an armoured ball as soon as the stun effect wore off. Rather counter to her predictions, the maneuver turned out not to be wholly defensive, as the monster began to roll toward her, picking up speed as it went.

"Oooh, shiitake mushrooms," Fey swore, jumping sideways as the live boulder crushed its way through where she had been standing, easily massive enough to cripple multiple limbs if she were too slow to dodge. Despite having its head tucked in, it appeared to be able to see her, turning and making a second attempt to flatten her.

The next three minutes were spent playing "don't get run over," which was certainly exciting, but not in a fun way. The volly could build up to quite a speed in a straight line but was slow to turn, so Fey ended up jogging in circles while waiting for the poison to do its work.

The monster eventually succumbed to the furyweed, uncurling and crumbling into pieces of black gravel that Fey skidded over while running in her circle, nearly stabbing herself in the eye when her arms moved reflexively to balance. (Remember, children, running around with an unsheathed sword is even more dangerous than running with scissors.) She sheathed her weapons with exaggerated care.

Coming to a stop, Fey dug through the gravel and found a few coins as well as a small, round crystal.

<Quartz stone (common): a low-grade enchanting component. Can be ground up for quartz dust.>

Analyzing the results of her fight (quote-unquote "fight"), Fey decided to send her pets back to the cave spiders, judging them unlikely to be of help against the thick-shelled vollies. "Don't forget to collect the loot," she told them as they set off in a small cavalcade, headed by Amethyst sitting on Boris's back. Fey took a snapshot of the cute arrangement before focusing on her own training.

Judging by the speed of the volly, Fey thought she could dodge two at once without too much trouble. She repeated her poisoned Vicious Strike against two monsters in a row, this time quickly sheathing her weapons to run. Contrary to her initial judgement, the spiked variation of the tortoise rolled less quickly than the bumpy version, making them easier to dodge and less dangerous.

For a time, everything went smoothly. Fey's skills and experience steadily grew with the effective attack strategy.

<Vicious Strike has reached level 3!>

<Vicious Strike has reached level 4!>

<Mana Blade has reached level 4!>

<Fey's stamina has increased to 102 (+1)!>

The easy times ended abruptly when the poison on her weapons wore off, and Fey found herself being chased by an angry volly with no poison effect in place.

"Nooo," Fey groaned, scrambling to think while continuing to dodge. Out of all her abilities, the only one with any chance of penetrating the volly's thick shell was Mana Edge, and she did not think it was yet at a high enough level to do so.

Seeing no alternative, Fey applied the effect to her sword and dagger before abruptly changing direction and charging at the volly. She slashed while running past it, aiming for the crack between shell segments.

The volly slowed and turned, giving no indication that it had taken any damage as it continued to chase her. With a mental shrug, she attacked, dodged, and attacked again and again.

<Mana Blade has reached level 5!>

Using Mana Edge added experience to the Mana Blade skill, of which Mana Edge was a subskill. At level 5, she could now ignore 15 points of defence, enough to start inflicting visible damage. Encouraged, Fey renewed her attacks.

Eventually, the volly collapsed, unable to maintain its curl and rolling attacks. Fey took advantage of its stationary position and unleashed a flurry of attacks until it crumbled away to gravel.

Panting, she immediately sat down. The speed of her movements in attacking and dodging was much higher than the previous jogging in a circle, and her (wimpy) muscles were collecting interest on the extra energy she had used up.

When she had mostly recovered, she dragged herself upright and went to go find Amethyst, her source of poison. She trekked through the intervening nine caverns between them, wishing she could private message her pets. (It's almost as if the game isn't designed for players to send their pets off on independent tasks.)

Just before she entered the cave spider cavern, Fey braced herself for the sight of mangled exoskeletons. She was rather surprised when she instead found a mostly empty space, occupied only by a cluster of her pets. With Amethyst's deadly bubble leading the way, the team (should we officially call them Feypets?) had quickly eradicated the entire population of spiders, with their looted bodies fading out of sight a few minutes after.

While waiting for the monsters to respawn, the pets appeared to be occupying themselves with an odd sort of shadow puppet contest, each of the glooms morphing their inky bodies into different shapes while Amethyst, Magic, and Boris served as judges. The judging showed a distinct lack of impartiality, as the three each supported a shadow copy of themselves.

"Excuse me," Fey interjected, picking up Obsidian, who had chosen to take on a miniature of Fey's shape, "you should all be voting for this one." Spotting Shadow, she changed her mind. "Never mind. This one wins, hands down." The ambitious gloom had replicated Leandriel's shape in incredible detail, down to the feathery texture of his wings and the engravings in his armour.

Ebony, the last gloom, had chosen to imitate a cave spider and waved two legs for attention.

"No. Just no," said Fey. "Stop it."

Deflated, Ebony relaxed back into a bunny shape.

Fun aside, Fey checked on the pets' progress. The glooms had reached level 12, and the senior pets were now level 16. "Very good," she praised. "You guys can train in the next cavern over if you run out of spiders." The level 12 monsters in the dungeon were giant rats[29] (or rodents of unusual size, if you prefer[30]), which had fairly balanced speed, attack, and defence. "Don't let anyone die," she told Amethyst, charging the eldest pet with the safety of the group after applying a fresh coat of poison to her weapons.

Amethyst squeaked cheerfully ("Of course, of course") before hopping onto Boris's back and trotting off. Before Fey could even finish stowing away the neatly stacked loot the pets had collected, she heard the squeaks and thuds of the rats being thoroughly beaten up. Crossing the rat cavern on her way back to the vollies, she winced and pretended not to see the bloody havoc being wreaked (like, quite bloody).

In the seventh cavern of floor B11, Leandriel battled level 107 chaos snakes. The creatures were as thick as his waist and four times longer than his height, with blood-red scales and eyes, and blood that flashed in hypnotic patterns that threatened to mesmerize him unless he activated his Battle Focus ability.

Lunging forward, he beheaded a snake with a powerful slash, but instead of dying, the creature sprouted two new heads, both of which hissed at him aggressively.

This was Leandriel's first time encountering chaos element monsters, and it was the most confusing and frustrating experience of his life. The snakes constantly changed their elemental affinities so that the same attack could end up doing double damage, half damage, or even heal. In addition, they had a 50 percent chance of reviving when their health reached zero, and had a bewildering array of special attacks depending on their element of the moment.

Proper strategy was out the window, and Leandriel was relying on his basic sword work, reflexes, and self-healing abilities just to survive. He made a mental note to congratulate the designer who had come up with the chaos element; the stated objective had been "confuse the hell out of them," and it had been implemented flawlessly. He also felt the urge to punch said designer right after that congratulations.

To make up for the difficulty of fighting them, chaos-type monsters were worth triple the experience of other monsters, but Leandriel thought the bonus would have to be closer to five times for him to even contemplate tolerating such an annoying experience.

Fey: Leandriel?

The private message distracted him enough that he misjudged his next dodge, allowing a snake to sink a fang into his arm, apparently temporarily able to completely ignore his armour. Fortunately, the attack ended up healing him instead of inflicting damage, though the paradoxical effect only served to annoy Leandriel more.

To avoid obscuring his field of view, Leandriel switched from text chat to audio chat.

"Fey? I am fighting right now. Do you have any objections to using audio chat?"

"No, of course not. Sorry, am I distracting you right now?"

"It makes little difference," Leandriel said in frustration, striking at a snake that instantly died but then spawned some kind of ghost version that he had no idea how to fight. "Sorry, I did not mean to sound dismissive. I am currently fighting a chaos monster, and all of my usual strategies are ineffective."

"Oh? What are they like?"

Briefly, Leandriel described his situation, his dark mood lightening when he heard Fey's delighted laugh. "What are you so pleased about?" he asked, voice softening.

"Oh, I just really like random things." (One could argue that our heroine has a high natural chaos affinity.) "Anyways, you're going about it all wrong."

"What do you mean?" Leandriel asked, slashing at a snake as he dodged its strike. The resulting wound began to emit a poisonous mist, from which he quickly backed away.

"Don't fight them normally. Do random stuff. Ideally, try things with opposite effects, like blessing and attacking at the same time."

Given that there were no chaos element monsters below level 100, Leandriel was certain Fey had never encountered one, but her voice was so assured that he decided to take her advice—he had little to lose, given his lack of success so far. Using a blessing on a monster for the first time, he cast Helping Hand while cleaving a snake's head in half. The creature pulsed, grew legs, then exploded in a cloud of chaos-coloured mist.

" . . . Huh."

"Did it work?" Fey asked.

"Yes, quite impressively." However, when Leandriel tried the same technique again, the snake doubled in size without appearing to come to any harm. "It does not appear that this combination is foolproof."

"Of course not; it's chaos. Just go with it, and do random things."

"Like what?"

"Um . . . Like, hug a snake. Tie them in a knot. Throw items at them. Sing a song. Just, random stuff. At the same time."

"Hug a snake," Leandriel repeated, picking out what was arguably the strangest suggestion of the bunch (though strong arguments could be made for the others as well).

"Haha, kill them with kindness, as they say. Do your best." Fey abruptly changed subjects, as she was wont to do. (Here the author has randomly introduced archaic wording, as she is wont to do.) "Anyways, the reason I messaged you was to let you know that I reached level 20 and I'm heading to the warrior trainers to learn my next skill. I'll be back after."

Leandriel nodded, then remembered that Fey could not see him. "I will likely still be down here when you return."

"Okay, see you later! Good luck with the random stuff!" Fey said cheerfully before disconnecting.

Alone with his thoughts, Leandriel contemplated Fey's suggestions while casting random spells and abilities and dodging attacks. *Such odd behaviours . . .*

While he was thinking, the snakes' attack initiative randomly cycled down to zero, causing them to ignore his presence.

Whether it was the influence of the chaos snakes or Fey's love of randomness, an uncharacteristic sense of abandon overtook him. Seizing a snake by the tail, he muscled it around a second snake and tied them together. One snake began to attack the other, and when the second died, Leandriel was credited for experience for the kill.

Smiling, Leandriel thought a silent thank-you to his elven friend and moved into action in a much better mood than minutes before.

CHAPTER 20
NEW TOYS

Fey collected her pets and headed out of the dungeon. It soon became clear that the glooms did not have a travel speed compatible with her walk; they either moved in small, slow hops or huge bounds (like bunnies). She finally resorted to holding the corners of her cape as a makeshift pouch to carry them on.

"Come on, get on," she said.

The glooms shifted uneasily, not wanting to touch the holy item.

"You're just going to have to get over it," Fey lectured sternly. "You can't walk around with such an obvious and easy weakness to exploit." She fully intended to make her new pets, the weakest dark elemental creatures around, develop the same resistance to holy attribute that high-level dark elementals had.

Reluctantly, the glooms hopped onto the blessed cloth, squeaking in protest when Fey fully wrapped them up and set off down the trail.

As usual, Fey spent her travel time experimenting and training abilities.

Now that Magic's Spore had reached level 10, he could choose which status effect to release. Holding out a hand, Fey asked, "Magic, can you make a pile of poison Spore?"

With his usual disregard of the precept of gravity, the mushroom hopped his way up to Fey's hand. With a cute expression of concentration, he produced a small pile of purple[31] powder.

Fey's Immunity was at a high enough level that she was able to handle the substance with impunity. "Here Amethyst, eat this."

<Amethyst has improved Poison Slime!>

The matter of transferring gloom poison over to the slime was trickier. While the shadow bunnies' bite carried a blighting effect, it did not seem to be transferred via any biological medium like saliva or venom. Fey resorted to having one of the glooms bite a leaf. (The individual in question was Shadow, not that Fey could distinguish the glooms without opening their pet menus. Bad owner.) Feeding Amethyst the blighted leaf was successful at teaching her the poison.

<Amethyst has improved Poison Slime!>

Hehehe. Fey felt smug from her successive successes (despite how minor they were). Feeling slightly invincible (whatever that means; you're either invincible or not), she decided to train Immunity with furyweed. At level 5, her ability could negate 2 damage per poison infliction, eliminating two-thirds of the damage she would take.

Confident in her math, Fey applied furyweed poison to her dagger and gave herself a small prick in the back of her hand.

(How pride goeth before the fall.)

<Fey has been poisoned!>

<Furyweed poison: –3 health/second.>

<Duration: 5 minutes.>

<Level 5 Immunity effect: decrease 2 damage per poison infliction.>

<New poison effect: −1 health/second.>

<Duration: 5 minutes.>

On paper, the experience with the poison went exactly as predicted. In reality, she had failed to take into account the physical symptoms of such a strong poison. An intense burning itch spread from the initial wound until her whole body was afflicted and she wanted to scratch her skin off.

Making a sound halfway between a moan and a scream, Fey started running, trying to distract herself with physical exertion before she actually started scratching herself bloody.

I repent! She wailed in her mind as she ran. (This is funny because she is not at all religious.) She now felt extremely sorry for all the poor vollies she had ignorantly inflicted such suffering upon, and thought they were superlatively justified in trying to squash her flat. The burning pain seemed to continue forever, and Fey pushed herself faster and faster, trying to replace the sensation with the bite of overexertion.

Subjective feelings of eternity aside, the poison wore off after exactly five minutes. Fey came to a panting stop, leaning against a tree and sliding gracelessly to the ground. For several minutes, the only movement she made was the effort of breathing; as that calmed, she seemed to stop moving at all.

Amethyst poked her owner concernedly with her bubble, not used to Fey's unnerving method of resting. Despite her dramaticism, the run had been short and Fey was soon back on her feet and trudging toward the village.

Damn, that's got more *fury than a woman scorned*[32]. Fey stretched her limbs, revelling in the simple pleasure of the absence of pain, her gait gradually regaining its normal ease as the aftereffects of the poison faded. With the increased regeneration from her Guardian's Blessing, she was restored to full health within ten minutes. Despite this, there seemed to be some lingering effects interfering with her decision-making abilities as, seeing that she still had a good distance to travel, Fey inexplicably chose to repeat her exposure to the poison.

What's wrong with meeee? She wailed mentally, finding herself running through the forest once again. (She asks that a lot, but usually follows it up with, "Don't answer that.")

<Fey's agility has increased to 41 (+1)!>

Fey arrived at the Moonwood sweaty and exhausted. Judging herself unfit for any activity other than her best impression of a boneless jelly (which implies the disturbing existence of boned jellies), she dragged herself over to the tavern and collapsed onto an empty bench, enjoying the cool feel of the table surface on her cheek. She was still in that position when the tavern-keeper came out a minute later.

"Miss?" Tallen asked tentatively, a bit nonplussed at finding an exhausted elf slumped over one of his tables.

Fey turned her head to look at him without lifting it off the table. "Hey, Tallen," she said in a languid voice. "Got anything to drink?"

Relieved at seeing Fey was just tired (as opposed to dying), he said, "I've just the thing," and bustled off to the kitchen, returning almost immediately with a glass of iced tea, which he placed just in front of where her head rested on the table.

Fey summoned the strength to sit upright and took a sip. As usual, it perfectly suited her taste, being heavily sweetened and peach flavoured. "You're the best, Tallen," she said appreciatively.

"Don't you forget it," he said with a wink, bustling off as players came and went, the establishment having become noticeably busier as more players entered the game.

Fey slowly sipped her beverage as she caught her breath, her energy returning much more quickly than it would have in real life had she overexerted herself to that extent. She allowed the background murmur of clinking cutlery and conversation to wash over her, enjoying her pocket of quiet within the noise.

"Hi," came an unfamiliar voice. (Alas, all good things come to an end.) It took Fey a few seconds to realize someone was talking to her, and she looked up to find a group of six elves had occupied the rest of the long table where she sat.

"Hi," she replied warily, feeling suddenly surrounded. (For the record, the players in question had not used any kind of stealth when sitting down and Fey was just really oblivious.)

"Remember us?" Before Fey could reply, he continued, "You saved us from the King Slime this morning."

Well, I remember the King Slime, anyway. "Oh yeah," she said in a vague tone. "Did everyone get away safely?" Looking around, she saw a mixed group of male and female elves. Something about their body language and features told her they were in their late teens despite the lack of the usual real-life clues such as clothing and hairstyle.

"I'm Eli," introduced the speaker, his body language indicating he was the putative leader of the group. The rest of the players introduced themselves, but their appellations failed to imprint themselves onto Fey's memory. (Our heroine is bad with both faces and names. Also, the author was too lazy to make up throwaway names that won't ever appear again.)

Fey adopted a neutrally pleasant demeanour and nodded at each elf. "I'm Fey," she said, demonstrating the full extent of her skill at small talk.

Clearly much more of an expert at the art of chitchat, Eli asked, "So, how long have you been playing *Fantasia*?"

Fey had to think for several seconds to come up with the answer. "Four nights." The flow of time felt strangely indistinct now that she was going from periods of consciousness to other periods of consciousness in a virtual setting.

"Cool, we just started today. Got any tips?"

"Uh, not really." Leaving aside the reliability of advice from a newbie to an even newer newbie, she doubted her "style" of adventuring (also known as "do random crap and luck into good outcomes") would be suitable for most people. "Just have fun," she said in the spirit of genericism.

With the threat of more idle conversation to spur her to her feet, Fey quickly finished her iced tea and stood. Tallen magically appeared at her elbow as she did so. "I brought you some travel rations," he said, handing her a neatly wrapped package.

"Thanks, Tallen," Fey said gratefully, having totally forgotten that she might become hungry in the future and might want to carry food with her.

"Can we pay your bill for you?" Eli asked. "It's the least we could do to thank you for saving our butts earlier."

"Uh" was Fey's (quick-witted) response, the fact that she ate for free throwing her for a loop at the offer. (Error. Does not compute.)

Tallen, in contrast, quickly capitalized on the offer. "That will be thirty-five gold," he said, including the cost of the travel food in the total. Fey slid a glance at the tavern-keeper and received a conspiratorial wink as the newbies dug into their pockets for coins.

"Thanks," she said, not having the heart to tell the players that they had failed to save her any money and were instead lining the tavern-keeper's pockets.

"No problem. See you around!" Eli and his friends waved cheerfully as Fey left the tavern.

Before heading to the warrior trainers, Fey stopped at the bank to store away her gold and items. Most people would have disposed of common items like spider fangs and rat teeth at the general store, but Fey was a hoarder at heart and the bank offered free safety deposit box services for up to a thousand different items. She cheerfully handed over her piles of (junk) items to be placed into storage.

Irrilana seemed to be standing duty alone at the designated clearing for warrior training that day. Fey was curious as to where her twin had gone but did not feel she was in a position to ask. (Instead, 10 percent of her cognitive processing started speculating about what NPCs did in their free time.)

Focusing on the business at hand, she said, "I've reached level 20 and have come to learn my next warrior skill."

Irrilana glanced at Fey, looking over her player stats and progress at the same time. "You have reached the correct level, but have not completed enough warrior feats to unlock the next skill."

"Warrior feats?" Fey echoed blankly.

Seeing that Fey had no idea how the class advancement system worked, Irrilana explained. "Each class has its own set of feats you can complete to show your progress in skill. They are worth different numbers of feat points depending on difficulty, and a certain number of points are required to learn each successive skill. In this case, you will need 20. When you begin to specialize at level 30, each sub-class will have its own set of feats to complete. You can find the list of feats under your class menu."

All of this information was included in the Advanced Gameplay section of the game manual that Fey had failed to read before diving into the virtual world. (To be fair to the heroine, the author had also failed to *write* the Advanced Gameplay section of the game manual before making this up shortly before starting this chapter. It is unsurprising that the two have a similar tendency to make things up as they go along.)

"Oh. Thanks." Fey called up the warrior class menu in her head.

<Warrior Stage I: unspecialized.>

<Warrior skills: Mana Blade (I) – subskill Mana Edge.>

<Warrior feat points: 14.>

<Points required for next skill: 20.>

Wondering how she had earned her 14 points, she scrolled through the long list of possible warrior feats.

<Who's the Boss?: defeat a boss monster in melee combat.>

<Point value: 10 points for boss of equal level; value increases or decreases if boss is stronger or weaker than the player.>

<History: Slime King (level 15) at level 11—14 points.>

Clearly, points were only awarded for the first boss of the same type defeated, or Fey would have more than enough points to unlock her next skill. She browsed the list for tasks that looked relatively easy to complete.

<Mad Skillz: become skilled at a melee weapon (until Weapon Mastery skill forms).>

<Point value: 10 points.>

"Does unarmed combat count toward weapon mastery?" she asked Irrilana. (If it did, she would already have the points, because she had formed the Kicking skill already, but we're not judging our heroine for her lack of deductive reasoning.)

"No, but it is easy enough to weaponize an unarmed fighting style with short blades in hand or attached to leg armour," the trainer answered.

Fey's eyes gleamed in interest. The idea of adding sharp and pointy emphasis to her punches and kicks was incredibly appealing and likely a much better strategy than trying to learn a standard melee weapon from the beginning. Even without a warrior feat as a prize, the suggestion was too good not to pursue. Thanking Irrilana for the advice, Fey made a beeline back to town.

Not sure whether bladed leg armour belonged in a weapons or armour shop, Fey decided to visit Senaia's armour shop first (because she had a discount there).

"Fey! Welcome!" Senaia greeted warmly. From the countertop, Topaz the yellow slime waved its bubble hello.

"Hi." Fey normally attempted to follow convention and force out a line or two of small talk before stating her business, but was so focused on her current objective that social niceties flew out the window. "Do you have bladed leg armour here?"

Senaia's expression went unfocused as she reviewed the store's inventory on a virtual screen. "That's not a popular type of armour, so we might not have any in stock . . . Yes, none. However, it would be easy enough to have a set made if you are willing to wait for a few days. A custom set would be best, anyway, given how exactly they need to fit."

"Yes, please." Fey wanted the weaponized armour yesterday but was willing to jump through whatever hoops it took to get it and make sure it functioned well.

The shopkeeper whipped out a notepad and pencil, which seemed like obvious props since she clearly had access to virtual screens to jot down notes. "May I ask your strength and agility levels?"

"Sixty-five and forty-one."

Senaia jotted the numbers down, then pulled out a measuring cord to take a much more comprehensive set of dimensions than what was needed for a simple pair of pants. In addition to waist circumference and leg length, she measured Fey's thigh and calf circumference at four different points, both with flexed and extended joints at the hip, knee, and ankle. She even took exact molds of Fey's feet using some kind of clay and had her display the full range of motion she needed to jump, squat, and kick in every possible direction.

With all the information written down, Senaia muttered to herself while crunching numbers. "Grade B steel, extra flexibility . . . The cost will be three thousand gold. Twenty-four hundred after your discount. Will that be acceptable?"

"Sounds good." The quoted price was considerably more expensive than a standard set of leg armour of the same material, but if it really could protect her while offering nearly the same mobility as simple cloth *and* sharp bits to slice at her enemies, it would be totally worth it. "Oh, I reached level twenty, so I should upgrade the rest of my equipment while I'm at it."

"Oh my, level twenty already? Congratulations! Would you like to see our standard options or add to your custom order?"

Fey thought about what parts of her upper body she would want to weaponize. Since her fists would presumably be armed with held weapons, that only really left her elbows. "Can you make armour with blades at the elbows?"

"Of course."

After a second flurry of measurements, Fey's total came to 4000g, a bit over half the money she had accrued thus far in her adventures. She went to the bank and brought the appropriate payment back, with the promise that the set would be complete in three days, which would actually be the next time she logged in due to the accelerated flow of time in game.

"Oh, punching blades really complement this kind of armour," Senaia advised. "You can find them in the weapons shop. I'm pretty sure Sylvannos will have a pair in storage somewhere."

Hmm . . . Fey had completely forgotten about the punching blades in favour of leg blades, as kicking was overwhelmingly her preferred mode of hitting things. Still, she had money left over and was due for a weapons upgrade, so she wandered into the neighbouring weapons shop.

The weapons shop was managed my Senaia's younger brother, Sylvannos. Physically, the auburn-haired male bore little resemblance to his sister, but he had a boyish, slightly frenetic version of Senaia's cheerful energy, as well as a slightly geeky obsession with the weapons he sold.

He rushed over as soon as Fey crossed the threshold of the tree-shop. "Welcome, how may I help you today?"

"I'd like to look at your level 20 short swords and any punching blades you might have."

The younger elf's eyes lit up with interest at the mention of the uncommon weapon. "Right away." He quickly retrieved the correct weapons out of dozens of racks growing out of the walls and brought them to the counter for Fey's examination.

Fey only gave the short swords a cursory glance; they appeared to be higher-quality copies of the one she already had. Most of her attention was on the unfamiliar weapons Sylvannos had brought over.

"These are punching blades?" Having never seen one before, Fey was not even sure of how to go about picking it up properly.

"Yes!" Sylvannos hefted one in demonstration, and the weapon suddenly made sense. A horizontal bar was held across the palm in a fist-like grip, with a spade-shaped blade curving out in front of the hand like the bladed version of brass knuckles. The metal on the outside of the arm flattened and extended out past the elbow into a gently curved wing that could be braced against the forearms.[33]

Fey could instantly see how the weapons would enhance the unarmed strikes she already knew with minimal modification of the techniques. The blades would add several inches of reach and a lot more weight and cutting power, while the wings would allow her to block heavy strikes and cuts without absorbing too much damage with her actual flesh.

Short swords forgotten, she picked up a pair of matched punching blades and snapped out multiple strikes in quick succession. Extremely well balanced, they felt almost weightless, like natural extensions of her arms.

"I'll take them," she said without asking about the price or attempting to bargain (#ItemLust).

"They are twelve hundred gold each."

When Fey immediately put down the punching blades and left the shop, Sylvannos thought she was protesting the price, which was admittedly fairly steep compared to more common weapons in the same material.

"Um, one thousand gold?" he said uncertainly, though by this time Fey was already out of earshot. Feeling rather deflated at the lost sale, he began to put the weapons back on the racks.

Fortuitously, he started with the short swords, as Fey returned a few minutes later, laden with money from the bank. She placed 2400g on the counter, picked up the punching blades and their accompanying sheaths, and left to go play with her new toys.

CHAPTER 21

FEATS AND FEASTS

Thanks to the chaos snakes' triple experience value and Fey's advice, Leandriel reached level 100 faster than expected. He had not quite begun to revel in the chaos, but her ideas had pushed him to think creatively and come up with a viable strategy. Since the snakes were equally likely to die whether he used his strongest or weakest attacks (or buffs, or debuffs, or heals), he ended up relying on his low-cost, area-of-effect abilities, with little consideration toward whether they were intended to be used offensively or not. He also found that switching between skills seemed to be more effective than using the same one repeatedly, giving some evidence to support the "fight randomness with randomness" approach.

Training target achieved, Leandriel ascended to the upper levels of the dungeon, finding Fey on B3, battling level 22 floating rays (the fish, not the electromagnetic radiation). He noted her change in weaponry; though the exotic blades in her hands were far from common, she used them with a level of comfort and technique that told him she had years of unarmed martial arts experience.

Giving him a friendly glance in greeting, Fey gradually fought her way closer to where he was standing, disengaging from battle when his passive intimidation was enough to keep the rays from even attempting to attack.

"What's up?" she asked casually, still several paces away.

"I reached level 100, so I came to see how you were doing."

When Fey failed to continue the normal course of conversation, Leandriel looked more closely and saw that she now wore an unfocused expression, her steps losing some of their previous grace as she continued to approach.

"Fey?" he asked, concerned.

The appellation elicited no response. Fey continued forward, stepping past normal conversational distance until she stood well within arm's reach. He certainly did not mind the closeness, but something out of the ordinary was certainly happening. Mystified, Leandriel allowed her to pick up his gauntleted hand and raise it to her eye level.

Following her fascinated gaze, Leandriel spotted a speck of multicoloured liquid flashing in hypnotic patterns just behind his wrist.

With chagrin, he realized he had inadvertently mesmerized his companion with the chaos snake blood still dotting his armour. Gently disengaging her grip, he quickly logged out and back in to cleanse his equipment, the process taking about a minute.

Fey blinked, rather disoriented. She seemed to have a small gap of time in her memories. The last thing she remembered was walking toward Leandriel, but the angel was nowhere in sight.

"What the . . . " she muttered to herself.

No longer deterred by Leandriel's presence, the floating rays resumed their attack against Fey. She had forgotten about them in her distraction, and failed to dodge in time to avoid being clipped in the head by a diving attack.

"Oww! You bleepers." (Yes, she actually said "bleepers." #Self-censorship) Fey swiped at the creature reflexively but missed, and it climbed in the air, out of range. She was glaring up at the monster with her hands on her hips when Leandriel reappeared.

"Oh, hi," she greeted as the angel's form solidified. "Where did you go?" (Nope, she's still totally oblivious to the whole not-an-NPC thing. Sorry.)

"I'm afraid I must apologize yet again," Leandriel said (apologetically). His armour was gleaming and clean after the logout, mesmerizing in its own way, but one in which Fey could remember and appreciate the sight.

"I returned with some chaos snake blood on my armour, and you were mesmerized for a short time until I recognized the cause."

"Oh." After a pause, Fey asked, "I didn't do anything weird, did I?"

"No, no," Leandriel hurried to reassure her. The speed of his denial made Fey suspect that she had indeed been acting odd.

Seeing her un-reassured expression, Leandriel started to explain. "All that happened was—"

"Noo, don't tell me," Fey interrupted. *I have enough cringe-worthy memories, thankyouverymuch.* Her imagination was conjuring up enough embarrassing scenarios without being reinforced by reality.

"Really, it was nothing bad," said Leandriel, raising an eyebrow at Fey's reaction.

"No good can come of me knowing," she said darkly, adding a touch of melodrama for humour.

Leandriel's lips twitched in amusement. "Okay, then."

"So, are you taking a break from training?" Fey asked, having missed Leandriel's earlier explanation.

"Yes. I have reached level 100, which was my goal for today." He did not actually need any rest, his stamina having reached the impossible figure of 250 after spending several days flying nonstop, but even fighting chaos snakes grew monotonous after a while.

"Congratulations!" Fey said, her automatic response to someone's announcement of a level-up in a game. (Well, normally, she would type "congrats," but saying the abbreviated version sounded weird. The even shorter "gratz" did not bear thinking of.)

"Congratulations yourself. Are you enjoying your new warrior skill?" Leandriel asked, reasonably assuming Fey had returned to the dungeon after accomplishing the goal she had left to complete. (Reasonable, but incorrect.)

Sheepishly, Fey admitted, "I didn't have enough warrior feat points to unlock it. After that, I got a bit distracted," she said, raising her punching blades. In acquiring equipment more suited to her pre-existing skills, she had made significant progress in improving the fighting abilities of her avatar, just not in the way she had intended. (Pretty typical of our heroine.)

"How many points do you still need?" Leandriel asked, easily falling into gamer strategizing mode.

"Six. I'm trying to get a weapons mastery skill to form." While Fey was certainly better at punching and striking with the punching blades than she was at wielding a sword, tae kwon do was about 70 percent kicking techniques, and she was still far from being proficient enough to form a weapons mastery skill.

Leandriel frowned slightly in thought. "That is one of the harder feats to accomplish. Which ones have you already completed?"

"Just one boss kill."

"The monster-killing feats would probably be faster to complete. Look up 'kill tree,'" he suggested.

<Kill tree: kill n monsters in a single blow (monsters cannot be more than 10 levels below player level).>

<Point value: $2n$.>

(Look, a variable!)

Didn't I already kill a monster in one hit? I guess it doesn't count if it happened before I joined the warrior class, Fey mused. (This is the author's way of oh-so-subtly explaining the discrepancy to discerning readers.)

With Vicious Strike at her disposal, Fey was sure she could kill one monster with a single, well-placed attack, but until she gained some kind of area-of-effect or chaining attack skill, killing groups of monsters at once would not be feasible.

"I don't think I can kill more than one monster at a time," she mused aloud.

"Well, if you can kill them quickly, you might try the 'mad minute' feat," Leandriel advised.

<Mad Minute[34] (I): kill 60 monsters in 60 seconds (monsters cannot be more than 10 levels below player level)>

<Point value: 5 points>

Hmm. If Fey could kill a monster in one hit, she saw no reason she could not do it sixty times. The only problem with accomplishing the feat was that many seconds would be wasted in moving between monsters. *Unless I can bunch them up somehow . . .*

Fey eyed Leandriel and the repelling effect he exerted on the floating rays in the cavern. "May I borrow your presence for a few minutes?" she asked the angel.

The unusual wording made Leandriel realize that Fey was planning something, but he acceded readily to the request. "Certainly," he said, without asking for specifics.

"Great!" With a final glare up at the floating rays and a mental note to return for revenge at a later time (#Vindictive), Fey led Leandriel to a different cavern.

Fey chose the level 12 lesser earth golems for her attempt at Mad Minute, mainly because they had a very obvious vital point, the animating crystal at the centre of their foreheads, something her short, stout punching blades could easily crack with focused blows.

She positioned Leandriel about a third of the way into the cavern. "Stay here, please." She continued forward alone.

Leandriel was highly amused when he realized that Fey was literally borrowing his presence in order to scare the golems into a smaller area. The animated creatures lumbered away from his repelling influence over two-thirds of the cavern, congregating into the farthest third. Smiling, he activated his Battle Aura ability, increasing both the strength and range of his intimidation effect and pressing the golems into an even smaller area.

Fey turned, startled to see Leandriel glowing an icy, fearsome blue, the colour calling to mind the ferocity of blizzards and the implacable immensity of glaciers.

"Is this better?" he called from his position across the cavern. In contrast to his intimidating appearance, his voice was warm and amused.

Fey had the unique experience of consciously noticing the influence of a fear effect. Rather than having an explicit stat debuff, the game's intimidation effects were designed to activate the adrenergic system based on the complex interaction between the attacker's intimidation ability, the recipient's resistances, and the player's individual stress response, affecting their concentration and performance the unique way fear did in real life for that person.

If Fey had met Leandriel on the opposing side of a battlefield, the obvious, overwhelming difference in strength between them and the presumed hostile intent from fighting on different sides would be plenty of reason to feel stressed, and she would not consciously question if the degree of fear she felt was more than she should feel without an intimidation ability being involved.

However, she *knew* this Leandriel to be only kind and helpful, even protective of her, someone she normally felt relaxed and happy around, so the gnawing fear in the pit of her stomach and the cold sweat affecting her palms felt like an extrinsically imposed effect, an irrational phobia. Breathing through it as best she could, she opened an audio channel, not quite up to yelling across the cavern.

"Hey, do you mind if we form a party? That aura is kicking my butt."

The effect vanished, leaving only the slightly shaky remnants of fear. Leandriel closed the distance between them before she could tell him she was fine. Pulling off his gauntlets, he grasped her hands, which were still cold and clammy with reaction.

"I am so sorry. I completely forgot that you might also feel negative effects," he said, looking more distressed than she felt now that the aura was off.

She made her body and voice relax, forcibly shifting the mood back to their earlier lightheartedness in a way that was only possible because she was somewhat naturally resistant to fear effects, rationality ruling her actions regardless of the state of her emotions (#Robot). "Hey, it's all good, I'm fine. We can just form a party and get this done."

He scanned her expression, and she focused on the pleasant warmth of his hands to keep her body language genuinely relaxed. "Okay, then," he agreed, reluctantly letting her go and returning to his previous spot.

<Leandriel has sent you a party invitation.>

<You have accepted Leandriel's party invitation.>

With the party formed, Fey gained immunity to any debuffing effects Leandriel cast, and he reactivated his Battle Aura without incident. Not only were the golems pressed into the farthest fifth of the cavern, but their movements grew uncoordinated as their minds were clouded with fear (or whatever the golem equivalent of fear was).

Glad to have a task to focus on to shrug off the last aftereffects of intimidation, she considered her course of attack. Given the golems' rocky bodies, none of Fey's pets (Feypets!) would be particularly effective in damaging the monsters. They also tended to introduce an unpredictable element that might drastically improve or worsen her time per kill, so she decided to have them sit the exercise out for a more reliable result.

Taking a deep breath, Fey mapped out the most efficient path through the golems in her mind. (Loading . . . Please wait.) Finding a comfortable grip on her punching blades, she burst into action.

Fey's Mad Minute, as typical of most of her physical activities, was not particularly graceful but got the job done. She repeatedly quick-stepped between each successive golem and delivered a precise and accurate[35] strike to the animating stone in its forehead, using a combination of Vicious Strike and Mana Edge to help her penetrate the hard surface. She also used Isolate to prevent the monsters from reacting to her attacks on other individuals, though she thought Leandriel's influence had much more of an impact on hindering their movements. She kept count as she felled each golem, going beyond her quota and stopping at sixty-two just in case she had miscounted along the way.

<Isolate has reached level 5!>

<Vicious Strike has reached level 5!>

Breathless, Fey checked the warrior menu, hoping she had been fast enough to complete the feat.

<Warrior Stage I: unspecialized.>

<Warrior skills: Mana Blade (I)—subskill Mana Edge.>

<Warrior feat points: 21.>

<Eligible for next warrior skill.>

<Recent feats: Kill Tree: One-Hit Wonder—2 points.>

<Mad Minute (I)—5 points.>

"I did it!" Fey exclaimed. The Feypets (muahaha, finally got the stodgy non-parenthetical narrator to adopt the term) cheered without really understanding what was happening. (They're still not very smart but make up for it in cuteness.) Spotting the collapsed remains of the golems, they began rooting through the stone for loot.

Leaving them to their thing, Fey bounded over to Leandriel in a state of excited victoriousness, the gait an irregular mix of running and skipping that made her look like a very tall ten-year-old. "I did it!" she repeated.

Leandriel could not help but smile back at her infectious enthusiasm, though part of him was still watching for any remnants of wariness caused by his earlier mistake. "Congratulations." By his observation, Fey was either a master of controlling her body language or had entirely forgotten about the earlier incident. (Having had the benefit of a lot more observations of our heroine, we can confidently declare that the first possibility is outside the bounds of Fey's abilities.)

"Thanks for all your help," Fey said cheerfully.

Leandriel almost apologized again, but the irrepressible buoyancy of her mood carried him upward until he let go of the worry and guilt weighing on his thoughts, their presence almost an insult to the vibrancy and joy before him. "You are very welcome," he said, a smile again tugging at his lips. "Will you head to the warrior trainers now?" he asked, imagining Fey rushing out of the dungeon with the same bounding gait.

Fey would indeed have normally headed out immediately to unlock her new skill, but she was hungry. "Actually, do you want to stop to eat?"

"Certainly."

The pair found an empty patch of ground to have an impromptu picnic. Fey settled easily into a cross-legged position, then watched with surreptitious fascination as Leandriel underwent the rather elaborate series of steps required for an angel in full plate to sit on the floor.

First, Leandriel used his Ex-quip[36] skill to magically replace his plate with flexible cloth garments. An auxiliary skill available to all warriors at level 30 in addition to the main skill, it was useful for donning and removing the complex and multilayered armour they often wore, and in the case of winged players, the only way to do so without two skilled assistants and half an hour of complex manipulations.

The angel next unfurled his wings, the massive appendages extending three and a half metres (that's 11.5 feet for you weirdo Americans) to either side of him. In a feat of grace and balance that Fey suspected was even harder than it looked, Leandriel carefully sat down, letting his wings relax against the ground once he had safely settled in.

As far as Fey could tell, having wings was rather inconvenient (but still really cool). "I'm not sure I could manage a pair of wings without a *lot* of clumsiness," she commented, opening her food packet and discovering that Tallen had packed a mix of fruits, hard candies, and dried foods that all catered to her food preferences. She happily selected a pear to munch on. (*omnom*)

Leandriel half smiled, half grimaced while pulling his own foodstuffs out of his pouch. "You should have seen me on the first day. It took me quite some time just to discover how to move them." Realizing the worries behind her comment, he added, "You would not have to deal with this level of inconvenience; avariel wings work differently."

Fey raised her eyebrows and made a questioning noise, her mouth still full of pear. "Mrh?"

Leandriel explained, "Avariel wings act as summoned entities that are attached to the body. They consume mana when in use but can be dismissed when not needed. Your body will also be transformed to be lighter, so the required wingspan is much more manageable."

Fey finished swallowing and said, "That's definitely worth it for someone like me."

It was Leandriel's turn to raise an eyebrow. "Like you?" (Sorry to all the people who can't raise one eyebrow who lack representation in this story.)

He bit into a cookie while Fey clarified. "I have pretty poor spatial awareness unless I'm really concentrating. When I was a kid, I'd constantly bang my head against the corners of furniture." (She still banged into furniture on a regular basis, but clipping a hip now and then is a lot less concerning.) She paused to reflect on how she had survived childhood, then noticed what Leandriel was eating. "Is that a cookie?"

"Would you like one?" Leandriel offered, pushing his container forward. He personally thought that Fey had above-average physical abilities, especially when it came to fighting, but he was not about to discount her evaluation of her own abilities, knowing that extensive training could overcome a lack of natural talent.

Fey promptly abandoned her healthy food in favour of processed sugar and chocolate chips. (She highly doubted that the game developers had bothered coding for long-term micronutrient deficiency effects.) She slid her own food forward. "Take whatever you want."

"Thank you." Leandriel politely selected a piece of jerky (though they both knew his food was better).

Suddenly realizing they were sitting on the ground, sharing snacks, Fey grinned. "I'm afraid I've dragged you down to my level."

"Which level is that?"

"The nine-year-old level. I never advanced beyond sharing snacks when it came to making people like me."

Leandriel smiled in deep amusement. "It is a simple and effective strategy. I see nothing wrong with it."

"I'll bring better snacks next time," Fey promised, drawing a chuckle out of the angel.

Finishing his cookie, Leandriel next reached into his near-bottomless pouch and pulled out a round cake with a hole in the middle.

" . . . Is that an angel cake?" Fey asked.

"Yes. The bakery apparently could not resist the pun." (Neither could the author.) In spite of the joke, the cake made for reasonable travel food, not having any icing or glaze and being suited for eating with bare hands. He offered the pre-sliced cake to Fey, who accepted a piece.

Having completed their looting, Fey's pets gathered with their haul of coins and miscellaneous items. "Thanks, guys," Fey said, accepting the tribute and storing it away. "Do you guys eat food?" she wondered aloud.

Magic clearly had no interest in cake (possibly because he had recently finished draining the life out of hundreds of rats and spiders). Instead of looking at the food, he hopped over to Leandriel (#AbandonOwner) and appeared to take a nap.

Boris sniffed disinterestedly at the cake before rooting out a bag of nuts in Fey's food pack and munching happily away.

Amethyst hopped onto Fey's knee and surveyed the food with the vague curiosity of a creature that had subsisted solely through cannibalism and poison ingestion up to this point. Fey figured that the slime could ingest just about anything without ill effects, so she pinched a piece of cake and dropped it into the slime's mouth. The slime did not do much in the way of chewing or swallowing, but the morsel, visible through the slime's translucent membrane, gradually dissolved over the course of several minutes. (She's just a giant bag of digestive enzymes, isn't she?)

The glooms hopped around, apparently curious about the food but not interested in eating. Ebony, who had earlier taken on the shape of a cave spider and badly lost the popularity contest, mimicked the shapes of several foods experimentally.

"People will eat you if you look like that," Fey jokingly warned an apple-shaped Ebony. The gloom squeaked in alarm and reverted to rabbit form.

Seeing the shapeshifting reminded Fey of the glooms' earlier antics. "Hey, go back to the shapes you had during your contest."

Six rabbit-shaped shadows morphed into tiny silhouettes of a slime, a boar, a mushroom, a Fey, a Leandriel, and a cave spider.

"Not you, Ebony," Fey added. The shadow bunny again reverted to its normal form but drooped to the ground, clearly discouraged.

"Aww, it's okay, I'm sure you'll find a nice shape soon," Fey soothed, picking up the sad gloom and sticking it on her lap in consolation.

Fey picked up Shadow, who had faithfully recreated Leandriel's form in full plate armour. "Isn't this cool?" she said to the (full-sized) angel. Shadow flapped his wings realistically. (Show-off.)

"That is . . . amazing," Leandriel breathed. Without thinking, he reached for the gloom, only to drop his hand when Shadow flinched at his holy aura.

"None of that," Fey chided the gloom. "Go on, you have to develop holy resistance. It's not going to kill you."

Reluctantly, Shadow hopped over to Leandriel's newly extended hand (the hop looking really weird in angel form). The gloom shivered in discomfort at the contact, angel form wavering at the edges.

" . . . Are you sure about this?" Leandriel asked. The gloom looked so miserable touching his skin that he wanted to let it go.

"If his personality is based on mine, he's fine."

"Your personality?"

"Er. Well. He probably is feeling uncomfortable, but not nearly to the degree he's displaying," Fey admitted.

Leandriel chuckled. "You are quite honest with yourself."

Fey and Leandriel talked and played with the pets as they ate, lingering far longer than such a snack break would normally take due how much enjoyment they were getting out of the interlude. Fey eventually made all of the glooms go sit with Leandriel, causing them to gain a percentage in holy resistance.

When Fey's alarm chimed, she reluctantly logged off to face the demands of daytime. Leandriel decided to follow suit.

◊◊◊

CHAPTER 22

LIFE HACK

Leander walked down to the IT department to deliver his daily report. Upon entering the building, which was the base of operations for several hundred programmers and their sophisticated equipment, he found an unusual flurry of activity in the group project room. Over fifty men and women typed furiously at the computer terminals where there might usually be a dozen or so having a casual meeting or brainstorm session. In contrast to the furious rate of work, at least half the people involved were grinning widely.

"What's going on?" he asked Kevin, the programmer he usually reported to, a young man with the pale skin, glasses, and slightly hunched posture of someone who spent too many hours staring at a computer screen without a break.

"Dream Life Enterprises is hacking us again, looking for our advanced AI software," Kevin answered, never taking his eyes off the screen or pausing his typing on the keyboard. He was one of the ones wearing the type of grin that would make Leander brace himself for a diabolical practical joke.

In the competitive world of virtual reality gaming, VirtualRealities indisputably dominated the market with the most advanced interfacing hardware as well as their simulation software, which was known for its multisensory realism, whimsically detailed worlds, and, perhaps hardest of all to emulate, their incredibly realistic NPCs. Their main competitor, Dream Life, had spent billions of dollars in research and development over the years, but never managed to close the gap, their NPCs falling just short of true realism into the uncanny valley that discomforted players. With a string of recent high-profile firings in the company, it appeared that someone had resorted to hacking. This was the third such incursion in the last few weeks that Leander was aware of.

Leander grinned, the expression holding a slight twinge of malice against people who would stoop this low. They would never find what they were looking for; the files did not exist in the company servers. "So what is everyone doing?" he asked. The expressions everyone wore clued him in that this was no simple defence.

"That half is making sure the intrusion doesn't affect our game servers," Kevin said, briefly sparing the use of his left hand on the keyboard to gesture at the half of the programmers who were wearing serious expressions. He grinned and continued, "This half is making sure they find the little surprise we left for them."

"A virus?"

Kevin grinned even more widely. "Better." He paused dramatically before continuing. "It's a copy of Dream Life's own AI software." The words triggered a round of laughter throughout the room. Leander joined in, the diabolical nature of the practical joke filling him with respect toward whoever had thought of it.

"I wonder how long it will take them to realize what they have," Leander said, still grinning.

"Well, considering we rewrote the whole thing to look different while functioning identically, a while."

"You evil, evil man."

"Well, everybody helped," Kevin said modestly.

Suddenly, someone yelled, "They found it!" and the room filled with cheers as if they were in a control room that had successfully completed an expedition to Mars. Objective (apparently) reached, the hackers ceased their intrusion, and within a few minutes, most of the people left the common room to return to their private offices for a quieter place to work.

Leander followed Kevin as the programmer packed up and headed toward his office. "So I saw you fought some chaos-element monsters last night. What did you think?" Kevin asked.

Leander paused, trying to find the right words to encapsulate the random, frustrating experience. After several false starts, he finally said, "You had better keep it a secret that you were the one who thought of the concept."

The words were said so seriously that Kevin stopped walking to look at his coworker. "What? Why?"

"If it were to become known, I am sure someone would find you and punch you in the face."

Kevin's worried look transformed to a mixture of worry and confusion when Leander added, "Probably right before or after hugging you."

⸺◇◇◇◇◇⸺

Arwyn came home from work tired and lacking the willpower to resist logging into *Fantasia* before a normal bedtime hour. Giving in to the game's seductive whisper—*"Come, come,"* it beckoned creepily—it was barely 9:00 p.m. when she slid on the game helmet and was transported to virtual reality.

◊◊◊

"Scanning. Player detected. Welcome back to *Fantasia*, Fey E'lan."

◊◊◊

Fey materialized inside the infinity dungeon. Leandriel was long gone, having warned her he had to return to his duties when they had said their goodbyes the night before. She was reminded that she had a set of new kicking gear waiting at the armour shop by a notification on her virtual menu and set off for the Moonwood at a comfortable jog. Boris kept up fairly easily at a trot, with Magic sneaking a ride on the boar's back, while the glooms bounded along like the rabbits they mimicked. Amethyst, as the leader (and also the one that happened to weigh the least) got to ride along on Fey's shoulder.

<Fey's stamina has increased to 103 (+1)!>

Hehehe. Fey thought that if people's fitness quantifiably increased when they exercised, they would be motivated to run around more. (If we're talking about motivations to exercise, having a world full of aggressive monsters out to kill you is probably a stronger motivation.)

Walking into Senaia's tree-shop, Fey saw that the elf was busy with another customer, so she found an out-of-the way corner to wait.

The Feypets, not having been forbidden from entering, wandered in through the shop's open archway. Seeing their owner just standing around, they began to explore the shop.

"Do *not* knock anything over," she hissed at them under her breath. It would be just her luck if any of them had inherited her accident-prone tendencies.

At the warning, the pets began to walk with exaggerated caution, delicately taking a step (or a hop, depending on the pet's state of leggedness) after a careful search for hazards, pausing between each step to repeat the process. This was possibly the cutest thing Fey had ever seen, and she took a short video of their explorations until one pet's behaviour caught her attention.

After inspecting an armour stand, Obsidian the gloom had morphed into a miniature replica of a boot. Fey picked up the shadow-boot with interest, examining it from all angles. "Can you do a full-sized boot?" she asked.

With a bit of straining, the gloom was able to expand to the correct dimensions, but the result was flimsy to the touch (*pokepoke*).

"Keep practicing," Fey told Obsidian, putting it back on the ground. The gloom reverted to its rabbit shape and hopped away to find other things to mimic (*hop* *pause* *hop*).

Having completed an order from the other customer, Senaia turned her attention to Fey. "Welcome, Fey! Hello, Amethyst," she greeted the player and the pet sitting on her shoulder. "I have your new armour already if you'd like to try it on."

"Yes, please," Fey said with enthusiasm, following the shopkeeper to a crate behind the counter (where Topaz was sitting cutely). Senaia pried off the lid and Fey peered inside.

"Oooh . . . " Fey said in admiration, seeing smooth curves of blackened metal accented with bright silver.

"Here, let me help you put it on." Senaia had Fey change into close-fitting leggings and shirt, then proceeded to set each piece of armour into the correct place. Everything fit perfectly, but the process still took over ten minutes.

"Ideally, you'd have the Ex-quip skill available for this kind of intricate armour, but it's not available until level 30," Senaia said while making sure all the fastenings were secured. Fey made a mental note to earn extra feat points for the optional skill, sure she would never be able to put everything on correctly on her own.

Finally, it was all in place. Fey twisted and turned in front of the mirror to fully inspect the leg armour. *This is so badass.*

Indeed, "badass" was an apt description of Fey's bladed leg armour. (Or would "kickass" be better?) Several important design features seamlessly integrated the offensive and defensive aspects of the piece.

The main body of the armour was made of a slightly more flexible metal in jointed segments that transitioned to woven strips for extra flexibility around areas that might normally be left with gaps. Four stripes of tougher metal ran down the front, back, and sides, connected at intervals by rings of the same material, designed to catch the brunt of any impacts without compromising the player's range of motion.

The front strip of metal going down the shin and top of the foot was particularly thick and reinforced, shaped into a raised, sharpened ridge that turned her leg below the knee into a cutting implement. The ridge extended into a robust, triangular point a few inches above the knee, ensuring that she would be well-equipped to do damage even in tight quarters.

The boots of the armour were designed more for blunt damage than cutting or piercing, with broad, flat studs attached to the toes and heels to concentrate the force of her kicks without risking getting caught in flesh or armour and upsetting her balance while fighting.

The rest of the armour covering her arms and torso was designed along the same theme, with similar edged ridges along her outer forearms extending past her elbows, angled and sized precisely to not interfere with the long wings of her punching blades. The entire waist portion was constructed from woven steel strips so that she truly had full range of motion. The helmet was a minimalist piece that covered the top and back of her head without obstructing her hearing or vision, while a separate gorget protected her vulnerable neck.

To top it all off, Senaia handed Fey a pair of weighted rings, about two hundred grams (half a pound) each. "What are these for?" Fey asked, fiddling with the latch mechanism that opened them.

"You can clip these to the middle of your foot to give your kicks more momentum," Senaia explained. "It makes running and jumping take a great deal more energy, so you should remove them when you're not fighting. Again, having Ex-quip would be ideal."

"I didn't pay you enough," Fey murmured worshipfully, knowing just enough about biomechanics to understand how much difference such small weights would make when attached to the end of a long lever arm (lever leg?).

"I take it you're happy with the product?" Senaia asked jokingly.

Fey was starting to feel a strong urge to start kicking things to see exactly what kind of damage she could do. To save Senaia's shop from a destructive rampage, she quickly thanked Senaia and jogged out of the shop. "Thanks so much, Senaia! These are really awesome."

⸺◦◦◇◦◦⸺

Senaia smiled at Fey's exuberance. "Have fun!" she called after the player, waving goodbye.

Turning to move the now-empty crate into the storage room, she nearly tripped over a gloom. "Oh my!" she exclaimed in startlement, not having noticed Fey's extra pets. As more and more pets came out of various nooks and crannies to run after their owner (who had just abandoned them to play with her new toys), Senaia's eyes became wider and wider.

"Did you just see that?" she asked Topaz as the herd of glooms was followed by a boar-riding mushroom.

The slime squeaked in agreement.

⸺◦◦◇◦◦⸺

Fey headed out of the village and quickly made her way to the nearby monster territories with a clear destination in mind. She wanted to test out her new gear on the level 5 poison mushrooms she had read about earlier and collect a new poison for Amethyst to learn at the same time.

Poison mushrooms had murky green caps with bright yellow spots to signal their toxicity[37] but otherwise had largely the same shape and appearance as blue mushrooms. Being poisonous at a level where almost no players had poison resistance, they were not popular training targets, and Fey had the whole herd[38] to herself.

After spotting the monsters, Fey ordered, "Anyone who isn't immune to poison, stay out of range." This caused a bit of confused squeaking amongst the Feypets as they worked out what "immunity" was (still not very smart), but eventually, Magic and Boris stayed behind while Amethyst and the glooms accompanied their owner forward.

Approaching a poison mushroom, Fey slammed an Axe Kick into its body, feeling the extra impact her armoured boot was making compared to the leather she was previously wearing. With a 16-level disadvantage, the mushroom immediately died and shrivelled up.

"Hehehe." Fey chuckled evilly, bending over to pick up a coin.

Sensing danger (if that's the way to describe reacting to a herd-mate being brutally killed with no attempt at stealth), the rest of the poison mushrooms began to squeak in alarm and hop away, releasing clouds of poisonous spores in their wakes.

<Fey has been poisoned!>

<Poison mushroom poison: −4 health/20 seconds.>

<Duration: 10 minutes.>

<Immunity effect: −2 damage per poison infliction.>

<Net effect: −2 health/20 seconds.>

<Duration: 10 minutes.>

Fey was pleased to find a poison that could affect her, ensuring that she would not have to subject herself to furyweed in order to continue training Immunity. The mushroom poison came with the side effect of somewhat blurry vision that mimicked mild myopia. Since Arwyn was severely near-sighted in real life, the effect was actually less difficult to navigate than walking around without her glasses on, and she serenely began a one-sided massacre of the poison mushrooms without any difficulty. If anything, the blurry vision helped her not feel bad about the cute creatures she was killing.

"Okay, Amethyst, start eating."

Amethyst opened her mouth as wide as it would go, somewhat resembling a purple version of a certain pink balloon-like video game character (Kirby) as she collected airborne poison spores. It took several minutes before she had a sufficient sample to analyze, but eventually:

<Amethyst has improved Poison Slime!>

<Poison mushroom poison: −4 health/20 seconds.>

<Duration: 10 minutes.>

Shortly after this, Fey stopped tormenting (massacring) the much weaker mushrooms. They posed no challenge at all, and their diminutive size meant that she was quite limited in the types of attacks she could try out.

Remembering yet another task she had left undone, Fey headed to the warrior training area to unlock her level 20 skill now that she had earned enough feat points to do so. This time, she found Irrilathan alone on duty. *Do they usually take turns?* she wondered.

Without waiting for Fey to state her business, the warrior trainer scanned Fey's progress. "I see you are ready to learn your next warrior skill," he said without preamble.

"Yes, sir," Fey said, reverting to the way she talked to her tae kwon do instructors without thought.

Irrilathan drew his longsword, a plain piece that was clearly meant to be used rather than admired; one had to look carefully to see the bluish sheen that indicated mithril alloy in the blade. "Watch carefully," he ordered. Holding his arm straight in front of him, he focused, mana the same colour as his platinum hair gathering just in front of the tip of the sword.

"Arc Slash." He swept his arm to the right, the single spot of glowing gold extending into a short arc of thirty degrees ($\pi/6$ radians for the math fans) that expanded as it moved away from its origin point, gradually fading away about two paces away.

"This is the basic form of Arc Slash," Irrilathan said as he sheathed his sword in an easy, practiced movement. "As you increase your mastery, it will evolve, increasing the arc angle and the distance it can travel. Try it now."

Fey hefted one of her punching blades in her dominant right hand, assuming that any edged weapon would be able to activate the skill. Visualizing the flow of mana, she was able to concentrate it and activate the skill just as Irrilathan had demonstrated.

<Fey has learned Arc Slash!>

The skill consumed 100 of Fey's current 231 maximum mana, but she considered it a reasonable cost given that it was her first skill that would be able to hit multiple opponents and that it would continue to evolve as she used it.

"Very good." The praise was overshadowed by the immediate next step. "Now try with your other arm."

Fey settled the second punching blade onto her left hand. It was naturally less dexterous but more than able to complete the simple sweeping motion the skill demanded. She thought that the difference in coordination would make little difference, but the left-handed version of Arc Slash covered a paltry twenty-degree arc and fizzled out of existence twice as quickly.

Aww, so lame (#Teardrop).

"You need to practice with your off hand more if you plan to dual wield," said Irrilathan. "Warrior skills convert mana into force by channelling it through the body. Your physical skills will apply a bonus or penalty to the base effect."

In that case, I should try activating it with a kick, Fey thought, making a note to experiment later, when her mana reserves were replenished. "Thank you for the instruction," she said, automatically bowing because it still felt like she was in tae kwon do class. Hesitantly, she asked, "May I see what Arc Slash looks like when mastered?" In real life, she was used to seeing what felt like inhuman demonstrations of physical prowess on a daily basis when the assistant instructors demonstrated an advanced form of whatever technique they were learning that day. The demonstrations were almost entirely aspirational; Arwyn did not think that she would ever be able to perform some of the harder moves even if she quit her day job and focused on training full time. (Look up "quadruple kick tae kwon do" and you'll understand.)

Irrilathan smiled at the request, for the first time showing more than businesslike calm in his expression. "While there is no such thing as full mastery. . . " (that's what all the masters say) " . . . I can show you the progress that I have made." He drew his sword once more.

Instead of pointing his weapon forward, the trainer started with his sword tip just above the ground. With a simple breath, he gathered his mana and began tracing a glowing arc in the air. Using his left foot as a pivot point, he steadily raised his arm while turning two full circles, creating a perfect corkscrew pattern that extended from his toes to the sword's length above his head.

Irrilathan let the attack hang in the air for a few seconds before cancelling the skill. "I would release the attack, but I'm afraid it would cause quite a bit of damage to the trees," he said. Belatedly, he added on, "And you." (Nice to know where people rank on the list of priorities. Elves.)

Fey's mind was too boggled to take offense at the lack of care toward her life and health. They were standing in a clearing large enough to run laps in, so she could imagine the range of Irrilathan's attack. She had naively imagined that Arc Slash would be "complete" once the user was able to create a full circle, but by moving the sword vertically as well as horizontally, the warrior trainer had gone far beyond that, essentially removing the upper limit of mastery. (Though after a certain point, the monsters probably won't notice a difference between being cut into twelve versus thirteen pieces.)

Her inner fangirl was acting up (*squee*) but Fey kept her external composure and thanked the instructor for the demonstration before leaving.

CHAPTER 23

GOOD FOOD, MEDIOCRE COMPANY

Fey was feeling pretty good. With her upgraded equipment and new skills (skill, singular, let's not exaggerate just because it sounds better, non-parenthetical narrator), she felt ready to take on more dangerous monsters in real combat (in contrast to the random assortment of things she's been doing for the last twenty-odd chapters to somehow make it this far without dying).

Maybe I should go find Leah, she mused.

In the world of *Fantasia*, monsters were naturally weaker in more developed areas and stronger in wilderness. Players could travel safely between major cities starting at around level 12—even earlier if they chose to use protected forms of transportation, such as the public coaches that connected most of the human lands. There was no clear linear progression of where to adventure as one's level increased, and where players went depended more on their inclination toward particular environments than anything else. Fey had a tendency to remain in familiar surroundings, and without the external pressure of uniting with her friend, she likely would have remained in the Elvenwood for quite a long time (driving readers looking for plot progression slowly insane).

She messaged Leah's avatar, Sirena:

<**Fey:** Hey. What level are you now?>

<**Sirena:** 18. You?>

<**Fey:** 21.>

(Yeah, Fey gained a level sometime after getting her punching blades. Just go with it.)

Sirena: *sigh* it's hard to catch up when I have to look for a new party to join every few hours when people log off or get bored of grinding.

Fey: Aww, poor baby. I'll come visit and all your "lone mage" problems will be solved.

Sirena: The idea of you playing tank does not make me feel safe in any way.

Without asking for any of the details of Fey's character build, Sirena had accurately guessed that Fey would tend more toward a "run away" style of fighting than the "stand and deliver" of a reliable tank.

Fey: Well, not tank exactly, but I could definitely draw the aggro . . . Yeah, never mind, make sure you specialize in quick-cast magic and are also able to run away while you cast.

(Fey was being honest with herself.)

Sirena: Way ahead of you. I'm going for priest so I can store up prayer points in advance.

Mages who chose to worship a particularly deity had part of their spell-casting costs borne by the deity they pledged allegiance to. (You had to pick only one; they *are* watching and don't take disloyalty very well.) In return for lower mana costs and faster casting times, religious mages had an additional Prayer bar that they had to fill with rituals and sacrifices, with spells no longer working once the player ran out of Prayer points.[39]

Fey: Sounds good. You keep training and I'll start travelling toward you.

Sirena: Excellent. If you waste time gallivanting across half the continent, I'll definitely catch up.

Fey: Um, excuse me, there will be no "gallivanting". I will be "rampaging" across the continent, leaving a trail of carnage in my wake.

Sirena: Of course, of course. Oh, looks like I found a hunting party to join; see you later!

Fey: Bye!

Fey was all fired up[40] to start her journey toward the ocean, except . . . she had no idea which direction it lay in. *The ocean is . . . east?* She vaguely remembered seeing a world map in her game manual, but had skipped over the illustration with barely a glance.

Fey opened her navigation menu, expanding the minimap that was always a translucent overlay in the corner of her vision. As she zoomed out of the local area she had already explored, the map gradually became less detailed, eventually turning a blank grey beyond the borders of the Elvenwood. *Useless.*

Fey logged off in order to do some research on the Internet.

◊◊◊

Arwyn sat up from her game chair and went to her computer desk. Turning on her laptop and logging in, she opened her favourite search engine and typed in "Fantasia world map."

Despite having only been launched for general play a few days ago, there was already a considerable amount of information about Fantasia available as players from a multitude of starting locations shared their experiences online. There were even written "starter guides," which she skipped over with a healthy dose of skepticism as to the wisdom of the advice contained within. *Puh-lease. Not a single one of the writers has even reached their first subspecialization.*

With a few clicks, she found what she was looking for: a detailed world map created by merging the information from many players' minimaps. There were still large patches of grey wilderness, likely filled with murderous high-level monsters, but all the major roads and the entire coastline were filled in.

The first thing Arwyn noticed about *Fantasia*'s main continent was . . . *It's shaped like an elephant* . . . [41] Indeed, despite some slightly jagged coastlines and a river system cutting lines across the land mass, the continent of Pantheel[42] was clearly recognizable as an elephant in profile; there was even a mountain chain that marked the curve of one huge ear.

Earth's largest land mammal was *Fantasia*'s largest mammal land; whimsical details like this were hallmarks of VirtualRealities' many successful game enterprises.

In the elephantine scheme of things, the Elvenwood was located on Pantheel's eye and ear, its great forests bounded on the west by the curved mountain chain delineating the ear. Beyond the mountains to the west, vast deserts covered the elephant's torso and back, largely unexplored beyond a few major settlements. On the belly, in the south, was the Dark Side, a volcanic area where constant ash clouds occluded the sun, perfect for demonic and undead races to thrive. The northernmost territory above the back was not land at all, but permanently frozen ocean that allowed travel and even settlement by a few cold-tolerant races.

Grasslands and plains suitable for human farming bordered the Elvenwood to the east, stretching to cover to the continent up to the trunk-and-tusk-shaped coastline. The merfolk colonies where Sirena was currently training were in the tropical waters southeast of the continent, partially sheltered by the long elephant's trunk peninsula that was prime beach land for those inclined to take a virtual vacation rather than running around doing quests.

The scale of distances on the continent was quite large, but Fey estimated that it would take less than a week to reach the southeastern coast if she took advantage of the coach system in the human lands.

In the course of her research, Arwyn was sidetracked several times, tempted into clicking on various interesting-looking articles and learning miscellaneous information about the world of *Fantasia*.

The horns of a monster are one of the most highly armoured parts of its body, but if you can shatter one, the monster generally falls unconscious.

Players who worship certain gods can refill their Prayer bar by burying or burning monster remains.

Merfolk race specialties: bonus to charisma-based abilities, 50% water affinity, racial ability to use telepathy, penalty to speed and stamina on land.

Between the necessary and very unnecessary research, Arwyn spent over an hour on the computer before logging back into *Fantasia*.

◊◊◊

As soon as Fey logged in, she received an unexpected audio chat.

"Where are you?"

Jumping in surprise at the disembodied sound, she belatedly read the notification that the sender was Blade. Grimacing, she answered, "Near town?"

"Want to meet up at the tavern?"

Not really, she thought acerbically. (Being spooked by sudden noises never put her in a good mood.) However, since the tavern was a good place to gather (free) supplies before her impending journey, she said, "Sure," and headed to the designated tree-building.

Fey was surprise to see that the interior of the tavern had undergone some major renovations. In order to accommodate the growing number of new players, Tallen had (literally) whistled up a second floor, complete with tables and benches grown out of the wood, a staircase taking up the space of a former table on the first floor.

In addition to the extra space, the tavern-keeper appeared to have recruited some extra help. While Tallen stayed in the kitchen, a young boy who looked approximately twelve years in age appeared to be in charge of seating and taking orders.

"Hello, my name is Todd and I will be your server today. May I direct you to a seat?"

Fey was highly amused at the boy's formal and clearly rehearsed lines that contrasted sharply with his youth and enthusiasm. Not wanting to hurt his feeling, she adopted an equally serious tone. "Actually, I'm meeting someone, but I'm not sure if he's already here."

"Oh!" Todd's eyes widened dramatically and he lost the artificially proper demeanour he had been assuming. "Are you Fey?" he asked excitedly.

"Why, yes I am," she said, somewhat taken aback. *Am I that famous here?*

"My dad told me all about you! Also Mr. Blade asked me to look out for you; he's upstairs." Todd had completely reverted to the excited and curious child that he actually was. Based on some similarities in their hair and facial features, she guessed that "Dad" was Tallen.

As he led the way upstairs, he chattered excitedly. "How did you get so many logs? My dad said he won't run out of wood for a year!"

"I had help," Fey answered with a smile at the memory.

"Was it Mr. Blade?"

"Nope," she said. (She tried not to sound too derisive and start corrupting the next generation with cynicism.) "It was a very nice angel who felt bad about crashing into me while he was flying and helped me with a quest."

"An angel! I've never seen one before. Did he look cool?"

"Very cool," she answered with sincerity.

On the second floor, Fey could see that Blade was sitting at a table that was curiously elevated a foot above the rest, the wood of the floor grown into a short platform extending a few steps from the edge of the benches.

"Why is that table higher?" she asked curiously.

"That's the reserved table. When the tavern is full, you can pay extra to be seated there instead of waiting in line. My dad said you and your friends can sit there for free because you're a VIP."

Stuck between expressing her admiration for Tallen's moneymaking ideas, denial that Blade was her friend (though he was on her friend list, so weak argument there), and confusion that she was a Very Important Person, Fey sat down across from Blade and merely said, "Ah, thank you, Todd."

"My dad said he'll be up with your food soon." Turning to Blade, Todd reverted to his amusingly incongruous server voice. "Would you like to see a menu, sir?"

Blade gave Fey a curious look as to why she seemed to have skipped ordering food, then said, "I'll have whatever she's having."

"Very good, sir."

Pfft. Hearing that particularly snooty waiter response come out in Todd's boyish voice nearly made Fey burst out laughing, but she managed to limit the outburst to a single cough. *He's so adorable.*

Dignity intact, Todd turned to return downstairs, then exclaimed, "There are monsters in the tavern!"

All heads in the busy eating-place turned to look, and hands went to weapons.

"They're with me," Fey said hastily, jumping out of her seat to grab her pets before someone tried to kill them. She dumped Magic and the glooms into a pouch made by her cape, then tucked Boris under one arm and retreated to her table. Amethyst was still riding on her shoulder.

In terms of remaining inconspicuous, the damage was done; most of the eyes in the tavern remained on her. Fey tried to brazen it out and kept her posture relaxed and nonchalant as she released Magic and the glooms from her cape, but she was acutely aware that the way they were hopping around was just attracting more attention. (Boris was sitting calmly on the bench beside Fey like the well-behaved pet he was. What a good boy.)

Instead of continuing downstairs, Todd trailed Fey back to her seat, waitering abandoned in favour of asking curious questions. "Why do you have monsters, Miss Fey?"

At the mention of her name, Fey's fame immediately increased.

<Fey's fame has increased to 53 (+30)!>

"They're my pets. I found them on my adventures," Fey muttered. In contrast to Todd's loud, carrying voice, her words were aimed to travel no further than Todd's ears.

"Cool!" Accepting the abbreviated explanation, Todd went back to work.

Blade was just as curious as the rest of the players. "What are these?" he asked, pointing at one of the glooms. Inkblot wriggled its ears in a rude gesture back, but nobody understood.

"Glooms," Fey answered, herding her pets to the side so they would not get in the way of the food that was coming. The glooms naturally migrated to the shady area under the table, leaving only three pets in plain view. Amethyst hopped down from Fey's shoulder and relaxed against the table, going from a teardrop shape to something closer to a pancake.

"Did you say 'gloom'?" asked an unfamiliar voice. It belonged to a player at a nearby table, an elf with an unstrung longbow leaning on the bench beside him. In a particularly forward move, he migrated seats to the VIP table, sitting to Fey's right with Boris in between. "Aren't glooms from the Dark Side? Have you travelled there already?"

"No . . . " Fey answered slowly, foreseeing a bunch of questions she did not want to answer.

"Where did you find it, then?"

"A dungeon . . . "

"A dungeon around here?"

"That's a secret," Fey said firmly. In addition to being an incredibly useful training area that would be annoying to be cluttered with players, the dungeon was enshrined in her mind as "the special place" Leandriel had shared with her, and it would take a lot more than social pressure to get the information out of her.

Thankfully for Fey, Tallen arrived upstairs carrying a large platter with several players' food, including two large, steaming bowls meant for Fey and Blade. "You can't sit there," he said to the elven archer. "This is the reserved table."

Before Fey could send the tavern-keeper a grateful look for kicking out the interloper, Tallen added, "It's ten gold a seat."

Ten gold was fairly expensive compared to the average food bill for a meal at the tavern, but a trivial amount of money for anyone above level 10, so the archer dug in his pockets for the required amount rather than argue.

Seeing a tavern-approved option to get closer, several other curious players also chose to pay the fee and moved to the VIP table. *I see why I'm a VIP,* Fey thought dryly, watching Tallen whisk away the coins with one hand while the other held the heavy platter of food steady.

Thoughts of cynicism fled when she saw the meal the tavern-keeper placed in front of her: udon noodles in soup broth. She inhaled appreciatively, the rich aroma of the steaming broth activating an appetite that was already hungry from not eating frequently enough to make up the energy she burned fighting monsters.

She dug in, slurping up the noodles. *Mmm . . . QQ.*[43] She used a term that referred to the bouncy, soft-but-chewy texture of foods such as tapioca pearls and udon.

A different player, a female elf armed with a long spear, asked, "How did you order noodles? I didn't see them on the menu."

Fey shrugged, stuffing herself with more noodles to avoid having to answer. (Not that she knew what kind of mind-reading voodoo Tallen did to come up with her favourite foods every time she visited.)

"Do you know?" the player asked Blade, who was eating, but not with the degree of enthusiasm that Fey was showing.

"I have no clue," said Blade. "I just asked for whatever she was having."

Not to be denied his fee-given right to ask questions, the first player pressed, "Is the dungeon nearby?"

Fey shook her head, leaving it up in the air as to whether that was a no to the question or a negative to answering in general.

Another player, this one dressed in mage robes, tried another line of questioning. "So how did you get monsters as pets? Is there a taming skill or something?"

"Yeah," Fey said, willing to share information on this less-secret matter.

This elicited quite a bit of interest. "How do you get the skill? Is it class-specific?"

"Not really. You just kind of be nice to them." She neglected to mention that most of her previous taming experiences involved nearly killing the creature in question before being nice to them.

"It can't be that easy, can it?" Blade asked skeptically.

"Not exactly." Fey did not have the words to accurately summarize the kinds of peculiar circumstances that had resulted in monster taming, so she did not try and ate more noodles instead.

"How many pets do you have?"

"Eight. Nine? Nine."

The surrounding players all looked at Fey strangely for not knowing her pet count, but she tended to lump all the glooms together in one shadowy pile (and so does the author).

"So it's just regular monsters in the wild? You don't have to trigger a quest or anything?" The question came from someone still wearing their newbie outfit.

"Yeah, I think theoretically, any monster can be tamed."

"I'm going to go try on a forest wolf!" One player headed out excitedly, triggering a mass exodus of around a third of the players in the tavern. Fey thought about advising them to start with a weak monster first, then mentally shrugged and continued her meal, the extra-large bowl still containing plenty of noodles despite the amount she had already consumed.

Having rested adequately under the table, the glooms started hopping restlessly around Fey's feet. She reached down and scooped the six onto the table, where they looked around or hopped as their individual natures dictated.

Fey was highly amused when Inkblot presented her with a shoelace, presumably pilfered from an unsuspecting player's boot.

"That's not really loot, you know." Inkblot tilted its ears curiously. "Loot comes from your enemies—generally dead enemies."

When Amethyst suddenly perked up at the words, Fey hastily added, "And killing players is bad." She sighed in relief when the slime relaxed again (#Pancake).

Enticed by all the cute pets, Blade carefully reached out and patted Shadow on the head. The gloom tolerated the contact for a few seconds, then hopped out of reach (#Rejected).

Blade went back to eating his noodles. "So what's up?"

"I'm heading to the east coast," Fey announced. "You're from Newtown, right? How long did it take you to get here?" The human starter city was about a hundred kilometres from the Moonwood.

"About a day?" Blade guessed. "Most of it was on coaches, but you have to walk the last twenty kilometres or so. Why are you going to the coast?"

"I'm meeting up with my friend Le— Sirena. She's a mermaid."

Blade pictured the underwater merfolk kingdom, tropical waters, coral castles, and of course, half-fish, bikini-clad girls. Unsurprisingly, the idea of visiting appealed to him. "Cool."

Fey polished off the last of her noodles, having eaten so much that her belly would have been protruding had her armour not been rigid enough to hide the bulge. "Let's go," she said to her pets. They hopped to the ground, with the exception of Amethyst, who used her bubble-arm as a grappling hook to hoist herself back onto Fey's shoulder.

Blade stood as well, looking disgruntled. "You could have asked me if I was coming along," he grumbled as he followed Fey down the stairs.

" . . . You're coming along?" Fey asked. She had assumed that the warrior would not want to return to the east, having just come from there.

"What, so I'm not invited?"

Fey sighed mentally. She did not understand why her conversations with Blade tended to take on the overtones of a lovers' quarrel. (Because the author thinks it's funny, duh.) " . . . Do you want to come?" she finally asked, calculating that it was the fastest way to end the conversation.

"Well, since you asked so nicely," Blade said with a joking grin.

Fey shook her head with 70 percent exasperation and 30 percent amusement before leading the way out.

Tallen met the group at the exit with a large package of travel food, enough to last for days. "I heard you were leaving," he said, giving the impression of being omniscient within his tavern. (Is it still an impression if it's accurate?)

"Yeah." Fey was awkward at goodbyes, and this was no exception. "Thanks for all the great food, Tallen. I'll come back to visit when I've met up with my friend."

"Looking forward to it. Bring me any delicacies you find on your trip."

"I will. Bye. Bye, Todd!" Fey waved across the room at the young waiter, who paused in the middle of writing down an order to wave enthusiastically back.

CHAPTER 24

WALK THE WALK

Let's go visit Kallara before we leave," Fey suggested.

Blade shrugged his agreement, and they headed to the healer's tree-shop, entering just as another group of players exited the establishment, presumably after buying potions. (Coincidentally, the only thing Fey hasn't done.)

Kallara looked up from the shop's till. "Hello, you two. How are you doing?" she asked with her usual smile.

"I'm great," Fey said. "I switched out my weapons and armour," she added happily, unable to refrain from showing off her new and deadlier equipment despite the fact that Kallara would probably be entirely unimpressed.

"Very nice," Kallara said (clearly humouring Fey). "And you, young man?"

"Oh, I upgraded my equipment, too. Nothing fancy." After reaching level 20, Blade had purchased another set of plate armour and a new sword in a slightly higher grade of steel. The only real change in his appearance was the addition of a small round shield on his off hand.

"Wonderful. You two look ready for adventure."

"Actually, we're going on a trip to the coast, to meet up with my friend, who's a mermaid," said Fey.

Kallara looked suitably sorrowful to see her favourite players leave the Moonwood. "Well, I'll miss you. Be sure to come back to visit."

Aww. Fey was moved by the healer's display of emotion. "I will," she promised. "I'll get a teleport key and visit from every town that has a teleportation gate." Teleportation gates could be activated by paying a moderate fee in gold with each trip or by buying a key, essentially an unlimited pass, with real-life currency.

"That's so kind of you," Kallara said with a (devious) glint in her eye.

In a much more businesslike voice, she continued, "I assume you will be travelling along the human roads?"

"Uh, yeah." Fey was rather confused by the sudden change in demeanour and watched curiously as the healer pulled out a sheet of paper and began to draw.

Aww, she's drawing me a map. The sketch revealed itself to be a fairly accurate rendering of Fey's planned route.

Kallara then proceeded to mark specific locations on the map and label them with letters. This made no sense until she flipped the paper over and drew a legend to explain the labels. Task done, she handed the sheet over to Fey while Blade looked on curiously.

Fey had to flip back and forth several times to cross-reference the information, but eventually figured out that the map and legend marked the locations and descriptions of various potion ingredients the apothecary wanted her to collect. "You sneaky . . . Sneaky!" she exclaimed, her name-calling abilities failing her.

Kallara's smiled mischievously. "You'll gain quest experience for each ingredient you bring me," she bribed, creating a quest offer.

" . . . Fine," Fey grumbled, knowing it was a good offer but feeling ill-used by the emotional manipulation.

Blade also accepted the quest, with considerably less moral outrage. Remembering his earlier herb-collecting misadventures, he asked, "Could we get the levels and abilities of the herb monsters?"

"Now, that wouldn't be any fun," said Kallara. "Where's your sense of adventure?"

"Is that your way of saying you don't know?" Fey asked.

"Of course not," Kallara said, eyes twinkling. "Just that I would not deprive you of the thrill of discovery."

Fey decided it would be a good time to make a melodramatic exit. "Let's go," she said grumpily.

"Wait!" Kallara pulled out a box of lesser healing potions, capable of healing 200 health each, and gave five to each player. (Yay, free stuff!) "Just in case," she said. (Not that this is foreshadowing or anything.)

Fey was slightly mollified by the bribe. "Thanks, Kallara. See you later!"

Choosing the correct trail heading east, Fey set off at her usual "going somewhere" pace, an extremely fast walk that rivalled slow jogging in speed. There was a particular trick to the gait that made it possible to go quickly without extra strain or tension, and she could maintain the pace all day.

Blade clearly had not mastered this particular trick, falling behind until he broke into a jog to keep up. "What's the rush?"

"I'm not rushing, I'm walking at my normal pace."

Blade dropped back to a walk and tried to match Fey's speed, straining to take faster steps without much success.

"You're doing it all wrong," said Fey (judgementally).

"I'm *walking* wrong?"

"Yes. Stop leaning forward, don't tense your muscles, and push off with your toes." Fey exaggerated the movement, rising completely onto the balls of her feet with each step in a childish walk that she mentally referred to as "tripping along." It was even faster than her normal walk, but it looked silly and resulted in calf cramps when maintained for too long.

When Blade failed to immediately grasp the intricacies of fast walking (not that Fey had actually explained all the intricacies), Fey sighed and dropped to a (slightly) slower walk. "You'll figure it out eventually." She had never explained the process before, but she had successfully trained several friends in real life, including Leah, to walk quickly by cruelly leaving them trailing behind until their bodies naturally picked up the trick.

"I can't believe I'm getting walking lessons," Blade muttered.

"If you could walk at a decent pace, we wouldn't be going this slowly," Fey countered.

Since she no longer had to focus on walking at top speed, Fey decided it was a good idea to multitask and train Immunity.

"Amethyst, poison mushroom slime."

The slime obediently secreted a layer of the toxin, and Fey's world became blurry as the poison took effect.

"Still poisoning yourself?" asked Blade.

"Why wouldn't I be?"

"Because it's [censored word]ing uncomfortable?"

"Oh, this one doesn't hurt at all," Fey assured him. "Wanna try?" She held Amethyst out by dangling the slime by the bubble.

Knowing he was probably going to regret it, Blade gingerly poked the still-poisonous slime.

<Blade has been poisoned!>

<Poison mushroom poison: −4 health/20 seconds.>

<Duration: 10 minutes.>

<Level 1 Immunity effect: −1 damage per poison infliction.>

<New poison effect: −3 health/20 seconds.>

<Duration: 10 minutes.>

"Gah! I can't see!" Blade exclaimed, coming to a halt. Having perfect vision in real life, Blade had no experience navigating a world of blurry blobs and splotches of colour.

"Sure, you can see," said Fey (in the tone of an adult reassuring a child that there were no monsters under the bed). "Look, I'm waving at you."

Blade could indeed see a skin-coloured blob moving back and forth, but the sight did not reassure him that he could safely navigate the forest trails in his present conditions.

"Oh, come on, it'll be fine." Fey pushed Blade back into walking. His arms came up uncertainly as if he were afraid of crashing into something at any moment. (Silly, he's much more likely to trip on a tree root.)

"If this is what you consider a mild side effect, I'd hate to see what you consider bad," Blade muttered.

"Furyweed," Fey answered immediately, some lingering horror making it into her voice.

"What's that?"

"You don't want to know," Fey said firmly. It was an experience that she would only wish upon her worst enemies, and Blade did not fall into that category. (He falls into "miscellaneous.")

After walking for a while, the glooms began lagging behind, their undersized ears drooping with fatigue.

"Poor babies," Fey said, gathering them up to carry. The six glooms were fairly light and insubstantial, but having her hands occupied making a pouch with her cape was rather inconvenient.

"Hey, you guys can change shape, right? Turn into rings."

Each gloom interpreted "ring" in a different way, morphing into a range of sizes from a thick manacle to a large hula hoop.

"Oh, you guys crack me up," she said in a highly amused voice.

Blade watched the interaction, seeing a softer, more affectionate side of Fey than he had so far experienced. (He wanted to complain about the unfair treatment but was aware of the lack of sympathy he would get.) "Want some help?" he offered, holding a hand out to carry some of the glooms.

"Mm . . . I got it, thanks." Fey found places for all the shadow-pets on her person, three acting as inky necklaces of different lengths, one wrapped around each of her forearms, and one going around her waist. "You can carry Boris if you want." The sturdy boar was still trotting along gamely with Magic on his back, but Fey thought it would be unfair for him to be the only one not being carried.

Blade picked the boar up, who settled down after a brief struggle for freedom. ("Lemme go! Aww, fine.") Magic transferred his sticking power onto Blade's smooth plate armour, hopping in circles around his torso like some strange planetary orbit.

"How is it doing that?" Blade asked, twisting around to see when Magic paused at the small of his back.

"No idea. It certainly isn't based on physics or biology." (Ninety-nine percent realism. Yeah, right.)

Inspection over, the mushroom jumped from human to elf, coming to a rest on Fey's head.

"You can't stay up there, you know," Fey said, keeping her head straight to avoid disturbing her pet's position. "My neck will get sore."

Magic squeaked cutely. ("But the view is nice from up here.")

"Fine. Twenty minutes."

"How do you know what it's saying?" Blade asked.

"I don't. I just make up fake dialogue," Fey said with a grin.

A few hours later, the group broke free of the forest. The thin hiking trail widened into a spacious road that could accommodate carriages passing each other in opposite directions.

A tall post bearing the logo of the travel coach company marked the travel stop, topped by a clock that was synchronized with all the other stops and waystations it ran.

"How often does a coach arrive?" Fey asked Blade.

"Every hour, I think? It depends on the route."

"On the hour?"

"I can't remember."

Fey was unexpectedly met with the fantasy game version of waiting for a bus. Fortunately, she also had fantasy-game options to occupy her time.

"Magic, cast attracting Spore."

A sweet-smelling cloud of particles diffused outward. After reaching level 10, Spore had improved its base range to fifty metres (164 feet). In the open air outside the forest, effects such as wind currents could take it even farther.

"Get ready," Fey told Blade, dropping her pets to the ground, clipping the weights to her boots, and drawing her punching blades.

"For what?"

"No idea." Fey seemed irresponsibly blasé about randomly attracting any monsters in range, but she reasoned that nothing particularly dangerous would live so close to something as urban as a major road.

"Great," Blade muttered, drawing his sword. Somehow, adventuring with Fey had made him start to dislike surprises.

The monsters that arrived first were the closest and weakest, cartoonish creatures that hopped and toddled out of the grass and nearby forest. (They shall not be further described because the author is lazy.)

Fey did not bother attacking. "Go," she said to her pets, who hopped and toddled forward to meet their wild counterparts. The Feypets were of a similar size and original strength to their opponents, but having levelled up far beyond their base level, were now considerably stronger. A (cute?) slaughter ensued.

While Blade walked around rather half-heartedly stabbing the tiny monsters, Fey occupied herself with ferrying Magic around while he used Drain, transferring the mushroom from dried husk to fresh victim so he could save time between attacks.

<Magic's Drain has reached level 8!>

<Poison mushroom poison has worn off.>

While Blade had declined to continue training Immunity after his first experience with blurry vision, Fey had continued applying poison effects whenever they wore off, increasing her Immunity to level 5.

"Amethyst, poison mushroom slime." She walked over to where the slime was cheerfully mashing some plant monsters into paste and poked the toxic secretions.

<Fey has been poisoned!>

"You're still doing that at a time like this?" Blade asked incredulously.

"A time like what?"

"Com . . . bat. Never mind." Blade had to admit that there was no danger or urgency in what they were doing. He was even starting to feel guilty about all the cute creatures he was killing.

"Besides, I can still kill things," Fey said, stomping on a brown monster in demonstration; with her vision impaired, she could only distinguish its size and colour. If anything, the blurriness was helpful because she did not have to see how cute it was.

A second wave of monsters appeared, slightly higher in level than the first group but still weaker than her level 12. Fey treated it as an opportunity to level up her and her pets' skills, able to spam repetitive attacks as the monsters lacked the intelligence to take advantage of their predictability.

Between fighting the weak monsters and collecting loot, the party passed a moderately productive forty-seven minutes until the travel coach arrived.

———◦◦◇◦◦———

(The author has banned the snarky narrator from this and all future Leandriel point of view scenes in order to preserve his dignity. Bye-bye.)

Leandriel was dithering. He was rather unfamiliar with the activity, being fairly decisive in most areas of life, but the word was accurate to describe his current state of uncertainty.

His ambivalence could be directly attributable to a certain female elf on his friend list.

He was deep in the Oré[44] Mountains bounding the Elvenwood to the west, several hundred kilometres from the nearest teleportation gate. His quarry at the moment was the first dragon he had ever hunted, the weakest level 100 bronze dragon.

Regardless of level, dragons were formidable boss monsters with high strength, devastating breath attacks, nearly impenetrable skills, and unparalleled magic resistance. They were monsters that entire armies banded together to attack, often only to be barbecued and eaten.

Despite the danger of his task, Leandriel was not particularly worried about his chances. Kevin had calculated that with his current abilities and equipment, he could win, and Leandriel trusted his friend's analytic capabilities, which had seen him through quest after quest.

No, the dilemma that occupied Leandriel's thoughts was whether to PM his new friend.

He was very aware that since he was busy with work and had no plans with Fey today, his normal behaviour was to leave her alone.

But . . . he wanted to say hi.

Leandriel's dithering had started a while ago, when the elf had logged on for the first time that night. She had quickly logged out again, and Leandriel had been able to focus on fighting his way toward the mountain where the dragon laired. Several in-game hours later, she had re-entered the game, and he was navigating the labyrinthine tunnel system that guarded the bronze dragon's hoard, dithering.

He could sense that he was getting close to his destination. Annoyed with himself, he finally decided to just send a PM. In his current distracted state, fighting something like a dragon would certainly lead to his death.

Leandriel: Hello.

Fey: Hi! What's up?

Fey's cheerful reply instantly removed any apprehension Leandriel felt about his course of action while simultaneously making him feel silly for being apprehensive in the first place.

Leandriel: I am hunting a bronze dragon.

Fey: Awesome! That's much cooler than what I'm doing.

Leandriel: And what would that be?

Fey: Sitting in a travel coach.

Leandriel: Are you travelling somewhere?

Fey: To Newtown, for now. I'm on my way to the merfolk colonies, where my friend Sirena is.

Leandriel assumed that Fey was referring to a friend from outside the game, as there would have been no opportunity for an elf to meet a mermaid in the beginner stage of *Fantasia*. It made him wonder about the kind of person Fey would befriend.

<**Leandriel:** Quite the journey.>

<**Fey:** Yeah. I'm pretty bored right now, sitting around like this. Tell me more about the bronze dragon.>

<**Leandriel:** Well, it is level 100, about 15 metres long, not including the neck and tail. Its elemental affinities are earth and metal, and its breath attack is a corrosive gas that damages both metal and organic materials.>

<**Fey:** Are you going to be okay?>

<**Fey:** Not that I don't think you can handle it!>

He smiled at the unnecessary worry.

Leandriel: Thank you for the concern. I am fairly confident of my chances, and I have dragonsbane with me.

Fey: What's that?

Leandriel: Dragonsbane is an herb that temporarily disables a dragon's breath attack when inhaled. It is fairly rare and hard to come by—it has to be imported from the southern rainforests—but invaluable when going on a hunt like this.

Fey: Oh, you're well prepared, then. Go kick that dragon's scaly butt!

His smile morphed into a grin at the colourful language.

Leandriel: Haha, I will. Safe journey.

Fey: I'd wish you luck, but you don't need it. Bye!

Well. If Fey had such confidence in him, he certainly could not disappoint a lady. Leandriel went to find a scaled behind to kick.

CHAPTER 25
SLAYING BOREDOM

W hy are you smiling?" Blade asked. He and Fey were sitting in a coach, making a somewhat bumpy journey over to Newtown. The setting did nothing to explain Fey's unfocused and somewhat goofy smile.

Fey blinked and refocused on her surroundings. "Mm, what? Oh, I was just talking to a friend through private messaging."

"Your mermaid friend?"

"Uh, no, another one." Fey shifted her jaw to the side in an effort to stop smiling, but the corners of her mouth refused to come down. *I'm a goner. My brain is mush after such a short conversation.*

Blade waited expectantly for further explanation but received only silence (made creepy by the fact that Fey's typical, relentlessly neutral expression was now an unexplained smile). Distracted by her attempts to control her facial muscles, Fey failed to notice the gaping hole in the conversation.

Shaking his head, Blade let the matter rest, displaying great wisdom in accepting Fey's odd behaviour without too much questioning.

(Therein lies madness.) He was displaying a necessary quality for anyone who chose to be friends with her: a high level of tolerance. Fey's unmodulated personality was like a force of nature in its difficulty to predict, wide range of outcomes, and inability to be quelled by any human invention. Rather than fighting it, her friends chose to go along with the randomness, with varying levels of amusement. In return, Fey offered deep and steadfast friendship, her support ranging anywhere from providing a sympathetic ear for complaints to verbally castrating her friends' enemies (Is the word "castrate" allowed in a PG context?), all the way to helping plan diabolical revenge plots that nonetheless did not break any laws, depending on the situation at hand.

The corners of Fey's mouth were still slightly higher than usual, but she had mostly managed to school her face into a semblance of neutrality. To distract herself, she pulled out Kallara's map. "It looks like one of the herbs is available right outside Newtown."

Blade nodded. "What's it called?"

"Tear grass." The accompanying illustration showed a blue grass, otherwise nondescript in appearance. (See how the author didn't otherwise describe it? Hahaha so clever.)

"I bet it cries when it's under attack," Blade joked.

"More like it makes *us* cry," Fey said, half-seriously.

(Tune in next chapter to see who's right.)

━━◦◦◦◇◦◦◦━━

(Okayokay, leaving. No need to push.)

Leandriel knew he was almost upon the dragon's lair when he heard the slow, deep breathing of an immense creature. Walking as quietly as he could, he went around a bend in the tunnel and came upon the bronze dragon's sleeping form.

Everything about the fantasy creature suggested lethal beauty. Despite its size, it was perfectly proportioned and delicately formed in a way that suggested sleekness and speed. Its scales had the metallic lustre of polished bronze, though Leandriel knew they were far harder than the metal it was named after. They armoured the dragon from the tip of its nose down to the end of its tail, the largest and toughest over its back and the outside of its legs, transitioning to smaller, thinner plates in areas that required flexibility.

Despite its reptilian body and bat-like wings, the dragon reminded Leandriel of a cat in the way that it was sleeping. Forelimbs with scimitar-like claws were tucked neatly under a head the size of an entire horse, membranous wings tucked neatly against its back, its long, flexible tail curled compactly around its body to nearly touch its nose.

Piled around it was its glittering hoard. Dragons in *Fantasia* had a stereotypically magpie-like love of shiny, glittering objects. The bronze dragon had collected a huge assortment of light-reflecting objects, anything from bits of iron pyrite and quartz scavenged from nearby rivers to ore-rich chunks of rock and rough gemstones gouged out of the nearby mountains. Amongst the natural treasures were the occasional bits of crafted items, pieces of plate armour from hapless adventurers or piles of gold coins from unfortunate merchants travelling through the area.

Leandriel carefully avoided the scattered minerals, his enchanted boots helping him make his way to the dragon's head with a minimum of noise. Stealth was not his class's strong suit, but he had enough intrinsic dexterity to sneak up on a creature whose quiet breathing was the equivalent of a strong wind.

He paused and centred himself before making his next move. It would take speed, strategy, and a good deal of luck to come out of the impending battle without major injury.

From his pouch, Leandriel pulled out a handful of dragonsbane. The dried plant was brittle and crumbled easily in his grasp. Timing it to one of the dragon's inhalations, he blew the herb powder into a draconian nostril.

The dragon sneezed, a thunderous burst of air that boomed like cannon fire and forced Leandriel back a few stumbling steps. The dragon sneezed again and again, so distracted that Leandriel was able to retreat behind a rocky outcropping and conceal himself.

It became clear that the dragon was having a classic allergic reaction, sneezing repeatedly and dripping tears and snot in a decidedly un-fantastical way. Leandriel stifled a chuckle. He supposed that was one way to stop it from using its breath attack. Fey would love it.

As the sneezing and accompanying gusts of wind died down, Leandriel drew his sword and launched his first attack.

"Holy Lance."

A beam of physical force shot out of the tip of his sword, turning it into a magical lance. The skill was especially suited for large, boss-type monsters, concentrating the force of his attack down to a single point rather than dissipating it in extended slashes.

The downside of the point attack was the difficulty of aiming. If the angle was off by a fraction of a degree, the lance tip would move critical inches away from his target. Rather than piercing the joint where the dragon's forehead met its body, he was a handsbreadth off, his attack glancing off the great scales over its ribs. The dragon roared, the sound deafening despite a certain muffled quality from its state of nasal congestion.

Leandriel leaped backward in a wing-assisted jump as the great beast snapped its jaws closed where he had been standing a split second earlier. He passed close enough to hit the dragon with his sword blade, but his strike connected with the bony ridge above its eye, barely leaving a scratch. As soon as it oriented on his new position, it struck again, then again, relentlessly fast and deadly.

Leandriel dodged and parried, moving at a speed that denied conscious thought. He was aware of nothing but the dragon, the ground and its various obstacles, and the sword in his hands.

Whenever he had the opportunity, he loosed Holy Lance, managing to inflict minor wounds that bled sluggishly.

Though the bronze dragon lacked the true intelligence of the greater dragons, it was not without its own cunning. As Leandriel became more accustomed to its attacks and more adept at inflicting wounds, the dragon abruptly changed tactics. Leandriel was suddenly struck from behind by a great lashing tail. It felt as if a tree had fallen on him.

Stunned and knocked off his feet, he was unable to dodge as jaws equipped with teeth the size of short swords closed around his torso. He felt a searing pain in his left wing, but his armour, made of a blessed titanium-mithril alloy, held against the crushing power of dragon jaws. There was a sizzling sound as the dragon's corrosive saliva went to work on feathers and metal alike.

Grimly focusing through the pain, Leandriel kept his grip on his sword and thrust into the only vulnerable spot he could reach: the dragon's right nostril. The dragon roared in displeasure, causing Leandriel to tumble to the ground. He forced himself to his feet, casting Cleanse to stop his armour from further degradation, and dropped into a fighting stance.

The dragon was still roaring in pain, the intensity of the sound a tangible pressure on Leandriel's skin. Hot blood dripped in a steady trickle from the dense network of capillaries in its nose, the most damage he had managed to inflict so far, but still trivial in the context of its immense size.

A dragon with allergies and a nosebleed, Leandriel thought, taking advantage of its distraction to take cover and cast Healing Light on himself. *Fey would really love it.* The spell repaired most of the damage to his flesh, but at least one broken bone had shifted out of place and was unable to fuse back together. The limb flared with pain every time he moved it, but it would have to do; the dragon was attacking again, angrier than ever.

He dodged as the dragon swiped at him with its great claws. It appeared that the beast was now wary of allowing its head within reach of his sword, forgoing its previous attempts to bite him in favour of wary, catlike swipes. He took advantage of the fear, shifting his aim to launch Holy Lance toward its head. The strikes missed more often, or glanced off the dragon's tough, bony jaw, but they caused it to flinch and lose offensive momentum.

Leandriel circled around to the dragon's side, positioning himself where it would be awkward for the beast's claws to reach him. The dragon started to reposition itself to face him square on, then abruptly reversed direction, whipping out its massive tail. He leaped over the first attack, but was still in the air when the tail reversed direction, crashing into his shins and knocking him onto his front.

In a feat of strength that would certainly be impossible in real life, Leandriel caught himself one-handed, the other still holding his sword, and pushed off hard enough to regain his feet. By this time, the tail was already whipping back for a third pass and he was barely able to turn to face the attack before it struck him full in the torso, whipping him into involuntary flight.

Leandriel instinctively beat his wings despite the broken bone and managed to slow himself enough that when he crashed into the cavern wall, no new bones were broken. His armour held, his helmet cushioning the impact enough that he did not suffer a concussion.

It was clear that he would have to do something to disable the dragon's tail if he wanted any chance of winning the fight. He scanned the appendage for weakness, zeroing in on the extra-flexible area where tail met body.

"Go kick that dragon's scaly butt!" he recalled. Perhaps there was some unintended wisdom in the words.

Leandriel charged. He angled his advance in a zig-zag pattern that kept the dragon's sweeping tail attacks in view, casting Holy Lance completely randomly, releasing light bolts in whichever direction his sword happened to be pointing as he ran. As sometimes occurred with random attacks, he managed to pierce the dragon's most vulnerable spot: a reddish, slit-pupiled eye.

The dragon roared and thrashed, its movements erratic and unpredictable. Leandriel was caught by its spasming tail, but, now nearer to its base than its tip, it lacked the power to do more than stagger him for a few steps.

He was now within direct striking distance. Wasting no time, he activated every ability he had to increase his attack power, reversed his grip on the sword, and plunged it down in a two-handed strike at the base of the tail. As it plunged through the smaller, weaker scales there, he launched a skill:

"Holy Impact!"

While warriors gradually increased the range of what was considered melee combat as they levelled up, their most devastating attacks remained when their weapons made direct contact with the enemy.

Holy Impact was a dual-purpose skill; when directed into the ground, it functioned as an area-of-attack skill that sent waves of holy force through the ground, stunning and damaging any monsters who were standing in the area.

In contrast, used directly on a monster, the shockwaves it generated reverberated within the body, building upon themselves with constructive interference[45] with truly devastating results.

With a huge boom and burst of light, Leandriel's attack shattered the dragon's vertebra and paralyzed its tail. The monster's sheer size kept it from dying from the attack, but it spasmed and shook, too dazed and disoriented to even roar.

The dragon was injured and stunned, but not yet dying. Leandriel repeated the attack, this time aiming for the joint where the hind leg met its body. With another explosion of light, he destroyed the joint and hit an artery, the leg spurting gouts of blood as it collapsed and unbalanced the massive creature.

Leandriel jumped back from the corrosive fluid, hearing it sizzle as it splashed over the rock floor—in a few cases cleaning gem-embedded rock chunks until the uncut gems fell gleaming to the floor. Backing up further, he watched the dragon's death throes from a safe distance, healing what he could without taking his eyes off the creature in case it rallied for a final attack.

He had to dodge a few blind charges, but the dragon was done; after a few minutes, it collapsed with a splash in a pool of its own blood. The impact shook the whole cavern with a boom.

<Leandriel has defeated the bronze dragon!>

<Leandriel has gained 6,600 experience.>

<Leandriel's earth affinity has increased to 5% (+5%)!>

<Leandriel's metal affinity has increased to 5% (+5%)!>

<Leandriel has earned the title Dragon Slayer!>

<Leandriel's fame has increased to 12,300 (+2,000)!>

Leandriel leaned tiredly against the wall, surveying the cavern as his breathing slowed. There was a hoard of minerals and treasures now scattered all over the ground, but the most valuable loot from a dragon by far was its body. Its nearly indestructible scales were invaluable components for armour, as strong as adamantium and imbued with innate magic resistance. Its magical, corrosive blood, which was even now etching its own pool into the cavern floor, could be mixed into war potions that could devastate armies. Even its flesh, prepared correctly, could be eaten for permanent stat boosts in strength, magic resistance, and elemental affinity.

He eyed the hulk before him. Even with his magical belt pouch that shrank and lightened its contents by a factor of 10,000, he was doubtful of his ability to fly while carrying an entire dragon.

He shrugged, wincing as the movement jostled his injured wing. He would not be able to set the bone by himself anyway. Gathering the spoils, he set off on the long but victorious walk to the nearest settlement.

—◆◇◆◇◆—

(*ahem* Let it be known that it is the opinion of this narrator that the previous scene could have been amusingly improved with the addition of snarky comments, and that this opinion was put forth to the author and summarily rejected without cause. And now on to our regular programming.)

Fey was bored sitting in the carriage. Really bored. One might call it "dangerously bored." Unable to feel sleepy in the game, her mind was clear and alert while having nothing to do. She slumped in a corner of the carriage, discontentedly poking Amethyst with a finger. The slime did not appear to mind.

<Amethyst's Double Membrane has reached level 9!>

Fey's eyes widened in surprise. It appeared that the slime could improve the strength of her membrane by means other than cannibalism.

She was immensely cheered by the idea that she could train skills other than Immunity while cooped up in the carriage.

"Here." Fey passed her pet to Blade. "Poke Amethyst for me."

"Huh? Why?"

"It's for training her defence skills."

"Oh. Well, in that case . . . " Blade extended his index finger and poked the slime. Amethyst's squishy texture was rather fun to compress; combined with his dislike of her tendency to poison him, he began to poke harder and faster. (*pokepokepoke*)

The rougher treatment did not hurt, but when Amethyst sensed that Blade was enjoying himself too much, she retaliated by secreting thornweed poison.

<Blade has been poisoned!>

"Ow! [Censored word]!"

Blade dropped the slime and shook out his hand, the side effect of thornweed being local pain to the area of contact. (This was somehow never mentioned in the six previous chapters where the poison was used.) "You little piece of slime!" (He didn't actually say "slime" there.)

Fey looked up from where she was busy poking and prodding the glooms, looking for some skill or ability to train. "If she poisoned you, just poke her harder," she goaded, not above manipulating Blade to train her slime more efficiently.

Blade snatched Amethyst up and poked her as if he would really like to punch her instead. After Fey winked at Amethyst, the slime tolerated the treatment without complaint. She did, however, continue to secrete thornweed poison whenever the previous effect wore off.

<Blade's Immunity has reached level 2!>

In this manner, Blade and Amethyst improved their abilities (at the cost of further deteriorating their relationship).

Fey eventually settled on rolling her glooms up in her holy element cape to increase their elemental resistance before moving on to looking for something for Boris to do.

"Hmm, a new skill, maybe?" The boar's only innate skills were Charge and Rage, both of which had activation conditions that did not suit the confines of a moving carriage.

Boris had all the features and proportions of a wild boar, with a heavy, muscular body; tough, bristled hide; and slightly curved tusks, all of which would make him a formidable opponent in combat—if he had the size to back it up. His miniature size meant that straightforward physical attacks would not be particularly effective against opponents above his weight category.

Fey pondered what would fit his natural inclinations and talents while putting him in less physical danger. "Hmm. An intimidation skill, maybe? Okay, Boris, stare at Blade like you're going to kill him."

Boris turned in the direction of the human and gave his best glare. The boar's eyes briefly flashed red.

<Boris has learned glare!>

<Glare: reduce the attack power and attack initiative of opponents you make direct eye contact with.>

The Glare skill was similar to Fey's Terrify (minus the weird screeching noise), but was limited to one opponent at a time, with a proportionally stronger debuffing effect.

"Good job!" Fey praised, delighted at the boar's quick progress. "Now just keep practicing."

Blade shivered, unsure what part was the naturally unsettled feeling he would get at seeing demonically red eyes and what was the ability's fear effect. "Does he have to glare at *me*?"

"Who else would he Glare at?"

"You."

Fey snorted. "Boris wuvs me," she said in a baby voice, giving the boar a hug. He snuggled briefly into her arms, then went back to practicing Glare on Blade.

In his state of discomfiture, Blade had neglected to continue poking Amethyst. The slime smacked him with her bubble to get his attention.

"Why you little—!" (*Simpsons* reference.) Abandoning a single-finger poke, Blade chopped at Amethyst with the edge of his hand. Amethyst's body contents were pushed to the sides in neat halves, but she bounced back from the strike no worse the wear. After a few chops, a renewed Glare effect distracted him, and Amethyst smacked him again. In this manner, the cycle of anger and fear continued until, finally,

<Blade has learned Fighting Spirit[46]!>

<Fighting Spirit: overcome intimidation and fear-based debuffs with the power of your emotions.>

(Apparently, being bullied has its benefits. What doesn't kill you really does make you stronger in *Fantasia*. Not that Blade was about to thank anyone for all the unintended ability development.)

Now Magic was the only pet not in training. Fey picked up the mushroom thoughtfully. "Well, you're already pretty badass." Between Drain and Spore, the mushroom just needed to continue levelling up to become a truly terrifying opponent.

Magic squeaked, eager to join in and be assigned some kind of training.

"I guess you could cast Spore out the window." (Approximately 999 of 1,000 people would advise against this course of action. No comment on who the last person would be.)

Fey's version of caution was to tell Magic to restrict his Spore effects to paralysis and sleep, reasoning that it would render any monsters unable to chase after the carriage. (If one thought about it more, one would come to the conclusion that it would just narrow the monsters coming after the carriage to the ones strong enough to shrug off the status effects.) Fortunately, the lands surrounding the carriage routes were clear of high-level monster spawns, and the party survived the particularly reckless decision without incident.

Seeing everyone else hard at work, Fey looked for something she could do. (Apparently, being constantly poisoned was a given at this point and training Immunity did not count.) She rummaged in her backpack and pulled out the large flask of water originally meant to let Amethyst train Osmosis. She figured she could practice Enchant; the spell itself could not be levelled up by repeated casting, but she had a small chance of increasing her intelligence attribute with each repetition, and the resulting enchanted water might come in handy later.

"Water."

Fey's maximum mana was now over 200 and she could do a proper iteration of the spell, but her Enchant still had a reduced effect compared to what Kallara had accomplished.

<Spell efficiency decreased due to magic-insulating equipment.>

Whazzat? Fey looked at her equipment menu, which summarized the physical and magical effects of each piece of armour she wore. Next to every single piece that contained metal, a penalty to magic was displayed.

In *Fantasia*, it was possible to belong to multiple classes and all attributes naturally increased with level, so it was very plausible that mages could have sufficient strength to wear heavy armour. Rather than use artificial class restrictions to limit what equipment players could wear to balance combat advantages, the game designers had introduced an extra property to materials not seen in the real world: magic conductivity.

Somewhat opposite to electrical conductivity, organic materials conducted magic the most efficiently, while metals generally acted as magic insulators. Therefore, to ensure their spells had maximum attack power, mages were relegated to the silk and cotton robes they stereotypically wore in games and books. Treated materials, such as leather, fell somewhere in the middle of magic conductivity, providing neither a bonus nor a penalty to spells.

With her custom armour, Fey was now wearing a great deal of metal. Sighing, she began the tedious process of unbuckling and unsnapping all the metal pieces, leaving her in a thin shirt and leggings.

"Uh, what are you doing?" asked Blade.

"Magic," Fey answered in a put-upon voice.

Magic the mushroom looked up expectantly.

"Not you, Magic," Fey said, patting the mushroom. He went back to casting Spore out the window.

"Ah." (Blade actually understood what Fey was talking about in this instance because he had read the entire game manual like a responsible gamer and knew what magic conductivity was.)

After divesting herself of metals, Fey cast Enchant again, purposely triggering it when her mana stores were just below the spell cost, because overdrawing her mana would be the best way to encourage her intelligence attribute to grow.

Thus Fey's dangerous levels of boredom led her party to becoming more dangerous as a whole.

CHAPTER 26

PETTABLE

"Freeeedom!"

Fey opened the carriage door and hopped out as soon as it was safe to do so. Players waiting at the travel post—marked by a literal post in the ground, complete with the company logo and signature clock—were treated to the unusual sight of the procession of pets that hopped and tumbled down the carriage steps after her.

Blade exited in a slower, more dignified manner. He had to hurry (in a much less dignified manner) to catch up to Fey, who was exercising her newfound freedom by walking rapidly into town.

Fey gazed around at the bustling settlement of Newtown. It appeared to be modelled after a village prior to the advent of industrial machinery, with cobblestone streets and one- to two-storey buildings. The tallest building in view was some kind of church with a clock tower and a huge bell, the stylized sun symbol it displayed not one she was familiar with.

Being the starter town for human players, the majority of people in view sported round ears and newbie outfits, but there were enough players who had upgraded their gear that Fey and Blade did not stand out too much.

"Ooh look, a pet shop!" Fey rushed over to a glass storefront lettered with "Ye Olde Pet Shoppe" in fancy font. Wanting to see what was available and get out of the crowded streets, she opened the door and slipped inside. (Blade was pulled along by the invisible but powerful herd instinct.)

Rather than live animals, the pet shop displayed many eggs of various shapes, colours, and sizes. Players who did not have pet-taming skills relied on the imprinting[47] instinct to bond with newly hatched creatures and had to raise them into adulthood before they would start gaining levels and skills.

Fey scanned the cards on the displays that indicated the species and price of each egg. There were more than a few creatures where it seemed implausible that they would be born from an egg, but Fey supposed magical handwaving could explain away all the inconveniences of biological accuracy.

The lowest price for common creatures such as ordinary cats and small birds was 5000g and quickly jumped into the hundreds of thousands for rarer magical creatures. For absolute beginners who had not yet amassed any savings, a pet egg was out of reach, and Fey's party was alone in the shop.

"May I help you, miss?" The pet shop owner was a generic-looking human male (because the author is a lazy noodle and doesn't bother putting effort into one-off characters).

"Uh, just looking around." Fey hated being stared at while browsing in a store, so she nudged Blade with her elbow. "You should get one."

As Fey had hoped, the shopkeeper turned his attention to Blade. "Anything look interesting, sir?"

⸻◦◦◇◇◦◦⸻

Blade was rather inclined toward buying a pet. He had a reasonable sum of money saved, his equipment upgrades considerably cheaper than Fey's due to opting for standard sword, shield, and heavy armour. "What would you recommend for a warrior?" he asked.

Sensing his first impending sale (after days of dealing with broke n00bs), the shopkeeper went from somewhat bored to extremely enthusiastic. "Of course! I can recommend pets to fit every budget and fighting style! For warriors, we have pets with magical attacks to help balance your damage type, fast pets that complement your attacks to add a little bit of extra damage, pets with high defence to anchor your party, and pets with ranged attacks of all kinds! We also have pets that are more useful out of battle, such as ones that can serve as mounts once they reach adulthood, ones with extra-keen senses for scouting and sensing traps, and pets with a whole variety of special abilities that are suitable for all kinds of environments!"

"Er . . . " Blade was struck with decision paralysis. He did not yet have a clear idea of his exact play style and the type of pet that would best complement it.

Fey chimed in with her opinion. "Get a fire-element magic type," she said, reasoning that you could never go wrong with setting your enemies on fire.

"Excellent suggestion, miss!" The shopkeeper went around the store and collected various eggs off the shelves to place on the counter. They ranged in size from smaller than a robin's egg to several times that of an ostrich egg. Most were in various shades of yellow and orange, some evenly coloured, some with spots and swirly patterns. ("Swirly" is such a fun word.)

Blade had no way of judging the unhatched pets based on their egg appearance, so he simply pointed at one near the top of his budget at 10,000g. "What's that?" (Holy crap, he's a much better saver than Fey is. It probably helps that he doesn't have a hoarding issue that keeps him from selling junk items.)

"Ah, you have an excellent eye! This is a fyrfalcon egg." (Rhymes with "gyrfalcon."[48]) "In addition to its keen eyesight and powerful flight, which make it ideal for scouting, it has formidable diving attacks that deal both physical and fire damage. At higher levels, it can even create tornadoes of fire."

"Sounds cool," Fey said. If it were her purchase, she would have immediately decided on the fire bird, but Blade insisted on hearing the description of every pet within his price range.

The shopkeeper went through the lineup one by one; every pet had the potential to become powerful magical creatures. (The author is too lazy to come up with descriptions for multiple pets, so just imagine a bunch of fire Pokémon.) The fyrfalcon was the only one who could fly, and Fey made compelling, rational arguments in its favour (while conveniently not mentioning the advantages of the other pets) until Blade agreed and went to the bank to withdraw his savings. Fey tagged along to clear her bag of the small coins and junk items she had accumulated on the trip (#Hoard).

"Thank you for your purchase!" The shopkeeper removed the stasis spell keeping the egg from hatching and provided a complimentary bottle of growth potion, enough to accelerate its development to adult size. "Just put a dab of this on the egg to make it hatch, then feed the rest to the bird," he advised.

"Thanks." Blade took the bottle and his new egg, now nestled securely in a padded box, and headed out of the shop.

"Let's go hatch this baby," Fey said, eager to see the new pet come out.

Blade walked toward an unoccupied bench on the street.

"Where are you going?" Fey asked in a big-sister tone.

Blade halted, particularly susceptible to the same tone that had featured prominently in his childhood. "Over there?" he said, the answer turning into a question against his will.

Fey sighed as if the obviousness of the bench's unsuitability weighed on her soul (#Melodramatic). "Don't you know that baby birds imprint on the first person they see? You have to go somewhere without any people." Fey had a limited knowledge of the imprinting phenomenon and assumed the instinct was as strong with all birds as it was with baby ducks. (The author has a minor obsession with baby ducks.)

Taking over, Fey kidnapped (egg-napped?) the egg and led the way out of town to an uninhabited field. "Here." She gave Blade the egg back and walked a short distance away so it would not imprint on her. As she left, she added, "You'd better not name it anything stupid."

Blade stared at the egg, trying to think of a name that Fey would not consider stupid. Without her intervention, he would have just named it "Fyrfalcon," in a move as generic as his avatar name.[49]

Finally, he unscrewed the bottle of growth potion. The cap conveniently doubled as a transfer pipette (colloquially referred to as an eyedropper), and he used it to dab a drop of potion onto the egg.

Almost immediately, small cheeping and tapping sounds could be heard from within the shell. The egg made small movements as the creature inside pecked its way to freedom, eventually resulting in a crack that widened until the shell split and the chick spilled out.

With its feathers still damp and plastered to its body, its resemblance to a two-legged dinosaur could be more clearly seen.[50] Blade thought the chick was an ugly kind of cute. "Hello," he said to the little bird.

<Blade receives a pet!>

<Please select a name for your pet:___>

"Firefly," he decided (which, by Blade standards, was very creative).

<Name confirmed.>

<Firefly: immature fyrfalcon.>

<Time until maturity: 30 days.>

Firefly opened its beak and cheeped demandingly. Blade fed it a few drops of growth potion.

<Firefly's growth was accelerated.>
<Time until maturity: 29 days.>

At the sound of the chick's demanding cries, Fey approached curiously. She examined the baby fyrfalcon, now noticeably larger than when it had just hatched. Its down feathers had dried (no idea why growth potion would speed up evaporation, but just go with it), and it was now more traditionally cute and fluffy, covered in pinkish fuzz.

"Cute," she appraised. "What's its name?"

"Firefly."

"Shouldn't you be named Malcolm, then?"[51]

"Huh?" (Clearly, Blade has never seen the very excellent show.)

"Never mind."

Firefly cheeped again and Blade fed it more potion. It had now doubled in size, clearly unable to fit into the discarded remains of the shell beside it.

"Looks kinda useless, though," Fey commented. The fyrfalcon chick's wings looked short and stubby, lacking the long, stiff flight feathers it would gain as an adult.

Blade felt that this was a rather unfair judgement of the bird, which was only a few minutes old. "I just have to feed it the rest of the potion." His efforts were stymied when the chick closed its beak, apparently full. "Aww, come on," he coaxed, poking its beak with the dropper.

____

Fey was highly amused to see Blade's struggles with the tiny, stubborn bird. "It looks like this is going to take a while." She would have been happy to settle down and spectate the entire frustrated process, but in the interest of productivity, decided she should go herb-collecting. "I'll go ahead and collect tear grass while you do your thing."

"Okay." The chick opened its beak long enough for Blade to get another few drops of potion in, then promptly closed it again. "Aww, come on," he said again.

Walking away. I'm walking away. Ahh, but this is so funny. Okay, for real, I'm walking away. Summoning all of her (meagre) self-discipline, she headed farther out from town, following Kallara's map to find the tear grass.

A few minutes out, she found a patch of grass distinctive in the fact that it was bright blue rather than the typical green. Kallara's instructions called for Fey to collect blades of grass rather than plant roots, so she grabbed a few and tore them free. She was entirely aware that this would likely trigger some kind of unpleasant defensive ability in the plant, but seeing no real way to avoid it, preferred to get it over with as quickly as possible.

The broken edges of the grass immediately began to release a white, smoky substance that spread out in a cloud. As if signalled, the surrounding undamaged grass followed suit.[52] Fey and her pets were quickly engulfed in the fog.

As soon as the smoke reached her face, Fey's eyes began to burn and water. Breathing it in caused uncontrollable coughing, much more irritating than actual smoke from a fire. (Get it? Tear grass? The author likes her dumb puns.)

Coughing hard and effectively blinded, she backed out of the cloud as fast as she could, sitting down as soon as she reached fresh air to catch her breath. Similarly affected, Boris followed, looking absolutely miserable.

The rest of the Feypets did not appear to be affected at all, their eyes looking more like cartoon animations than real eyeballs in sockets and completely lacking any form of lungs. Incensed at the affront to her owner, Amethyst attacked the grass with Whip, leaving fairly deep divots in the ground but not materially changing the grass's ability to generate more of its toxic gas. Magic was more effective, using Drain to leave circles of dead grass the size of his stem as he hopped around.

Not satisfied with the small circles Magic was creating, Amethyst squeaked commandingly and the glooms started rolling the mushroom around, causing much larger swathes of death wherever he touched. They were rather haphazard in rolling him (think rabbit soccer) but eventually managed to kill the entire patch of grass. The irritating clouds gradually dissipated.

When Fey eventually stopped coughing, she wiped her streaming eyes and looked around to see the environmental destruction her pets had wrought. "Overkill," she said fondly, petting them as they crowded near her, vying for praise. (Please note that neither Fey nor the author endorse the wanton destruction of the natural environment in real life.) She gathered up the grass, far more than Kallara probably needed, but she figured she might as well take it all since it was already dead.

Shouldering her backpack, she headed back to Blade and his new pet.

Firefly the fyrfalcon had molted away its fluffy chick down and now had the plumage of an adult falcon. Its coloration was a red-tinged version of a typical gyrfalcon, with grey and brown replaced by dark carmine red and rusty red-brown mottling.

Fey stared at the bird, who was perched calmly on Blade's arm, much more settled than she would expect a young falcon to be in real life. *So this is what a normal pet looks like.* Even at rest, the fyrfalcon's size, sharp gaze, and even sharper claws made it very clear that it was a predator who could do serious damage, in sharp contrast to Fey's pets, who tended to look cute and cuddly even when unleashing their most deadly attacks.

"Hi, bird," she said, her voice somewhere between the cutesy high voice she used to talk to her own pets and the somewhat unenthusiastic low tone she used to talk to Blade. Firefly did not respond vocally, though the bird's head posture was tilted in interest.

"Are you a boy bird or a girl bird?" she wondered aloud, her vocabulary dropping in difficulty to match the age group she would normally address with her tone of voice. Firefly certainly appeared rather large to her eye, and she knew that female birds of prey tended to outgrow their male counterparts by a significant margin, but she had no idea if the game developers had upsized the entire fyrfalcon species to make them more deadly in combat.

Blade stared at his pet as if that would glean him the information. "Dunno."

"Let's go ask the pet store owner."

"Sure." As they walked into town, Blade added, "So what are your pets? Male or female?"

Fey smiled wryly. "Neither, most of them. Amethyst appears to be some kind of oversized, undifferentiated animal cell that probably reproduces through mitosis. Magic is a fungus, so I guess more accurately both male and female, rather than neither. The glooms seem to be made of animated dark element that likes to take the shape of a bunny for no reason, and I have no idea how they reproduce. Boris is definitely male, though."

" . . . I see." Blade was fairly certain that he had not heard the word "mitosis" since high school, and biology had not been one of his favourite subjects. He could tell that Fey knew a lot more than him, but that knowledge could range anywhere from "read a few articles online" to "has a postdoctorate in biochemistry" and he would not know the difference.

The sun was nearing the horizon, growing dim enough that one could make out Amethyst's slight bioluminescence with careful observation. The glowing purple slime interrupted their walk by jumping down to the ground and bouncing excitedly, pointing her bubble down a different path away from town.

"King Slime?" Fey guessed.

Amethyst squeaked an affirmative.

"Okay, let's go." Fey bent down to pick up her pet and carry her to the slime territory, but Amethyst hopped over to Boris and Magic. Squeaking meaningfully, Amethyst made an encompassing motion with her bubble that included the three senior Feypets.

Charades was not Fey's strong suit, but she did her best. "You want to go kill it yourselves?"

The pets nodded confidently.

The three pets were now all level 17, so Fey judged they would be able to hold their own against a level 15 monster, even if it were a boss. "Okay, off you go." (*sniffle* They grow up so fast, don't they?)

Magic and Amethyst hopped onto Boris's back, and the miniature boar trotted off.

"Uh, do you think it's okay to let them go off like that?" Blade asked.

Fey shrugged. "How much trouble could they get into?" (Ah, how the irresponsible pet ownership goes on and on.) She called after them, "Stay in the slime area and we'll come find you!" Amethyst waved her bubble in acknowledgement.

Considering the plan to regroup an adequate amount of caution and planning, Fey continued strolling toward Newtown, the picture of insouciance. Blade glanced worriedly at the diminutive, retreating figures of the Feypets, exchanged a glance with Firefly (who, being about an hour old, likely had very little opinion on the matter) then followed uncertainly after Fey.

—◦◦◇◦◦—

(This narrator is very pleased to introduce the very first scene written from the pets' point of view! *throws virtual confetti that doesn't have to be cleaned up* Enjoy!)

Amethyst was hungry. She had gained multiple levels in Double Membrane from being forcefully poked on the carriage ride, without any food to fuel the changes. If she had had a stomach, it would have growled in anticipation as the panicked yells of running newbies indicated the presence of her favourite food: King Slime bubble.

A player came into view, running directly at Amethyst and her companions. In the deepening shadows of evening and blinded by fear, the newbie failed to notice the diminutive pets despite Amethyst's faint glow.

Judging that if the player was allowed to continue his forward trajectory, he would trample them underfoot, Amethyst (conscience-lessly) snapped out a Whip attack, neatly shattering the player's right kneecap (#ExcessiveUnnecessaryViolence).

Crippled mid-stride, the newbie performed a spectacular example of the phenomenon knowns as "faceplanting," falling down with a yell of pain that was abruptly muffled by the ground.

Magic squeaked. ("Nice aim.")

Amethyst squeaked. ("Thanks.")

Boris, having remained at a steady trot throughout the whole affair, carried them past the player (now writhing in pain) and grunted. ("I could have dodged that, you know.")

The idea of dodging had never occurred to the slow-moving mushroom and slime. Amethyst squeaked. ("Good idea. We'll do that next time.")

Magic politely disagreed with his own squeaking. ("But this way, you train more.") The Feypets had gained much of their owner's drive to spam skills to increase their level, so even one extra Whip counted (more than the well-being of some newbie).

Boris acknowledged the point by nodding, but added his own counterargument with a grunt. ("Yeah, but we're also not supposed to get in trouble.")

Amethyst and Magic digested the idea of avoiding trouble as an entirely new concept.

Magic squeaked. ("It's okay as long as we don't get caught, right?")

Amethyst brightened. She squeaked. ("Yeah! That guy didn't scc us at all!")

Boris grunted skeptically. ("That was luck. You didn't sneak at all.")

Amethyst squeaked, clearly chastised. ("I'll be more sneaky.")

(We will leave it to the reader to decide what it means about Fey's psyche that her pets considered it more important to not get caught doing things that might lead to trouble rather than avoiding doing those things in the first place.)

The trio came upon their opponent in the form of an orange King Slime, highly visible with its glow against the dark of twilight. Boris stopped as soon as they spotted the boss so they could begin battle preparations. Magic hopped off the boar's back and into a patch of tall grass to hide, ready to provide support from a distance.

All the newbies had successfully escaped the area (or had been turned into streaks of light that then left the area), so the boss monster was just hopping around, for all the world like an enormous normal slime without any goals or real thoughts in its head. Local slimes had come out of hiding to gather admiringly around their huge cousin-monster.

If Amethyst had had a nose, she would have snorted at the celebrity worship. Instead, she squeaked derisively (whatever that sounds like).

Copying one of Fey's earlier actions, Amethyst coated her bubble and Boris's tusks with furyweed poison. After having experienced its effects herself, Fey would no longer use the painful toxin (unless someone really deserved it), but Amethyst had no such qualms (#Ruthless).

Amethyst rolled around on the grass to wipe off the remaining poison coating her body, then hopped onto Boris's back and squeaked her readiness.

Boris's muscles bunched and tensed as he broke into a gallop and began a Charge attack. A property of the skill was that the boar continuously gained speed as long as he continued running in a straight line, so by the time they hit the King Slime, they were traveling at a prodigious speed. Amethyst flattened herself against the boar's back as they blasted through the side of the King Slime, tearing a giant hole in its membrane. (Innocent bystander slimes were also trampled to death in what would have been a gory scene had they had blood instead of faintly bioluminescent slime. As it was, the effect was fairly festive.) As they continued forward past the boss, Amethyst blasted a Whip out behind them to deal further damage and speed their escape.

The King Slime gave a relatively low-pitched squeak of pain at the injury and the furyweed poison diffusing through its cytoplasm, turning to launch a counterattack. The fight became a game of dodgebubble as Boris made skillful evasive maneuvers to avoid the boss's oversized version of Whip. (Many more common slimes were subsequently trampled to death or splatted out of existence by their cousin-monster.) Amethyst pitched in by smashing the King Slime with her bubble whenever they were in range and she could do so without upsetting Boris's balance, the added momentum of her Whip occasionally adding the extra boost of speed they needed to dodge a particularly close attack.

From a distance, Magic sent out clouds of Spore laden with every debuff he could produce, but the boss was large enough that it was able to avoid the full status effects. (In contrast, many of the regular slimes who had escaped the direct area of battle succumbed and died.)

Things appeared to be working out well for the pets as they whittled away the King Slime's health until Boris dodged in the wrong direction and took a direct hit from its massive bubble-arm. The heavy sphere caught him under the ribs and threw him into the air for a short distance before he landed heavily in a groaning heap.

Amethyst squeaked in alarm as her mount was knocked out from under her. Seeing her ally unable to stand, she attacked before the King Slime could finish him off. Jumping as high as she could, she opened her mouth enormously wide and engulfed the boss' giant bubble, attempting to digest it alive.

Squeaking in pain, the King Slime tried to dislodge Amethyst by repeatedly slamming her into the ground. A normal slime would have exploded at the first impact, but Amethyst's Double Membrane was strong enough to keep her intact, though not without pain. She grimly hung on, willing her digestive enzymes to work faster.

Seeing his oldest friend's ordeal, Magic hopped out of hiding, but his rate of travel was so slow that he doubted he could reach the boss before Amethyst's health reached a critical level. He sent out every kind of Spore within his abilities, which somewhat weakened the King Slime's attacks, but was not enough to defeat it.

In desperation, Magic combined his Drain and Spore abilities to create Drain Spore[53]. A cloud of life-sapping particles settled all over the King Slime and went to work.

Between the furyweed poison, extensive gashes in its membrane, and the Drain Spore, the King Slime quickly weakened. Amethyst dropped to the ground as she finished digesting its bubble, and speeded up the boss' death by snapping Whip out repeatedly, riddling it with even more holes.

Finally, the King Slime lost its structural integrity and collapsed into a puddle of goo.

(Pets don't receive system notices, so the expected messages will not be displayed.)

Amethyst tensed, then relaxed as she saw movement emerging from the remains of the King Slime. Magic's Drain Spores had been growing larger as they stole health from the monster and now resolved into a troop of blue mushrooms each about the size of a marble, a hundred times smaller than Magic but otherwise very similar in appearance. They hopped off and disappeared into the tall grass, presumably looking for more food to eat.

Magic watched what was technically his offspring hop away without much interest. (Yeah, the parental instinct is completely lacking in fungi.) Instead, he squeaked at Amethyst. ("You okay?")

If the slime had had any blood vessels, she would be severely bruised. As it was, she simply wanted to stay still until she healed. She squeaked tiredly. ("I'll be okay. Go check on Boris.")

Magic hopped over and squeaked at the boar. ("You okay?")

Boris grunted. ("Think the leg is broken.") He had landed badly, folding his left hind leg at an unnatural angle, and was holding very still to avoid the sharp jolts of pain that occurred at the slightest movement.

With his comrades out of commission, it looked like it was up to Magic to collect the loot while they waited for rescue. Having neither limbs nor a pouch-like mouth to store items, he was particularly unsuited to the task but did his best, hopping around laboriously. He was helped by the fact that he could apparently make coins (mainly from the hapless bystander slimes) and other small items stick to him at will.

In the King Slime's remains, Magic found an unusual object: a small gold crown the size of a finger ring. He pushed it over to Amethyst with a squeak. ("Look at this.")

Amethyst felt extremely drawn to the object. Extending her bubble-arm, she picked it up. The crown-ring was of a size that she could just squeeze her bubble through. It slid down the length of her whippy arm until it landed on her head, where she felt it fuse with her membrane as if it were meant to be there.

Magic squeaked. ("Looks nice.")

Amethyst squeaked. ("Thanks.")

The pets settled down to wait for Fey's arrival.

CHAPTER 27
JOY

Fey and Blade walked to the local slime territory to find her pets, having ascertained at the pet shop that Firefly was a female. (Avian girl power!)

"Amethyst! Magic! Boris!" she called once they were in the vicinity, following the resultant squeaking to their source.

Magic hopped up and down in greeting. In the night, he was harder to see than the bioluminescent Amethyst, but his bright blue cap and white stem were still much more visible than Boris's dark brown colour.

"Hello," she said to the mushroom. "I take it you beat the King Slime?"

Magic squeaked what she assumed was an affirmative.

Fey checked the pet menu. "Huh. Magic learned a new subskill," she commented.

<Drain Spore: release health-draining spores that grow into immature blue mushrooms; drained health does not go to the caster.>

<Subskill: takes draining rate from Drain, effect range from Spore.>

Fey looked but did not see any other blue mushrooms hopping around. She shrugged and moved on. (Apparently she didn't have much in the way of parental instincts, either.)

She checked Amethyst's pet menu next. The slime's Double Membrane had reached level 10 and evolved into Triple Membrane,[54] tripling her physical defence so that it now required thirty times the force to do any damage.

Finding the slime, Fey noted the new accessory. "What's this?" she said, poking the tiny crown Amethyst was wearing, which did not appear to be removable.

<King Slime Crown: crown granted only to slimes who have defeated the King Slime in direct combat (+10 fame). Grants the wearer authority over slimes, increases Charisma by 5, and allows the wearer to temporarily take on the King Slime's size. Size increase can be used once an hour and lasts as many seconds as the slime's level.>

"Wow." Fey made a mental note to hunt down the boss versions of her other pets to see if they could get similar bonus items. "Your Royal Purpleness," she said jokingly to Amethyst. The slime waved her bubble in a queenly manner.

Fey's pleased mood disappeared as soon as she found Boris and opened his pet menu. That his Charge skill had levelled up went unnoticed; all her attention was drawn to the status effect notification:

<Broken leg: unable to walk or run until healed.>

"Ahh!" Fey yelled, rushing over to Boris's dark outline on the ground. "Why didn't you guys tell me his leg was broken??"

Magic squeaked. ("Well, I tried.") It was one of the few times Fey had radically misinterpreted her pets' squeaking.

Ignoring the mushroom, Fey focused on her injured pet. "Aww, poor baby. Let's get you to the healer's." She carefully shifted Boris onto her cape as a makeshift stretcher, then ran off toward town, even forgetting to pick up Magic and Amethyst in her haste.

"Fey, your other pets . . . " Blade called, trailing off when it was clear she was not listening. He looked down at the tiny pets, who were conferring in squeaks now that their primary and secondary means of transportation (Fey and Boris, respectively) had left them behind.

He could see the exact moment when they settled on him as their next-likeliest means of transport. Amethyst lassoed the hilt of his sword with her bubble-arm and pulled herself up, while Magic simply hopped up his leg. Both Feypets earnestly squeaked at him what he assumed were variations of "go." (To be exact, Magic said, "Gogogo!" while Amethyst said, "Hurry up and follow Fey-Fey, meat-shield-man!")

Sighing at the absurdity that was his life, Blade walked back to town.

Fey ran to the shop that displayed both the apothecary's potion bottle and healer's cross on its overhanging sign. She shouldered open the door, reflecting that human buildings were much less convenient than elven tree-shops with their open archways when one was carrying an injured pet. (Probably more convenient when it rained, though.)

"Hello? I have a pet with a broken leg—" Fey stopped abruptly. "Kallara?"

The healer inside Newtown's potion shop smiled. "You must have met my colleague in the Moonwood. My name is Kalinda. People often remark on the resemblance, but we are not related." Indeed, despite the striking similarities in feature, Kalinda had the round ears of a human.

"A broken leg, you say?" Kalinda continued. "Please put him on the examination table."

Remembering the more urgent matter at hand, Fey eased Boris onto the table. The boar bore the inevitable jostling with remarkable stoicism. (Where he picked up that trait is a mystery, given how whiny his owner is. Good boar-boar.)

Kalinda examined the boar's leg, which was bent at an angle that was clearly unnatural. Without ceremony, she began treatment.

"Numb."

Kalinda's spell was the equivalent of a local anesthetic. Boris relaxed as the nerves in his leg were disabled and stopped sending pain signals to his brain. (Totally not thinking about scary healer abilities that would be really hard to fight in combat.)

Grasping the injured leg firmly, Kalinda pulled it into alignment. Fey cringed at the sound of shifting bone.

"Bone Heal," came Kalinda's next spell. Compared to regular healing spells, it restored relatively few health points, which strongly correlated with blood loss, but was more effective at repairing disabling injuries like broken and dislocated bones. In more urgent situations, the spell could be used without manually setting the bones in the correct position, but this took considerably more mana.

Kalinda removed the Numb spell and handed Boris back to Fey. (*Pokémon healing center sound*) "There you go; all better."

"Thank you so much." Fey hugged Boris to her chest, causing the boar to perform the porcine version of "teenaged boy embarrassed by his overly affectionate mom."

Around this time, Blade entered the shop carrying his own pet and his two uninvited passengers. (The author just realized she completely lost track of the glooms in this scene but we'll just assume they were hanging out somewhere upon Fey's person.)

"Hello! How may I help you?" Kalinda greeted.

"Oh, I'm with her," Blade said. As if to prove his words, Amethyst and Magic hopped over to their owner and started scolding her in indignant squeaks over her abandonment of them.

Noticing the healer's facial features, Blade commented, "You look a lot like the healer in the Moonwood."

Kalinda smiled as if at an inside joke. "Indeed, many have commented on the likeness. I am told I resemble the healers in other cities as well."

Well, at least they didn't name you Joy,[55] thought Fey.

Fey bent down and pacified her squeaky pets. "Sorry guys, but it was an emergency."

The slime and mushroom grumbled for a bit longer but settled down, recognizing that Boris's injury did take precedence over their distaste at having to ride Blade back to town.

"Oh, you have three pets," Kalinda commented in surprise.

"Er, actually, nine," Fey said. At her words, Onyx, Inkblot, Ebony, Shadow, Midnight, and Obsidian reverted to their rabbit forms and dropped from their respective positions hanging around Fey's person. (See? Now it looks like the author definitely kept track of everyone the whole time.)

"That is quite the number of glooms. What caused you to seek out so many of the same pet?" Kalinda asked curiously.

" . . . It was an accident, actually. I saved them from total annihilation, and they decided to become my pets."

"Annihilation?"

"Holy light from a high-level celestial," Fey clarified.

"Ah. That would do it."

Blade had never heard the story before, having learned that questions rarely led to answers and given up on trying to get straight answers out of Fey. Having now heard the half story, he had to ask. "What celestial? Are there any in the Elvenwood?"

Leandriel's existence was not exactly a secret, but Fey was irrationally reluctant to discuss the angel. "Oh, you know," she said in a vague non-answer. "Aaanyways, thanks for all your help!" she said to Kalinda. She handed the healer a 100g piece, collected her pets, and hustled out of the shop before anyone could ask her any more questions.

"Have a nice day!" Kalinda called out cheerfully, deciding that Fey had meant to give her a very large tip since the elf had not stopped to wait for change.

"Know what?" Blade asked as he caught up to Fey.

"Know what?" Fey repeated quizzically, having forgotten her earlier verbal dodge.

"You just said, 'You know.'"

Fey shook her head dismissively. "Obviously, you *don't* know."

"What?" Blade asked, starting to get confused.

Fey grinned. Blade was the perfect target for her silly sense of humour. (She also had a sadistic facet of humour, but she did not hate Blade enough to subject him to it.) She patted his arm consolingly. "Too easy."

Now Blade was deep in confused territory. "What?" he said again.

Fey started to feel mildly guilty at Blade's good-natured and honest reaction. He was still genuinely trying to communicate with her, not a hint of annoyance in his expression, while she was purposefully obstructing his understanding of events. She decided to compromise with an extremely abbreviated description of events. "There was a guy casting Purifying Light in a gloom territory, and these six hid in my shadow to survive. After I got him to stop, they spontaneously became my pets."

"Oh. Cool." Blade paused to consider the story. "How did you get him to stop?"

Fey grinned. "I asked him politely," she said in a tone that implied that the way that she asked had been anything but polite. The fact that she had very literally asked nicely only added to her amusement. (We shall classify this as the "double meanings/puns" facet of her sense of humour.)

"Oh," Blade said, a distinctly worried tone colouring his voice. He could see that Fey did not have a Player Killer tattoo—a drop of blood—on her forehead, but his imagination spun up various violent scenarios in which she was the diabolical aggressor.

Fey laughed. "I really did ask politely," she said in a much more relaxed voice.

Blade did not look convinced. "Okay."

I should probably stop joking about violence until he gets to know me better, Fey reflected. Her dramatic shifts in tone probably appeared to be a sign of mental and emotional instability rather than her random sense of humour.

Deciding that further reassurance of her non-violence (and sanity) would have the opposite effect, she decided to log off a few minutes early. "Gotta go. Go train your pet or something. See you tomorrow." She popped out of existence.

⸺◦◦◇◦◦⸺

Blade looked at Firefly. "Sometimes, that girl scares me," he confided to the bird.

Firefly nodded without much understanding, still at level 1 with a commensurate level of intelligence.

Despite Fey's possible insanity, Blade decided her suggestion to train his new pet had merit. He still had a bit of time until he had to log out, so he headed back to the slime territory with Firefly on his arm.

⸺◦◦◇◦◦⸺

(And now, the author will demonstrate that she understands the concept of "skipping time for the purposes of advancing the plot." Behold, the "summary"!)

The rest of the week passed in stable routine. By day, Arwyn went to work and did other tedious adult things to keep her life running smoothly; by night, Fey and Blade travelled steadily toward the coast. The party got into the usual types of mishaps collecting herbs for Kallara and exploring the land while waiting between travel coaches, Fey reaching level 23 and Blade level 24. As promised, Fey purchased a teleportation key and went back to the Moonwood to deliver their harvest whenever they passed through a town large enough to have a teleportation gate.

Out of curiosity, they visited the healer in every town they passed; each one had a name that started with a K and bore strikingly similar, though not identical, facial features.

Blade noticed two curious behaviours from his party-mate on a regular basis. One, she was strangely distracted and smiley every day around the time they logged in, which he eventually figured out was related to talking to someone via private messaging. In sharp contrast to a sometimes brutal level of honesty about any other topic, she became extremely cagey and evasive when he asked who she was talking to, and he finally left the mystery alone, just waiting for the few minutes it took for her to regain (relative) normalcy before he talked to her.

The second behaviour occurred whenever circumstances forced them to share a travel coach with other players. Fey would suddenly shift her body language to indicate that Blade was the party leader, directing the strangers' attention to him. The first time it happened, he was caught off guard, but he became accustomed to being in charge of making polite conversation with other players, something he rather enjoyed.

Fey certainly did not enjoy talking to strangers, especially for the extended periods of time they spent cooped up in the travel coach. Since she had a convenient human to whom she could divert the social interaction, she did. She had no problem pretending to be shy if it meant she could sit in the corner and amuse herself by training her pets and her skills rather than summoning the energy to talk about generic topics that held no interest for her. She kept her eyes lowered and her voice soft when she did have to speak, which had the amusing bonus effect of making Blade quite confused whenever players entered or left their company.

Fey did develop somewhat of a fondness for the human warrior and the way he good-naturedly navigated all of the weirdness thrown his way. Her attitude toward him softened imperceptibly, which essentially meant that she continued to mess with him when it was amusing to do so, but with a slightly more affectionate expression in her eyes. In contrast, Blade's relationship with Amethyst continued to worsen, exacerbated by long periods of "training" where they frequently came to blows under the pretext of helping each other train skills.

The pets steadily closed the gap between themselves and their owners. The glooms turned out to be extremely effective at killing plant-type monsters due to the blighting effect of their bites, and reached level 20 at the same time as Amethyst, Magic, and Boris. (It's totally plausible that this would happen and is not just because the author is too lazy to keep track of different pet levels.) At this level mark, they gained another boost in intelligence and developed more distinct personalities.

Firefly reached level 10 very quickly and continued to grow to level 15 by their last day of travel. Her personality from an early stage was noticeably different from the Feypets', her behaviours much more dignified and restrained. The fyrfalcon had yet to display any manifestation of fire or magic, her attacks consisting of diving strikes with beak and talons. When not in combat, she perched quietly on Blade's shoulder or arm, gripping the leather accessory he had purchased to fit over his heavy armour.

Friday night, Arwyn logged into *Fantasia* early, anticipating her arrival at the coast before virtual nightfall.

NOTES

1   Drizzt Do'Urden, dark elf from the book series *Legend of Drizzt* by R. A. Salvatore.

2   Drinking untreated water, such as from a lake, river, or stream, can result in a variety of waterborne infections, including parasitic infections such as giardiasis.

3   An environment is hypotonic when the solute concentration in the environment is lower than that inside the cell. This causes a net influx of water into the cell, which, in the absence of a rigid cell wall such as in plants, can swell to the point of bursting (lysis).

4   Slimes in *Fantasia* are modelled after somewhat unrealistic undifferentiated animal cells with incredible adaptive abilities. They divide mitotically and are asexual in nature, but for ongoing narration purposes, Amethyst will be referred to as "she" due to the gender conventions of the name.

5   When calling them "huge," the author is referring to the individual fruiting bodies of a fungus typically thought of as mushrooms. Fungal organisms can form networks stretching several kilometres in area and weighing hundreds of tons, the most famous being the honey mushroom *Armillaria ostoyae* in Malheur National Park, which holds the Guinness world record as the largest single organism.

6   Placebo effect: improvement of a patient's condition in response to treatment, but not directly due to the treatment. In treatments for pain, the effect of a placebo can be significantly larger than the actual treatment's effect.

7   This is a play on the word *radar*; however, Fey is actually navigating by the standard minimap system common to many games.

8   *Sequoiadendron giganteum*, commonly known as the giant sequoia, giant redwood, or Sierra redwood, is a species native to the western slopes of the Sierra Nevada mountains in California. They are known as the most massive trees, with the largest tree in the world by volume, the General Sherman Tree, measuring 83 metres in height, with a base diameter of 11 metres.

9   As with other invertebrates, slugs lack a true brain. Their nervous system is instead controlled by small knots of neurons, called ganglia, each of which is responsible for the control of a different body part or system.

10   As with other invertebrates, slugs have a more primitive circulatory system, in which circulatory fluid called hemolymph is pumped directly to tissues and organs rather than being separated from extracellular fluid by capillaries. They also have a simple two-chamber heart rather than the four-chamber heart seen in vertebrates.

11   Chitin, a polymer made of N-acetylglucosamine, forms a key component of cell walls in fungi, exoskeletons in arthropods, scales in fish, and skin in amphibians.

12   Steradians, or square radians, are the SI unit of solid angle used in three-dimensional geometry. A full sphere subtends 4π steradians, while the spikester's attack fills the half-sphere above the ground subtending 2π steradians.

13   In nature, resistance or immunity to a specific toxin does not generalize to other, unrelated toxins. This has been simplified for the sake of game mechanics.

14   "Pome" is the scientific name for fruits like apples and pears, and *Malus* is the genus containing the apple tree species.

15   Gamer abbreviation for "over-powered."

16   Extirpation, also known as local extinction, refers to the loss of a species within a certain geographic area, with at least one other population surviving elsewhere.

17   Divining, also called dowsing, is the use of various equipment such as sticks or metal rods to locate resources such as fresh water or metal deposits based on the random movement of the equipment. This method has been shown to be no better than random chance at actually locating the resources in question.

18   Mucous membranes such as the eyes, inside of the nose, and mouth are generally more permeable to chemicals and toxins than the rest of the skin.

19   Chronotype refers to individual variation in the sleep-wake cycle, where "early birds" tend to wake up and fall asleep early in the day and "night owls" naturally stay up later and wake up later. These sleep patterns are associated with different times of peak focus during the day.

20   The Valsalva maneuver involves increasing the intrathoracic pressure by bearing down against a closed glottis (i.e., without exhaling), and this can lower the heart rate by increasing vagal (parasympathetic) tone.

21   Irony that is inherent in speeches or situations of a drama and is understood by the audience but not the characters in the play. dramatic irony. (n.d.). *Dictionary.com Unabridged*. Retrieved August 19, 2014, from Dictionary.com website: http://dictionary.reference.com/browse/dramatic irony

22   Satisfaction or pleasure felt at someone else's misfortune. schadenfreude. (n.d.). *Dictionary.com Unabridged*. Retrieved October 23, 2014, from Dictionary.com website: http://dictionary.reference.com/browse/schadenfreude

23   This is a reference to the song "Magic" by B.o.B ft. Rivers Cuomo, which is a super-catchy song that does not actually reflect the author's music preferences.

24   The full line from Shakespeare's play *Hamlet* is, "The lady doth protest too much, methinks" (Act III, Scene II).

25   Toxins that work through being injected into the body are often referred to as venom rather than poison, however this distinction is rather blurry, as most poisons are venomous and most venoms have at least a mild negative effect on contact.

26   This refers to when two people try to one-up each other with excessively delightful and thoughtful gifts; in an odd turn of phrase, the loser is the person who receives the better gifts.

27   Readers may or may not recognize this as the name of a darking in Tamora Pierce's book *In the Realms of the Gods*.

28   Phylogeny refers to the study of the evolution of species, with species grouped based on shared common ancestors. The term "bugs" generally includes species belonging to the phylum *Arthropoda*, which share the characteristics of being invertebrate animals with exoskeletons and segmented bodies; however, crustaceans such as crabs and lobsters are generally excluded from the term despite belonging to the phylum.

29   These monsters can be commonly found in the MMORPG *RuneScape*.

30   This is a reference to *The Princess Bride* by William Goldman.

31   There is no intrinsic property of poison that would make it purple; this was chosen solely because the move Poisonpowder in Pokémon is depicted as purple.

32   From William Congreve's play *The Mourning Bride*; the original lines are: "Heaven has no rage like love to hatred turned/Nor hell a fury like a woman scorned" (Act III, Scene VIII).

33   Though the details of this weapon have been changed, the original idea was inspired by a weapon in the Noble Dead series by Barb and J. C. Hendee. In terms of actual traditional weapons, punching blades are somewhat similar to a combination of the katar and the tonfa.

34   This is a reference to simple math worksheets commonly assigned in elementary school that tested students' abilities to do simple addition, subtraction, multiplication, and division quickly. Each sheet is meant to be completed in one minute. The curious can find an online version here: http://www.webmathminute.com/default.asp?

35   With regards to scientific terminology, accuracy refers to the closeness of measurements to the true value, while precision refers to the repeatability or reliability of measurements. A common comparison would be to describe a group of shots on a bullseye target as accurate but not precise if they roughly hit the target and on average are near the centre, precise but not

accurate if they are closely clustered but are off to one side of the target, and both precise and accurate if they cluster near the bullseye.

36   This name is taken from a magic featured in the manga *Fairy Tail*, the most famous user of which is Erza Scarlet.

37   The strategy of using conspicuous characteristics such as colouration, sounds, or odors as a warning signal against potential predators in organisms with strong defence mechanisms such as toxicity is known as *aposematism*.

38   A group of mushrooms is properly called a troop.

39   A lot of the magic system in *Fantasia* is the result of an interesting discussion that I had with my reader Aetheo. <You have earned the title *Fantasia Game Developer!*>

40   *Fairy Tail* reference.

41   This is a tribute to the author's favourite bad pun, "Everything that is not an elephant is irrelephant."

42   This is an anagram of the word *elephant*, because the author is bad at naming things.

43   *QQ* (pronounced kyoo-kyoo) is a term originating from Taiwan to describe the bouncy, soft-but-chewy texture of foods such as fish balls, tapioca pearls in bubble tea, and certain types of noodles, including udon noodles and jian mien. It derives from a similar-sounding word meaning "chewy."

44   This is a double pun. The Oré mountains are rich in minerals suitable for mining, and this also sounds like "oreille," which means "ear" in French. This is the mountain chain that outlines the curve of the continent-elephant's ear.

45   Constructive interference is a phenomenon that occurs when waveforms such as light and sound move in phase and their wave amplitudes add up to form a resulting wave with a larger amplitude (in the case of sound, louder, and in the case of light, intensity), used in applications such as multi-speaker sound systems and stereotactic radiation therapy. Conversely, destructive interference occurs when waveforms move out of phase and the opposing directions of oscillation cancel each other out, which is the principle behind things such as noise-cancelling headphones and anti-glare coatings.

46   This ability name is taken from *Legendary Moonlight Sculptor*, but the details are different and the *Fantasia* version adds no attack power to the player.

47   Imprinting is a form of rapid learning during a specific phase of development, the most common example being that of baby birds imprinting on the first moving object they see (including inanimate objects) and following it around. This instinct appears to be stronger in birds that leave the nest shortly after birth, such as chickens, ducks, and geese, compared to birds that are reared in the nest for a period of time before leaving.

48   Gyrfalcons are the largest species of falcon and have been used by nobility in falconry for centuries.

49   The author of this story spent a full three weeks unable to start writing before she found and settled on Blade as the ultimate in blandness and genericism to name this character.

50   Birds are the only lineage of dinosaurs to survive the Cretaceous-Paleogene (K-Pg) extinction event approximately 66 million years ago. This extinction event is hypothesized to have been caused by a massive asteroid impact that resulted in the production of massive ash and dust clouds that impaired the function of photosynthetic organisms and caused dramatic global cooling in addition to severely limiting the supply of available food. This resulted in 75 percent of the species in the fossil record disappearing, including most species that had larger, more energetically expensive body plans, such as the non-avian dinosaurs.

51   This is a reference to the TV series *Firefly*, in which Captain Malcolm Reynolds commanded a Firefly-class spaceship named *Serenity*.

52   Plants can send a variety of signals to other plants through the release of volatile organic compounds, as in response to damage that induce upregulation of defensive mechanisms in neighbouring, undamaged plants.

53   This is the author's fungus version of the Pokémon move Leech Seed.

54   The cell membrane consists of a phospholipid bilayer where the hydrophilic phosphate groups face outward and the hydrophobic lipid ends face inward, anchored and stabilized by a variety of cell proteins and sterols. It makes no biological sense for slimes to have either a single or a triple membrane, and it amuses the author greatly to make lame biology jokes like this.

55   In Pokémon, all the nurses at Pokémon Centers are identical cousins named Joy, and all police officers are identical cousins named Jenny.

Chapter title credits:
thirst (3), Lord Vitor2510 (7). Book-kun (8), Vibe (9), epithetic (10, 28, 33), Red (13).

ABOUT THE AUTHOR

unice5656 is a gynoid robot designed to pass the Turing test. She writes fiction with elements of comedy, adventure, and fantasy, but which is ultimately thinly disguised romance. You can join her Discord server at https://discord.gg/teHrrw79VP.

DISCOVER
STORIES UNBOUND

PodiumAudio.com

www.ingramcontent.com/pod-product-compliance
Lightning Source LLC
Chambersburg PA
CBHW021806110726

47902CB00006B/1676

9781039428140